Blood Vengeance

by Tessa Dawn

A Blood Curse Novel
Book Seven
In the Blood Curse Series

Published by Ghost Pines Publishing, LLC
http://www.ghostpinespublishing.com

Volume VII of the Blood Curse Series by Tessa Dawn
First Edition Trade Paperback Published April 27, 2015
10 9 8 7 6 5 4 3 2 1

ISBN-13: 978-1-937223-15-1
Printed in the United States of America

Author may be contacted at: http://www.tessadawn.com

This is a work of fiction. All characters and events portrayed in this novel
are either fictitious or are used fictitiously. Any resemblance to actual
persons, living or dead, business establishments, events, or locales is
entirely coincidental.

Ghost Pines Publishing, LLC

Credits and Acknowledgments

Ghost Pines Publishing, LLC., *Publishing*
GreenHouse Design, Inc., *Cover Art*
Lidia Bircea, *Romanian Translations*
Reba Hilbert, *Editing*

Blaze of Glory – by Bon Jovi
House of the Rising Sun – This song was recorded several times by various artists prior to the most-recognizable version by the Animals in 1964 (sung by lead singer, Eric Burdon). There is some controversy as to who wrote the lyrics, with one theory being George Turner and Bert Martin. The song is in the public domain.

To Becky M ~ for being my son's most formidable sentinel.

The Blood Curse

In 800 BC, Prince Jadon and Prince Jaegar Demir were banished from their Romanian homeland after being cursed by a ghostly apparition: the reincarnated Blood of their numerous female victims. The princes belonged to an ancient society that sacrificed its females to the point of extinction, and the punishment was severe.

They were forced to roam the earth in darkness as creatures of the night. They were condemned to feed on the blood of the innocent and stripped of their ability to produce female offspring. They were damned to father twin sons by human hosts who would die wretchedly upon giving birth; and the firstborn of the first set would forever be required as a sacrifice of atonement for the sins of their forefathers.

Staggered by the enormity of The Curse, Prince Jadon, whose own hands had never shed blood, begged his accuser for leniency and received four small mercies—four exceptions to the curse that would apply to his house and his descendants, alone.

ψ   Though still creatures of the night, they would be allowed to walk in the sun.

ψ   Though still required to live on blood, they would not be forced to take the lives of the innocent.

ψ While still incapable of producing female offspring, they would be given one opportunity and thirty days to obtain a mate—a human destiny chosen by the gods—following a sign that appeared in the heavens.

ψ While they were still required to sacrifice a firstborn son, their twins would be born as one child of darkness and one child of light, allowing them to sacrifice the former while keeping the latter to carry on their race.

And so… forever banished from their homeland in the Transylvanian mountains of Eastern Europe, the descendants of Jaegar and the descendants of Jadon became the Vampyr of legend: roaming the earth, ruling the elements, living on the blood of others… forever bound by an ancient curse. They were brothers of the same species, separated only by degrees of light and shadow.

Prologue

Tiffany Matthews cleared away the remaining scattered toys from the front parlor of Prince Phoenix's suite of rooms. She took several steps back and skimmed the wide-planked, hardwood floors, her eyes searching up and down each slat of wood, one at a time, scanning for the missing *Bobee*, a stuffed purple dragon that Phoenix clung to like glue. The child needed the dragon to sleep—or at least he thought he did—and as of three o'clock that afternoon, Bobee had gone missing.

It was an utter catastrophe in the making.

She furrowed her brow and glanced beneath the formal settee. Nothing there. She spun around and checked beneath the mission-style end tables. Nothing there, either. She got down on her hands and knees and tried to view the room from a child's point of view—still nothing reared its dragon-head.

She sighed. She had two financial reports to *peruse* before morning, a ledger full of new accounts to enter into the computer database, and here she was, on her hands and knees like a ninny—or a nanny, to be exact—searching for a purple dragon.

"Still nothing yet?" Brooke asked, stepping quietly into the room. The queen was as tired as she looked, considering the fact that Phoenix had not taken a decent nap all day. "Napolean says he picked up the dragon in Romania the last time he was there to check on things at the University—he can't possibly get another one here in the States."

Tiffany rolled her eyes and huffed in annoyance. "Great. Just great. I don't suppose the child would settle for Barney?"

Brooke drew back, appalled. "Oh gods," she uttered. "Just the thought of it. I think he would have a royal meltdown."

Tiffany laughed, and then she clutched at her forearm. "Agreed." She scratched her wrist and stood up from the floor. "I swear; I have looked everywhere, even in the most ridiculous of places, like the refrigerator, the bathtub, and the pantry, just to rule it out. Where the heck is Bobee?"

Brooke rubbed her tired eyes and slowly shook her head. "You looked in the refrigerator?"

Tiffany squared her shoulders and leveled a warning glare at her best friend. "Don't go there, Brookie."

The queen looked off into the distance. "I think Bobee's dead."

"No!" Tiffany nearly shouted, spinning around on her heels. "Watch your mouth, *milady*." They both giggled at Brooke's formal title. "To even speak of it is treason."

Brooke held up both hands in surrender. "*Sorry*. Hey, why don't you go ahead and make your way to the guest house. It's already going on six o'clock, and I know you have a lot of work to do for DMV Prime. I'll keep searching for the missing toy, and I'll let you know if I find it." She breathed a plaintive sigh. "Who knows: Maybe someone will send a ransom note, and we can pay for Bobee's safe return."

Tiffany laughed wholeheartedly. "Oh, if only we should be that lucky." She tucked her arm to her chest, rubbed it against her shirt, and headed toward the front door of the parlor. "Now, if I could only find my car keys."

"You lost them *again*?" Brooke asked.

Tiffany moaned. "I swear; I would lose my head if it wasn't firmly attached to my shoulders." She squeezed her left forearm with her right hand and absently began to rub tight circles over her wrist with her thumb.

"What's with your arm?" Brooke said, frowning. She gestured toward the cradled limb.

Tiffany frowned. "I don't know." She held it up and turned it over in order to take a closer look. "I think I must have bumped it against the furniture." She noticed several red welts, swelling near the junction of her elbow, and winced. "Or maybe it's an allergy of some sort, a really bad rash. Maybe I came in contact with some dust or pollen, trying to hunt for Bobee."

Brooke gave her a mock look of insult. "Are you saying my house is filthy?"

Tiffany chuckled. She waved her hand around the room and smirked. "House, Brooke? Your son has a *suite* of rooms. This is a mansion, not a house." She angled her chin in a playful, haughty manner.

Brooke sneered at the amusing gesture. "Don't change the subject. Are you saying my *less than humble abode* is dirty?"

Tiffany curtsied. "No, *milady*." She laughed. "Although I might be saying it would help if you would quit firing your cleaning staff."

"Who?" Brooke demanded in a surly voice. "Please tell me you are *not* referring to MaryAnn, the so-called human servant?" She made disdainful air quotes around the words *human servant*.

Tiffany regarded her with mirth.

"Oh dear gods," Brooke clipped, "the woman was trying to seduce Napolean."

"You don't know that for a fact," Tiffany said.

"She was dusting the furniture in the nude!"

Tiffany burst out in laughter and tucked a lock of her short blond hair behind her ear. "Well, maybe she was just being *organic*." She snickered then. "Besides, can you blame the poor woman? She's human. It must have been like being restricted to a really bad diet of celery and tuna, and then all of a sudden, you stumble across a huge chunk of meat, filet mignon: fresh, juicy, and right off the grill. What was the poor woman to do?"

Brooke stepped forward and punched her friend playfully in the arm. "Yeah, more like filet Mondragon." She winked conspiratorially and laughed. "Besides, Carlotta is still with us."

Tiffany knew the human servant well. She belonged to a kind, loyal family, one who had served the Vampyr for almost nine generations, and she was an invaluable asset to the house of Jadon. "Yes, but she's a governess and an all-around magician, not a housekeeper."

Brooke rolled her eyes, apparently refusing to take the conversation any further. She was just about to turn away, start searching for Bobee again, when she eyed the raised ridges on Tiffany's wrist *again*. "Tiff, that is really flaring up. Let me see."

Tiffany held out her arm and grimaced. *Yikes, it did look bad.* Well, not in a gruesome sort of way, but there were dozens of little lines crisscrossing along her skin like a cryptic diagram, parallel points that intersected in such a way that it almost looked like two dancing kids linking arms. "Maybe I should take some Benadryl."

All at once, Brooke's mouth shot open, and she took an unwitting step back, still grasping Tiffany's arm.

"Hey, that is attached, you know," Tiffany protested.

Brooke gazed up at her friend in blank stupefaction, looked down at her wrist once more, and then gulped. *"Tiffany... "*

"What?" Tiffany's voice rose in alarm. "You think it's something serious, don't you?"

Brooke ran her fingers over the bright, mysterious lines and blanched. "I think... I think... " She covered her mouth with her hand.

"What?" Tiffany insisted, staring down at her arm in concern. Holy crap, there really was something funky going on.

"That's not a rash or an allergy, Tiff. It's a constellation. *A celestial deity.*"

"What do you mean?" Tiffany said, her voice rising with distress.

Brooke slowly shook her head as she took another look. "Correction. That would be celestial deities, as in plural. That's Gemini, the twins."

"Gemini who?" Tiffany shrieked, squeezing her arm with her hand. Her face suddenly felt hot, and her stomach felt queasy, although she didn't quite know why. Well, other than the fact that she was dying of the plague. "Oh, God. How do you catch Gemini? Is there a medication for it?"

Brooke held both hands out in front of her and toggled them up and down as if to say, *Okay, let's just calm down*, and then she gaped at Tiffany's arm once more. "You are so not following me right now, Tiff." She began to speak slowly and evenly, measuring her speech as if she were talking to a child, while over pronouncing her words. "The-mark-on-your-arm-is-the-sign-of-a-Blood-Moon. It's a replication of a deity, one that belongs to a male from the house of Jadon. A vampire. Tiffany, it's the mark of a vampire's *destiny.*"

There was no need for the moron's version of CliffsNotes, nor the repetitive explanation—Tiffany heard her friend loud and clear—although, the full meaning of the words did not quite sink in. And not because Tiffany was too slow to process the English language. On the contrary, she heard it, understood it, and moved right past understanding to *denial*.

No way.

No how.

Not today.

Not even tomorrow.

She marched very calmly to the nearest window, pulled back the blinds, and peeked up at the moon. As her eyes struggled to focus on the bloodred orb that hung like a neon sign in the heavens, her mind swirled around in a dizzying maelstrom, trying to dissect the far-too-obvious clues: mainly, the brilliant cluster of stars and meteors, the complex network of lines and planes, all coalescing in a unified pattern to form the image of a set of twins, two young children, linked at the wrist, staring off into space at a blackened sky.

Gemini.

Tiffany looked down at her arm.

Then she looked back up at the moon.

Then she looked back down at her arm—

And she let out an appalling string of curse words.

"Who is it?" she demanded, all hints of good nature gone from her voice. *This wasn't funny, not in the least.* This was beyond upsetting. It was horrific.

Impossible.

It simply was not happening.

Brooke strolled to Tiffany's side and glanced at the sky.

For a moment, the beautiful brunette simply stared at the stars in awe, and then she fell into immediate formal protocol. "We need to go find Napolean." She spoke softly and deliberately. "Whoever the male is, he has to be close by. Close enough to find you… if he searches."

Tiffany spun around on her heels, her eyes darting back and forth across the room like frenetic lasers. She half expected to see Count Dracula himself hanging from the ceiling. "No!" she exclaimed, to no one in particular. There was absolutely no way they were going *to go find Napolean* in order to offer her up as the virgin sacrifice to a vamp. Okay, well, not necessarily a virgin, but a sacrifice just the same. "That is not going to happen."

Brooke nodded gravely and lowered her voice. "Okay, so what would you like me to do?"

Tiffany glanced around the room and shuddered. "Give me your keys, Brooke. I need to get out of here."

"And you want to take my car?"

Tiffany glowered at her best friend, and if looks could kill, Brooke would have been six feet under, with rigor mortis already setting in. "Damnit, Brooke! I'm not playing around. The guest house is three miles away! Do you want me to walk?" She spun around again and eyed the back door of the parlor, the passage that led to Phoenix's private portico. "*Give me your keys.*"

Brooke took a slow step backward and sighed. "Sweetie," she nearly crooned, "I get it—you're scared. Believe me, I understand. But you and I both know that you can't run away from this. What we need to do is—"

"We?" Tiffany cut in. "Seriously, Brooke? *We?*" She took several steps back, gravitating toward the door. "No. There is no *we* in this. And I get it, too: You're in love with the vampire king, and your life has been a thousand times better since Napolean claimed you, since you came to Dark Moon Vale. Bully for you." She sighed, trying to catch her breath. "And so has mine—I'll be the first to admit it—but *that* is as your graphic designer, your best friend, and your son's impromptu nanny. Not as some creature's *destiny.*"

"Some *creature?*" Brooke looked mildly offended.

"Don't do that, Brooke," Tiffany said. "Seriously, not right now. That's not even fair. You know I have supported you… and Napolean… and Phoenix." Her voice rose in proportion to her angst. "Hell, I've committed myself to living in Dark Moon Vale, knowing full well that I can never go back, not now that I know about the Vampyr, not now that I've placed myself under their protection and care. But"—she held up her hand to silence any protest before one could be made—"but *this* I cannot do. I will not do. I'm not you, Brooke. These guys scare the hell out of me on a really primitive level, if you know what I mean. So please. *Please.* Just give me your keys." She held out her hand and waited.

Brooke looked positively ill. The turmoil in her eyes was unmistakable, the angst on her face, excruciating. "Oh, Tiff," she whispered. "You are my best friend in the entire world." She straightened her spine and raised her chin, although her confidence didn't register in her voice. "And there is nothing I wouldn't do for you, but what you're asking… " She glanced at the door to the hall and then the door to the portico, each one in turn. "As your friend, as someone who *loves* you, I know that you're in danger if you go off alone." She sighed. "And as Napolean's mate, a member of the house of Jadon—hell, *as the queen*—I also know that whoever this male is, if I help his *destiny* escape—"

"His *destiny*?" Tiffany interrupted, hardly able to believe her ears. "So is that what I am now? *His* destiny?"

"No," Brooke argued. "I mean, *yes*, obviously, but—"

"Don't, *milady*. The indecision does not become you." Tiffany knew she was being cruel, but she just couldn't help it. She was also running out of time. Gritting her teeth, she steadied her resolve and changed tactics. "At least tell me this: Who's here, at the manse, right now? Which of your *subjects*? Which one of the males?" She instantly regretted the sarcasm, but it was too late to take it back.

Brooke looked momentarily stunned, perhaps even hurt by the sharp delivery, but to her credit, she collected herself and tried to answer honestly. "Um… I don't know." She shrugged her shoulders in exasperation, her soft blue eyes clouding with distress. "There's no one… no meetings… no counsels." She dropped her head and ran her hands through her hair, as if physically seeking the answers from her mind. "The only one who stops by this time of night, unannounced, is Ramsey Olaru, the sentinel. He sometimes drops in to compare notes with Napolean, but it all depends on what's up."

Tiffany felt her knees go weak beneath her. "Ramsey? *Olaru*? The six-foot-five walking pit bull? The one who fights with a *pitchfork*?"

"It's a trident," Brooke mumbled weakly, "an archaic weapon that—"

Tiffany leveled a spiteful glare at her friend. "The guy who spit out a toothpick on Napolean's floor, the one who smashed his enemy's head into smithereens by bashing it against the side of a cave wall?" She winked at her friend sardonically. "That's just… lovely." She nodded her head in quick, short bursts. "Remember, Brooke—*it's me*—the one you tell all your secrets to." Her eyes glazed over with tears, and her voice hitched in her throat. "Just give me your keys, Brookie. I'm begging you."

Brooke turned the color of stale, curdled milk. "Tiffany, *listen*."

"*No.*"

"*Please*, just listen. Let's you and I go somewhere *together*, anywhere you'd like. I'll tell Carlotta that I'm going out, so she can look after Phoenix; and then I'll get my car and come around the back. You can meet me by the trellis. We'll go to a hotel or a cabin—hell, we can go to another town—and I won't call Napolean until you tell me you're ready. At least this way, someone will be with you."

Tiffany pursed her lips and nodded her head derisively. "Yeah, because Napolean Mondragon can't just reach into your mind, or follow the trail of your blood, or just beam himself into any room you're standing in like Captain Kirk, right? Because his queen can just walk away undetected… " Her voice trailed off. There was no point in exploring this angle any further.

Tiffany was out of time.

She wiped a single tear from her eye and reached for her jacket, a soft, form-fitting cloak hanging on a polished bronze hook beside the portico door, and she quickly shrugged into the garment.

"What are you doing?" Brooke asked, her face an ashen mask.

"I'm leaving."

"On foot?"

"Can't fly. I'm human."

Brooke lunged forward, and in that terrifying moment, her unnatural vampiric speed as well as her supernatural agility completely caught Tiffany off guard.

"Don't!" Tiffany shouted, raising her hands to ward off her friend as if she were about to tear out her throat with her fangs.

Brooke drew back in surprise and gasped.

And all the tears Tiffany had been holding at bay began to stream down her cheeks in desperate rivers. Her voice caught on a sob. "You're stronger than me, Brooke, and you're faster. You could stop me, but it would kill me. Do you understand what I'm saying? This is a line you can't cross." She swiped at her tears with the heels of her hands and sniffled. "I'm not asking you to break an oath, to help me get away, just turn your back and—"

"Brooke!" Napolean's deep voice rose in a thunderous crescendo as the ancient king began to make his way down the hall. Undoubtedly, he had sensed his mate's distress and was on his way to investigate the cause.

Shit, shit, and more shit! Tiffany thought, glancing at the door. She had to get the hell out of Dodge… and now.

As Brooke turned around to answer the king—her lethal, vampiric husband—Tiffany dashed for the door. She wrenched open the handle in a fevered rush and flew out onto the patio, frantic to make an escape, flinching as the door slammed shut behind her. She immediately eyed the trellis and gave it less than a moment's thought before leaping over the rail and dashing down the steep hill toward the open meadow below.

Oh, thank the gods of horses and war!

She breathed a sigh of relief as she eyed the majestic Percheron still searching for patches of grass in the snow-covered meadow at the base of the hill. Nearly eighteen hands of muscle, strength, and speed awaited her devotion, and she couldn't help but marvel at her sudden good fortune: Prince Phoenix had wanted to see *da pwetty pony* earlier that day, if that's what one could call the magnificent, intelligent beast, and the king's gift to his son was still saddled and neatly tied beneath a temporary shelter, awaiting Napolean's private trainer to return him to the stables.

Tiffany was not much of a rider—okay, so she could barely

sit straight in the saddle—but what the hell: Desperate times called for desperate measures. She eyed the Percheron cautiously, approached with gentle ease, and slowly raised an outstretched hand, careful not to frighten the horse away: "Here, horsy. *Here, horsy!* Come, *please*. Just… come."

The horse looked up at her with luminous, haunting eyes. He tossed back his head and pranced in place, as if showing off his power and pride.

And then he went back to eating.

Tiffany's heart sank into her stomach. *Not now, Mr. Horse. Please… not now.* She held out her hand, palm side up, as if she had a delectable piece of sugar resting in the center, and she tried again. "Here, beautiful prince"—maybe he preferred an appeal to his ego—"here, you gorgeous, magnificent gladiator. Come see Auntie Tiff… *please*."

She waited with bated breath.

And to her utter surprise, the horse trotted over in her direction. Truth be told, he probably came out of pity.

She waited until he was within an arm's length before slowly reaching up to stroke his neck, just beneath his mane. "That's a good horsy," she murmured, feeling more than a little foolish. She sauntered up to his left side and eyed the dangling stirrup, marveling at the barely leashed power emanating from the horse's breast, and praying all the while that he wouldn't trample her, or worse, take off running while she tried to mount. She reached for the reins and softly slid a foot into the stirrup. Okay, so she had to jack her knee up to her chest just to reach the perilous leather hoop, but she did it as gracefully as she could. "Okay, Mr. Horse, I'm counting on you to save me," she whispered.

The stallion snorted in reply, and she took it as a *yes*.

With that, she grabbed the shoehorn, pulled herself into the saddle, and kicked him in the flanks.

*

Napolean Mondragon burst into the parlor in a maelstrom, his glorious long hair whipping behind him as if stirred by a mystical wind. His eyes were narrowed in concentration; his face was a mask of concern; and his no-nonsense tone made it abundantly clear: He wasn't playing around.

Brooke opened her mouth to speak, but she didn't have a chance.

"What's wrong?" he demanded, staring at her with unconcealed concern. He reached out, took her hands in his, and then quickly released them. He ran his palms up and down her arms, while perusing her body from head to toe with a dark, penetrating gaze, his eyes scanning for gods-knew-what. "Are you hurt, my love?"

"No," Brooke answered. She tried to speak in a calming voice. "I'm... I... It's just—"

"Where's Phoenix?" He immediately strode toward the back of the parlor.

"He's in his room. He's in his crib. *He's fine.*"

Napolean turned back around and visibly eased up. "Then why are you so distressed?"

Brooke took a deep breath and answered bluntly, "It's Tiffany."

"Tiffany?" Napolean furrowed his brow. "Has something happened to your friend?"

Brooke shook her head in denial. "Have you seen the moon, milord?"

"*Milord?*" Napolean frowned, and then he reached out to gently stroke her cheek with the back of his hand. "That's rather ominous, *rather formal*, coming from you."

"Have you seen the moon?" she repeated.

"Of course," he answered sternly. "A Gemini Blood Moon. It belongs to Ramsey Olaru, but his *destiny* is yet unknown. I was with the sentinel just moments ago in the living room, trying to figure it out. We were about to search for Carlotta when I felt your distress... "

"It's not Carlotta," Brooke whispered cautiously.

Napolean's dark eyes lit up with instant understanding. "*Tiffany?*"

Brooke bit her bottom lip and nodded in a barely perceptible gesture.

Napolean drew back in surprise. "Where is she?"

Brooke took a deep breath and shook her head. "Gone."

"What do you mean, *gone?*"

Brooke turned to face the back of the parlor and pointed toward the still-open door. "I mean, *she's gone.* She ran off. I couldn't make her stay."

"And why is that?" Ramsey Olaru's deep, husky tenor reverberated through the room as the huge, fearsome male sauntered into the parlor. "Forgive my bad manners, milord, but I felt the circumstances warranted the intrusion."

Napolean nodded. "Ramsey," he said by way of greeting. "Then you heard?"

Ramsey inclined his head. "I heard."

Brooke shuddered, recognizing the precarious situation for what it was: Not only had Tiffany taken off into the valley like some kind of escaped convict, but Ramsey Olaru was a Master Warrior, a dangerous and hard-nosed sentinel of Dark Moon Vale; and he was standing on the precipice of a perilous cliff, where his life hung in the balance beneath a centuries-awaited Blood Moon. The male was not only hyped up on adrenaline—if not downright feral—he was more dangerous than ever before, and his eerily calm exterior only emphasized that point.

Brooke sought to diffuse the situation as tactfully as possible. "I'm sorry, Ramsey," she whispered. "Tiffany was terrified, and I tried—"

Ramsey held up a large, rugged hand to silence her as he turned to face the king. "Milord, have you taken Tiffany's blood?"

A low growl of warning rumbled in Napolean's throat, and the king's nostrils flared in disapproval. "What the *hell* was that?"

Ramsey lowered his gaze, as respectfully as he could. He glanced up at Brooke and declined his head in apology. "Forgive me, milady. I meant you no disrespect." Then he set his jaw and turned to Napolean. "Milord, by all rights, I should not even be standing here right now. A Blood Moon trumps all other protocol. So please, just tell me: Have you taken Tiffany's blood?"

Oh gods, he really sounds... upset, Brooke whispered to Napolean telepathically. She didn't want to aggravate the situation, but she was growing increasingly concerned for her friend.

It's okay, angel, Napolean replied in a gentle but confident psychic tone. *He is dealing with an overwhelming sense of urgency. It is to be expected.*

Of course, Brooke said. *I understand. I just... are you sure he's okay?*

Napolean nodded, and then he cleared his throat. "Miss Matthews is under the protection of the house of Jadon," he said to Ramsey. "She has been initiated as a human loyalist. Of course I've taken her blood."

Ramsey shifted his weight from foot to foot and slowly stretched his back. "And?"

Napolean shut his eyes, as if trying to maintain his cool. His hand twitched almost imperceptibly, and his face grew taut— but his expression remained composed. "And she's about three-quarters of a mile into the northern forest... on a horse. She's heading due east."

"On a horse?" Brooke cut in, immediately regretting the irrelevant outburst.

Ramsey's top lip twitched several times in a row, and the tips of his fangs began to extend from his gums before he quickly caught the involuntary reaction and reined it in. His eyes deepened to a darker hue, the hazel tones expanding to amber; but otherwise, he showed little reaction. "Phoenix's Percheron?" he asked, incredulous.

"Yes, on Viking," Napolean confirmed.

Ramsey nodded solemnly, and then his entire body stiffened; his spine grew straighter; and he appeared to grow two inches taller. "If that is all, milord."

Napolean inclined his head, and Brooke nearly swayed where she stood.

Oh gods, Napolean; will she be okay? For the first time that night, she truly feared for her friend, and not because of the Dark Ones or any other supernatural creatures that went bump in the night. Brooke was afraid of Ramsey.

She will, Napolean replied in her mind. *He will find her and retrieve her…*

Faster than she can say his name, Brooke uttered, swallowing her fear. A blind man could see Ramsey's determination. The sentinel would not be denied.

Indeed, Napolean replied. And then he turned to face the powerful vampire before them. "Warrior, do you want—"

Ramsey clenched his fists at his side and then slowly released them, but he held his tongue out of respect… and waited.

"Julien… our tracker?" Napolean persisted.

Ramsey sucked his teeth and exhaled. "Nope."

"Your brothers, Saxson or Santos?"

He rolled his shoulders and popped his neck. "*Nope.*"

When Napolean held out both hands, palms facing down, parallel to the floor, and then gently splayed his fingers as if to calm a wild beast, Brooke's heart nearly skipped a beat.

"You are one of only three valley sentinels," Napolean said ceremoniously, "a member of my private guard, a warrior entrusted to protect this vale. So I need not express to you the many dangers that could arise."

Brooke clung to Napolean's hand and shuddered. By all that was holy, Ramsey's eyes were like hot, focused lasers as he locked them unerringly with the king's. He didn't interrupt him and he didn't cut him off, yet his silence spoke volumes: He was itching to get on with the search.

"Very well," Napolean said. "Then you also know I can only give you so much time before I interfere. Until we see you *both* home safely."

Brooke's stomach did a tiny flip. *See them both home safely?* Oh gods, the reality was truly sinking in, and she didn't like the implications: Both Ramsey and Tiffany could be in very real danger. Perhaps she should have tried harder to stop her friend...

Ramsey cleared his throat with a raspy inflection. "If that is all, milord."

Once again, Napolean declined his head in a regal gesture of formal dismissal. "That is all, warrior."

"That's it?" Brooke squawked out loud, forgetting to hold her tongue. *No please be gentle? Try not to frighten her out of her wits or yank her arm out of its socket? Maybe you should take another vampire along, like Braden or Nachari?*

"Milady?" Ramsey inquired solicitously, although his voice was as hard as stone.

"Nothing," Brooke said quickly. "I was just thinking out loud." When Ramsey didn't reply, Brooke ducked beneath the safety of Napolean's arm, nestling closer to his chest.

Perhaps she was just imagining things.

Perhaps Ramsey was just on edge.

Or perhaps the warrior was truly miffed by the fact that Tiffany Matthews was supposed to be one of them: While human, she understood the Curse and the consequences of failing to fulfill it. She worked in Dark Moon Vale for the royal family, and she also knew Ramsey personally, if only through passing interactions; yet and still, she had chosen to run away, to risk the sentinel's life.

She made no such conscious choice, Napolean said telepathically. *She simply reacted in fear. He knows this.* Having revealed the fact that he was reading her thoughts, he tightened his arm around her waist and pulled her closer. "This male will not hurt his *destiny*, my love." He spoke aloud for Ramsey's benefit, and then he turned back to regard the keyed-up vampire. "Fifteen minutes to find her; thirty to retrieve her; and then... your brethren will step in."

Ramsey nodded in obeisance. "As you will, milord."

Brooke watched in angst-filled suspense as the ruthless sentinel stalked to the back door of the parlor; threw open the panel, using only his mind to do so; and drew some sort of crude weapon from a sheath at his belt. "And just what the hell is that for?" she whispered beneath her breath.

"We have many enemies, my love," Napolean answered calmly, shifting his hand to the small of her back, where he could rub it softly. "And Ramsey is a sentinel. He hunts Dark Ones. He protects the people. He dispatches enemies, of all types, *at my command*. He is not an ordinary member of the house of Jadon. He must take extraordinary precautions."

Despite her mate's explanation, Brooke Adams-Mondragon cringed.

It had only been fourteen months since she and Tiffany had first come to Dark Moon Vale to attend a routine conference. It had only been fourteen months since the two of them had been hurtled into a world beyond comprehension, into the realm of the Vampyr, against their will. And as she thought about it, she had to admit: Napolean had been rather *intense* when she had *met* him as well. For heaven's sake, he had stopped a cab with the palm of his hand, ripped the door off the hinges, and ordered Brooke to get out of the backseat, while Ramsey had driven the "getaway" car. Well, no wonder she still feared the male like the grim reaper... with fangs.

She drew in a deep breath of air and tried to calm her racing heart.

In the end, it had all worked out, and Brooke had found happiness beyond her wildest dreams. She had been gifted with peace, security, and love—surely, Tiffany would find the same.

But with Ramsey Olaru?

As she stared at the open door, shivering from the cool, ominous breeze that wafted through in Ramsey's wake, she marshaled her courage and summoned her hope. And then she said a prayer to the celestial god Gemini: *Please let Tiffany be okay, and please don't let Ramsey... harm her sensitive soul.*

She knew her best friend well, just as she also knew the vampire...

And this was not going to be an easy Blood Moon.

one

Ramsey Olaru shimmered into view beneath the narrow, spindly branches of a Ponderosa pine. He plucked a thin pine needle from a low-hanging branch, stuffed it between his teeth, and slowly turned around in a circle.

He was scenting, once again, for the presence of Dark Ones. He was tuning into Nachari and Keitaro's recently placed lycan-wards, making sure the supernatural wolf-detectors were functioning. He was checking for the presence of vampire hunters, human miscreants, or general threats of any kind: bears, cougars, wolves, anything that could threaten his *destiny*.

His destiny.

Tiffany Matthews.

What in the hell had just happened?

He looped his familiar spiked bola into a thong at his waist—the last thing he needed to do was frighten the blond graphic artist any further—and tried to determine his next move: Tiffany was riding up a steep, rocky grade about fifty yards away, and by the harried look on her face, she was barely keeping her seat. Somehow, she had found an old riding trail, one that wound its way through the steep Rocky Mountains, and unbeknownst to her, she was heading for an imminent bluff, one with an abrupt seventy-foot drop-off.

The horse was holding his own, *and damn, wasn't that the understatement of the century?* The Percheron was a magnificent sight to behold. But even the young, powerful steed was having a hard time keeping his footing on the gravelly trail, and Ramsey couldn't help but consider what would happen if the 1,400-pound steed actually fell. He grit his teeth around the reed and focused his thoughts: There were more pressing matters to attend to.

Like how to retrieve his *destiny* before she encountered something she couldn't defend against... before she led the horse to the edge of the waiting cliff.

He sighed, mentally preparing himself for the confrontation. No matter how he turned it, it wouldn't be pleasant, and frankly, that wasn't his foremost concern. Tiffany would come with him one way or the other; best to just go ahead and get it done.

He whistled low, mimicking the call of a native swallow, just to get her attention in the least abrasive way, and then he slowly stepped out from beneath the tree and began to make his way up the steep embankment, choosing his footing with ease.

Tiffany froze in the saddle. She pulled back on the reins to halt the horse and sat up straight to listen. A wisp of her harshly layered, short blond hair fell into her eyes as she turned her head from side to side, trying to home in on the sound.

"Over here, behind you," Ramsey drawled, stepping into the moonlight.

Her eyes immediately darted to where he stood, and she took a quick intake of breath. For a moment, Ramsey thought she would fall out of the saddle in fright, but she quickly regained her composure and held out a hand in a gesture of *stop*. "Don't come any closer, Mr. Olaru," she warned.

Ramsey spat out the reed and smiled. "Now, you know that's not going to happen, Miss Matthews." He tried to keep his voice soft, but it came out as a rasp just the same. "Why don't you come down from that horse, and let's talk this over."

To Ramsey's utter surprise and horror, she kicked the

Percheron in the flanks and tried to gallop up the mountain. *Oh hell*, he thought, putting a little urgency into his own step as he followed like a stalking raider behind them. *Whoa, boy*; he sent a telepathic call to Viking. The horse was clearly nervous, undoubtedly responding to the presence of a predator, and the animal's tightly coiled power could be unleashed at any moment. He snorted, pranced in place, and then took a powerful leap up the mountain, nearly bounding to the top of the hill.

And that's when Ramsey shifted into overdrive. He dematerialized from where he stood and instantly reappeared at the top of the bluff in front of the horse, holding both hands out in front of him. "Whoa, Viking!" His tone was deadly serious this time.

The horse reared up before settling into a restless stance, but Tiffany kept her seat. She tightened her hold on the reins, lifted them slightly upward, and glanced over her shoulder, noticing the cliff for the very first time. "You take one more step forward, and I'm going to back him up," she said, her voice belying her resolve.

Ramsey frowned and assessed the situation. *Hells bells, would she really take herself and the horse over the side of a cliff—just to get away from him?* He held his arms out to the sides and whispered, "You don't want to do that, baby girl. I can assure you; that's not the better option."

Tiffany raised her jaw in defiance and leveled a murderous glare his way. "Don't test me, Mr. Olaru. I will do it." The horse whinnied as if to say, *what the hell are you people doing*, and then he tossed his head in disobedience to create some slack in the reins. Tiffany gathered the slack and drew the leather taut, pulling back ever so slightly to regain control.

Ramsey regarded the massive beast with caution. He was much too close to the edge for Ramsey's liking, and while the impressive stallion had grown up with vampires from a colt, he was like any other animal, any other person for that matter: There were just some souls he liked better than others. And Ramsey Olaru? Not so much.

He sent a warm, peaceful ray of comfort radiating in the horse's direction and then turned his attention back to Tiffany. "Why don't you call me Ramsey, baby girl, and *let's talk this over.*"

Tiffany sneered. "Talk this over? Seriously?" She squared her jaw. "No, I don't think so. Why don't you just walk away?"

Ramsey shook his head slowly and frowned. "Not going to happen." He relaxed his shoulders and tried to appear less threatening, however that worked. "What seems to be the impasse?"

Tiffany practically snorted then, her vivid sea-green eyes darkening with contempt. "The impasse? Oh my gosh; you have got to be kidding." She looked up at the moon and then glanced at her wrist, all the while still holding the reins, and then she almost snarled. "The *impasse* is you. And me. That moon and my wrist. It's not going to happen, Ramsey. I'm sorry to tell you... and I hate to do this... but I'm not like Brooke, and it's... it's just... *not going to happen.*" Her voice rose in proportion to her angst, and for a moment, Ramsey thought she might start hyperventilating. *Damn, was he really that scary, just on the face of things?*

He grimaced, already knowing the answer: Yeah, he was.

Ramsey Olaru was known as one cruel and ruthless son of a viper, and he had a reputation for being an unforgiving hard-ass, even when it was easier to take another route. But heck, what could he say? It was part of the job, being a sentinel. He was a guardian, an executioner, and an enforcer all at once; and one didn't do that well without drawing a hard line somewhere along the way. "I'm not so bad with females," he offered in an attempt to soften the truth.

Tiffany laughed, yet the sound was curiously hollow. "*Females?*" she mimicked him again. "You don't even live in the twenty-first century, Ramsey." When he started to object, she immediately spoke over him. "Hell, you still fight with a pitchfork."

"It's a trident," he said nonchalantly, "an archaic weapon that—"

"Oh, hell, you sound just like Brooke!" She rotated her wrists, seizing up on the reins. "It's a farm utensil, Mr. Olaru! And it's barbaric."

The horse responded to the barest hint of pressure on his bit and took a nervous step backward, toward the cliff. "Whoa!" Ramsey said, speaking once again to the horse. "Tiffany, you need to watch what you're doing."

Her eyes glistened with tears, and she shivered, for the first time displaying some healthy fear of the bluff. "I know exactly what I'm doing, Ramsey, and I'm sorry." She bent her head to look over her shoulder, to stare down at the perilous drop-off, and in that brief, telltale moment, something dangerous flashed in her eyes: decision, determination… resolution. The willingness to end her life.

Ramsey licked his lips and took a measured step forward, not far enough to frighten the horse, but close enough to lunge if he had to. "You would kill that beautiful animal?" he asked, appealing to her conscience. "What would Phoenix think of that?"

Tiffany blinked back her tears and steadied her resolve. "Phoenix is only thirteen and a half months old."

"And you're what? Twenty-nine or thirty? You would end it all right here, right now?" He glanced up at the sky and gestured with his chin. "Over that moon?"

Tiffany's features grew strained. "It's not the moon, Ramsey, and you know it. It's the Curse and all the blood. The violence and the endless threats. It's the sacrifice and the *fangs*. You're a vampire, Ramsey, one that can hunt and maim and kill without hesitation, and I don't want to be what you are. I like being human, and I still have a soul… as well as free will. So, don't speak to me like I'm an idiot or a newbie. I'm neither."

Ramsey nodded slowly, acknowledging the fact that he had

heard her words. "You took on this entire world when you stayed in Dark Moon Vale, baby girl," he said without mincing words. "When you chose to keep your memories and serve our king. You knew the deal back then, and you knew you could never go back—but you stayed. So, what's changed?"

Tiffany sighed deeply. "That was for Brooke… and Phoenix… for me." She shrugged, almost apologetically. "But that's not the same as giving up my humanity, giving myself *to you*."

Ramsey considered her words carefully—way too deep of a subject to get into at this juncture—there was no point in having this discussion now, not here, not while they were balancing on the edge of a cliff, quite literally. He chose to take another tactic. "Okay, well, look at it this way, then: If you back that horse off that cliff, I'll just have to jump over and catch you." He raised his shoulders in a matching gesture. "But the real question is: Could I catch both you *and* the horse?" He toggled his hands up and down as if pondering the possibility. "Possibly… *probably*… " He sniffed. "It's not so much the weight as the size that might be difficult, trying to hold you and the horse at the same time. More than likely, you would have to go back and tell Phoenix that Viking didn't make it—that you killed his pony."

"Would you shut up!"

Ramsey chuckled low in his throat, and the corner of his mouth turned up in what he knew was a wicked smile.

"Is this funny to you?" Tiffany asked, her voice filled with anguish and maybe even a little regret.

"It's a little bit funny," Ramsey retorted, though his voice was as serious as a heart attack, "in a tragic sort of way." He narrowed his gaze, and he *felt* his eyes flush with heat. He knew they had flashed crimson before settling back into their normal hazel hues. "But I'll tell you what isn't funny, Miss Matthews… " He drew a deep breath and practically growled the words. "Underneath us right now, about two to three miles beneath the surface, is a colony of vampires from a very different house, and if they could get to you, they would, just to eliminate me. And I'll tell you something else, baby doll: The shit they would do to you if they caught you would make jumping off a cliff look like a real good option. And while I *can* jump over the side of this mountain and catch you before you die, I don't know if I can fight more than a couple of Dark Ones at a time. So I'm going to ask you once more, *nicely*, to get off that horse and back away from that cliff. And then, I'm gonna come get you."

*

Ramsey's chilling words brushed over Tiffany's skin like a pair of skeletal hands reaching from the grave. The wind was beginning to howl, the thick scent of pine was wafting to her nostrils, and the moment seemed utterly surreal.

She gulped, and then she shivered. The dangerous sentinel was not playing around. He was not offering her an olive branch or a half-dozen roses, and he was not trying to gently romance her into his arms. And somehow, in that terrifying moment, she knew that all of her fears were warranted: Ramsey Olaru was not Napolean Mondragon. He was not one of the Silivasi brothers or even the former Dark One, Saber Alexiares. He was a *feeding*, hunting, killing machine; and he would offer her no quarter, make no allowances, spare her no indignity just to make it easier.

Despite his uncanny, model-worthy good looks, his somewhat civilized mannerisms, and his obvious keen intelligence, he may as well have been a Viking himself, a relic from a time gone by. Ramsey Olaru was all hard muscle and grit, stout bearing and implacable resolve. He was six feet five inches of stunning, almost unnatural beauty, and he was hard as granite, inside and out.

What was worse, he believed without hesitation that Tiffany *belonged* to him, and he wasn't about to let her walk away. Not that she could blame him—his very life depended upon her acquiescence—but still, he could have at least tried to ease her mind, perhaps assuage her fears, or even appeal to her heart. Yet he had done none of the above. He had *ordered* her to get down off the horse and laced it inside of a threat.

Tiffany struggled to swallow her fear, as impossible as that was, and then she tried a different approach. "You're really kind of scaring me, Ramsey," she whispered.

He frowned. "Yeah, and you're really kind of starting to tick me off." He drew up to his full, imposing height. "Get down off that horse, Tiffany. I'm not going to ask you again."

She knew that he meant it, and she couldn't win this battle.

Not here.

Not now.

Not today.

She kicked the horse a few paces forward—away from the cliff—placed her hand around the horn, and slowly dismounted from the saddle. As Ramsey sidled up beside her to take the Percheron's reins, she sidestepped out of his way and hugged her arms to her chest. "Do you even have a conscience?" she muttered in a surly tone.

He led the enormous animal away from the cliff, while she took slow, hesitant steps behind him, and then he glanced over his shoulder to meet her questioning gaze. "You ever listen to 'Blaze of Glory' by Bon Jovi? The lyrics?"

Tiffany drew back in surprise. "What?" *He was asking her about a retro rock song? Now?* "Yeah, I've heard it a time or two," she said. And then she tried to recall some of the words: *I'm a devil on the run, a six gun lover, a candle in the wind…* Seemed appropriate enough, in a disturbing kind of way, but what in the world was he trying to tell her?

Ramsey suddenly stopped walking and turned to face her. He reached out with a surprisingly gentle hand, cupped the side of her face with his fingers, and brushed his thumb ever so softly against the warmth of her cheek. "*You ask about my conscience, and I offer you my soul.*" The words were a mere whisper of sound as he held her gaze with his, his stunning hazel eyes revealing the barest glimpse of vulnerability, the soul inside the sentinel.

Tiffany drew in a sharp intake of breath and tried not to shiver, even as chills shot down her spine and settled in her toes.

He knew he had nothing refined to offer.

He knew he was a *hardened* vampire, all rough, jagged edges and hard-lined planes.

Yet, he offered her…

His soul?

She brushed his hand away. The touch was too intimate to bear. And then she fell into a silent step beside him as she followed him back to the vale.

two

Deep in the bowels of the Dark Ones' colony, Salvatore Nistor glared at the infernal cube beside his bed. Earlier that night, it had revealed a *Gemini Blood Moon*, another male in the house of Jadon receiving his undeserved due. As far as which male the gods were blessing, the cube didn't say. Now, the crazy, inconsistent thing was glowing luminescent blue and pastel purple, which meant something entirely different: It meant *she* was at it again: the idiotic, confused human female.

The one with dyed red-and-black hair—peculiar choice, to put it mildly. The more she tried to conjure spirits in her piteous attempt to engage her idea of the *underworld*—the more she tried to summon a dark entity with her dangerously limited knowledge of what she was doing—the more her errant vibrations appeared in the globe's murky depths.

He sighed and grasped the familiar cube in both palms: *What to do*? *What to do*? Should he oblige the silly human in her misplaced fantasies, appear as the dark, mysterious entity she so desired to conjure, or should he command the crystal to never… *ever*… show him this vile human female again?

He lifted the cube from its perch on his bedside table and cradled it in his lap, lovingly, trying to reason the whole thing out: On one hand, Derrian was not getting any younger. Salvatore's nephew was now sixteen months old and some change, and the sorcerer could certainly use another full-time nanny, considering what had happened to the last one: such an unpleasant business involving chains, a test tube, and a dull knife. Salvatore cringed. On the other hand, he was hardly ready to father a dark offspring of his own, to take on a lifetime of responsibility and obligation. Not to mention, destroying such an uncommon woman by using her as a disposable breed mate would certainly be a waste of a rare opportunity, a dark, malleable human soul.

He had to admit, this was a rare and exquisite opportunity to say the least.

The confused woman was ripe for the picking.

She was dabbling in energy she couldn't possibly comprehend, and she was committing abhorrent acts of wantonness and vulgarity in her endless attempts to attract a malicious spirit: slaughtering chickens and kittens and birds; drawing bizarre chalk diagrams on her kitchen floor in an attempt to summon a demonic entity; and sleeping with as many human men as she could bring home, offering her body wantonly to please these elusive shadowy *beings*, whoever she thought they might be.

And, most recently, in a moment of pure desperation, she had offered her immortal soul in trade for a lifetime of truly depraved power.

And this had grabbed Salvatore's attention. It had grabbed the attention of his cube.

It was well known that the males in the house of Jaegar had been cursed without the benefit of the *four mercies* afforded their self-righteous cousins who lived above the surface: The males in the house of Jaegar had no *destinies*; they could never walk in the sun; they took the lives of the innocent *at will* in order to feed their bloodlust… and both their children were born wholly evil.

Evil.

Well, wasn't that just a relative term?

Relative and preposterous.

The Dark Ones simply preferred… *and enjoyed*… a different lifestyle.

Still, the starkest difference between the Dark Ones and the house of Jadon was the presence of females in their daily lives, mates who shared in the duty and responsibility of rearing the young, and bedfellows who warmed the sheets at night, as if Salvatore could ever be truly content with only one partner.

Once again, *partner* was such a relative word: Salvatore Nistor had no equal, and women were mere objects of temporary pleasure, never partners.

He sighed, feeling overwhelmed by the quandary. "What shall I do about you, Miss Tawni Duvall? Do you have any idea how close you are standing to an eternal edge of darkness? An utterly hellish precipice? Ready and willing to careen into the depths of the abyss?" He laughed, a low, maniacal sound that reverberated in the dark underground lair, shaking the magnificent antique chandelier above him. "While the only way a human can be converted to Vampyr is to be born to the privilege, a female *destiny* marked by the gods—and only for the males in the house of Jadon—there are two exceptions my dear, Miss Duvall: a child, like Braden Bratianu, born to a human *destiny*, who already possesses celestial DNA; and a human stupid enough to trade his *or her* immortal soul for the glorious opportunity, which makes you fair game for all." He licked his lips as if he had just partaken of a delicacy. "And you are just such a human, are you not, Miss Duvall?" He cradled the cube to his heart and moaned in pleasure, considering the possibilities.

No, he didn't want her as an individual, *not at all*: He didn't want to deal with all her occultist nonsense, nor would he tolerate all her inane sacrificial pets. And the endless orgies with human men?

That was definitely out.

But…

And this was really the point worth considering…

She could prove to be very useful, indeed.

After all, a mere woman could go where a Dark One could not, like straight into the heart of the house of Jadon. She could even knock on Napolean's front door. Hell, she could take a job in one of the various industries: at Marquis's beloved casino or the Dark Moon Stables, at the Dark Moon Lodge or even DMV Prime, working for the queen or her blond-haired friend. Or she could just beat down someone's door while wielding a chainsaw, bloody but effective. The possibilities were truly endless, and the Light Ones would never suspect a thing. They would never see her coming.

Why would they?

As long as she stayed away from the wizards, those who might detect her malevolent aura, those who might suspect that she was somehow Vampyr after all…

Salvatore placed the cube back on his bedside table. He stood up and exhaled a deep sigh of resignation: Some things just had to be done for the good of the whole, for the brethren he so adored, for the beloved house of Jaegar.

Leaning over the cube, he whispered, "Yes, Miss Tawni Duvall, I believe it is time for you to succeed in summoning a demon—or a vampire. Tomato, tomahto. There are some things a male of honor simply must do, and tonight, I believe I will *do…* you."

three

Ramsey pulled into the long, sloping driveway that led to his modern cliff-side estate and finally brought the roomy Cadillac Escalade to a halt in front of the spacious five-car garage. "Home sweet home," he muttered to Tiffany, who continued to stare out the window like a zombie being led on a leash.

He climbed down from the cab, circled the vehicle, opened her door, and took a judicious step back, trying to avoid any further intimidation. "Carlotta is packing some of your things," he said casually. "She'll have them sent tomorrow. Anything else you need, we can pick up this week."

Tiffany shrugged with indifference. "And that's that?" she said caustically. "No garish castle-tower in which to lock up the captured princess?"

Ramsey reached out and ran his fingers through an errant lock of her wispy blond hair, and then he smiled a wolfish grin. "Too short to be Rapunzel," he said. "How would I ever get to you?"

Tiffany flicked his hand away and drew back. "I would appreciate it if you wouldn't touch my hair—*or me*—without my permission." Her voice contained a confidence her posture didn't match.

Ramsey cocked his head to the side. "So I take it that means sex is out, at least for tonight?"

Tiffany visibly recoiled. She placed both hands on her hips and glared at him, which only brought a twinkle to his eye. Rolling her eyes, she gestured forward and then followed him through the garage, toward the back door of the house, where he placed the palm of his hand against a strange-looking panel—it appeared more like a ward than an alarm. "What is that?" she asked, her curiosity getting the best of her.

"Just something to keep the boogeymen out," Ramsey replied. "I'll have Nachari calibrate it to include your palm later this week."

Tiffany shivered, but she didn't reply. When they entered through a long hall, passed an elaborate butler's pantry, and stepped into a stunningly designed modern kitchen, her jaw dropped open, and she simply gaped. "Holy... shit. All of this for a male who doesn't even eat?"

Ramsey watched as her eyes swept around the room, taking in the double gourmet ovens and side-by-side refrigerators, the smooth granite counters and the glimmering stainless-steel appliances, as she appraised the intricate hand-painted mosaics and the light travertine floors. Everything was modern lines, sleek design, and contemporary elegance. "Housekeepers and gardeners, pool hands and window-washers all eat food, or at least accept a drink," he commented wryly. "So do human servants and occasional human guests. We don't live alone in this valley, Miss Matthews."

Tiffany just shook her head in what looked like bewilderment.

"You hungry?"

She clenched her eyes shut and grimaced. No doubt, she was thinking about the prospect of blood, letting her imagination get the best of her. She blinked several times, turned her attention to a built-in wall cooler, stocked heavily with rare bottles of wine, and frowned. "Do you drink... *other things*?"

"Occasionally," Ramsey said, glancing at the cooler door. "Would you like some wine?"

She shook her head. "No." And then she remembered her manners. "Thank you." Her eyes met the floor, and she waited to follow him further into the house.

Ramsey sighed, feeling very much like the predator he was, as he strolled further into the luxurious domicile. "This is the living room," he said brusquely. "Well, one of them."

As Tiffany walked tentatively across the gigantic space, Ramsey couldn't help but appraise her shapely legs and absolutely perfect derriere, though he wished she were wearing one of those killer pair of stilettos. *Sue him*—she was a truly beautiful woman. When she got to the floor-to-ceiling glass panels that flanked the entire northeastern wall, she stepped forward to check out the view. "Do you own stock in Windex?" She placed a perfect, deliberate fingerprint on the glass. She eyed the door to the outdoor patio circumspectly and then stepped away, apparently thinking better of it. "Is there a barbeque outside? For the occasional human guest?"

Ramsey shook his head. "Nope. Waterfall, fire-pit, eight-man hot tub, but no barbeque."

Tiffany sighed. She walked further into the room, gazed up at the fireplace that reached all the way to the vaulted ceiling, and then gaped at the eighty-five-inch-screen TV that might have been missed if she hadn't stared straight at it. The furniture was ultra-modern, all clean lines and linear angles, tasteful… expensive. "Bachelor pad," she commented absently.

Ramsey pointed to an adjoining room, connected to this one by a wet bar and a decorative art-niche, with three consecutive arches. There was an exquisite pool table and four more flat-screen TVs anchored tastefully to the hand-textured walls in the parlor. "What gave it away?"

Tiffany shrugged, apparently still hiding inside her defensive shell. She peered down the hall toward the dual master suites, then turned toward the lavish staircase and grimaced. She didn't have to say a word; what she was thinking was obvious: *Where will I sleep?*

Ramsey took a deep breath and dove in with both feet. "My master is on the main floor at the end of this hall, to the left. The second master is across the hall on the right. I haven't decided yet whether or not I'm willing to let you out of my sight, even for a moment." It was the truth, and there was no delicate way to put it, at least not that Ramsey knew of. "But I'll show you both rooms, just in case." He pointed to a perpendicular corridor that shot off to the right, about five or six feet forward of the second master bedroom. "There's a library and another unused bedroom to the right, down that hall, plus a half bath just to your left. Any other guest bedrooms are upstairs." He gestured toward the staircase. "Six in all."

"Bathrooms?" she asked, seemingly confused by the complexity of the floor plan.

"Six bedrooms, eight baths," he replied.

She gawked. "Good lord, you don't do anything in moderation, do you?"

"I'm not a moderate guy," he said, his voice sounding far more insinuating than intended.

Tiffany must have taken it as a threat because she took an unwitting step back and grasped both arms with her hands.

"Tiffany," he said, growing increasingly frustrated, "come here." He held out his hand.

She shook her head emphatically. "No, Ramsey. I—"

"C'mon," he repeated, and he felt his pupils radiate with heat, a result of the unfair compulsion he had just given her, the vampiric command.

Tiffany shuffled toward him—she really had no choice—and he could literally hear her heart thundering in her chest. When, at last, she stood before him, he reached out and cupped her face, noticing how large and rugged his hands appeared, contrasted against her delicate skin. "Look at me, Miss Matthews," he rasped, not really knowing how to speak softly.

She stared up at him, and her sea-green eyes glimmered like jewels in the dim light of the living room.

"I'm a lot of harsh things, little lady, definitely rough around the edges, but I'm not an animal. And I'm not a rapist. I am not going to hurt you." He bent to place an innocent kiss on her forehead. "Not ever."

She grasped his hands where they held her face and shivered. "Ramsey, I can't… I can barely… breathe."

He sent a pulse of warmth into his thumbs and gently rubbed her cheeks, well, as gently as he knew how. "Better?" He tried *hard* for a softer voice. "How about now?"

She drew in a deep, unsure breath and nodded. "A little."

And then, gods forgive him, he took her in his arms.

He knew it was too soon, and he didn't have the right, but *propriety be damned*. What the hell was he supposed to do with her? She was like a frightened mouse in the paws of a lion, and he was at an utter loss for words. He tightened his arms around her slender frame, careful not to crush her with his rock-hard body. He slid his hands down to her waist and let them rest on her hips, unmoving, as she slowly settled down. "Like I said before, there's another unused bedroom next to the library, catty-corner from the second master suite. Tomorrow, we'll turn it into an office so you can work from here, keep doing the things that are familiar for DMV Prime."

Tiffany swallowed her fear, and perhaps she swallowed a sharper retort. "Then I have to stay in these four—*these fifty*—walls?" She frowned. "Like a prisoner?"

Ramsey shook his head. "No, you can work at Napolean's—when *I'm* at Napolean's. You can work at the DMV offices, when *I* go into town."

She stood quietly for a moment, perhaps collecting her thoughts. "And what about you?" Her voice was muffled as she spoke into his massive chest. She was only moderately tall compared to his towering frame. "Are you going to keep *working* as a sentinel, for now?"

His lip twitched unintentionally, and he hoped he didn't look like a stray pit bull, the kind that was just about to eat a little white rabbit. "Damn, that's a hard one." He considered the question and the implications. "Some things I still have to attend to. But others?" He cocked his head to the side. "I might be able to let them go *for a while*."

Tiffany squirmed in his arms—she clearly wanted to be free—but something inside of him was not ready to let go. Not just yet. He relaxed his hold, hooked both thumbs into the forward belt-loops of her jeans, instead, in order to keep her close, and then he waited her out.

She sighed. She shifted her weight restlessly from one foot to the other. And then she awkwardly looked down. "So… just what is it that you do, Ramsey? I mean, *specifically*. What does your job entail?"

He chuckled at the awkward change of subject. "You don't want to know exactly what I do, baby doll. Trust me; you'll want no part of that business."

She used her own thumbs to unhook his from her jeans, and then she drew back and stared at him with a mixture of surprise and concern in her expression. "Then how will I get to know you? I mean, if everything remains a secret?" The words were so soft, so tentative, that they tugged at the iron-strings of his heart: Was she willing, if only a little, to actually *get to know him*?

He placed the tips of his fingers gently on each side of her waist. "We'll take it one day, one step, at a time. Trust the celestial gods to sort it out."

She seemed to measure his words carefully, and then her eyes sparkled with a hint of mischief, if only for a moment. "Are you saying you have faith in the gods, Ramsey Olaru? In something other than violence and blood?"

He meant to chuckle in reply, but the sound came out like a muted growl. Hell, he was a little bit rusty. "In the gods… in my king… in my weapons. Yeah, I have faith."

Tiffany froze.

All at once, her shoulders stiffened, her stomach clenched, and she set her jaw in a hard, implacable line. "*Ramsey…* "

"What?" he asked, instinctively sending his six senses outward, searching for impending danger.

"Your hands," she whispered.

He looked down, gazing over her narrow, elegant shoulders, past her gracefully arched back, to that gloriously round derriere. Sure enough, his hands were planted firmly on her rear, each massive palm resting possessively on a respective globe. *Shit*, he swore inwardly, quickly bringing them back to her waist. "My bad," he whispered.

And then he let her go…

For now.

*

Tiffany literally trembled in her French-heeled boots.

The vampire could not keep his hands off her, even when he tried.

She had never felt more cornered, more uncertain, more threatened in all her life.

Well, maybe when she was hiding in Kagen's clinic with a bunch of half-wit vampire hunters, or soon after, while she was waiting for Nathaniel and Marquis Silivasi to rip out her heart for daring to attack their women. She had never touched Ciopori or Jocelyn, but still…

This was overwhelming in a way that defied imagination.

Ramsey Olaru was overwhelming in a way that defied reason.

And her head was virtually spinning.

When they had first climbed into Ramsey's truck, she had

felt like she was being led to the gallows, following an ice-cold executioner to her death. And all along the drive, on the way up the secluded switch-back to the steep, imposing house on the cliff, she had wanted to dive out of the luxurious SUV and take her chances, plummeting over the rocks. And now that they were inside his house, his modern, architectural wonder of design and technology, the reality of it all was as overwhelming and intimidating as the man himself.

Correction: the male.

The vampire.

On one hand, his home was breathtakingly beautiful, just like Ramsey—his features, his mouth, and that body? *Dear Lord.* But on the other hand, it was also foreboding, just like the vampire, stunning on the outside yet somehow distant, closed off, and unwelcoming on the inside, all in some intangible, elusive sort of way: guarded yet unassuming; harsh yet also inviting; surprisingly gentle, yet powerfully imposing.

Confusing!

Tiffany thought about his voice, the way he walked, the way he maneuvered all that hard, unyielding muscle, and then she thought about the kiss to her forehead and his pacifying words: *I'm not an animal or a rapist. I will not hurt you… ever.*

And still, she shivered.

He offered to set up an office for her, to give her a sense of the familiar, yet he told her in no uncertain terms that she would not be going anywhere without him.

He didn't hesitate to use his powers when it suited him—to compel her to come forward, to use his eyes and his voice to control her—yet he sent gentle streams of warmth into her cheeks with his hands in an effort to try and soothe her.

He tried to hold her, to somehow give her comfort, yet and still, he had cupped her ass!

The male was a barbarian trapped in a GQ model's body. He was a primal, instinctive being, trying to play at being a gentleman… if only for her comfort. And Tiffany had no idea which part of him would emerge dominant, which base instinct would eventually win.

Stepping back from his contradictory embrace, she turned toward the kitchen and sighed. Human guests, indeed. "I think I'll have that glass of wine now." To hell with propriety: What was she supposed to do with him? How would she ever get through this? "In fact, just bring a bottle, if you don't mind."

Ramsey chuckled, deep, low, and gravelly from the throat. *Would you please stop doing that?* He took a few steps toward the kitchen. "Red or white?" His voice was positively lethal.

Tiffany cringed at the unspoken implication: red or white? *Blood or wine?*

"White," she quickly asserted. And then she inadvertently eyed the stocked pine-and-glass bar situated next to the parlor. "Unless you have something stronger." What the hell, she was not too proud to self-medicate.

His lips turned up in a wicked grin as he sauntered to the bar instead, grabbed a thin plastic toothpick out of a crystal jar, and stuffed it between his ridiculously pouty lips. "Now you're speaking my language," he mumbled around the toothpick. "Name your poison."

Tiffany searched for the nearest seat in the living room, whichever chair was small enough to seat only one person at a time. *Poison?* Oh yeah, the male hardly understood the power of his words. Or maybe poignancy was a better term. "You choose," she said evenly. And then she watched as he set about creating the perfect mixture of *poison* in an exquisite, monogramed glass.

Geez, could the male be any more of an enigma?

She buttoned her tailored blouse to the very tippy-top and waited for her drink.

four

Tawni Duvall set down her chalk on the kitchen counter and checked the time. It was 11:00 PM, and the moon was an unusual shade of pale coral, almost as if it had some kind of red dye in it. She stared at the immaculate crisscrossed lines outlining the carefully drawn, five-pointed star which made up her latest diagram, and she frowned in spite of the perfection. She was at her wits' end, honestly. As in, what did the elusive entities of the underworld want from a faithful servant in order to grant her an audience? Hells bells, she was beautiful, college-educated, and willing to delve as deeply into darkness as the devil himself.

What kind of minions were the demons looking for these days, anyway?

She stared at the diagram and practically seethed with rage and frustration. Tawni had read every book she could get her hands on about conjuring dark spirits, and she had performed every nasty ritual imaginable, including sacrificing several cutesy little furry animals. *So what!* She had loved every minute of it. The surge of power she had felt as the creatures shivered in her hands, the thrill of possibility that washed over her when she thought about the absolute command she held over their lives— all of it absolutely titillated her, and she made no apology for her actions. She had even gone so far as to park her POS clunker outside of an elementary school the other day, just to watch the prim and proper children exit the building and get onto the little yellow school bus. There was a particularly cute kindergartener in pigtails who caught her eye, all flawless skin and big blue eyes, but she had been too much of a chicken to approach the girl.

Tawni had not crossed over into harming humans yet, not ever, but she was willing to consider it if she had to. Eventually, *something* had to work. She was getting tired of all the endless waiting.

She stepped into the center of the diagram and opened the tattered book of spells she had purchased in some corner dime-store shop in a quaint little village, the last time she'd been in Europe, and began to read a highlighted passage: "Dark shadows, wayward souls, I summon you now before me. With my free will and power, I bid you: *Appear*. Come to me. Come to me. Come to me."

She waited quietly with bated breath.

When nothing happened, she read it again, this time placing undue emphasis on the last three phrases. "*Come to me. Come to me. Come to me.* Now!" She added the last word for effect.

All at once, an icy breeze swept through the kitchen window, as if from a sudden gust of winter wind—but the window wasn't open—and a dark, evocative presence began to take shape in front of her like a specter rising out of a fog. She spun around on her heels to stare at the front door, as if a summoned soul would need to use a door.

She bit her bottom lip, barely realizing that she was doing it.

And just like that, the entity appeared in her living room, on the other side of the tiny bar that divided the room from the kitchen. The being was about six feet tall, imposing, definitely muscular, and he had the most glorious demonic-looking hair she had ever seen: It was halfway down his back, swirling in an unseen wind, like a host of living snakes, each coiled band shimmering midnight black or a deep blood red.

It was magnificent.

Creepy.

Unlike anything she had ever laid eyes on before. And bless the darkness, but unlike hers, it did not look like it had been dyed! She gasped and met his dark sapphire eyes with approval. They glowed with lethal intensity, and then he winked at her, his thinly arched brows furrowing from the gesture. "You called?"

She bowed her head in reverence. "Greetings, Dark One." Her voice was trembling, and it caused him to smile. *Smile.* A grin of pure, unadulterated wickedness.

"You have no idea how truly *accurate* that salutation is." His forehead creased with interest, and he gazed directly at her from beneath a pronounced widow's peak before speaking once more in a heavily laced voice: satin, fire, and brimstone. "Greetings, Miss Duvall."

She gulped. "Greetings." And then her voice came out in a thin, fearful chirp. "Wh… what am I so accurate about?" She could barely contain her excitement, despite her mounting fear.

"The term you used: *Dark One*," he lilted, almost singing the words. "It is fitting on so very many levels. It is, indeed, my correct title."

She felt her knees grow weak beneath her. Tawni had anticipated this moment a thousand times in her mind, the excitement, the titillation, finally coming in contact with *true* dark energy, but nothing had prepared her for the sheer breadth of power that radiated about the creature now standing in her apartment. He practically oozed malevolence; cruelty emanated from every pore of his skin; and the taint of evil expanded and contracted with every flex of his muscles, accentuating his hard-cut body. His aura contained three distinct colors, inky gray, sickly purple, and a garish shade of yellowish green; and it swirled in and out of his thick mane of hair as if mating with the illusionary snakes.

He took a step toward the kitchen, gliding like an upright

cobra, and every cell in her body trembled with terror. *Oh shit. Oh shit. Oh shit. What had she done?* This demon was death on two feet, and if he wasn't intimately pleased with her efforts, she knew she would never live to see the light of day. It was written all over his beautiful, *terrifying* face.

"My liege… my lord… Dark One?" Oh hell, she had no idea how to properly address him going forward. "I'm honored that you came. Thank you for responding to my summons." She bent to one knee and bowed her head, too terrified to hold his piercing gaze.

"You may call me *master*," he drawled lazily, and then he entered the kitchen noiselessly, though she never saw him move.

"Yes, master," she whispered, feeling like she might just empty her bladder. *Oh, please, no. Not now. Not here.* She clenched her Kegel muscles as tightly as she could and bent her head even lower.

He took another step in her direction, stopping just short of stepping on her hair, and his presence, so near and domineering, was more than her quaking body could handle.

She fell prostrate on the floor, her forehead pressed to the cool, dirty tiles, trying desperately to staunch her rising nausea. The genuflecting wasn't planned or even intentional. It was simply instinctive, occurring on a deep primal level. Somehow, Tawni just *knew* she had to become smaller, weaker, make herself less and less significant before him. She had to demonstrate her utter and absolute surrender… if she wanted to live.

He chuckled sardonically. "Very good, Miss. Duvall. I see you know your place."

"I do," she whispered, imagining what it would feel like if he actually touched her.

"I do, *what?*" he growled in that inhuman voice.

"I do, *master*," she repeated, pressing her face further into the tiles. *Good lord, he was scary… and sexy as all get-out.*

He crouched down to eye her more closely, and she nearly fainted with anticipation. And then, he snatched her by the hair, yanked upward to force her gaze, and released a pair of wicked-looking fangs. "Look at me, human!"

Tawni's scalp blazed as if it were on fire. His fingers were as strong as forceps, and her roots were burning. "My lord?" she asked, shocked by his sudden violence and anger. *What had she done wrong?* "I mean, Dark One, *master*?"

He chuckled deep in his throat. "Your place, *Tawni Duvall*, is as a grub beneath my feet. You don't summon me. You don't *summon* anything. You are nothing more than a paltry, insignificant worm, an ameba that I could crush in an instant, a vessel that I *will* use for my perverted pleasure—and your unspeakable pain—whenever I so desire. You are a mere tool within my hand, one that I may devour, destroy, or defile at will." He looked down at her faded blue jeans and frowned. "And if you lose your bowels on this floor, in front of me, I will tear this hair from your head, wipe up your excrement with your scalp, and stuff it down your insignificant throat. And then I will snap your bones, one at a time, starting from your head to your toes, while I force you to eat them, before I let you die." He paused, as if considering his next words carefully. "So, if you need to use the restroom, I suggest you do it now."

Tawni froze.

This was nothing like she had envisioned.

He was nothing like she had imagined.

Perhaps she just needed to try harder to please him, to win his regard and affection. She could do that. She was born to do just that. She did have to urinate, but she wasn't about to tell him that now. She could hold it. *She would hold it.*

He released his grip on her hair and stood up.

"Thank you," she whispered, struggling not to massage her burning scalp.

"Get up!" he ordered.

She stumbled to her feet, took one hard look at his face, and nearly passed out.

He caught her by the arm and steadied her, maintaining his iron grip until she regained her balance. "Now then," he drawled, "your *master's* name is Salvatore Nistor, and I have come in answer to your *request*, not your summons."

She started to reply, but he held up his forefinger to silence her, waggling it back and forth in warning.

Enough said.

No problem.

She waited like a silent lamb.

"The entities you seek do not exist as you have sought them, at least not in the way you imagine. Your human demons are inside of you, projections of your fears, manifestations of your own inner guile and bitterness. They are the living, breathing creations of so much envy, self-revulsion, and hate, born of your errant, contrary vibrations. Without your *summons*, they would not appear. Do not get me wrong: Such demons do, in fact, exist. They exist for those humans who desire, feed, or fear them, and they take the form of the monster that lives inside. They become that which you believe... or need... or create."

Tawni frowned, not understanding his words. "Then... then what are you?"

"I, sweet Tawni, am the real thing." He laughed so loud that the foundation of her kitchen shook. "A monster unlike any you have ever envisioned: Vampyr... Nosferatu... a creature of the night. And I make the grotesque demons in your human art, your restless dreams, your furtive imagination, look like fairy tales, mere hoaxes that go bump in the night." He narrowed his diabolical gaze. "I can assure you, I am very real. And in my world, the dark lords are real as well." He reached out, produced a claw on his first finger, and began to carve a mock diagram, like the one she had drawn on the kitchen floor, into the front of her chest, just below her collarbone, just above her breasts. The pain was excruciating, yet somehow exquisite, and she bit down on her tongue to keep from crying out. And then, once he'd finally finished, he stepped back and tasted her blood, sucking suggestively on the tip of his finger. Her stomach clenched in reaction.

"So, think long and hard before you choose to trade your soul for the power I offer you," he said. "For once you do, there is no turning back."

Tawni glanced down at her bleeding chest and gasped at the perfect insignia. It was all she could do not to sway in place from the blistering pain, but she was determined to be strong… and to think. She placed her open palm over the bloody diagram and tried to regulate her breathing as his words sank into her soul: *Think long and hard before you choose to trade your soul for the power I offer you; for once you do, there is no turning back.*

She needed to ask more questions.

She cleared her throat and reached for her courage, and then she looked him straight in those demonic sapphire eyes. "I want it more than words can say," she began, "but maybe I should find out a little more about what *it* is… first."

He smiled in a deceptively gracious manner. "Ah, then you are not *quite* as stupid as you look."

She nodded, but she didn't reply.

He clasped her jaw in his hands, and his fingers bit into her cheeks. "Just so that we are crystal clear: Do you wish to trade your *soul* for power?"

She nodded again, still trying to catch her breath. If only he knew—that was *exactly* what she wanted, what she had *always* wanted—it was the stuff that had fueled her dreams as a child, given birth to her rebellion as a teenager, fed her fantasies as a fully mature adult. But he still wasn't being very specific. "Yes, my soul for power… and for immortality." She raised her jaw and boldly held his gaze. "I hate this weak, pitiful society I live in. I hate their trivial rules and their petty laws and their self-righteous ways. I hate their fake, ugly faces, their hollow platitudes, and their meaningless, empty lives. I want more, much, *much* more."

He cocked an eyebrow with interest. "Such as?"

She drew in a deep breath for courage. "Such as power… domination… and immortality. I want to be at the top of the food chain."

He nodded, far too slyly, and his smile was almost seductive in its duplicity—but for the life of her, she couldn't detect any obvious deceit. "You wish to be dominant over other *humans?*" he echoed for clarity. "To possess an immortal body, with the potential to live forever? You wish to be at the top of the food chain, a mammal amongst mammals, physically superior to your planet's animal and human inhabitants? Be explicitly clear, Tawni Duvall: Is this what you seek?"

She couldn't think.

Her head was positively spinning with the possibilities, but yes, that sounded exactly right: Tawni wanted superiority over all the beasts of the earth, human and animal alike. She nodded emphatically, and he covered his mouth with his hand as if to stifle a laugh. She measured him sideways—what was so funny about that? Her throat was suddenly dry, and she cleared it for emphasis. "Can you, or can you not, give those three things to me, Master *Salvatore?*" She waited, hardly able to contain her hope as his eyes twinkled with amusement.

And then, just as rapidly, his face grew deathly calm and severe. "Oh, indeed, I can." He waved his hand absently through the air. "And before all that is unholy, I promise you the exact three things you have asked for: power unlike anything a human may possess, absolute domination over the planet's mammals, and a body that is capable of living forever. All three are mine to give."

Tawni could hardly believe her ears. She knew there was a catch—there was always a catch—but so what? If she had that kind of power, who could stop her? If her body was immortal, then what could she possibly have to fear? And if she was at the top of the food chain, then well, that kind of said it all. Granted, he had called himself a vampire, some kind of Nosferatu, or something like that, but that wouldn't pose a challenge, not if she was one, too. She swallowed hard and asked her last remaining question. "And in return?"

"In return?" He licked his lips like they were coated in honey.

"Yes." She cleared her throat again. "What do you want from me in return?"

Salvatore Nistor pursed his lips and furrowed his dark brows magnanimously. "Everything," he answered plainly. "From the moment you consent, you are mine: your body, your soul, and your allegiance. And there is no going back."

For a split second, something in Tawni's spirit registered an infinite and lethal warning: *Danger! There are words beneath his words; there is a threat beyond the fantasy; duplicity, brutality, and deception are laced on his forked tongue.* But as it stood, all she heard was the promise of power: the allure of a future without vulnerability; the ability to take and destroy and dominate, at her leisure, each carrot dangled so temptingly before her as if suspended from a golden string. "I understand." She spoke firmly.

"Oh," he snickered, "I don't believe you do, but you will." He winked as if they were partners in a devilish conspiracy, and then he waved his hand to dismiss both the words and the gesture. "That is of no consequence: All that I need to know right now is whether or not you *consent.*"

Tawni thought about it.

She *really* thought about it for a moment. And then she slowly arched her back, squaring her shoulders to this terrifying being. "And just out of curiosity, if I don't? Consent, that is? What then?"

"Then… " He drew out the word. "Then I will kill you, Miss Duvall." He spoke without pretense. "Slowly, painfully, simply for wasting my time, *but*"—he reached out and placed his forefinger over her lips to make sure he had her full attention—"and it's a very important *but*; fear of death cannot be the justification for your decision." He shrugged as if his promise to kill her was no more significant than the weather. "You should have thought that through before you *summoned* me. No," he warned, "it is far better to die with your soul intact than to relinquish the one thing you can never reclaim out of fear of temporary suffering. If you trade your soul for what I have to offer you, you do it freely and without reservation. You do it because it is your true heart's desire, or you don't do it at all."

Tawni's knees grew weak beneath her, but fortunately, they didn't buckle. She marshaled her strength and sidestepped past him, praying that he wouldn't swat her like a fly for the insult. And then she wandered into the living room, where she felt like she had a little more room to breathe, and began to pace in tight little circles, all around the cluttered space. To her utter surprise, he left her alone. In fact, he simply watched like an innocent bystander.

And waited.

As if even he, in all his dark, brooding malevolence, understood the gravity of the decision, the sacredness of the moment.

She ran her hands through her hair and thought it over: True, she did not want to die. And there was no question in her mind that Salvatore would kill her, and when he did, it would be a grisly and painful death. But he was right. It was better to die than to make the wrong decision. No, she had to do this because it was truly what she yearned for, truly what she wanted, not because the six-foot lethal demon would torture her mercilessly.

She drew in a deep breath and returned to the question: Was this what she wanted? Not just now, but for all eternity? A chorus of nervous laughter escaped her throat, and she bit down hard on her tongue to make it stop. May propriety and convention be damned: *It was.*

This was exactly what Tawni wanted, and she didn't need to think it over any further: Salvatore Nistor was the stroke of luck Tawni had been waiting for her entire life. Since the day she had turned five years old and drowned her birthday kitten, since the time she had entered the third grade and begun setting things on fire, since the day she had been mocked and ridiculed and called a witch by a group of teenage girls in the cafeteria—the day she had let the hatred burn, fester, and develop into a full-fledged obsession for vengeance—she had wanted nothing more. From the day she had begun listening to jarring music and imagining wicked scenarios, the day she had chosen hate over forgiveness, self-pity over survival, and to use her imagination to create pain rather than possibility, she had made the decision. Truth be told, Tawni Duvall had relinquished her soul a long, long time ago. Whatever happened today would be a mere formality.

"I do want this," she said with absolute certainty. "And I freely give my consent."

There.

She had said it.

She rubbed her hands together nervously, turned toward the kitchen, and waited for Salvatore's reply.

*

Salvatore stared at the ridiculous human woman in utter stupefaction.

He could hardly believe what had just happened, the words that had left her mouth, and every muscle in his body was twitching to react: to strike, mutilate, and punish, just for the hell of it. He wanted to fly into the living room and tear her skin from her body, one bloody strip at a time, just to hear her scream. He wanted to rip out her throat with his fangs, drain her body of blood, while sucking, biting, and guzzling, just to watch her writhe. He wanted to take her back to the colony, chain her to his huge iron bed, and violate her ever-so-slowly, creatively, *painfully*, in order to teach her a lesson, her *true* position on the food chain. And then he wanted to draw out her conversion for days, perhaps weeks, just because he could. He wanted to watch her plead for mercy. He wanted her to beg the god she clearly despised for salvation, knowing all the while that it was much too late, her plea would be denied, for she no longer housed a soul.

Salvatore practically salivated over the endless possibilities as he watched her, waiting so patiently for his reply.

And honestly, *how stupid could one person be?*

He sighed, forcing all of his instincts to heel, clamping down on the need to terrorize.

As badly as he wanted to sacrifice the lamebrain offering before him—she did *consent* to relinquish her soul, after all—he knew he had to be careful. He knew he had to be smart. Right now, in this present moment, this woman could still walk in the sun, and that meant she was a valuable commodity, indeed. *Very valuable.* He needed to act with both wisdom and deliberation. This was not an opportunity that knocked every day.

Salvatore shut his eyes and imagined himself wading in a calm, peaceful stream…

Perhaps he could split the difference.

Perhaps he could take Tawni home, back to his lair, and enjoy her later, within limits.

Perhaps he could give her a mission to complete, a simple but effective task to demonstrate her *enthusiasm*, something that involved the house of Jadon, before he gifted her with immortality.

Perhaps Tawni needed to prove that she was worthy of her torment… first.

Yes, Salvatore mused: a simple but demonstrative task was precisely what Tawni needed.

five

Tiffany leaned forward in the large, overstuffed armchair, placed the back of her hand against her forehead, and tried to discern her temperature… or something like that. She was unusually hot, or was she cool, clammy, perhaps catching a cold? She shook her head to clear the cobwebs, and the room began to spin around in wild, dizzying circles. Okay, so maybe downing four drinks in a row had not been the best idea. What time was it anyway? It had to be at least one o'clock in the morning.

Ramsey squatted down in front of her chair and stared at her intently. The ground seemed to rise up to meet his booted feet, before shifting back and forth, then settling in place. "Hey, baby girl," he drawled in that infuriating, far-too-masculine voice, "I think you've had one too many. Can you stand up? Think you can walk?"

Tiffany furrowed her brows, deeply pondering the question. She placed her forefinger on her chin, inflated her cheeks with air, and then slowly blew it out, right in Ramsey's face. He didn't flinch. "Hmm?" she finally asked. "What was the question?"

His pouty lips turned up in a smile, and she leaned in closer for a better look, marveling at the sheer perfection of the lines, the way they accentuated his perfectly sculpted mouth. And then reality sank back in: Oh yeah, this wasn't some Adonis kneeling before her in supplication. It was Ramsey Olaru, the pitchfork dude, and he was using his deep, gravelly voice to do something sinister to her. Just what, she wasn't sure.

"Don't you play games with me, Farmer John." She slurred the words, all the while pointing a stern, accusing finger in his general direction. "'Cause I need it. *See it.* I mean, I know what you are doing."

Ramsey nodded his head, leaned back on his heels, and bit the inside of his cheek, continuing to stare at her like she had cake, or frosting, or something on her nose. She knew that she didn't.

So, ha!

"Damn," he grumbled. "I wish you would've told me you were such a lightweight, Blondie. I would've made you something else."

Now this felt like a direct assault… or an insult… something clearly nefarious. Tiffany sat up straight and tried to hold his iron stare with one of her own. "You can't make me *anything*, Mr. Olaru!" There. *She'd told him!* She sat back in the chair, crossed her arms over her chest, and huffed. "Besides, my mother made me, not you! So, deal with that." Although she meant every word in earnest, this somehow made her giggle.

Ramsey averted his eyes and simply nodded, again. "All right, Blondie," he said, his voice absent of challenge or insult—peculiar, that. "Tell you what: I think we need to find some pj's, maybe head for the shower, and then tuck you into bed."

Tiffany gasped. "Don't you dare put the shower in my bed! I know how to do it *all* by myself." She stood up abruptly and almost toppled over sideways before he caught her in his arms, his large, rugged hands anchored, once again, on both sides of her waist. She knew where this was headed, right down to her… bottom!

"Is that a fact?" he said, before she had another chance to speak. He lifted her as effortlessly as he might have hefted a sack of potatoes and then gently tossed her over his shoulders, so that she was now hanging upside down.

"Ohhhh," she moaned, reaching for the pockets on his blue jeans and tugging in earnest. "I think I'm gonna puke on your butt." He quickly set her down, steadying her on her feet by her shoulders. She leaned forward and rested her head against his chest. "Oh, God… why did I drink so much?"

"Tiffany," he whispered, taking one hand off her shoulder to place it on her cheek. "Look at me. Maybe I can help."

She drew her face away from his hand and held it at an awkward angle, tilted to the side, and then she narrowed her eyes into a squint and glared at him from her peripheral vision—yet she said nothing.

He moved both hands to the ridge of her elbows, providing moderate but surprisingly effective support, and then he frowned. "What the hell is that?" he asked, scrunching up his face in confusion.

"What?" she demanded.

"That look. Your face. What the hell are you doing?"

She grit her teeth, pursed her lips, and tried to glare at him like a vampire—it seemed like the appropriate thing to do at the time—and then she snorted. "I'm giving you a warning," she said tersely. "You. Are. Not. Going. To. Get. Away. With. This."

Ramsey whistled low beneath his breath, almost sounding like Nathaniel Silivasi, and then he slowly shook his head. "Wow… okay. I think we're done for the night." He placed one hand beneath her knees, the other around her waist, and lifted her to his chest. "C'mon, baby girl; it's time to go night-night." He started toward the hallway… and the bedrooms.

"Hey! I thought I toooold youuuu—"

"Yep, you told me, all right. C'mon, Miss Matthews." He continued down the hall until he reached the second master bedroom, the one across from his own room, and then he used his telekinesis to open the door. "It's time to hit the sack."

Tiffany tried to protest, but it wasn't worth the energy. All she wanted was for him to stop walking, stop moving, so the room would stop spinning.

He somehow managed to hold onto her with only one arm, while pulling back the covers with the other, and then he gently laid her down on the soft memory-foam mattress—well, as gently as Ramsey did anything. Put it this way: He didn't throw her or drop her on her head.

Tiffany moaned and crawled further onto the mattress, trying to quiet her stomach. She so did not want to vomit. "Ohhh, Godddddd," she repeated.

"Sh, Blondie," he said, and then she heard him walk away. All of a sudden there was water running in the en suite bath, and a few minutes later, he was back with a cool washcloth. "Roll over," he said, waiting as she rolled gingerly onto her back.

"There," he grumbled. His bedside manner left a bit to be desired, but all in all, he was pretty gracious.

He placed the cool cloth on her forehead, and she sighed. "Thank you."

He grunted something unintelligible, and she assumed he probably nodded, but her eyes were closed and she had no intentions of opening them again, not until, maybe, the next century. Perhaps he could convert her and get on with the whole nasty business of the Curse while she slept, blissfully unaware. The thought drifted off into the same fog as her mind, completely enveloping her consciousness and ushering her into an alternate, hazy plane. Several minutes passed by, and she could have sworn she heard something, someone, making another trip to the bathroom and running the faucet again. She no longer remembered exactly where she was or who, precisely, she was with. And for some reason, it didn't matter. All that mattered was sleep: blessed, peaceful *sleep*.

The washcloth was placed on her forehead again, and she welcomed it. When she felt her legs elevate above the bed, her pants slide over her hips, and her blouse slip off her arms, she thought she should probably say something, maybe protest, but it was far too much effort to try. Instead, she wriggled out of the garments and luxuriated in the most glorious sensation in the world: crisp, clean sheets enfolding her body, being tucked up to her chin, and a soft but heavy blanket enveloping her in its comforting warmth. "Mmm," she murmured. And then she turned onto her side. "Ramsey," she said absently, wondering if it was the brutish Master Warrior who was actually tucking her in.

"Yeah, babe?" The deep, silken voice seemed to drift from the ether. Perhaps Ramsey was somewhere else. Perhaps he was somewhere using his supernatural powers to communicate like a vampire—could they actually do that? She thought she mumbled a reply, but maybe it was just a dream.

When the mattress depressed beside her, a large hand supporting the weight of an even larger body as it bent over her languid frame, she burrowed deeper into the pillow, placed her arm beneath her head, and nestled against the crook of her elbow.

A pliant but firm set of lips brushed her cheeks, and then the weight was gone.

"Sleep with the angels, baby girl," she heard from that same, foggy distance. She raised her knee to get even more comfortable and slid her free hand under the pillow.

Sleep with the angels?

Nah, that was definitely *not* Ramsey Olaru.

six

The next day

Fortunately for Tiffany, Ramsey had some important business in town the next day, and he had agreed to drop her off on the top floor of DMV Prime, at the executive suite of offices, so she could gather some of her things and make a few calls while he met with his *associate* in the lobby.

Needless to say, her head was pounding—she had already taken two aspirin, consumed sixteen ounces of water, and downed two cups of coffee, just for good measure—and to say she felt embarrassed by the turn of events would have been an understatement. Tiffany had never been a heavyweight drinker, but still, last night had been pathetic. She wasn't sure if Ramsey had mixed actual poison in those drinks, or if the stress of the whole situation had compromised her judgment. Either way, it didn't really matter. She had made an utter fool of herself; she had awakened wearing nothing but her panties and underwear; and Ramsey wasn't saying much of anything about it, which was actually preferred as far as Tiffany was concerned. She figured he was either trying to be a gentleman, sparing her some major embarrassment, or in the worst-case scenario, he was a complete lecherous predator, and if that were the case, she would soon find out… in about forty-eight hours.

She rolled her eyes. Somehow, she knew that the latter scenario was not the case. What had he said? *I'm a lot of harsh things, little lady, definitely rough around the edges, but I'm not an animal. And I'm not a rapist.* She shuffled a few papers around on her desk and turned her attention back to the matter at hand and Ramsey's explanation for coming into town: He had to meet with an associate.

Associate, her behind!

Ramsey was meeting with Julien Lacusta, the valley's most gifted tracker, and from what she had overheard, it had something to do with a potential teenage Dark One. Someone was going around the valley killing little kittens and birds and draining them of blood, and Saxson, Ramsey's twin, wanted Julien to make sure the Dark Ones' hunting packs weren't feeding too close to home.

Whatever that meant.

Ah well, at least it was an opportunity: a temporary respite if nothing else, a chance for Tiffany to organize and gather her work, collect her wits, and try to call Brooke in private.

The two hadn't spoken since the night before, the night Tiffany had tried to make a run for it on Prince Phoenix's 250,000-dollar horse, and she was pretty sure the royal family was not all that pleased with her at the moment, let alone impressed with her powers of reasoning.

Hell.

Who were they to judge?

Even the king had nearly killed Ramsey once for insolence, insubordination, and just plain ol' badness. Surely, they could understand Tiffany's angst.

She sighed.

She stuffed another group of files in her bright blue backpack, grabbed her rolodex and the charger for her laptop, and sank down into the plush leather chair behind her smooth mahogany desk, wondering when she would see it again. And what would her life be like then?

She blinked away the inner turmoil before her eyes could fill with tears, and then she drew her cell phone out of her purse and hit the pre-programmed button for Brooke.

The phone rang four times before the beautiful, brunette queen of the house of Jadon answered. "Tiff, is that you?" Brooke sounded positively tormented.

"It's me," Tiffany said, getting the perfunctory greeting out of the way.

"Oh gods," Brooke exhaled, not bothering to hide her concern. "It's so nice to hear your voice."

"Yeah, yours, too."

There was an awkward pause before the queen finally asked, "So… how's it going?"

Tiffany sighed. "How do you think?"

"That well, huh?"

"Just peachy," Tiffany said. "Last night he made me alcoholic beverages, and I had four in a row."

Brooke gasped, and Tiffany could almost see her recoil in her mind's eye. "Ramsey got you drunk?"

Now this made Tiffany laugh, *inside*. If Brooke only knew; Tiffany had gotten *herself* drunk. "Completely blitzed," she said, "and then he threw me on the floor and ravaged me against my will." She didn't know why she said it; it just seemed like a clever way to break the ice.

Brooke inhaled sharply. "*No!* No? *He didn't.*" She took the phone away from her ear. "Napolean!"

"I'm kidding!" Tiffany rushed the words. "*Just kidding.*" Sort of. *Oh hell, that was all she needed*: Napolean to confront Ramsey, and Ramsey to confront her. And what was with this *run-and-tell-hubby-stuff* anyway? What was the king going to do about it? "Sorry," she whispered.

"Not funny," Brooke said wearily. "I've been out of my

mind with worry." And then, in the background: "No, sweetie. Everything's fine. Really. It was just a miscommunication. Yes, I'm sure. Thanks anyway. *Love you.*"

Yikes, Tiffany thought. *Really dodged a bullet there, especially if Brooke was throwing in 'I love you,' just for good measure.* "You know better than to even hint that you're upset about something to that vampire," Tiffany said, preaching. "You have to stop doing that, Brooke. Seriously. If we're going to talk, you can't do that."

"If we're going to talk?" Brooke echoed.

"*When* we talk," Tiffany reassured her.

"And you have to stop making up such horrible stories about Ramsey. I mean, I know he's a bit harsh, but Tiff, that was quite unsettling."

Tiffany grew quiet.

A bit harsh?

"Tiff?"

She rubbed her face in her hands and tried to force some fake cheer into her heart. Couldn't do it.

"*Tiff?*"

"I'm here."

Brooke sighed. "Oh, Tiff, I'm sorry. You're right. I shouldn't have said anything to Napolean just now. I overreacted... especially when I know you so well."

"Meaning?"

"*Meaning,* whenever you lead with snarky jokes and inappropriate humor, it means you're dangling on the edge. You're not okay, are you?"

"I can't go there right now, Brooke. I honestly can't." She fought to keep her voice steady, and Brooke waited about two or three seconds before regrouping.

"Okay... so... where would you like to go, then? You lead, and I'll follow."

Tiffany managed a faint smile, truly appreciating her friend's words. "Are *we* okay?" she asked sheepishly.

"You mean *you and me*?" Brooke asked. "Always, in my mind, but you tell me. The last time I saw you, I know you were rattled. We both were. And I know you felt like I should've given you my keys, and maybe I should have—I don't know—but like I said, we were both so rattled." Brooke took a deep breath, like she was trying to avoid mixing up the order of her words. "And I'm sure you aren't happy that I told Napolean about your wrist, that you were Ramsey's *destiny*, but Tiffany, you have to understand: I was truly concerned for your safety. And Ramsey? He wasn't going to be denied—"

"Brooke—"

"Not by me. Not by Napolean. And not by the laws—"

"*Brooke…* "

"That govern the house of Jadon. Ramsey knew that Napolean had taken your blood, and he insisted on having him track you."

"Brooke!"

"What?" she murmured in a low, conciliatory voice.

"You're rambling."

"I know."

"It's okay. I mean, it's not okay, but you didn't do anything wrong. You were in an untenable situation. I get it."

Brooke let out a deep sigh of relief. "Do you?"

"Sort of. That's all I've got right now."

"Will you ever forgive me?"

Tiffany felt her eyes dampen with moisture. This was such a mess, this whole damn thing, *the whole damn Curse*; and now, it was affecting her relationship with her dearest friend.

"Tiffany? Will you?"

"I will. I have. *I do.*" She pinched the bridge of her nose as if such a thing could stave off tears. "I just wanted to call and let you know I'm alive, let you know that I don't hold what happened against you, and I'll be in touch."

"Don't go," Brooke urged rapidly, her voice growing thick

with compassion. "Tell me what's going on. Please. Tell me how I can support you."

"There's nothing you can do right now," Tiffany said honestly. "There's nothing anyone can do. I just need some time to—"

"Carlotta packed all your clothes, and they're being dropped off by courier, even as we speak."

Tiffany slumped in her chair. Brooke was going to continue rambling. She would do just about anything to keep the connection open at this point, which meant she was still feeling insecure. "That was nice of her," Tiffany said, staring out the window at the beautiful horizon of trees and mountaintops framing an immaculate, well-designed parking lot. She wanted to be *available*, but she wasn't ready to talk about Ramsey or this particular Blood Moon, and she wasn't able to fake cheer or sweep all her very real concerns under the rug. "So, I'll call you in a day or two then?"

"Oh, Napolean found Bobee!"

Tiffany couldn't help but bite. "Really? Where was he? I swear, I looked everywhere!"

"He was in Napolean's master closet, stuffed inside a pair of steel-toed boots."

"Huh?" Tiffany asked, utterly perplexed. "Why would the little prince put him there?"

"Well, from all that we could piece together, Phoenix associates those boots with Daddy working, with Daddy going to kick some—"

"Ass."

"Exactly. And since he thinks of the purple dragon as a protector of sorts, he thought—"

"Bobee would go with Napolean and keep him safe."

"That's what I think, anyhow. He just said, 'Bobee fight wif Papa.'"

Tiffany smiled—actually smiled—and then she broke down

in tears. *Oh hell,* what the heck was happening to her now, and why was *this* the thing that finally sent her over the edge?

"Don't cry," Brooke urged. "I found your car keys, too. They were in a laundry basket."

Tiffany was just about to come up with a hard-nosed, irrefutable excuse to get off the phone, when a haggard-looking woman with thick, multicolored hair came to the doorway of her office and stood in the threshold, looking more than a bit disheveled.

She appeared entirely lost.

Tiffany wiped her eyes and sat up straight in her chair, swiveling around to face the stranger. "Hold on, Brooke, there's someone here at the office." She held the phone away from her ear and cocked her eyebrows. "Can I help you?"

The woman didn't respond immediately. She just stood there looking disturbingly freaky, in her poorly dyed black-and-red hair, an awful choice for a lot of reasons.

"Hey, Brooke, let me call you right back." Tiffany hung up the phone without waiting for an answer, and then she posed her question again. "Excuse me, *may I help you?*"

The woman blinked in surprise, as if she hadn't heard Tiffany the first time, or she hadn't expected her to actually have a voice… Okay, this was getting weirder by the second.

"Yes." The woman stared at the placard on the door. "Tiffany Matthews?"

Tiffany nodded her head. "That's me."

"Oh, oh, wonderful. May I come in for a moment?"

Tiffany frowned. "What's this about?"

The woman sauntered through the door as if she didn't hear her, again, and for the first time, Tiffany got a real good look at her eyes… and her clothes… and her demeanor. And all of it screamed *walking tragedy*.

The woman appeared to be young, late twenties, early thirties, and she was pretty enough, but she looked like she had really been through the wringer: There were bags under her eyes, her fingernails were dirty, and her hair was curiously disheveled. On top of that, she was wearing a man's silk white shirt, at least several sizes too large, over a pair of—were those actually *pajama bottoms?*

Tiffany did a double take, trying to make sense of the material: Granted, the pj's looked like they cost at least a hundred dollars—they were satin and pleated, for heaven's sake—but still, they were definitely pajama bottoms. Men's pajama bottoms. *What the hay?* "Are you in some sort of trouble?" Tiffany asked.

The woman looked positively rattled by the question, and she quickly shook her head. "No, *no*, not at all. Nothing like that." She looked down at her clothes, absently smoothed her expensive shirt, and walked confidently to Tiffany's desk, where she held out her hand in greeting. "My name is Tawni Duvall."

Tiffany took her hand and shook it cautiously. "Hello, Tawni. I'm Tiffany."

The woman threw back her head and laughed then—*inappropriate much?*—and then she sighed with apprehension. "I know I must look a mess. Oh my gosh, I can't believe I'm still wearing pajamas." She tried to cover the snafu with another inappropriate giggle. "Please, let me explain." She looked at the black marble container full of business cards resting on Tiffany's desk, and boldly reached out to take one: "*Tiffany Matthews, Graphic Design & Marketing...* " She read it out loud with a smile. "You see, I'm new in town, and I'm also a graphic artist. And I was hoping to apply for a job."

Tiffany coughed into her hand to subdue a harsher reaction. *She was job hunting in a man's shirt and pajamas?* "Um... well... we only hire from the inside."

The woman nodded. "I see. But I was kind of hoping to get some sort of contract work. You know, to provide remote assistance, if possible. I can do just about anything, and I work from home. So—"

Tiffany reached toward her desk phone. She was about to

call security, which, honestly, was the last thing she wanted to do since Ramsey Olaru was still parked downstairs in the lobby, all six-foot-five, mean-as-hell inches of the warrior-sentinel; but this woman was truly weirding her out.

The woman stretched out her hand and held it over the phone. "Don't! *Please*… don't call security." She looked positively scared to death, and then she withdrew her hand and took a cautious step backward. "Look, the truth of the matter is this: My boyfriend beat the crap out of me last night, so I'm a little bit out of sorts." She looked down at her clothes. "And yes, I realize that I'm wearing pajamas and my hair is a mess, but I was just downstairs in the car… *with him*… and I had to get out and run, somewhere, anywhere. So I came into the building. Then he followed me, so I took the elevator upstairs. And then I wandered into your office, hoping to stall for some time." She wandered to the window and peered out at the parking lot below. "It looks like his car is gone, so no worries. I'll just get out of your hair."

Tiffany felt oddly conflicted.

Normally, she would feel enormous compassion for someone in this woman's predicament, but there was just something *not right* about her. She stood up abruptly and gestured toward the hall, beyond the open doorway. "Are you sure that he's gone?" Even as she asked the question, she had a hard time believing that such a creepy guy could just slip right past Ramsey and Julien, both coming and going? That seemed utterly impossible. She reached once more for the phone. "We should call the police, Tawni."

"No!" the woman protested. She hugged her arms to her chest and took several steps back, heading for the door. "Please, believe me; that will only make matters worse. You have no idea just how much worse that would make matters." She forced an insincere smile and practically curtsied in her pj's. "I'm so sorry to have bothered you like this."

Tiffany frowned and waved her hand. "No, not at all. You did what you had to, to get away from danger."

Tawni let out an exaggerated sigh. "*Thank you.*" And then she shrugged. "For what it's worth, I really am a graphic artist, and any contract work I could do would go a long way to helping me get the heck out of Dodge, if you know what I mean." She held up Tiffany's business card. "So if you don't mind, I'll keep this. Maybe I can send you my resume or something, some samples of my work. No pressure. Just a thought. And if you like what you see, that'd be great. If not, I totally understand—crazy woman stalking the office, not exactly a vote for confidence and dependability." She straightened her shirt, took a few steps forward, and held out her hand. "Thank you again, Tiffany. And I really am sorry for freaking you out."

Tiffany stared at the proffered hand and frowned. What if this woman was telling the truth? "Tawni, you should really let me call someone for you. If you're not comfortable with the police, then maybe we can find a shelter nearby, a nonprofit that works with these types of situations."

Tawni just shook her head sadly. "He'd find me, Miss Matthews." She straightened her shoulders and tried to perk up. "But if you really want to help me, then keep your eye out for my resume. The thing I need most, right now, is a job, just a chance at independence."

Tiffany watched as the strange and deeply troubled woman strolled quickly out of the door and practically jogged down the hall. If she'd had a better relationship with Ramsey—well, any relationship at all—she would have almost considered calling him, just to ask him to follow the woman for a little while, see what was going on.

But that wasn't going to happen.

She sat back down in her chair and tried to shake it off, the chills and the overwhelming sense of foreboding that came, and left, with the peculiar woman.

Shaking her head, she tried to get a grip: *Good grief,* her own life was nothing but one chaotic mishap after another. Or at least, so it seemed. The last thing she needed was to get involved in some stranger's domestic violence situation—her own domestic situation was more than enough to handle right now, no matter how pitiful the woman had seemed.

Tiffany quickly dismissed the subject from her mind.

She had more than enough to concern herself with, and while some bizarre-looking woman wearing hundreds of dollars of silk over a pair of men's pajamas, and running away from some psychopathic boyfriend, may have been tragic, it really wasn't her problem

Not today.

She could only wish the lady well.

*

Tawni Duvall ducked into the nearest bathroom, pressed her hand to her lower belly, which was aching like the dickens, and darted into the closest stall. She held Tiffany Matthews's business card in front of her face like it was made of pure gold, and then she raised it to her mouth and kissed the font, right over the woman's name, before carefully placing it in her right pajama pocket.

In *Salvatore's* right pajama pocket.

She leaned back against the smooth gray metal door and sighed: Talk about thinking quick on your feet! *Holy crap, that had almost ended in utter disaster*, in failure, discovery, and imminent death.

Hers.

She brought her hand up to her mouth and bit into it, trying to calm her nerves as she thought about her impossible situation. Things had not gone well with her master last night, to put it mildly. In fact, this whole thing was turning out to be a never-ending nightmare, nothing like she had hoped or dreamed.

After returning to the colony, the term Salvatore used to describe the truly gothic, underground labyrinth where he made his home, the sadistic vampire had taken Tawni to a dusky underground *lair*, carved out of limestone and granite, littered with stalagmites and gargoyle-shaped candles, all over the floor, and that wasn't even the part that had bothered her. She was all about the creepy, occult-looking symbols. After all, she had tried to summon a demon, and she had fully expected to explore the unseen bowels of hell, to descend into the depths of depravity…

What she hadn't expected was to be chained to a massive iron bed on a garish raised platform and then beaten within an inch of her life, just to be healed again with venom, over and over… *and over*. The entire scene had been terribly savage, her master's way of demonstrating his superior vampiric powers and inherent male supremacy. She hadn't expected to be used like some cheap, two-bit whore. Sure, she had expected her master to want sex, and she had even hoped she might enjoy it—after all, Salvatore Nistor was drop-dead gorgeous, despite his blackened soul—but what had transpired between them last night had been so brutal and violent, so debasing and painful, that even in her demented imagination she could not find a way to reconcile it. She had not expected for her womb to still ache or her thighs to be covered in mottled bruises, even after his *after-glow* healing. And who the heck wore three condoms at once, anyhow? Something about avoiding pregnancy at all costs: babies with claws, ribs exploding, and a foul, distasteful smell that her master wanted to avoid.

Tawni shivered and quickly dismissed the thought. There was no point in recalling all the horrific details. The truth of the matter was simple: Salvatore Nistor had a rare and demented sense of humor, to be sure, and she had just made the biggest mistake of her life, one she could never take back. She drew in a deep breath and slowly exhaled. It was a little late for regrets.

Now, as she stood in a lonely bathroom stall in the Dark Moon Vale executive suites, she closed her eyes and just let the terror, anguish, and grief sweep over her. As it ran up and down her legs like a dozen tiny spiders, traveled along her spine in an ever-expanding web, and ricocheted throughout her head like a host of animated silk sacs, she struggled to accept her new reality: a life without pardon or even a moment's peace.

"Stop it, Tawni," she whispered. "This is what you asked for. This was the bargain you made." *Besides*, she added silently, *maybe Salvatore will actually be pleased with you for once. Maybe he'll actually do the soul extraction and the conversion, sooner than later, and you'll have powers of your own to fight him with.* She stroked the outline of the business card, rubbing her thumb over the thick, expensive paper, and hardened her resolve. *Just stay strong, and concentrate on the assignment.*

The *assignment* Salvatore had given her had been ill-advised, way too soon, and dangerous as hell, not to mention just plain stupid: Tawni had no idea what she was doing yet; she had no idea what Salvatore really wanted from her; and she had almost screwed it up. That woman was far too smart and perceptive to fall for her pathetic story—her boyfriend had just beat her up in the parking lot…

Yeah, right.

All Tawni knew was that Salvatore was hell-bent on testing her, making her prove she was worthy of his gift of immortality before he bestowed it, and he had ordered her to take a cab to DMV Prime, find Tiffany Matthews, and engage the woman at once: try to make some positive inroads, start up a friendship, see if she could even get a job. According to *his highness*, Tiffany was the key to Tawni's salvation, as it were, because the woman had access to the second most important vampire in the house of Jadon, Prince Phillip… or Pharaoh… or something like that. And more than life itself, Salvatore Nistor wanted to strike at the heart of the house of Jadon by destroying the little prince.

Whatever.

All Tawni knew was that Salvatore was utterly and completely mad, as in crazy as a loon. She had tried to explain that she needed to wash her hair, groom herself, especially if she hoped to apply for a job. Hell, a skirt and blouse would do nicely as compared to a pair of baggy pajamas and a too-expensive silk shirt, but her comments had only stoked the fire of his anger. His madness. And after two more rounds of Salvatore's version of sex play, Tawni had been willing to crawl into Tiffany's office naked if necessary, plead for the woman's mercy, and demand to know where to find Prince Pharaoh at gunpoint, if that's what it took.

Salvatore had given her one imperious directive: "Come back with Tiffany's business card as proof of your success, or die a slow and painful death without ever knowing immortality." Even now, Tawni shuddered as she remembered the threat. Salvatore had not been kidding—the vampire didn't kid. And since he had taken her blood, running away was not an option. According to him, he could track her anywhere on earth, and she had no reason, whatsoever, to doubt him. As far as Tawni was concerned, the male could make it rain, thunder, and lightning. He could probably spin straw into gold or reverse the sun and the moon if he chose to, let alone hang them in the sky.

The male could do anything.

Well, that wasn't entirely true…

Salvatore Nistor could not go out in the sunlight, and that's why he had sent Tawni, instead. That's why he had refused to make her immortal, like him.

At least not yet.

She sighed, once again rubbing her hand over her pants pocket to feel the edges of the card, so safely tucked inside. And then she checked her watch—it was only 10:45 AM, so she still had lots of time. As it stood, she would have to take a cab to the outskirts of the Red Canyons, hike a couple miles in, until she came to a series of crumbled caves, and then wait like an idiot for her master to come and claim her, once the sun went down.

So be it.

This was her new life.

In the meantime, she would use the wad of cash Salvatore had given her to buy a decent pair of pants, and then she would swing by the local library to use their computers, see if she could google Tiffany Matthews, learn more about her soon-to-be best friend.

And after that?

Well, if she still had time, she would try to buy some marijuana at a nearby dispensary and maybe even score a couple bottles of ibuprofen. She would need all the pain relief she could get, and if she had to get through the next few days by remaining high, then she was all for the prospect.

One way or the other, she had to survive just long enough for Salvatore to convert her.

And to do that, she *had* to help the ancient Dark One kill the little prince.

Unless she appeased her new master, she was as good as dead.

And there was just no way—*no way*—she was going out like that.

Not when she had come this far.

seven

"Close your eyes, baby girl." Ramsey planted both hands on Tiffany's shoulders, turned her in the direction of the third main-floor bedroom, and gave her a gentle shove forward.

Tiffany tried not to stiffen in reaction to his touch as she reluctantly complied, taking several stutter steps forward. "Okay," she whispered, forcing herself to go along with whatever this was: After several fruitless hours of trying to work while utterly distracted, they had just returned from DMV Prime, put her clothes away in closets and drawers, and Tiffany was a taut bundle of anxious nerves, to put it mildly. Despite herself, she couldn't help but wonder *what came next*, and if going along with Ramsey's latest surprise would get her past that hurdle, that ever-present fear of the unknown, then so be it. She was game.

To an extent.

As it stood, there was no point in pretending this Blood Moon wasn't happening, no matter how badly she wished she could remain in denial. And opposing Ramsey Olaru at every turn was a bit like trying to walk an elephant backward when it wanted to go forward. Truth be told, Ramsey was always in control, even when he tried to pretend he wasn't, which, really, when did Ramsey *pretend* anything?

She held her breath, waiting.

"Open them," he said gruffly.

Tiffany opened her eyes and blinked several times, staring into the open room. And then her jaw dropped in genuine surprise. It was no longer a bedroom, but a beautiful, exquisite office. She took an unwitting step forward as she gazed at the luxurious accouterments: Toward the rear of the room, nestled in front of a huge picture window, was the most gorgeous mesquite desk Tiffany had ever seen, with a plush, ergonomic swivel-chair nestled beneath it. To the right of the desk was a high-tech drafting table, and perched atop the desk was a brand-new PC with a sleek HD screen that matched the gorgeous surroundings in artful design. Anchored on the opposite wall, toward the left, was a second flat-screen monitor that appeared to provide both TV and computer broadcasting. Basically, she could access her computer from the desktop screen or the television monitor while she worked, depending upon her mood.

She turned around in a semicircle, still in awe of what she was seeing.

On the adjacent wall to the monitor were a series of polished mesquite shelving, housing everything from reference materials to art supplies. There was a soft reading chair with a matching ottoman placed inconspicuously in the forward, right-hand corner, beside a gently flowing waterfall, and an acoustic-wave stereo with Bose speakers at her disposal in the corner shelves behind her desk. And the artwork on the walls—there were three of her favorite paintings: Monet: *Nympheas* (1926); Greco: *Toledo* (1599); and Rousseau: *Sleeping Gypsy* (1897). *How in the world did he know?* Despite her persistent uneasiness with Mr. Olaru, she spun around to face him. "When did you do all this?"

She stepped further into the room and began to walk around leisurely, taking meticulous note of the smallest architectural and design details. "You did *all of this*... for me?"

The corner of Ramsey's mouth quirked up in a self-satisfied smile, and for the first time since she'd been taken from the forest, he nearly took her breath away. *Good Lord, he was stunning when he smiled.*

"You like?" he drawled.

She swallowed hard, caught her breath, and nodded faintly. "Well, of course."

He followed her into the room. "Brooke told me what you'd like"—he pointed to the three art pieces—"and Saxson brought in a team of contractors while we were in town today to knock out the work." He ran his hand over an intricately carved design in the apex of the waterfall, a gorgeous baroque garland crafted in lime-wood after Grinling Gibbons' work, etched seamlessly into the framework of the piece. "This... the definition... Saber did it."

Tiffany's eyebrows shot up in surprise. "Saber? *Alexiares?* The Dark One?" She quickly caught the error. "I mean, the guy who's mated to Princess Vanya?"

Ramsey nodded. "One in the same." He eyed the woodwork appreciatively. "He's pretty damn talented."

Tiffany stared at the baroque garland, marveling at the detail in the flowers, grapes, and leaves, and nodded. She couldn't disagree, but what really surprised her—no, stunned her actually—was the fact that Ramsey Olaru had gone through all this trouble for her, that he'd even had enough forethought to arrange it. When? How? *Why?* She was utterly speechless.

He shrugged. "I thought it might make your... imprisonment a little more tolerable."

Tiffany grimaced. Geez, she really had been acting like a captured POW, hadn't she? She wanted to apologize, but she couldn't. Nothing had changed, at least not in terms of how she felt about being his *destiny*, how intrinsically she feared him, the way she primarily saw him. Yet and still, he had gone out of his way to accommodate her in something so very important, recreating a beautiful—*no, positively magical*—work environment so she could at least feel at home. The least she could do was offer an olive branch of her own.

She took a deep breath for courage, ran her hand through her immaculately groomed hair—and, of course, it just occurred to her that they both had that in common: blond hair—and strolled to the desk to try out her chair.

Ramsey leaned back against the solid pine doorframe, crossed his feet at the ankles, and folded his arms over his massive chest. He looked like he was posing for a *GQ* centerfold, maybe one entitled "Dark, dangerous, and decadent eye-candy."

Where had that thought come from?

She shivered and placed her hands, palms down, on the desk to feel the smooth, grain-filled wood beneath her fingers. It was positively exquisite. "Thank you," she said, meaning it.

"You're welcome." If he was nervous, she couldn't tell. And then he just continued to stand there, staring at her like she held the secrets to the universe in her eyes, his own piercing hazel gaze penetrating her inner armor like a beacon of light invading the dark.

She wrung her hands together and shifted nervously in the chair. "So," she said quietly.

"So," he repeated.

She exhaled slowly. "Am I allowed to ask you a question? Any questions?" She decided to walk it back a bit. "Basic questions?"

His features tightened a bit, but other than that, he remained calm, cool, and collected, at least on the outside. "Of course," he said in that typical deep rasp of his, probably not meaning to sound like death in black jeans, although he did. He just... did.

She shook her head briskly to dismiss the thought. "About anything at all?"

He cocked his head to the side, and that interminable lock of blond hair that often hung over the corner of his right eye shifted, unveiling his steely gaze like a magician's revelation. "That's probably only fair." His perfectly sculpted nose twitched, almost imperceptibly, and Tiffany couldn't help but wonder how... *why*... when had the gods decided to pack all that lethality and brutality into the statue of a Roman god?

She stared down at her desk to avoid his unsettling gaze. "So... " She may as well start with something *real*. Test the waters. See if he was as willing to open up, just a little, as he pretended. "Do your parents still live in Dark Moon Vale?" She bit her lip, only half expecting an answer.

"My parents don't still live... anywhere," he said, so coolly, so distantly, that it genuinely surprised her. "They passed away centuries ago."

He never even paused before answering, and that brought Tiffany up short. Good heavens, he was so blunt. She swallowed her rising discomfort. "Oh, I'm sorry." He nodded, and she waited for him to elaborate. When he didn't, she decided to dive in and ask another question, not at all certain that he wouldn't just leap across the room and snap her neck for daring to be so brazen, so intrusive. "Do... um... is it okay to ask... what happened?"

His stunning, evocative eyes flashed several shades darker, but only for a second. "My mother was staked through the heart by vampire-hunters, and five years later, my father was killed by a Dark One when he was ambushed in a cave."

Tiffany gulped.

Oh, heavens. That was awful.

She opened her mouth to reply and then closed it, completely at a loss for words. She reached up to scratch her ear. "So, it's just you and your brothers: Saxson and Santias?"

"Santos," he corrected.

"*Santos,*" she repeated. Well, this was getting more and more awkward by the moment. She was just about to excuse herself to use the restroom, maybe try to kill a couple hours by soaking in the jetted tub, when Ramsey cleared his throat.

"There are very few families intact in Dark Moon Vale, at least not from the earlier generations." He paused, and it really looked like he was trying. "While tragic, my story isn't that uncommon."

Despite herself, Tiffany asked the next obvious question: "Why is that?"

He seemed to settle back into his own skin, as if it required a great amount of *shifting* to answer. "How much do you know about the history of the house of Jadon?"

Tiffany softened her voice. "Um, some, I guess. Not much."

He nodded then. "How much do you want to know?"

She laughed nervously, and then she thought about his parents, what he had just told her. No doubt, the history had a lot to do with who Ramsey Olaru was, and if this was her fate, as impossible as it was to reconcile that fact in the present moment, the least she could do was try to understand what had made him who he was. "I'd like to know," she said, wishing she sounded more like her usual, confident self.

He nodded. And then he ran his hand through his hair and slowly exhaled. "Back in 800 BC, at the time of the original Curse, things were… a lot different than they are now."

Tiffany leaned forward in her seat. "How so?" It was a sort of silly question, but she wanted to keep him talking.

"The vampires. The culture. Life." He settled into his stance as if sinking deeper into the conversation, and she waited quietly for him to continue. He sighed heavily; again, as if it were an enormous amount of information to try and organize in his mind, let alone convey, while standing at the threshold of Tiffany's new office. "Right after the males were cursed," he began, "there was nothing but chaos, confusion, and bloodlust."

Her palms began to sweat.

She could only imagine.

"You gotta think about it from the point of view of those who were there." He reached into his pocket, drew out a small sterling-silver case with the letters *RDO* engraved in the front, from which he withdrew a *toothpick*, and stuffed it between his full, sculptured lips. Turning back to the subject at hand, he continued. "For centuries, they had been privileged beings, half human, half celestial, favored by the gods; then just like that"— he snapped his fingers—"they were turned into these supernatural creatures with all these strange and powerful abilities. But mostly, they were just overwhelmed with bloodlust. Absolutely crazed and out of control."

Tiffany tried to envision what that would have looked like, been like, but it was hard. "What did they do? I mean, right after it happened?"

Ramsey chuckled low in his throat. "Oh, they preyed on humans; they destroyed each other; and they died by the hundreds."

Tiffany glanced away, slowly shaking her head. What a statement. "I don't completely understand. I mean, some of it is obvious, but… " Her voice trailed off, and Ramsey shrugged.

He glanced out the window and stared off into the distance, as if he was seeing the picture in his mind. "First, it depends on which house you're talking about, Jadon's or Jaegar's, and you have to keep in mind: There were no formal *houses* back then, just half-crazed men—*males*—who had pledged their allegiance to one prince or the other. The followers of Jadon blamed Jaegar's supporters for the Curse, and the followers of Jaegar blamed Jadon's loyalists for the same. So it was pretty much open season."

Tiffany nodded. It made sense. She decided to ask about the house of Jaegar first, perhaps save the best for last. "Tell me about the Dark Ones then. What happened next… with them?"

Ramsey blew out a short, derisive breath and rotated the toothpick to the other side of his mouth, using only his teeth. "The followers of Jaegar did four things pretty consistently: They murdered as many males from the house of Jadon as they could; they fed on humans, openly and indiscriminately, like the earth was an endless buffet table—which caused dozens of human vampire-hunting societies to emerge—they repeatedly burned in the sun because they forgot they were immune; and they reproduced like rabbits, raping human women with the ferocity of locusts devouring stalks in a field of grass. According to the history, Prince Jaegar wanted to wipe all of Prince Jadon's progeny from the earth as quickly as possible, but his own followers were too crazed, too out of control to manage… or organize."

Tiffany shuddered all the way down to her toes. She rubbed her forehead in consternation and frowned. "So, what did the house of Jadon do? How did they survive?"

Ramsey rolled his shoulders in a slow, languid stretch. "Well, as you know, both tribes were banished from their homeland, *from our homeland*, so they slowly migrated to North America—"

"Why North America?" She immediately regretted this second interruption—she and Ramsey were not that familiar with each other, not by a long shot. "Sorry," she whispered.

He smiled.

And it was a genuine smile…

"Well, I think part of it was the fact that the newly made vampires could fly, so they were able to travel the world in a way they had never done before, and they were drawn to the Rocky Mountains because of the vast similarities with the Transylvanian Alps. They were drawn to an isolated, mostly uninhabited *continent*. Not to mention, the wizard Fabien had already been here a time or two—*think Ciopori and Vanya*. I happen to believe the gods were already lining things up, knowing what the future would hold, making sure Marquis would one day be close to Ciopori. Basically, the followers of Jadon came first, and then Prince Jaegar's loyalists followed."

Tiffany nodded, feeling herself drawn in by the history. "Whatever happened to the wizard Fabien?"

Ramsey shrugged. "No one knows. Apparently, he took the princesses across the sea, placed them in an enchanted sleep to be awakened later by Prince Jadon, and no one ever heard from him again. Perhaps he traded his life for the power and magic he needed… nobody really knows."

"And the princes?" Tiffany asked. She just had to know. "Whatever happened to them?"

Once again, Ramsey shrugged. "Same deal. Nobody knows for sure. Legend has it that they died in an epic battle back in Romania, that both warriors, *both vampires*, beheaded each other at the same exact moment, but no one has ever found their tombs."

Tiffany clenched and unclenched her fists several times, trying to wring out her hands, release some tension. "*Shit,*" she murmured. What else could she say? "And the house of Jadon? How did it survive?"

Ramsey bit down on the toothpick, *hard*. "One word: Napolean."

Tiffany braced her palms on the edge of her seat, angling her body even further forward, riveted by the tale. "Napolean?"

At this point, Ramsey pushed away from the wall, sauntered to the open armchair, and took a languorous seat. He placed both booted feet up on the ottoman and leaned back, once again crossing his arms in front of his chest. "When Jadon's followers first got to North America, they were dealing with all the same crap as the house of Jaegar—they were also consumed by bloodlust and learning how to feed for the first time without inflicting wholesale slaughter, and while many of the males came directly to the Rocky Mountains, a lot more scattered from one end of the continent to the other. Over time, as more and more humans migrated to the New World, they also attracted and encouraged human vampire-hunting societies here. Since the house of Jadon's males had to wait on their *destinies*"—he eyed her meaningfully—"they reproduced a lot more slowly, and a lot of males were taken by the Blood for failing to complete the requirements of their Blood Moons." He placed one ankle on top of the other. "Luckily, they—*we*—had the sun *and Napolean,* a time to regroup when the Dark Ones couldn't hunt us, and a leader who would step forward and rebuild all that was once right with the ancient civilization, a leader who knew what that civilization once looked like."

Tiffany twirled her fingers through her hair, tugging on several strands behind her ear, enraptured by the story. "So, how did you end up here... together... all in Dark Moon Vale? And what did Napolean do?"

Ramsey's eyes lit up with both recognition and respect, and for the first time, Tiffany got a glimpse of why the powerful sentinel served the king with so much loyalty. "The numbers of first-generation males in both houses, the followers of Jaegar and the followers of Jadon, had dwindled down from thousands to hundreds, maybe even less, when Napolean took it upon himself to try and save our civilization. Rumor has it, he was partially influenced by one of the Silivasis' ancestors after his own father died, and when that male passed away, he got real serious about reinventing the wheel: Apparently, he had made some sort of vow to this guy, Timaos. Anyhow, he slowly began to gather the males from one end of the mainland to the other, relocating them in one central place. He started to compile information, keep track of what worked and what didn't, what we needed to exist as a self-contained civilization in a new world, and he began to envision a cohesive society where we could function as vampires while still remaining true to our celestial origins. In short, he invented the house of Jadon. He drafted the laws and the covenants. He had the best warriors train the others, and ultimately, he went back to Romania, to the original castle of King Sakarias, to set up the University. While we weren't allowed to live there, there was nothing in the Curse prohibiting us from going back and forth, as long as we didn't stay, reestablish our community in Europe. Basically, he saved our species from imminent extinction by carving out a way for us to live, a place for us to thrive, and a code of honor to live by." He paused, as if wondering how much detail he should go into. "You may have noticed that there are a helluva lot more warriors than wizards, healers, or justices in Dark Moon Vale, right?"

Tiffany nodded. "I have."

"Well, that's no accident," Ramsey said. "While Napolean may have conceived of all four disciplines right from the start, his initial emphasis was straightforward: The house of Jaegar could reproduce at a far greater rate than we could, and in order to survive, we needed skilled Master Warriors, a lot of them, males who could fight better, stronger, faster, and with more efficiency than the Dark Ones. That took some serious training and time. It wasn't until a few centuries ago, after we attained true stability and our numbers stabilized, that Napolean gave the nod to more than a handful of males to pursue the alternate disciplines. In other words, what you see now? It didn't happen all at once. In fact, it took centuries to create the society you see today, but eventually, Napolean did it. And it's worked ever since." His eyes grew darker, more focused, and his upper lip drew back in a very subtle snarl. "For the longest time, we thought the Dark Ones were still scattered, living like animals in hidden caves and arroyos, but now we know better. They were right here… *beneath us*… all this time, and they developed their own advanced society, despite their degenerate ways."

Tiffany took a moment to let it all sink in, the history, the implications. When she was finally ready to push on, she chose to address a more personal subject: "And so your parents—they lived during a time of great turmoil and danger, before things were as established as they are today?"

Ramsey nodded, seemingly impressed with her quick grasp of the account. "Exactly. The first few generations of vampires rarely survived the battles, the bloodlust, the Curse, or the vampire-hunting societies." He shrugged, although it was not indifferent. "Kind of in the same way that early humans didn't survive the plagues, childbirth, or territorial wars of expansion. It takes time and understanding, science and civilization, to learn and to evolve. Napolean is the only original male left from the time of the Blood Curse, and while my parents came a few generations later, Dark Moon Vale was not an established stronghold, a sanctuary for our kind, at the time. Like so many of the vampires who would now be over one or two thousand years old, they fell prey to the world we lived in, before we knew how to navigate it."

Tiffany closed her eyes and tried to gentle her racing heart.

She had never given the history of the house of Jadon more than a cursory thought, and she was humbled by Napolean's ingenuity as well as Ramsey's retelling of the past. "I *am* sorry, Ramsey," she said softly. "So sorry."

At the mention of his name, his eyes locked unerringly with hers, and then he nodded in acknowledgment. But he didn't speak.

"So, that's why you serve the king so faithfully?"

Ramsey declined his head in a hard, definitive nod. "That's why we *all* revere him so deeply."

Tiffany understood. "And how did you come to be a sentinel?"

Ramsey's features relaxed as he digested the question. "We volunteered… a long time ago."

"You and your brothers?"

"Yeah."

Okay, so he was getting a little more tight-lipped now. She held his gaze with unwavering determination. "What do you do? I mean, as sentinels?"

He made a speculative gesture with his hand, as if to say, *a little of this—a little of that*. In other words, he evaded the question.

She braced her elbows on the desk and leaned forward in persistence. "*Ramsey*, what do you do?"

He looked away and frowned, and then he stood up from the chair with the silent grace of a jungle cat and nearly slinked across the room to her desk, where he bent over, placed both hands flat on the top panel, and stared directly into her eyes. "Very rarely, but on occasion, there are members of the house of Jadon who do not comply with the laws." His expression hardened. "I mete out justice for Napolean." He held her gaze without blinking. "And also rarely, but not unheard of, there are humans who do not respect the boundaries, not just leftover vampire-hunting societies, but criminal types, those who"—he seemed to be searching for just the right word—"those who take an interest in the casino or our other financial holdings, those who hear about the precious gems, the mines, and want a piece of our wealth for themselves. I make them go away." He licked his lips apathetically. "You already know that I hunt Dark Ones and fight lycans, when they occasionally rear their ugly heads, but I also do the king's bidding, whatever it may be, whether that's an execution, barring the door to the sacrificial chamber after a male has failed to fulfill the terms of his Blood Moon, or seeing to it that a firstborn, dark twin does not get a chance to grow up because his parents are having second thoughts. I'm a mercenary, an enforcer, and a protector. I make sure that the house of Jadon *survives*."

Tiffany felt all at once nauseous, her stomach turning over in roiling waves. *Dear gods, he was a killer*, a straight-up killer. She had always known this on some level, but for some reason, his words had driven it home. She cupped her hand over her mouth to stifle any emotional outbursts, to try and hide her fear. She wanted to duck under the desk, run from the room, anything, just to get away from his fearsome presence. And she knew that it wasn't fair.

After all, Ramsey Olaru had shown her three very important things that afternoon: First, that he wasn't some barbaric caveman who could only spit out one-syllable words. He was intelligent as hell, even eloquent, when he wanted to be, both articulate and organized. Second, that he was as loyal as the day was long, and despite the brutal nature of his work, he was driven by an internal code based on his own intrinsic idea of right and wrong. And last, that he had overcome great tragedy in his own life. He wasn't impervious to what it meant to suffer.

And all that had to count for something, didn't it?

Yet and still, Tiffany remained terrified.

Why her?

Why had the gods chosen her for this particular, petrifying male?

She glanced up into his bottomless hazel eyes and struggled to hold his gaze. "And now you want me to be a part of that world, of your world, knowing what it's about?"

He shook his head slowly, the object in his mouth going still. "No, baby girl, never that. I don't want you to share in the brutality or the ugliness. Never, *ever* that."

She frowned, confused. "Then what? What do you want from me?"

He removed the toothpick from his mouth and leaned in so close that, for a moment, she actually thought he was going to kiss her—she prayed that he wouldn't.

She just wasn't ready.

Oh gods, was she ever *not ready*…

"I want you to do for me what Napolean did for the house of Jadon," he said evenly, his typical rasp, softened a bit.

She held his searing gaze, and it felt like the air simply left her body. "And what's that?" Her words were barely audible.

"I want you to provide me with a sanctuary from all the madness."

Tiffany sat back in her chair and gulped. She had to create some distance between them. She had to get out of that room. "Ramsey, I… I—"

"And in return"—he spoke over her, his voice as close to a whisper as it had ever been before—"I promise to give you the world, Tiffany Matthews. To insulate you from all the stress and uncertainty of life, to protect you from even the thought of disappointment."

She reeled in her seat.

She pushed back against the floor with her toes until the

stubborn chair rolled a couple feet away, and then she stood up abruptly, rounded the desk, and hightailed it out of the room.

It was childish.

Maybe even immature or beneath her, but she just couldn't help it.

Ramsey was right on her heels.

He caught her by the arm, spun her around, and pulled her beneath his powerful frame, her much narrower shoulders folding effortlessly into his broad, all-encompassing chest.

"Ramsey, *please...* "

"Shh," he instructed. "Don't run." He kept his left arm at his side, even as his right arm slipped around her middle, pulling her tighter into his chest, and then he nuzzled his chin in her hair. "Don't think." He kissed the top of her head. "Can you feel my heart beating, Miss Matthews?"

She gulped again.

"I do have one, you know," he said in a satin voice. "And it is yours." He lowered his head until his warm breath wafted over her earlobe. "I want you, Tiffany. And not just because the gods have decreed it. Not just because my life now depends upon it, but because of your rebellious spirit, because of your incredible eyes, because the entire universe lights up when you smile." He pulled back a bit, giving her some room to breathe. "The first time I met you, I was working, making sure that the king's Blood Moon went off without a hitch. I remember erasing your memories and sending you back on your way to San Francisco, but I didn't have time to stop and enjoy the view. The first time I *really saw you* was several months later, at Napolean's mansion. You were sitting on the sofa in the front room in a pair of killer stilettos. You had half a dozen toys wrapped up in your arms, a ballpoint pen tucked behind your ear, and your makeup was smeared along the corner of your left eye. And I said to myself, *Holy shit, Ramsey; now that's one fine-as-hell woman*. If I hadn't been bound by this Curse, and you hadn't been the queen's best friend, I would have been all kinds of all over you." He chuckled deep in his throat. "Point is: *I want you*, Tiffany. And I always have."

Tiffany's stomach did a tiny little flip, and she lifted her chin to gaze up at him—she couldn't help it, and she couldn't avoid it. She felt like a moth drawn to an infernal flame, and her heart literally fluttered in her chest. "I d-d-don't even know what to say."

The corner of his lip turned up, and she flinched, still terrified that he was going to try and kiss her, that she was utterly incapable of stopping him.

That maybe she didn't want to.

"Just answer one question." He spoke with confidence. "And that's all I'll ask of you, for now."

She averted her eyes and nodded abruptly, hoping he would just say his piece and let her go. Gods help her, but she felt like a mouse shivering in the paws of a lion.

"All the bullshit aside: Are you attracted to me, baby girl?"

Tiffany nearly swooned, and she wasn't the type to swoon. *What kind of question was that?* Any woman who had eyes, ears, or warm blood coursing through her veins couldn't help but be attracted to Ramsey Olaru. On a scale from one to ten, with regard to physical perfection, he was a five hundred, a demi-god. "Yes," she uttered.

Why lie?

He nearly groaned, and she felt his body instantly harden. But to his credit, he didn't make any type of salacious move. "Then we'll get there," he said unemotionally. And with that, he slowly released her waist, held her gaze a moment longer than was reasonable, and sauntered out of the room.

eight

Tawni cowered in the corner of Salvatore's lair, trying to tuck her body into a small insignificant ball. She wanted to become invisible.

Hell, she wanted to become extinct.

Her right hand was broken, each and every finger at each and every joint, and her body was still covered with ghastly snake bites, a result of spending the entire afternoon in the colony's Chamber of Cobras with her new sadistic master. She shuddered at the thought of the horrifying chamber, where black smoke swirled around flaming candelabras, walls undulated like copulating men, and serpents slithered from the hollows of stony walls, before striking their helpless prey; and she tried to back even further into the corner.

Salvatore rose from his kingly perch on the bed and sauntered in her direction, his massive, powerful hands plastered over his ears. "Would you please shut up!" He was either referring to her constant, low-pitched, keening wail or her heavy, desperate pants. She rotated back and forth between the two, trying to withstand the pain.

He stopped about three feet in front of her, and she ducked to the side, covering her head. "Please," she pleaded. "I'm sorry. I'm sorry. *I'm sorry.*" She was angry. She was desperate. She was at her wits' end.

He raised his hand, drew it back, and just held it there, allowing the threat to linger in the air. "I mean it, skank. Shut up."

She bit her lip so hard she drew blood, and then she simply kowtowed before him, trembling and waiting for the next bout of torture to come.

When he didn't strike, she peeked up at him through dirty, disheveled hair. "Please," she whispered in desperation, "just convert me. *Please.* I've done everything you asked."

He scowled, his top lip matching the angle of his widow's peak. "No."

"But why?" she pleaded.

He licked his lips and retracted his hand, each gesture both confusing and terrifying her. "You know why," he snarled. "You can still walk in the sun."

She nodded agreeably. "I know. I know. And I understand why that's so important. *I do.* It's just—"

The blow caught her off guard this time, sending her front left tooth spiraling across the floor. She shrieked and curled into a ball, tucking her head into her lap.

Salvatore watched the tooth roll across the marble floor, ricochet off a stalagmite, and finally come to a full stop, with measured indifference. He rolled his seedy, dark eyes, sauntered over to the tooth, and then bent to pick it up. Scowling, he released a dollop of venom from his incisors, coated the tooth in the viscous fluid, and tossed it at her feet. "Put that back in before you're stuck like that."

Tawni snatched the tooth with her one good hand and tried to wedge it back into her gums. She sat there silently, waiting for the venom to take effect. Once the tooth attached, she sighed. And then she began to sob.

She couldn't help it.

The pain was unbearable.

The torture was never-ending.

And the crazy-as-hell vampire was driving her to insanity.

"Why don't you just kill me?" she blurted.

Remembering that he had left a dagger on the floor earlier, after carving his name into her thigh, she crawled the two or three feet necessary to retrieve it, grasped it awkwardly in her left hand, and placed the point of the blade directly against her carotid artery. "Convert me, or I'll end this now."

Salvatore's thin brows rose in amusement, and his cruel mouth curved up in a smile. "Oh, will you, little rabbit?" he hissed. He nicked his own throat with a fingernail and laughed. "Can you do it quickly? So quickly that I can't stop you first?" He cocked his head to the side. "Or will you fail miserably and provoke my punishment?"

Now this set Tawni off.

By all that was dark and unholy, what did she have left to lose?

"Provoke your punishment?" she mocked him, imitating his facial expression. "*Provoke your punishment!* Are you kidding me?" She forgot the condition of her broken hand and waved it wildly through the air, wincing from the sudden stab of pain. "All you do is punish me. All day. All night. Every second that I breathe. What the hell do I care if you try to punish me?" And then she did something that surprised even her—she drew the blade across her throat. As awkward as the angle was, she sliced her gullet from ear to ear and immediately began to gurgle. Her eyes bulged and her jaw shot open as she clutched at her throat and choked.

Salvatore harrumphed. "Hmm. Well, I suppose that answers the question." He strolled across the room once more and squatted in front of her, staring absently at the wound as sputtering pools of blood welled up from the gash and spilled onto the floor. And then he bent even lower, to taste the bright red substance, moaning in delight.

Tawni shook like a leaf now, completely stunned by what was

happening: So *this* was how she was going to die? *How long does it take?* she wondered, emitting ever more violent choking sounds.

Salvatore sank back on his heels and continued to watch her. Obviously, he could not have cared less one way or the other. He placed his hand on his jaw and rubbed at the five o'clock shadow that had just started to sprout that morning. "Well, let's see," he pondered. "I could heal you"—he reached forward and poked an extended pair of fingers directly into the wound, causing her to gag on the sharp, added obstruction, and frowned—"Or maybe not. That is a fairly nasty wound, and you are yet human." He scrunched up his nose and shook his head in disgust. "I could convert you"—he pressed his forefinger to his lips as if really giving the idea a lot of thought—"but then, that would be a lot like giving a spoiled child her way, very poor parenting, very poor indeed." He sat all the way down on his bottom, brought his knees up to his chest, and hooked his arms around his shins. "What should I do, Miss Duvall?"

Tawni began to feel the room sway and tilt. The light was fading, and the pain? Well, it was beyond imagining, beyond enduring. It was otherworldly, and she prayed for death.

Salvatore hissed, a long, drawn-out sound that seemed to come from far away. "You are really trying my patience this time, Tawni." He extended his incisors to a grotesque-looking length, punctured his palm, and began to rapidly fill it with venom until it swelled up like a blowfish. And then he released a claw on the opposite hand, tore a long, deep gash in the swollen flesh, and shoved it against her throat, applying the substance like a poultice.

Tawni swiped at his arm.

She tried to hit him, punch him, to push him away, but her right hand was useless, and there was no strength left in her body.

No!

She would have screamed to the *heavens* and back if she could have.

Noooooooooooooo!

She was so close to death, so close to being free, so close to being released from this hell, if only to descend to another one. *Oh, God, be merciful, please let me die!* she pleaded inside.

Salvatore snickered out loud. In fact, he guffawed so uproariously that the opulent chandelier at the center of the lair shook, and a pair of stalactites fell to the floor, crashing in an ear-piercing explosion of calcite.

He was listening to her final thoughts.

"Not final," he said. "And really, Tawni: *God, be merciful? Please, who are you kidding?*" He bent so close to her face that she could smell his breath, and then his expression turned dark and lethal, more sinister than it had ever been before. He wasn't playing around anymore. He was infuriated. He was livid. "*I am the only god in your life now.*" He pressed his hand harder into her throat. "*I hold the power of life and death over you, and I dictate the quality of both.*" He lowered his head and pressed a harsh, bloody kiss on her mouth. "If you ever defy me like this again, all that you've gone through up until now will seem like a blissful stroll through the park. I will break you. I will annihilate you. I will hurt you in places you don't even know you have." He grit his teeth and snarled. "Do. You. Understand?"

Tawni took her first breath of air in what felt like forever, her heart sinking with the realization that her throat was healing, she wasn't dying, and all she had done was anger her master—and he was a merciless son of a scorpion when he was happy. She sighed, getting a feel for her newly constructed throat, and then she tested her voice. "Yes." It was a piteous whisper.

"Louder," he demanded.

"Yes," she barked, and then the strangest impulse overtook her. She scrambled to her knees, bent as low as her body could stoop, and pressed her nose against the cold marble floor, peeking through the corner of her eye. "My lord?"

Salvatore sat back, eyeing her curiously.

"*My lord?*"

He humored her. "Speak."

"I am not worthy of you. I am not worthy of your patience or your perfection. I am not worthy of your time." She gazed up at him with seeking eyes, and beseeched him with every cell in her body. "I am not strong enough to endure your exquisite torture, and I am not smart enough to learn from your tutelage." She averted her eyes in acquiescence. "I know this. I do. And that is why I disobeyed you, out of weakness, not defiance. *But*"— she strongly emphasized the last word—"but make me as you are, and I promise: I will find a way to get to the woman you have chosen, even without the sun." She sat up, just slightly, and pressed her open palms together, literally *praying* to the monster. "Salvatore… *master*… I have already convinced her that I'm a battered woman." She laughed half-heartedly and shrugged. "And that's really kind of true. But the thing is: *I can use it.*" She looked at him then, pleading with her eyes. "That woman is *never* going to befriend me. She is *never* going to give me the time of day, let alone a job. But she did pity me—*she does pity me*—because she has a generous, compassionate heart. And if I call her and ask for help, beg her to help me escape my batterer, I believe that she will help me. No, I *know* she will help me. I won't stop trying until she does. And so what if it has to be after dark, after the sun goes down. That makes sense, right? I can't get away during the day. I have to plan some elaborate escape after my boyfriend falls asleep… drunk." She waved her left hand through the air, dismissing the details, and then she dared to reach up and stroke his chin, lovingly.

"Salvatore, *master,* please… I swear on my blackened soul, I will not fail you. And I will make her feel every ounce of pain you have gifted to me." She thought about his hatred toward the king and his ultimate goal, and she quickly revised the pledge. "I will do to the prince what you have done to me, before I take his life, but I need vampiric powers to do it. Just stop this endless procrastination and give me a chance to murder him. *Soon.*" She rubbed the pad of her thumb over his bottom lip and groaned with desire. "Please, master… *please*."

Salvatore took a long, slow, deep breath and stroked his groin. He reached out to place his palm on the top of her head and slowly caressed her matted hair. "Oh, my pet, my pitiful, little pet." He twirled his fingers through the bloodstained locks and hissed. "Break your other hand."

She gaped at him in shock… and dread.

How?

She certainly couldn't use her shattered hand to do it, and she most definitely did not want to refuse him. She placed her left palm against the marble floor, splayed her fingers wide, and bit back her shriek as she slammed her right elbow down against her hand.

It wasn't hard enough.

It didn't break.

She grunted and shouted and did it again… and again, wielding her elbow like a hammer until her bones finally snapped.

Salvatore smiled.

He reached for the bloody dagger and held the hilt out to her while pointing the blade at his own belly button. "To the hilt," he instructed. "Do it… to yourself."

Tawni whimpered to no avail. She shut her eyes and tried to breathe as beads of sweat coalesced on her forehead from concentration. She fumbled with the hilt of the dagger until she finally grasped it between her wrists and brought it to her naval. It fell to floor, three separate times, and she had to start over again. When, at last, she had it in a secure grip between the heels of both broken hands, she ground her molars together and roared as she fell forward onto the blade, arching her back as she struck it to make sure it lodged to the hilt.

Her body jerked in agony, and she fell sideways onto his lap, keening once again in unbearable pain, a piteous animal sound that frayed at her ears. "I'm sorry I'm so weak," she sobbed.

Salvatore was finally satisfied.

He hovered over her ruined body, grasped her face in his hands, and pulled her upright, drawing a tortured scream from somewhere deep in her exhausted throat.

And then he kissed her.

Slowly.

Tenderly.

Deeply.

Drawing both his affection and her suffering out as long as he could.

When he finally pulled away, he brushed her hair behind her shoulder and stared at her blood-streaked neck. "What a pity," he droned. "And to think, I just healed that awful mess." He smiled, releasing his canines to a lethal length. "Very well, I will convert you, Tawni. And you will find a way to get through to Miss Matthews—and to execute the little prince—or I will rip out your heart and behead you. *Vampirism* is not your salvation. You will *never* be my equal."

"Never," she repeated, nodding frantically. "Never."

He kissed her once more, and then he snarled, sounding more like a rabid dog than a vampire. "Say goodbye to your soul, Miss Duvall," he whispered.

And then he opened his mouth and tore out her throat with his teeth.

*

Salvatore stared at the utter disaster before him, wishing he could just go play pool, or perhaps watch a good movie, instead of having to clean up this mess. It wasn't as if the dagger had been insufficient, so why had he insisted on even more carnage?

And…

If he was really being honest with himself, then he also had to admit that the moment Tawni had given her consent to be transformed, the instant she had relinquished her immortal soul, all he had to do to convert her was inject her with venom.

Yeah…

It was the venom that destroyed the human cells, one by one, and it was the same venom that replaced them with superior, vampiric cells. In truth, the whole dramatic suicide-murder scene had been unnecessary, extraneous. Just something to keep him entertained.

He sighed.

He was tired.

He was bored.

And he was thoroughly unimpressed with the pitiful specimen he had chosen for a "bride," as well as the anticlimactic letdown of her torture. Besides, HBO was airing a Clint Eastwood marathon all week. Now *that* was worthy of his time and attention.

Ah well, what else was there to do?

He released his incisors and bent over Tawni, trying to get comfortable. He needed to start the conversion before she bled out. After all, the tramp was still human—*for the moment*—which meant, if her heart and brain stopped long enough, she would die.

For real.

And then all this wearisome nonsense would have been for nothing.

Damn, this crack-pot had better be worth all his trouble.

nine

Later that night, around 7 PM, Ramsey knocked lightly on Tiffany's office door. "Can I come in?" His guttural rasp, which was becoming more familiar and less disconcerting, reverberated through the thick wooden panel and settled in the room like a light mist after a forest rain.

Tiffany sat up straight in her chair and raised her gaze, taking it away from the monitor. "Sure, what's up?" She was trying to at least be cordial.

Ramsey cracked the door open and peered in, taking a cursory look around the room. He seemed to notice every little change she had made: the photograph of her parents she had placed on the bookshelves; the crystal paperweight she had set on her desktop; and the framed picture box, containing dried, pressed wildflowers, on the wall behind her. "Looks nice," he commented offhand, and then he pursed those gorgeous lips. "So we're about to get a game of pool going, me and the guys. I think you should join us." He raised his brows as if to say, *Now hear me out.* "It's a good way to let off a little steam, just relax and have a good time for a while."

Tiffany leaned back in her chair and considered the invitation. *So he was still going on with his daily life, still honoring plans or commitments he had made before he "claimed" her.* She figured it made sense. After all, she wasn't a newbie. She had been around the house of Jadon and its various inhabitants for a while now, and she already knew who they were, what they did, and how they inadvertently projected their power. It wasn't like Ramsey had to bring her up to speed on the basics.

Her attention naturally switched to Napolean and Brooke, how the ancient king had gently and deliberately brought her best friend into the house of Jadon, following the emergence of their Blood Moon. According to Brooke, Napolean had sat her down in the living room, explained who and what he was, answered all of her questions, and given her a bunch of material to read and think over while she slowly took her time digesting the strange new world she was soon to be a part of. In other words, he had employed a direct but fairly gentle tactic in order to make the transition as smooth as possible on Brooke. It wasn't his fault that the Dark Ones got involved with their evil possession plot and made the entire initiation a nightmare…

She sighed.

This was clearly not going to be the case with Ramsey.

Granted, he had shared some really personal information about his parents, and he had given her some valuable insights into the house of Jadon, but he was no Casanova. And it didn't appear as if he planned any slow, methodical seduction. Nope. Ramsey's idea of bringing her into the fold was far more simple: Let's relax for a while, play some pool, and have a good time.

She tapped her nails on the desk, returning to the root of his question. "By *me and the guys*, who might you be referring to?"

Ramsey chuckled. "Mmm, I might be referring to my brothers, Saxson and Santos; Julien Lacusta, if memory serves; and possibly Saber Alexiares, if he shows up this time."

Tiffany gulped.

Talk about Daniel—*er, uh, that would be Tiffany*—in the lion's den.

Was Ramsey really asking her to come shoot pool with four of the fiercest, most intimidating males in the house of Jadon? She felt a bit overwhelmed. "You want me to play pool with Julien Lacusta and Saber Alexiares?"

His firm lips turned up in a crooked, devilish smile. "I want you to play pool with me, baby girl. They'll just happen to be in the room." He winked, using those striking hazel eyes like props, for effect.

Tiffany looked down at her desk and stared at a sticky note, pretending not to notice the flirtatious gesture or the overtly solicitous tone of voice. "I'm not very good at pool."

He pushed the door further open and took a couple steps forward, into the room. His massive frame immediately filled up the space, almost as if he was utilizing all the oxygen. "That's okay. It's all in fun."

She held her ground and cocked an eyebrow. "*Right*. So you're saying that Napolean's sentinels, his tracker, and Saber Alexiares are not going to get *fiercely* competitive during this relaxing game of pool?"

Ramsey chuckled openly then. "Yeah, all right. Maybe a little bit." He held his thumb and forefinger about a half inch apart. "But you don't have to participate in the rivalry. Just shoot some pool and go with it."

She straightened the Post-its, pushed them off to the side, and just generally diddled with small objects as she thought it over. "Uh huh, so you guys can have fun with the inexperienced human, while taking full advantage of your supernatural powers." She smirked. "Let's see: You can use telepathy to whisper behind my back"—she placed the word *whisper* in air quotes—"you can use telekinesis to move the balls around the table, *perfectly*, and you can use superhuman strength and speed to propel the balls more quickly into the correct pockets. Sounds like a total setup for humiliation to me." She smiled, jokingly. "Maybe I'll just watch."

Ramsey shrugged, seemingly undaunted. "I'll take what I can get, sweetheart."

Tiffany rolled her eyes and shook her head. "Don't call me sweetheart."

"Okay, *baby girl.*"

"Not that either."

"All right." He backed out of the room, way too slowly for her liking, and then gently shut the door behind him. Speaking through the panel, he said, "See you in five, Blondie." She could hear his irritating laugher all the way down the hall, and despite her annoyance, she chuckled.

Tiffany was beginning to understand Ramsey Olaru just a little bit more.

If not who he was on a deep, intimate level, then at least his personality, the casual, take-it-as-you-go interior beneath the hardened, tough exterior. Ramsey was like a steady, flowing river, persistent and unyielding even in his fluctuations, while Tiffany was more like the solid, polished rock beneath the surface, the one that had been tossed haphazardly into the river by a passerby. Slowly, deliberately—almost imperceptibly—he would just keep washing over her with a steady current of appeals, until he slowly wore her down, got under her skin. Little did he know, she wasn't that easy to move, despite her congenial nature.

Tiffany had always had horrific luck with men and relationships, and that was putting it mildly—that was with human males. Try as she might, she just could not see herself with a vampire, let alone the son of Dracula.

She shut down her PC and turned off the monitor, gathering her papers into a neat little pile, almost as an anxious afterthought. Rising from her desk, she stretched her back and tried to steady her nerves. And then she slowly made her way out of the office, took a deep, cleansing breath for courage, and headed toward the parlor.

It was just a game of pool, after all.

And she would only stay for five or ten minutes.

What harm could there be in this one minor concession?

*

Santos, Saxson, and Julien were standing toward the back of the room, each one leaning lazily against the wall, either chalking or holding a pool stick, when Tiffany entered the room. They immediately straightened in reaction to her arrival, rising to their full, imposing heights, and she took one hard look at each intimidating male, made fleeting eye contact with each vampire in turn, and almost ran out of the room.

The raw power emanating from that corner was a bit like a twister hovering lazily in the sky, rotating in a deceptively mild pattern as it prepared to wreak havoc on the land: The males were pure, unadulterated energy, swirling, building, existing in suspended animation, until they flew into action and laid waste to every living and non-living thing in their path.

Namely, her.

She inhaled sharply, trying to bring her imagination under control.

"Welcome, sister." Saxson spoke first, and his deep, resonant voice sent chills down Tiffany's spine.

Sister?

Oh… God.

She swallowed her growing trepidation and forced herself to meet his penetrating gaze. She could do this. *She would do this.* After all, she had seen each one of these males, more than once, at Napolean's manse. The only difference was—she hadn't been asked to interact with them, then.

"Saxson, right?" she said, trying to sound polite. *Professional.*

His soft hazel eyes instantly darkened, the nuclear specks of gold deepening to bronze, and for the first time, she realized that Saxson's eyes were the exact same shade as Ramsey's. The shape may have been a little different—Saxson's were a bit more almond, whereas Ramsey's were more oval—but other than that, they were the same.

"You got it," he drawled, and then he winked at her beneath a slightly mussed head of hair, the light-ash locks deliberately trimmed to fall slightly longer in the front than the back, and his shoulder muscles bunched as he placed one palm on the corner of the pool table and stretched out his arm in a casual lean. It was almost as if he were allowing her time to study him.

She forced a tentative smile, and he winked at her… again.

So this was Ramsey's twin.

Before she could ponder the similarities between Saxson and Ramsey any further, Santos took three graceful strides forward and held out his hand. "We've met, but not formally. I'm Santos."

Tiffany stared at the large proffered hand suspended so congenially before her, and forced herself to take it. "Hi, I'm Tiffany."

He smiled, and when he did, his pearly white teeth almost sparkled, like a string of perfect jewels laid out in a display case. He held her hand longer than propriety required, meeting her firm grip with a gentle pressure of his own, and then he simply let it go and glided, more than he walked, back into the corner.

She shivered, hoping it wasn't that noticeable.

And that's when Julien Lacusta cleared his throat.

Like a granite statue suddenly coming to life, he shifted his weight from one foot to the other, his back remaining against the wall, and tipped his chin in an informal gesture of greeting.

Okay, so words were not even necessary with this guy.

Tiffany responded in suit, slowly nodding her head. "Julien, I presume," she said, wishing she hadn't.

The corner of his mouth quirked congenially, but it wasn't actually a smile, and his haunting, moonstone-gray eyes seemed to stare right through her, as if he were measuring her soul instead of her features. He brushed his hand lightly over his classically tapered hair, which was the oddest hue of mahogany, and murmured, "Julien Lacusta."

That was all he said, and for all intents and purposes, he may as well have said *Death on Two Feet* or *Grim Reaper*, instead. His tone and his countenance had the same chilling effect.

Wondering just what this guy's story was, Tiffany took an unwitting step back and bumped right into Ramsey. The Master Warrior placed his right hand firmly on her hip and gave her a reassuring pat on the arm with his left. She allowed the contact. In fact, she used it to take a few deep breaths and reboot her courage. And then she smiled at Julien. "I've seen you several times at Napolean's," she said softly. "So, I guess we're not really strangers."

He continued to stare at her with those deep-set, mystical eyes, but he didn't reply.

Not a single word.

Alrighty then. Maybe he only speaks gargoyle.

The awkward silence stretched out until Tiffany thought she might just scream to pierce the quiet. "So you guys like to play pool, I see." *Wow. Now that really sounded intelligent.*

Ramsey dropped his head. Was he amused by her? Embarrassed? And Saxson's mouth curved up in a sardonic smile. Santos just stood there, hanging out, as cool—*and disinterested?*—as a cucumber.

Fortunately, Julien didn't seem to notice the uncomfortable moment. He simply smiled—or at least his lips bent in a general upward direction—and then he sauntered over to the bar, took a shot glass out of the cabinet, and poured some sort of 151-proof gasoline in it.

Tiffany was about to shudder, but the front door swung open and the clamor jolted her out of the moment, brought her attention to the sparsely decorated entryway.

Good Lord, could she really handle anything else at this moment?

Saber Alexiares strolled into the house like he owned the entire planet, all six feet, 185 pounds of his lean but muscular physique moving forward with equal stealth and swagger. He had a custom-made pool stick in his hand, and there were several intricate carvings etched into the base. His wild black-and-red hair fell about his shoulders like glistening waves of ether, and the entire visage brought Tiffany's stomach into her throat.

It was just too much.

That subtle, almost cruel-looking scowl.

The way he prowled instead of walked, like a normal male should. Those intense, coal-black eyes, focused straight ahead like twin lasers on a flame gun, searching out their next target…

All of it was just too much.

She backed further into Ramsey and stifled a gasp.

"It's just Saber, Blondie," Ramsey drawled in her ear. "Not a Dark One." He bent forward to make contact, sort of brushing the base of his chin against her hair. "And he likes to bring his own pool stick," he whispered.

"As if that's gonna help," Santos chimed in from across the room, making no bones about the fact that he could hear Ramsey's words.

"Jealousy does not become you, Santos," Saber chided, stepping up to the bar. He exchanged a nearly gangster-looking nod with Julien, and then poured himself a drink—it looked like some sort of gin or vodka, and he mixed it with the contents of a small silver vial that he retrieved from his pocket.

Tiffany turned up her nose and groaned inside.

Ew. You so have to be kidding me—was that blood in the vial?

"Yeah, well, you're late," Santos retorted.

"So sue me," Saber barked, never looking up.

"Did you stop by Nachari's?" Saxson asked, lazily changing the subject.

"Yep."

Julien looked up from his place at the bar, made fleeting eye contact with Saber, and cocked his eyebrows. "Well?"

Apparently, he could speak—to other males.

"Well what?" Saber asked.

"Well, did he figure it out?" Saxson reached for the billiard rack, placed it in the middle of the pool table, on top of the velvety *red* surface, and started racking the balls.

Saber laughed then, and the sound was as surprising as it was disconcerting coming from the terrifying male.

"Figure what out?" Tiffany whispered to Ramsey, peering over her shoulder to look at him, while angling her head to the side. *As if all vampires didn't already have super-acute hearing.*

As if to make her point, Saxson took it upon himself to answer her question from across the room. "A human cop-ward," he said, like that statement simply made sense to the masses.

Tiffany was curious, but she wasn't sure if she should ask…

Oh hell, why not?

"A what?" she said, scrunching up her nose.

"A supernatural radar detector of sorts," Ramsey clarified. "It's for Saber's Viper."

This time, Tiffany rotated her shoulder to look directly at Ramsey. "What the heck is that?" She took a measured step to the side, hoping to force his hand from her hip—what had started out as reassurance was starting to feel a bit more possessive, perhaps some sort of unconscious male territorial thing, and she wasn't having any of it. "Besides," she added, "I thought he drove a truck." The off-hand comment slipped out before she could catch it.

"Now just how would you know that?" Saber asked, finally sauntering toward the pool table, his macabre drink in his hand.

Tiffany felt slightly faint. *Was he angry? Just because she thought he drove a truck?* "I… I… just heard—" She caught herself and stopped abruptly.

"You just randomly *heard* that I *drove a truck*?" he asked.

She started to recoil but caught her reaction and tried to minimize it at the last second. "Well, no, but… uh, yeah. Something like that." She cringed at her stuttering, and the

Dark One, the redeemed one—hell, the *lost boy*—laughed. *He actually laughed.*

"Yeah, what you *heard* was that Vanya slashed the tires on my Ford F350, right?"

Tiffany looked down at the ground. *Holy shit, how did he know that?* That was exactly the story Brooke had told her, and from the way Brooke had explained it, everyone in Dark Moon Vale had heard, and retold, the story, probably a dozen times.

She tugged at her earlobe nervously and shrugged. "I might have heard something kind of like that."

"Yeah… yeah," Saber groused. "You and everybody else." This time, he turned that devil-may-care smile directly on her, and she immediately felt more at ease. At least a little bit. "It's all good."

Santos *and Julien* laughed out loud, and frankly, that weirded her out—*could gargoyles actually display humor?*

"I heard she carved her name into the seats," Saxson said.

"And smashed out the headlights," Julien added.

Saber rolled his eyes, and there was a mischievous glint in their depths. "You guys listen to too many country-western songs, and you sound like a bunch of teenage girls, all that gossiping." He growled, and Tiffany couldn't tell if he was playing or not. "Drop it already. *It's over.*"

Ramsey started to laugh with the others. "Aw, is someone getting a little *sensitive*? Maybe a bit defensive? Touchy issue, Dragon?"

Saber scowled and shook his head. "Nope. S'all good." He set his drink down on the edge of the table, right on top of the black Italian granite, grabbed a cube of pool chalk, and began to chalk his cue. "But speaking of sensitive issues, since you wanna *go there…* " He leveled a slow, thoughtful gaze at Tiffany, then an equally measured glance at Ramsey, each one in turn. "Tell me, Chief: How are the *two of you* getting along? Everything roses in paradise?"

Ramsey stiffened, ever so slightly, but he didn't reply.

"Damn, that's cold," Saxson uttered, his voice betraying a hint of humor.

Julien chuckled with abandon—apparently, this was the tracker's idea of good humor—and Santos quickly looked away.

Ramsey snickered in a smooth, seamless recovery. "Don't worry about it, *soldier*." He punctuated the last word for effect—everyone knew that the Dark Ones referred to themselves as soldiers, not warriors, so it was par for the course in terms of their underhanded banter. "And if you must know, we're getting along swimmingly." He pressed a quick, soft kiss on the crown of Tiffany's head and smiled. "Aren't we, baby girl?"

She jumped…

And Saber laughed. "I can see that."

Ramsey drew back his shoulders, stretched his traps, and then popped his neck, rotating it from side to side. "*Anyhow*," he said with undue emphasis, "back to the cop-ward." He leveled his gaze at Tiffany, who knew she had to be staring at him like he had two heads about now. "Saber's truck was only a rental. He drives a Viper now, and rarely under one hundred miles per hour, by the look of things."

Santos removed the billiard rack from the balls and surveyed the table with his head bent sideways. "He seems to have a habit of attracting every human police officer within a fifty-mile radius," he said. He reached toward a mounted boxwood cue-holder, grabbed a thick maple cue stick, with a burgundy base, and tossed it to Ramsey, who caught it with two fingers and brought it down to his side. "Apparently, Nachari Silivasi has the same problem with his Mustangs."

Ramsey jacked the stick up in his hand and took a measured step toward the head of the table, leaning over to eye the triangular set of balls. "While it's no big deal for a vampire to use mind control on a cop, tell him to go away, advise him to stop writing that ticket—"

"Make his car careen off the road," Saxson inserted wryly, "it's still—"

"A royal pain in the ass," Ramsey said.

"Ain't nobody got time for that," Saxson said, chuckling.

Tiffany drew back and stared at the comical vampire. She opened her mouth to comment on Saxson's turn of phrase and then closed it, thinking better of remarking. These guys were finishing each other's sentences, and she wondered if the twins even realized how seamlessly they did it.

Ramsey slowly pulled back on the pool cue, slid it back and forth with a lethal grace, running it effortlessly over his elongated bridge, and then blasted the rack of balls at breakneck speed, following through immaculately, hitting the one-ball dead center. He continued to talk while eyeing the new formation of the remaining balls. "So anyhow, apparently Nachari figured out a way to put an energetic ward over the license plate. The moment a police officer runs the plates—"

"Or points his radar gun at your car… " Saxson chimed in.

"The ward tells him or her to get lost, and they never pull you over to begin with," Ramsey finished.

"Nice break," Julien grunted.

"Thanks," Ramsey said. He turned back to Tiffany. "So now the wizard has to install wards in half the cars in Dark Moon Vale."

Saxson grinned playfully. "Word spreads fast."

Tiffany nodded. She felt like she was watching a game of verbal ping-pong instead of pool. "I see." She took a step toward the table and gawked at the perfect break Ramsey had just orchestrated—he immediately sank five balls. "You cheated," she whispered. "You had to."

There was a collective gasp around the table as several of the males looked away.

She frowned. "What? Did I say something wrong?" She pointed at the remaining balls and raised her shoulders. "You used mind control."

Saxson grimaced. Santos began to rub his chin. And Saber stared at Ramsey like he was about to bite him, raising his eyebrows in question.

Ramsey moved toward Tiffany, even as she took a couple of cautious steps back. "What?" she repeated, starting to get concerned.

Ramsey placed a reassuring hand on her shoulder. "Nothing, baby girl. It's just… we take cheating pretty seriously around here." He exchanged a knowing glance with his twin. "Since there are so many ways for a vampire to get over, we employ some pretty strong deterrents in our games."

Julien shook his head. "You don't call *cheating* unless you're sure."

Tiffany grimaced. Okay, that sounded ominous, if not barbaric. She stared at Ramsey expectantly, waiting for him to elaborate on these so-called *deterrents*. When he didn't speak, she turned to each male in turn, noticing how quickly they looked away. Now this was definitely concerning. "Ramsey," she spoke pointedly, "what do you do to cheaters?"

He shrugged, stepped up to the table, and bent over. "Six-ball, corner pocket." He lined up the shot and made it with ease.

She waited quietly until he finally missed a shot and Santos stepped up to the table.

"Ramsey," she whispered, staring implicitly at him. "Tell me."

"Tell you what, sweetie?"

She shook her head in annoyance. "Don't play games with me. Tell me what you do to *deter* cheating?"

Tuned into his twin as always, Saxson pointed at a mid-sized mason jar nestled in the corner of the parlor on a high, decorative shelf. "You just have to pay the piper, that's all," he said.

Tiffany stared at the mason jar. *Money?* They took each other's money?

That seemed harmless enough.

Unless…

"How much?" she asked.

"How much what?" Ramsey echoed.

Okay, so he was still playing stupid. "How much do you have to put in the jar every time you cheat?"

This time it was Santos, not Saxson, who answered. "Just one."

Tiffany gaped at Santos, suddenly confused. "*One*? One dollar?" She turned back to Ramsey. "How is that a deterrent?"

If Ramsey could have cringed while still looking cocky, he probably would have. As it stood, his expression was more like that of a kid who had just got caught with his hand in the cookie jar. Taking a deep breath, he mumbled, "It's a finger jar, baby."

Tiffany tilted her head to the side and paused.

She looked at Ramsey; then she looked at the jar; and then she turned back to the vampire and frowned. Holding both hands up in the air, she said, "Okay, so what gives?" She just couldn't quite comprehend what he was saying.

"Oh, *hell*," Saber Alexiares jumped in. "You cheat, you put a finger in the jar."

Tiffany literally squinted at Saber. That was the weirdest thing she had ever heard. Unwittingly placing both hands on her hips, she squared her shoulders to Ramsey. "Okay, so let me get this straight. If someone is caught cheating, they basically go to time-out. They stand in the corner and hold their hand in that jar… well, a finger?" She scrunched up her nose for punctuation.

Julien started to laugh then. "Damn, Ramsey. Just tell her."

Ramsey sauntered over to the shelf, reached behind the jar, and withdrew a pair of gnarly-looking pliers. No, shears. He held them up and smirked. "You put a *finger* in the jar."

Tiffany's jaw dropped open as she gasped. "Are you kidding me?" She held up her left hand and pointed to her fingers, each one in turn. "You cut off a *finger*—an actual finger from your hand—and put it in a jar?"

"Sometimes it's the third finger," Saxson offered, "which makes it a little less—"

She glared at Ramsey's twin, and the room grew quiet. "And then what?" she demanded. "You just keep on playing, with one less finger, until the game is over?"

Julien shrugged, and she almost lost her composure. "You're serious?"

"It reattaches with a little venom," Saxson said, more sheepishly this time.

She turned to glower at Ramsey and then each of the males, one more time. "What is wrong with you people—you *non-people*?" she demanded, slowly backing away from both Ramsey and the table.

Saxson blanched, and then he glanced at Ramsey for…

What?

A hint?

An answer?

When nothing was forthcoming, he muttered, "I don't know. Abandonment issues? Separation anxiety?"

Santos nodded. "I was a late developer, I think, maybe by a couple of months?" He eyed Ramsey inquisitively.

Julien snorted. "And we all know Saber spent eight hundred years in Satan's army, so—"

"You think this is funny?" Tiffany interrupted, no longer caring that she was dealing with a gathering of lethal vampires.

"A little?" Saxson said, and they all started to chuckle beneath their breath.

Ramsey dropped his head and sighed. "Damn," he muttered.

Tiffany ran her hand through her hair, messing the perfect layers up. "That's crazy."

Ramsey tried to smile and shrug it off. "Tiffany… "

"Seriously," she said. "That's absolutely insane. Barbaric. Unnatural." She turned to Saxson and narrowed her gaze. "How many fingers have you lost in one game?"

He looked at Ramsey and held up both palms, clearly afraid to answer.

"Never mind," she said. "I really don't want to know." She frowned at Ramsey and slowly shook her head. "Well, I know one thing you can be sure of."

"What's that?" Ramsey whispered.

"I will never, *ever* play pool with you!"

Saxson made an apologetic face and mumbled, "It kind of goes for poker and water-polo, too."

"Oh hell," Ramsey snarled, shooting a murderous glare at his brother.

Tiffany spun on her heel and walked as briskly as she could without running out of the parlor, toward her office. She had to get away, if only for a moment. She had to gather her wits and collect her thoughts. Maybe it was just the entire situation, the Blood Moon, the inherent apprehension she felt as a human female in the presence of so many powerful, dangerous males, but at that moment, she was certain she had just stumbled into a den of hungry lions—and it was more than she could take.

Ramsey was close on her heels.

In fact, he caught up to her in the hall before she had a chance to step into her office. "Hey," he called brusquely, his voice no longer reflecting *any* humor or light-heartedness. "Blondie, *stop*."

He put an extra emphasis on the word *stop*, and she felt as if her feet suddenly faltered. Maybe he had used compulsion, maybe he hadn't, but after what she'd just learned, it wouldn't surprise her. Her eyes clouded with tears as she turned around to face him. "Just give me some space," she said. "I just need a minute—"

"Whoa… *whoa*… hold on. Now wait a minute." He stepped right into her personal space, grasped her by both wrists, and held her hands up to his mouth, where he kissed her knuckles with extraordinary gentleness. "I would never cut off one of your fingers, woman." His troubled eyes deepened in both intensity and color, and his jaw set in a hard, indomitable line. "And I would wipe the floor with any male—*with anyone or anything*—who ever dared to hurt you. Don't you know that?" He gestured toward the parlor, his powerful hand growing rigid from the veracity of his emotion. "Who we are, what we do; that's just males being males. We aren't human, Tiffany. We don't think, feel, and act in all the ways you might be accustomed to, but we don't hurt women. And we sure as hell don't hurt our *destinies.*" He released her hands, reached out to cup her chin, and firmly but softly forced her gaze. "*Baby...* " he whispered.

She stared at him, transfixed by his emotion, waiting to hear his next words. When nothing was forthcoming, she wet her dry lips and croaked out a barely audible word: "What?"

"I'm sorry," he said. And he sounded like he meant it.

She shook her head, not truly understanding. "For what? For doing what you've always done... with your brothers, with your friends? Or for the fact that I saw it, that I found out?" A single tear escaped from her eye, a show of weakness and vulnerability that made her feel as frustrated as she was ashamed—hell, why was she acting like such a frail, delicate flower?

None of it made any sense.

Ramsey reached out to brush the tear away. "For that," he said, bringing his thumb to his mouth to taste her tear. "*For that.*"

Tiffany shuddered, and then she lowered her head in regret. "No," she whispered, "I'm sorry." She clutched her face in her hands. "I completely overreacted. I freaked out over something that has nothing to do with me. I guess... I'm just... *shit.*" She ran her hands through her hair, just like she'd done in the parlor, and sighed heavily. "I'm just overwhelmed," she said, speaking more freely than she had dared since the moment he'd retrieved her from the forest. "I think I'm just... *shit.*"

"No, baby," he said, pulling her into his arms. "You're not *shit*. Feces never looked that good."

She laughed, in spite of herself, and laid her head on his rock-hard shoulder. For a moment, it almost felt...

Right?

"You're just wound a little too tight, baby girl; and I pushed you too far… too soon." He planted a chaste kiss on the top of her head and whispered, "What you are is beautiful, Tiffany. Beautiful, and sensitive, and a whole helluva lot of things that I've never been, but with the gods as my witness, I swear this to you: you are also safe." He gently massaged her back while drawing her even closer, and she let him. "In my home, in my arms, with my family." His voice was pure, uncensored velvet. "With me."

She tried to nod, but her heart had nearly stopped beating.

"Do you hear me, Blondie?" he pressed. "I said, *you are safe.*"

She nodded again, this time a little more convincingly.

"Say it," he prompted.

She smiled, and her lipstick smeared on his shirt, making her feel self-conscious, as well as ridiculous.

"*Say it.*"

She sighed. "I'm safe." The words were barely audible.

"Again."

"I'm safe," she repeated.

He relaxed his grasp around her shoulders and pulled back just a bit. "That's right, baby. You are."

She pulled away more decisively and stared at him, forcing herself to hold his seeking gaze, and for the first time, those deep hazel eyes were more than just stunning, model-like features, or alluring props, or even tools of compulsion. They were windows to his soul. They were utterly brimming with sincerity, and the visage left her breathless.

She tried to dab at her lipstick with her fingers, and only managed to smear it deeper into the fabric of his shirt. "Sorry," she whispered.

"Don't be," he said.

"I mean, for what I did in the parlor."

"Don't be," he repeated.

She sighed, feeling the first true wave of relief. "Do you think I offended your guests?"

Ramsey chuckled heartily then. "Those brutes? Nah. *No.*" He grasped her by the shoulders and gently spun her around, until her back rested against his chest and she was facing the front room. "Tell me what you see," he said. "Don't think it through. Don't analyze it, just whatever comes to mind."

Tiffany stared down the hall, peered catty-corner across the front room, and glanced into the parlor. She shook her head, not really understanding what he wanted. "I don't know. Your brothers. Julien, a tracker. Saber. Vampires?"

Ramsey nodded. "Yep, a bunch of territorial, savage males who aren't like any humans you've ever known, virtual thugs who shoot pool, drive way too fast down country roads, and drop their hacked-off fingers into a mason jar just to keep it interesting. Now ask me what I see."

Tiffany turned her head to the side, briefly glancing back at him. "What do you see?" She lowered her gaze and waited for his answer.

"I see four males who I trust with my life, brothers, one way or the other, who are just crazy enough to snap off their own fingers over the most insignificant breach of honor or integrity, over a *game*. And I see five warriors who would take a life, or lay down their lives, *for you*, without hesitation. So whatever you *do* have to fear, baby girl—and no one is making light of your feelings, because only you know what it's like to stand in your shoes—it's not in this house. Not tonight. Not ever." A low, barely audible growl rose in the back of his throat, and his muscles tightened against her hyper-aware shoulders. "'Cause frankly, may the gods help *any* soul—man, woman, or vampire—who ever dares to lay a *finger* on you, Tiffany Matthews. The way I see it: If we're that brutal over a game, what do you think would happen with some real stakes?"

Tiffany leaned back against him—she couldn't help it, and she didn't want to—as his words swept over her like water in that metaphorical stream, making real, measurable headway against that stubborn, lone rock, slowly wearing her down. Ramsey Olaru might be a lot of things—and he might do *a lot* of crazy things—but he was certainly a male of conviction.

And more and more, it looked like he was also a male of honor.

One thing was for certain: He meant every word he was saying, at least in this moment, and as he encircled her waist with his arms, almost for emphasis, the strangest thought entered her mind, much like a vision or a flashback. For reasons unknown, Tiffany suddenly saw a vivid image of the woman who had come into her office earlier, the one who had introduced herself as Tawni and asked for a job, the one who had been dressed in men's pajama bottoms and a white silk shirt; and she shivered.

Ramsey was right.

These males would destroy *anyone* who tried to hurt her.

They would cut that person down like a weed in a beautiful garden. They would chop a threatening finger off an offending hand before it had a chance to strike… or cheat. And they would do it in good humor.

They would do it for her.

Tiffany swallowed her fear and resolved to be a little more rational, a little less volatile.

A lot more accommodating.

Ramsey could have called her out for her dramatic behavior; he could have gotten angry or forced her to stay in the parlor. Hell, he could have just swiped the information from her mind and left her standing there like a dolt, completely unaware and disrespected in front of his brothers and friends, but he hadn't.

He hadn't.

He'd come after her like a determined sentinel, like a caring soul who wanted to protect nothing more than her sense of well-being…

Than her heart?

Perhaps there more to Ramsey Olaru than Tiffany once believed.

ten

The next morning

Tiffany stumbled out of bed at about eight o'clock in the morning and rubbed her temples in contemplation. The Dream Weave, the name her nana had used for her rare and unique ability to view the past, the future, and layers of mysteries through collective, unconscious symbolism while she dreamed, had been hyperactive since the night Ramsey brought her home.

She got it.

She did.

Her emotions were all over the map. Her barely suppressed fear was bubbling to the surface in her nighttime slumber, and her Dream Weaver was trying to bring this to her attention, letting her know she would have to deal with it one way or the other, soon.

Still, the continuous references to danger, the escalating warnings, the repeated symbol of a wolf in sheep's clothing, the theme that appeared in each and every dream was getting a little redundant. What did Spirit expect her to do about it? Yes, Ramsey Olaru was very much like a wolf, an instinctive, almost savage, beautiful creature with very sharp, dangerous teeth. And yes, he was definitely dressed in sheep's clothing. Hell, if the wool got any prettier, it could be sold for a million dollars a yard. Just the same, knowing it didn't change it. She got the warning: Beware. Now, all she could do was try to reconcile her hidden fears with her burgeoning reality. She could hardly shoot the wolf.

She rose from the bed, shrugged into her fluffy white robe, stuffed her feet into some soft, warm pink slippers—thank goodness Carlotta had been kind enough to pack her clothes— and began to pad her way to Ramsey's kitchen.

She needed a cup of coffee.

Now.

Halfway through the living room, on her way to the open-concept kitchen where Ramsey kept a killer, stainless steel single-cup coffeemaker, she yawned and turned her head to the side. And then she abruptly halted.

Ramsey Olaru was sitting in the large vaulted room, as silent as a *wolf* and just as mysterious, his back stretched out in a huge, marbled-gray chair, his massive arms lumbered heavily atop the armrests, and his feet propped lazily on an ottoman. He was staring right at her, yet he hadn't made a sound.

Tiffany cleared her throat. "Good morning."

"Morning," he replied.

She waited for him to say something else. He didn't. "Were you up all night?" she asked.

He chuckled then. "I'm nocturnal, Miss Matthews. I usually work at night and sleep during the day." He eyed her overtly, taking clear note of her loosely tied robe and the cutesy little slippers. "Looks like we're on different schedules."

Tiffany stuffed her hands in the robe's pockets. "Uh, yeah." *Looks like we're on different species' lists, actually.* She pointed toward the kitchen then, eager to make an escape. "Coffee. Can't live without my morning caffeine."

He *grunted.* "Mm, that'll change."

She halted abruptly, turning to gaze at him. *Heavens, did he always have to be so blunt?* The last thing she needed at eight in the morning was to be reminded of all the ways her life was about to change. She forced a congenial smile. "Well, it hasn't yet, so… "

She continued to the kitchen, searched through the cupboards for a mug, and then took a premeasured cup of java out of the nearby coffee rack to place in the brewer. She had to admit, the male had common sense as well as good taste; it was easy to find things in his kitchen—their placement just made sense.

She waited as the dark coffee brewed, luxuriating in the decadent aroma, until her mug was finally full. Fumbling through a few more cupboards to find some cream, sugar, and a spoon, she fixed her coffee just the way she liked it—with enough cream to turn the coffee beige and enough sugar to make her glucose levels shoot through the roof—and took her first, revitalizing sip. "Mmm, that's good," she mumbled beneath her breath, praying that she wouldn't lose her taste for the beverage in the future, or the familiar pick-me-up it gave her as a way to start the day.

She thought about sitting down at the bar, with her back turned to Ramsey, while she enjoyed the rest of her drink, but quickly thought better of it. She would feel those wolfish eyes boring through her back the entire time, and she would never be able to relax. Rather, she padded awkwardly across the living room, determined to pretend she was in control, and stopped just shy of the tinted patio doors. She glanced over her shoulder at the immense, brooding male. "Do you mind if I step outside to drink this?"

He eyed the double doors behind her. "Not at all." And then he rose from the chair, way too silently, way too fluidly, almost like the Loch Ness monster emerging from the sea. "Do you mind if I join you? I'd kind of like to talk with you about a couple of things."

Tiffany stiffened.

Now, that sounded ominous.

Had he been waiting to corner her for this *talk*, all morning? She took an absurdly large gulp of coffee, almost burning her tongue, and nodded with some hesitation. "Sure." It was not like he was going to take no for an answer.

Ramsey strolled across the living room in his typical lazy-cat way, unlocked the patio doors, and slowly slid them open before standing off to the side. "Ladies first."

She hurried past him, finding a convenient spot by the rail. Despite her newfound trepidation, she had to admit, the view was utterly spectacular, and the woodland scents that rose up to meet her were positively divine: She could smell pine, wet grasses, and cool, fresh air in every direction. It was almost like stepping into a little slice of heaven, other than the six-foot-five slayer that was lurking behind her, of course.

Tiffany leaned on the rail, looked out into the distance, studying a beautiful grouping of purple flowers, and tried to relax. "So, what was it you wanted to talk about?"

He strolled to the edge of the deck, copped a nonthreatening lean only a few feet away, on her left, and then sure enough, he reached up to a nearby pine, tugged on a low-hanging branch, and plucked a needle off the limb, stuffing it between his teeth.

Oral much? she thought.

"Extremely," he answered, curving his mouth in a sly little grin.

Tiffany huffed. "Don't read my thoughts."

"I wasn't trying to—you were projecting."

She crossed her arms and shook her head. "Ramsey, *I'm serious.*"

He shrugged. "So am I." And then he quickly held up a hand to pacify her, to try and stop the banter from escalating. "But I hear you, and I'll try harder."

She nodded. *Wow.* Well, that was kind of easy. She took another sip of her coffee and waited.

"So, here's the thing, Blondie. I'm not really one to beat around the bush or play a bunch of cat-and-mouse games. Frankly, I prefer to just shoot straight from the hip, and I don't know if it's because I'm a sentinel or what, but there are a couple of things that aren't sitting very well with me."

Tiffany angled her body toward him to gauge his facial expression and almost drew back in alarm—he looked so damn serious.

This could not be good.

Had she done something wrong already?

Well, other than running off on Phoenix's horse the first night, getting drunk as a skunk later on, and overreacting to the *finger-jar* during the pool game. *But frankly, who wouldn't?*

She watched as he stretched his back against the resistance of the railing, bracing those powerful arms against the posts, causing every single muscle beneath his fitted black tee to flex, and she hoped she wasn't gawking. "You're scaring me a bit," she said.

He shook his head, and his chin-length hair shifted, settling cross-wise over his right eyebrow. "No need to be scared. Although, I will say this: You're not gonna like it much."

She took a deep breath for courage and tried not to frown. "Whatever it is, just say it, Ramsey." Her own mood was growing increasingly morose.

"Conversion," he muttered. Just one word. As if that said it all.

Tiffany felt her heart begin to race in her chest, but to her credit, she didn't react prematurely. "What about it?" she asked, turning away. There was no way she could look at him right now, *no way*, especially with those damnable hazel eyes staring daggers straight through her.

Ramsey chewed a bit on the pine needle and then leaned forward, once more, against the rail. "I just... I have a real uneasy feeling about this Blood Moon of ours, Tiffany." He measured her with a sidelong glance. "Again, maybe it's because I'm a sentinel, but something is just really rubbing me the wrong way. I feel like we don't have the kind of time we think we have. Like, even though you're already up to speed with the house of Jadon and the whole damn Curse, something that should actually give us *more* time to work with, we somehow have less." He shrugged his shoulders, pushed off the rail, and turned around to lean back against it instead. This way, he could eye her directly.

Good heavens, the man was a presence, a force to be reckoned with: so straightforward and direct, so squarely grounded in his own powerful skin, and he was right—his words were more than just a little unsettling.

"Are you… " She paused, wanting to choose her words carefully. "Are you saying you think something bad is going to happen to you… or to me? And what exactly does this have to do with conversion?" She couldn't believe she had brought the subject full circle, mentioned the C-word all on her own, but there was just something in his voice. This wasn't Ramsey playing around. This was a Master Warrior trying to explain a misgiving.

"I'm saying, I'd feel a helluva lot safer, better about the next twenty-seven days, if I were to convert you sooner than later. As in *today*."

Tiffany gasped and almost dropped her mug over the railing. She spun around to face him, certain that the terror she was feeling reflected in her eyes.

He didn't wait for her to speak. "You're too damn vulnerable as a human, baby girl, and it isn't sitting well with me."

She rubbed her neck anxiously. *Oh shit, this was not happening.* And it was not going to happen, not today. She floundered for a moment, searching for a way to express her thoughts. "Vulnerable, how?"

He sighed. "In all kinds of ways."

"Like?"

He flicked at a piece of straw that had settled on the rail, possibly dropped by a bird. "You're vulnerable to our enemies, Tiffany—Dark Ones, lycans, hell, humans with bad intentions." He inclined his chin, gesturing toward the forest. "You're even vulnerable to the wildlife, baby girl." He smiled then, making somewhat light of the last statement. "And in some very real ways you're also vulnerable to me."

"*To you?*" Her voice rose in angst. *Oh, dear Lord, someone just shoot me now.* "How am I vulnerable to you?"

He frowned, as if the answer was plainly obvious. "Do you really need me to say it?"

"Yes," she answered, "apparently, I do."

"Pregnancy, Tiff. If I make love to you before I turn you, I could kill you."

She literally gulped and fumbled her coffee mug again, this time catching it just before it hit the deck, but not before the contents spilled out all over the rustic stain.

Had he really just gone there?

And since when did he call her *Tiff?*

Apparently, Ramsey thought they were much closer than she did.

"Are you saying you could hurt me physically, *sexually? What the hell…* " She almost choked over the words. "You think you would break me like a twig?" The thought made her want to dive right over the railing.

Ramsey eyed the dirty-beige liquid, now seeping into the wood beneath her feet, and chuckled, removing the pine needle from his mouth. "No, that's not what I'm saying. I would be very careful not to *break you like a twig*, although, yes, vampires do have to be *very* careful with human women, but that's not the issue I'm bringing up. The true danger is much more straightforward: In a nutshell, I have no idea how much self-control I have—how long I can wait—to be with you. And I have no idea how much self-control you have, how long *you* can wait."

Now this made Tiffany see red as well as silver, a nice polished steak knife sticking out of his arm. "You have no idea how long *I* can wait… for sex… with you? *How long I can wait?*"

He grinned for all he was worth, seeming to get a great deal of amusement out of her discomfort and her ire. "Yeah… how long *you* can wait." He paused. "I'm just keeping it real."

She snorted. "Well, you arrogant ass."

He toned his mirth down a little. "It's not even like that. I'm just saying—"

"Yeah, I know what you're saying, Ramsey. And frankly, you may as well be spewing diarrhea out of your mouth right now, because this is utter refuse, *garbage*, nonsense!" She marched over to the low-hanging pine branch, plucked a stiff reed off the tree, and tossed it at his chest. "Here, why don't you stuff that back in there instead." She snatched at the branch again, more forcefully this time, and plucked about five more reeds, tossing them wildly behind her back, one at a time, before spinning back around. "In fact, why don't you just *suck them all*."

Ramsey took a judicious step back, ignoring the flying debris, his sweet hazel eyes turning molten with determination. He looked mildly offended, yet defiantly confident, and Tiffany desperately wanted to remove that smug, self-assured look off his face. In fact, she wanted to remove it so badly it hurt.

"And for the record, Mr. Olaru, since you prefer to shoot straight from the hip"—she tapped her lower right side in a mocking gesture—"from where I'm standing, you're doing anything *but* keeping it real. In fact, you're somewhere out in la-la-fantasy land where *real* hasn't even entered the hemisphere. The *reality*, Ramsey, is we're nowhere near the possibility of having sex. And furthermore, as far as I'm concerned, I don't even think we've approached the valley of holding hands, the county of brushing up against one another, or even the casual province of staging a thumb war." She squared her jaw and took three deep breaths, realizing that she was breathing way too heavily—in fact, was she panting?

And, gods be merciful, but was that perspiration beading above her upper lip?

What the hell was happening to her?

He took a slow, leisurely step toward her, moving more like the wolf from her dreams than a man, and gently, intoxicatingly, bit down on his lower lip. "Are you always this easily flustered?" he drawled.

"I'm not flustered!" she hissed, taking a long, measured stride backward until she bumped into the rail.

"Oh, you're flustered, all right," he said.

"Stick. To. The. Subject," she griped.

He bent over and braced both arms against the rail, anchoring them on either side of her waist, thus caging her in. "Oh, yeah, the subject: We're not even close to holding hands... brushing up against each other... " He pressed his hips way too close, without actually touching his pelvis to hers, and then he dropped that gorgeous head, allowing all those perfectly layered, dark blond locks to fall forward into his face, and purred like a freakin' lion.

She gasped and tried to shove him back.

He didn't budge. "From where I'm standing," he murmured, "I'd say we're about *this close*"—he brought his hand up between them and held his forefinger and thumb about a centimeter apart, right at eye level—"to *brushing up* against one another... real hard."

She gulped, and he lowered his head even further so that his lips were hovering just narrowly above hers, so close that she could taste his breath on her tongue. Her heart was literally racing in her chest.

"In fact," he said quietly, "I'd say we're only one impulsive, reckless heartbeat away from the town, valley, and meadow of down-and-dirty, soul-searching, hair-pulling, name-calling, ecstasy-inducing *animal sex*." He licked his bottom lip and growled, this time like a wolf. "What do you think?"

Tiffany stammered like a child, just trying to form a consonant. Hell, she would like to buy a vowel! She was trying to remember her name, let alone how to speak, and if she had been any braver, she would have slapped him.

If she had been any more honest, she would have kissed him.

But as it was, she could only stand there panting, her mouth gaping open, her palms sweating, and her heart racing, completely aware of the fact that her forehead was now... perspiring?

Ew...

She wanted to die of mortification.

He reached out to touch the pad of his thumb to her bottom lip, lightly tracing it, as if he owned it, and she literally trembled with confusion and need, utterly enthralled by the tangible power of his desire.

He withdrew his thumb and took an unhurried step back. "I wasn't saying that you were acting *sexual* with me, baby girl, although if someone were to light a match around us, the whole damn forest would go up in flames. I was simply saying that the mere possibility of a pregnancy, even the chance of a fleeting, passing thought in that direction, is a very real danger, considering how I feel when I'm around you. Yes, my self-control is on a razor's edge, and yes, if I lose my willpower, I can and will seduce you, *bring you to the exact same level of heat I'm feeling* in minutes, if not seconds." He turned away, strolled across the deck, and took a seat in a nearby chair, giving her some room to breathe. "But mostly, I'm trying to say that something's just not right. Something isn't sitting well with me. I don't know what. I don't know why. I only know that you're just too damn vulnerable right now in your human form."

Tiffany pressed her hand to her heart and waited while the organ slowed down, finally stopped pounding. She took a deep breath to purge her thoughts and then just stood there, trying to process everything Ramsey was saying. She didn't want to touch the whole *I can seduce you whenever I want* comment with a ten-foot pole. Not now. Maybe not ever. She tucked her hair behind her ear and decided to stick to the safer subject: his desire to ultimately protect her. "I hear you, Ramsey. I do. So now, I need you to hear me, too." She leveled out her tone, making each word solid, deliberate, and poised. "The first contact I ever had with a vampire was with Napolean, watching him rip the back door of our cab off its hinges. The next contact was with you, when you erased my memories, supplanted them with something else, and sent me home, without my best friend."

He shrugged. "Baby girl, I was just doing my job."

She held up her hand to silence him. *Yeah, she really did that.* "I know. *I know.* That's not the point. The next contact I had was in the basement of Kagen's clinic, when Kristina Silivasi tossed me across the room and broke my arm." She shuddered at the memory. "Granted, I was hanging out with a bunch of lowlife, miscreant, vampire-hunters who had just staked Ciopori through the heart and shot Jocelyn multiple times, but still—" She stopped abruptly. "It's not important. Besides, it's a long story."

He held her determined gaze. "I know. I was there, upstairs, remember?"

She nodded. "Oh yeah, you were, weren't you? Guarding Ciopori after the attack."

He offered an affirmative nod and then waited for her to continue.

She wiped her palms on her jeans and pressed forward. "But the point I'm making is this: I'm not ready, Ramsey. I'm really, truly not ready. Not for the pain and suffering, not for what it means, not for all the terrifying events that come after. I'm just not ready."

He rubbed his jaw and sighed. "And so you're asking me to let you wait?"

She paused, trying to control her temper: *Let her wait?* "Let me? Are you serious?"

Ramsey frowned. He rose from his chair and started toward her, but then he stopped, stepped back, placed his foot on the chair, and braced his elbow on his knee instead. "Look, before you get all worked up, start calling me an ass and plucking leaves off the trees, let me explain. This is not about some antiquated caveman attitude. It's not about me controlling you as some dominant male or trying to ride roughshod over you as a vampire. It's about my role in the house of Jadon. It's about my role as your protector and your mate. If a male vampire senses danger, Tiffany—*when* a male vampire senses danger—you'd better believe he's gonna get his hackles up, jump right in the middle of the danger, and try to get between his female and the threat. He's not gonna feed, sleep, or chill out until whatever it is, is handled. That's just the way it is. That's the way it has always been, and that's the way it'll always be. That's not up for debate."

Tiffany sighed. She brushed her hand through her hair and looked down at the ground. "You, Tarzan. Me, Jane?" she echoed, reducing all of his words to that one simple refrain.

He frowned. "*Tiffany…* "

She met his eyes once more. "Ramsey, please… I'm *asking* you; don't push this too soon. I hear you, and I'll be careful. I promise. Just, can we wait?" She took several tentative steps forward and forced herself to place her hand on his massive shoulder, albeit very gingerly. "Please, *vampire,*" she lowered her voice to a delicate hush. "*Let me* wait."

He blew out a frustrated breath and glanced at her hand. "*Damnit.*" And then his eyes turned impassive, his shoulders stiffened, and he locked that steely gaze with hers. "Three days. I'll give you three more days."

Tiffany virtually trembled inside.

Three days was nothing.

She had only been with him for three days so far, *for heaven's sake.*

She studied his face, analyzing his hardened expression, noting the implacable resolve, *seeing* the sentinel before her. If she were smart—and she was—she would take the three days and run with it. Because truth be told, if she pushed him any further right now, he might just convert her right outside on the deck.

Besides, who knew what might happen in the course of

three days? Perhaps they would make some inroads… as friends. Suppose his heart softened just a little bit more? Just maybe— *what if*—in three days, she could barter for a couple more?

Three days were better than no days.

"Okay," she whispered reluctantly, at last giving in. "We'll revisit this in three days. I promise."

He frowned. "Revisit it?"

She sighed. "Ramsey… "

He nodded. "Fine. Three days."

*

Ramsey escorted Tiffany back down the hall, where she ducked quietly into her bedroom to get dressed, and he ducked lethargically into his, to get some sleep.

He would be of no use to her whatsoever if he didn't let his body rejuvenate at some point, and his irrational concern over her safety was definitely interfering with his rest.

Just why, he had no idea.

Ramsey was not the type to worry.

He didn't chew his nails. He didn't pace back and forth across the room. And he didn't let *what-ifs* and *could-bes* haunt him. He just dealt with things as they came and kicked ass when it was needed. But this was somehow different.

Paramount.

This was about his future, his very life…

His destiny.

Shrugging out of his T-shirt and tossing it across the room to hang over a dark gray upholstered chair, he slid out of his jeans and reclined on the custom, hand-crafted bed. He crossed his arms behind his head, overlapped his feet at the ankles, and let his chest rise and fall in deep, soporific breaths as he thought about the decision.

He would give her three days, and then he would convert her.

End of story.

There would be no *revisiting* the debate.

He shut his eyes and tried to make peace with the determination.

By the grace of his ruling moon, Gemini, he hoped he wasn't making a mistake by waiting.

eleven

Tiffany thumbed through Ramsey's guest-room closet, *her guest-room closet*, trying to pick out something comfortable for the day. She was just about to select a pair of light blue chiffon caravan pants, with a matching tunic, when her cell phone chimed in the background, playing the familiar upbeat ringtone that alerted her to an incoming call.

She frowned, wondering who it was. Brooke's ringtone was the theme to *Game of Thrones*, and calls made from her parents rang to Tom T. Hall's "Who's Gonna Feed Them Hogs," so this had to be coming from an outside line. She took three quick steps toward the bed, scooped up the phone, and stared at the display: *local area code, unknown number.*

Hmm.

She paused before hitting the call button, hoping it wasn't a salesman, and then she placed the receiver against her ear. "Hello?"

"Tiffany?" The female voice was hushed and urgent, a noticeable panic in the tone.

"Yes?" She waited, her curiosity rising.

"This is Tawni."

She frowned. "Tawni?"

"Tawni Duvall, the woman you met the other day in your

office." The woman fumbled with her phone, clearly dropping it, then she picked it back up. "The one who was wearing pajamas."

Tiffany drew back in surprise. A clear image of the disheveled *mess* popped into her mind. "Yes, Tawni, how can I help you, and how did you get my private number?" The moment she posed the question, she realized she had forwarded her calls for the week. She had been waiting to hear back from an important client and was not willing to risk missing the call.

"Is this your private number?" Tawni asked, immediately sounding apologetic. "Oh, I'm so sorry. I thought I dialed your office."

Tiffany winced—she was the one who'd more or less given out the number. "No, no; that's okay. I forgot: I forwarded the line. What… how can I help you, Tawni?"

The woman began to cry *hysterically*; she really sounded like she was losing it.

"Tawni?" Tiffany didn't know if she should hang up or what. Not to be cruel, but it was really creeping her out. *"Tawni… "*

The woman sniffled in the phone. "Yeah… yeah… I'm here. I'm sorry. It's just… " She lowered her voice. "Oh god, I think he's coming!"

Tiffany tightened her grasp on the phone. "Who's coming? Tawni, what's going on? Maybe you should call the police."

"No," the woman choked out, her voice still wavering from fear. "Just hold on… please, just for a second." Tiffany heard some movement in the background, the sound of a door slamming closed—*was it a closet door?*—and then Tawni began to whisper. "Okay, I'm here. I'm hiding." She didn't wait for Tiffany to reply. "Miss Matthews, I really need your help. My boyfriend is going to kill me if I don't get away, and I don't have anywhere else to turn."

Tiffany recoiled. "Tawni, you really need to call the police. Get out of the house and call… *right now.*"

The woman continued to plead with Tiffany even as she struggled to keep her voice hushed. "I can't get out, Tiffany. Not during the day. He won't let me out of his sight, at least not until he passes out, drunk, usually somewhere around midnight. The only other time he lets me out of the house is when he takes me to my babysitting job—I watch a toddler from eight to ten on Tuesdays and Thursdays while his mother goes to the gym, and sometimes Sal—*Saul*—will drop me off at the park for a half hour or so, and his mother meets me there. But as for the cops? His brother is on the force, and his uncle is the Chief of Police. So there's no way I'm getting a fair deal there. They both know he beats me."

Tiffany felt the weight of the woman's distress, as well as her impossible dilemma, and her heart filled with sympathy. "What about a shelter? Maybe a friend or someone could meet you at the park and pick you up, take you to a safe house."

Tawni sniffled. "Maybe. I just… I just don't know who I can trust. I don't really have any friends, and Saul's brother is just like him—they both abuse their partners, and he has so many connections in Silverton Creek. I'm just… oh god, Tiffany, I'm so desperate. I'm sorry I called you like this, but I don't know what else to do. Who else to turn to. *He's going to kill me.*" As if right on cue, there was a loud clamor in the background, and someone shouted Tawni's name. "Oh god, oh god, he's in the room."

Tiffany held the phone away from her ear and listened in suspended animation, horrified to think that she might actually hear this volatile man kill a woman on the other line. *"Tawni."*

The woman didn't answer.

"Tawni!"

Still no reply.

"What park do you go to?" Tiffany rushed the words. "Can you get there tonight? It's Tuesday—maybe I can meet you there and take you someplace safe."

"Tall Pines Village Park," Tawni whispered, and then she obviously cradled the phone in her hand, made a tunnel for her mouth and the mic, and lowered her voice to a barely audible sound. "Yes, yes I can! If he doesn't kill me before then, he might drop me off—oh, but he'll know that something's up the moment he sees you. He'll know that I called someone for help and—" She stopped abruptly. "Unless, unless we can make it look like a coincidence. Do you know any kids? Maybe someone around one or two years old? There's a toddler playground on the south end of the park, so it wouldn't look suspicious if there was another mom already there. If you just happened to be hanging out with a child, maybe pushing her on a swing or something, Saul might overlook it. He might just drop me off, watch for a couple of minutes, and then leave. But if he suspects something, even for a minute—*and he's really paranoid*—then he'll never let me out of the car."

"Where the hell are you, bitch!" Something heavy and glass exploded in the background, like someone had tossed a lamp against a wall, and Tiffany almost screamed.

Oh my lord!

This was all happening way too fast.

She didn't have time to think, and it wasn't as if Ramsey Olaru was going to let her waltz out of the house, head to a toddler park in Tall Pines Village, and meet with some pajama-wearing, abused woman whom she had just met in her office the day before.

Yeah, that was really going to fly.

But if she called the police, and the woman was killed…

Well, she didn't want to watch that headline on the news, knowing that she had turned her back on a stranger's cry for help.

And as for a shelter, she might be able to find one and take Tawni there, but again, Ramsey would have to be intimately involved.

And then it finally hit her: *Well, duh! Ramsey Olaru was a vampire.* And a kick-ass Master Warrior at that.

He could crush this evil man with the flick of his wrist, not that she wanted to get in the business of arranging executions, but this guy sounded like he needed a real rude awakening, if not a straight-up beat down.

But…

She had only heard one side of the story.

What if the woman was exaggerating?

Or crazy?

What if she was psychotic and making half of it up?

Still, that broken glass didn't sound fictional to her, and Ramsey would be able to pull any truth he needed out of Tawni's mind, or the boyfriend's, in seconds.

If need be, he could wipe their memories or implant a compulsion in Saul's thick skull, replace his rage with undying servitude, tell him to never harm Tawni again. Bottom line: Ramsey could do the same thing to this jackass that he had done to Tiffany, the night Napolean had claimed Brooke: send him on his merry way with all his memories wiped clean, never to bother Tawni again.

It was a hell of a lot more simple than involving human agencies.

She bit her bottom lip and nodded.

While it felt like she'd been deliberating for minutes, the entire process had actually only taken seconds—Tiffany had synthesized dozens of thoughts in a flash. "Tawni, are you still there?" She spoke forcefully into the receiver.

"I'm here," the frightened woman whimpered.

Lords, she sounded so, so terrified.

"Meet me at the park at eight o'clock tonight," Tiffany said.

Tawni inhaled sharply, as if she didn't dare to hope. "Are you sure? Can you get there? Do you know a kid you can bring with you?" Her voice rose in angst. "Because I swear, if he figures it out, he might just shoot me in the car."

Tiffany cringed.

Well now, this was an unexpected twist. Saul had a gun?

Yeah, she could probably bring Phoenix, as long as Ramsey and Brooke knew what was up, as long as the prince had solid protection, but she couldn't exactly stand there with an entourage, just waiting to take the batterer down.

Talk about tipping Saul off…

It didn't matter.

She didn't have time to work it out in her head.

There was a terrible commotion; the door to the closet—*or whatever it was*—flung open, and Tawni began to scream.

Tiffany's heart pounded in her chest. "Tawni! *Tawni?*"

"Who the hell are you talking to?" *Saul's voice.* The guy sounded murderous. Tawni had not been exaggerating.

"Eight o'clock, Tawni," Tiffany practically panted the words. "I'll be there with a child. Do you hear me? *I'll be there.* I promise. Hang in there. Don't—"

The phone went dead, and Tiffany held her breath, slowly lowering the device from her ear. Maybe Saul had already injured Tawni; maybe the phone had been disconnected in a scuffle; or maybe Tawni had wisely hung up before Saul could hear their plans. There was no way to know for sure.

Still reeling from the sudden rush of adrenaline, Tiffany tossed her cell across the coverlet, sat down on the edge of the bed, and just stared at the disconnected receiver for what felt like eons. Finally, she braced her head in her hands and exhaled, letting out a long expiration of anxiety: How in the world was she was going to convince Ramsey Olaru to go along with her promise, let alone convince Brooke to loan her precious son, like some stage prop for a potentially violent play?

There was no way, *absolutely no way* she was going to put that child in danger, even if she had to pack an entire arsenal herself to ensure his safety. But she had given Tawni her word, and her word was her bond.

To Tiffany's way of thinking, the best way to handle it would be to arrive at the park early, place Phoenix in a swing, and try to look as natural and unthreatening as she could. Meanwhile, Ramsey could be waiting *right there*, on the side of the road, in his Escalade, for Tawni and Saul to pull up; and the moment Saul got out of the car, or let Tawni get out on her own, Ramsey could take control of the human's mind. Hell, jump in the backseat if he had to.

There would be no need to wait.

And there would be no real danger—they were only dealing with humans after all.

For a fleeting moment, an image from last night's dream popped into Tiffany's mind, and she shivered: a large alpha wolf, standing on the edge of a high rock outcropping, with its tail tucked into a poorly disguised casing of wool.

The wolf in sheep's clothing.

Again.

Her mind was so clouded that Tiffany couldn't reason, but clearly, there was something *else* there: Yes, Ramsey was a predator, lupine in his every gesture and movement. And yes, he was as lethal as the most alpha member of any pack, but maybe there was something else—maybe he was more volatile, more dangerous, than she knew. Maybe he wouldn't erase the man's memories and send him on his way; maybe he would just slaughter the lowlife in front of her. Maybe he would bite *her*—Tiffany—just for suggesting the scenario.

She swallowed hard, trying to ease her fears.

She had given Tawni her word.

Her word.

And she wasn't about to let the woman die at the hands of a madman, crazy or not, stranger or friend.

Besides, Brooke would feel the same way once Tiffany called her, once she explained—

The door to Tiffany's bedroom flew open, and she shrieked, scrambling back on the bed. Ramsey Olaru stood in the doorway, all six feet, five inches of him, wearing nothing more than his skivvies, and by the arctic look on his ruthless face, he hadn't stopped by to chat.

"I could smell your fear all the way across the hall from my bedroom," he snarled, "and your *heartbeat* woke me up. What the hell is going on?"

twelve

Brooke Adams-Mondragon stood on the front veranda of the royal manse, watching as Ramsey and Tiffany made their way up the lengthy drive. While she certainly had a few misgivings about the potentially messy situation, as a whole, it was truly no big deal.

Correction: It was certainly a big deal for the poor battered woman, but it was never a big deal for a vampire to corral, contain, and control a group of humans. A vampire's powers were just too immense. She brushed a stray lock of hair behind her ear and smiled as the dark Escalade came to a complete stop, and then she made her way to the back door, strapped Phoenix's carrier into the middle seat, and efficiently plopped the child in the SUV, all before Ramsey had a chance to jump out and help her.

"I would've done that for you," Ramsey said in a polite but no-nonsense tone.

"I know," she replied. She waved enthusiastically at Tiffany and then shrugged apologetically at Ramsey. "I'm an old hand at this," she explained. "I don't even wait for Napolean—it drives him to distraction."

The sentinel nodded, lowering his chin and averting his eyes in a gesture of respect, even as Tiffany sat upright and waved her hand wildly, clearly thrilled to see her best friend. "Hey, Brookie!" the pretty blonde called.

Brooke's heart lit at the sound. "Hey, Tiff." It was so nice to be on good terms with her *bestie* again. Just the same, Brooke immediately saw through all that outward good cheer: Tiffany Matthews was clearly wound as tight as a drum, and this new situation couldn't be helping. Brooke double-checked all of the carrier belts to make sure the connections were secure, and then she swiftly buckled her toddler into the fortified seat. "All set."

"Hey there, Phoenix," Tiffany cooed in a soft, high-pitched voice as the child settled into the seat.

"Be still," Brooke admonished, when he immediately began to bob up and down like a hyperactive buoy in response to Tiffany's greeting.

"What is he wearing?" Tiffany asked, scrunching up her nose in mirth.

Brooke chuckled. She had bundled Phoenix in a warm winter jacket, a cozy wool hat, and a pair of padded mittens, all of which were totally unnecessary for a fourteen-month-old vampire who could already regulate his own body temperature, especially when it had been sixty degrees at noon, even if it was December. She threw her hands up in exasperation. "Oh, heck; at least he won't get cold." What else could she say—she just couldn't help it? Those latent human impulses still kicked in from time to time? Probably not the best thing to say to Tiffany right now, considering that conversion was undoubtedly a touchy issue.

"Well, you're definitely right about that," Tiffany teased.

Brooke gave Phoenix a wet and noisy kiss on the forehead, told him to be good, and then nodded once more at Ramsey, who was waiting rather restlessly in the driver's seat. He probably wanted to get the whole sordid affair over with. Taking her cue from his demeanor, she decided to cut straight to the chase: "So, you're sure this is a good idea?" She posed the question at both of them.

"No," Ramsey replied.

"Yes," Tiffany said, at the exact same time.

Great.

So, they were clearly in agreement.

Brooke chuckled inwardly, and then she waited patiently for one or the other to elaborate.

Ramsey shifted anxiously in his seat, and Tiffany shrugged.

"Okay, well, it's a bizarre idea at best," Tiffany began, "meeting in a park, after dark, but if the goal is to help the lady get away from her *situation*"—she cleared her throat and eyed Ramsey cautiously—"and to do it with the least amount of human interference or intervention possible, then I think the sentinel is our best bet."

Ramsey snorted, and Brooke almost cringed.

The sentinel?

So it was like that?

Still?

Brooke flashed her most gracious, queenly smile at Ramsey, hoping to lessen the tension, and then she nodded. "I'm sure Tiffany is right."

Ramsey arched his back, ostensibly to stretch. "Ever the diplomat, I'm sure Tiffany would rather approach the situation with subtlety and tact; however, I plan to simply attack it hard and fast." He narrowed his gaze at Brooke. "Rest assured, milady, it'll be handled swiftly and with finality."

Brooke winced and turned to regard Tiffany, hoping to read her expression. *So...* Tiffany wanted to feel it out, let the situation unfold naturally, and only intervene when necessary— erase the jerk's memories and send him on his way, only do it with kid gloves for the sake of the woman's emotional state. Whereas, Ramsey wanted to pull up in the Escalade, wave his hand over the whole damn park, freeze everyone within a three-block radius exactly where they stood, and then handle the business with a swift and brutal mind scrub. Perhaps they would meet somewhere in the middle.

As if reading her thoughts, Tiffany offered, "He's going to walk right up to the boyfriend, scrub his memories of the woman, of Tawni, and then tell him to relocate to Alaska, no questions asked."

Brooke frowned. "Alaska?"

Tiffany shook her head as if to say *don't ask*; then she took a deep, measured breath and smiled. "The whole encounter shouldn't take more than five minutes, once I've made contact with Tawni in the park, and Ramsey's either lured the abusive bastard out of his truck, climbed in the backseat, or followed him around the corner. Either way, I'll tell Tawni that she and I are going to wait at the playground until her boyfriend leaves—let's give him plenty of time to pull away—and then my own friend, who's waiting nearby, will help her escape. Depending on how it unfolds, Ramsey will just have to erase her memories, too." She turned to face Prince Phoenix and reached over the console to give him a pat on the lap. "Our little one should only be out of the truck for a couple of minutes."

Brooke nodded. "Are you sure you don't want backup?"

Ramsey frowned. "Santos and Saxson are working tonight, and Julien needs to hunt—the male hasn't fed in a month."

"Right," Brooke said, "but what about Saber Alexiares?" What she couldn't share, not even with Tiffany, was the fact that Napolean had a sixth sense about the fearsome male who used to be a Dark One. He was watching Saber closely, seriously considering him as a potential fourth sentinel, hoping Saber would come to the conclusion on his own. Of course, nothing would happen unless and until the stubborn vampire finally made a full commitment to the house of Jadon, unless and until he finally placed that crest ring on his finger and took the public oath. Still, he was probably available. "I'm sure he wouldn't mind," Brooke said. "He'd be happy to accompany you, if you asked."

Ramsey grew unnaturally quiet, as only a vampire could do. He was undoubtedly thinking the same thing. "Thought about it," he bit out, "but... *that ring.*" He shrugged. "Don't get me wrong: I trust the male as much as one predator trusts another, and he's even starting to grow on me as an individual, but—" He sighed, letting his hunched shoulders relax. "Until I see the insignia from the house of Jadon sitting on his fourth, right-hand finger; until I watch him bleed for the people and hear him vow to die for the same; I'm not going to extend that kind of invitation to him." He cocked his head to the side in reflection. "He needs time? That's cool. But so do we."

Brooke leveled a private gaze at Tiffany, and the two exchanged an *alrighty-then, perhaps-we-should-just-leave-this-subject-alone* glance, before returning to a companionable silence.

After a few awkward moments had passed, Brooke adjusted Phoenix's straps one last time and kissed him once more on the cheek. "Well, he is just a human, this abusive boyfriend. Even little Phoenix here could probably get the best of a mortal."

Tiffany glared at her then, thumbing her own chest in an exaggerated gesture. "Um, speaking as the resident *human* in the car, let's not be rude."

Brooke chuckled, and Ramsey quirked his lips in a subtle but affable smile. "Right," Brooke said. "How soon we forget." This invoked an even harsher glare from Tiffany, which made Brooke decide to back off, drop it altogether. She kissed Phoenix a third time, drawing a somewhat impatient glance from Ramsey, and the child squirmed. "Be good, my brave little Justice, and look out for Auntie Tiff."

Phoenix bounced up and down excitedly in the seat and shook his Bobee back and forth—*thank all the gods of providence, the stuffed toy was back in its master's arms.* "Auntie Tiff!" he squealed, causing the brooding blonde to laugh.

"And on that note," Brooke said, stepping back from the

open door, "I will let you guys get to it, and I'll see you back here within the hour."

Tiffany glanced at Ramsey, and they exchanged an unspoken understanding. *Yep, they were closer than they pretended to be, more deeply bonded than they realized.* "The way Ramsey drives, we'll be back in a half an hour," Tiffany said, and then she laughed.

And so did he.

"Don't worry. We'll be quick about it," he added.

Brooke nodded. "Very well." She smiled at her best friend. "You're a good person, Tiffany. This woman was lucky to have met you."

Tiffany simpered. "Yeah, I guess. I really shouldn't be getting involved, but *damn*; how do you do nothing when you can do something, ya know?"

"You learn… in time," Ramsey said evenly.

Brooke winked at Tiffany. "Napolean is pretty strict about the laws, the ones that govern our interference with human concerns, but I think in this instance, he would understand. This woman approached you—at the executive Prime offices, no less—and now, she's calling you at *home*? As far as I'm concerned, that approaches house of Jadon business. Better to send them both on their merry way than to let the situation continue… or escalate." She shut the door with a crisp thud and stepped away from the Cadillac, waving once more at both Tiffany and Phoenix, while biding her time.

Indeed, Ramsey could handle a lone, rotten human being, and even Phoenix could bite, fly away, or assert his will over a mortal female, as long as he understood what that *will* was; but—and wasn't there always a *but?*—Brooke had made the call without consulting Napolean. The king was busy on official duty, and she hadn't wanted to interrupt his engagement. Still, that raised her personal level of responsibility and accountability, as well as her general concern. She wasn't about to leave things to chance, even if there was *zero* chance, really, that a human could ever get the best of Ramsey Olaru.

She watched as the Escalade rounded the curved apex of the driveway, made a right-hand turn onto an unpaved road, and disappeared into the distance. And then she headed straight for her own sapphire-blue Jaguar. She would be right behind her best friend and her best friend's new mate, following them to Tall Pines Village Park, where she would wait, and watch, from a distance.

The couple would never know she was there.

She sighed.

Well, maybe Ramsey would figure it out in some preternatural, vampiric way, but even if he did, so be it. He would just have to understand.

Brooke loved Phoenix more than life itself, and she felt pretty much the same about her smart but impetuous friend. Tiffany might still be learning the ropes; she might still be getting her toes wet in the house of Jadon's deep internal waters—after all, she'd only had three days, so far, to make the adjustment—but Brooke was no longer an acolyte. If Ramsey needed some backup, another vampire who could kick some ass, *and the bait being used was Prince Phoenix?* Well then…

Brooke was momentarily startled by the deep, feral growl that rumbled in her own throat.

Enough said.

She climbed into her car and placed her key in the ignition, chuckling a bit at her own foolish antics. Who did she think she was? One of the sly female detectives from one of her favorite mystery novels? *Oh well*, she thought, *what can I say?*

Where the little cub went, Mama Bear was sure to follow.

thirteen

Ramsey Olaru scanned the entire dimly lit park in the breadth of two heartbeats. The playground was empty, the benches were abandoned, and there were no other humans present, no cars parked nearby for several blocks, and that meant it would be easy to keep an eye on Tiffany and Phoenix.

There would be no distractions.

He stilled his mind, tuning out all other senses for the moment, and concentrated solely on the layout of the park. There were two logical entrances, which meant only two exits: one, on the south perimeter, where he and Tiffany were parked, about 200 yards from the playground, and the other, on the opposite side of a grassy field, in the north, which led to a narrow, winding path, edged on both sides by a series of short, well-trimmed bushes, more or less restricting patrons to the designated trail. Visibility to the actual playground was unobstructed from his vantage point.

He glanced at Tiffany, watching as she climbed from the cab of the SUV, opened Phoenix's door, and began to unbuckle the little prince, wishing he could get out, too, without potentially scaring the boyfriend or provoking a jealous rage, at least too soon. "Keep your eyes and ears open," he told her. "If anything feels off, if anything makes you even the least bit uncomfortable, you hightail it back to this spot: Understand me?"

Tiffany visibly shivered. "Yes, Ramsey," she replied, lifting Phoenix from his seat. She headed back toward the passenger door and peered in at the warrior. "I'm just going to be right there"—she pointed at the playground—"near the swings with Phoenix." The child also pointed at the swings and giggled, and Tiffany's face lit up with satisfaction. "He'll have a good time, one way or the other."

Ramsey nodded. He gestured toward the bramble-lined pathway, on the other side of the park, and inclined his head. "Your friend, *this woman*," he corrected, "she's either going to approach you from that path or from right here. Don't turn your back on her—it's just not good form." He felt his hackles rise, and he forced himself to settle down. *Good lords; was this what it was like to finally have a* destiny? To be consumed by defensive instincts and overprotective impulses? He dismissed the thought. It wasn't like he didn't possess more than his fair share of both attributes, already. "I'm going to stay right here in the truck, hopefully out of sight from the boyfriend, but rest assured, I'll deal with him the moment he steps out of his car, unless he remains seated and tries to watch, of course. In that case, I'll just show up in his backseat and handle it." He pointed at the opposite one-way street, located behind the playground, on the other end of the park. "If he does drive off too quickly, then I'll follow him, so you may be alone with her for a couple of minutes, tops. Are you good with that?"

Tiffany made an affirmative gesture with her hand. "I think I can handle one single confused and frightened woman, Ramsey."

He chuckled, easing the tension. "Ah, so we're on a first-name basis now?"

She rolled her eyes and hauled Phoenix even closer to her side. "Besides, I have a few protective instincts of my own, Mr. Olaru." She instinctively kissed the child on the top of his head, nuzzling him with her nose.

Females, Ramsey thought.

It was as if they were all given an extra dose of kindness where little ones were concerned. He sure wished the gods would've given Tiffany a little extra *something* when it came to him, and then he immediately regretted the short-sighted thought. Of course they had. She was his *destiny* after all. It just might take a little time for her to connect to it; that's all.

He brought his attention back to the moment at hand and snorted. "I'm sure you do." And then he immediately switched back to *all-business* mode. "Just the same, I'm here for a reason. Don't be a hero. If this woman makes you feel uncomfortable in any way, pick up Phoenix and walk away." He paused, considering his next words. "And damn, I hate to break it down like this, because I know Phoenix is a prince, not a dog, but just the same, he's a vampire. And he *can* bite. If the woman does anything erratic, and I mean anything, however insignificant, something that makes you feel physically threatened before I'm done with the knucklehead, tell him *Ia-i sangele*."

Tiffany wrinkled up her nose. "Ia-i sangele?"

Ramsey searched for an adequate interpretation. "Loosely translated, it means to seize or claim." He sighed. "It means, *take her blood*." Tiffany recoiled, and he immediately threw up his hand, trying to head off another debate. "As a vampire, Phoenix is always aware of the pulse, the heartbeat, the movement of blood through any given human's veins. We all are. If you are projecting fear or urgency, and you tell him *Ia-i sangele*, it will trigger a natural instinct. It'll at least make him feral."

Tiffany took a step back, away from the SUV. She looked like she wanted to plant her hands on her hips and give him a piece of her mind, but luckily for him, her arms were full with the toddler. "Are you serious?" she said, anyway. "I mean, really? You want me to tell this sweet child to eat the woman?"

Ramsey bit back a snicker. "Blondie—"

"That is not my name," she interrupted.

"*Baby*," he interjected, "it's not that serious, or unnatural. All I'm saying is—"

"What's your middle name?" Tiffany asked.

"Excuse me?"

"Your middle name. What is it?"

"Demetrios." He sounded as hesitant as she felt.

"Well then, *Ramsey Demetrios Olaru*: I will not tell this child to become feral or to seize, claim, take, or drink a human's blood. Oh, and while we're at it"—the *ew* factor practically coated her suddenly tight lips—"thank you very much for making me uncomfortable with my best friend's son for the very first time in his life."

Ramsey shrank back, just a tad, and then he bit down on his tongue, leaving an indentation in the tip. He needed a toothpick. The woman was way too sassy for her own good—someone needed to tame her one day, and he was looking forward to the challenge. "Just remember what I said," he intoned calmly, and then he instinctively glanced to the left. There was a dark gray sedan approaching from the northern side of the park, a BMW 750i, no less. Apparently, the dysfunctional couple wasn't hurting for money. "Looks like your friend is here."

Tiffany quickly backed away from the door, her gorgeous sea-green eyes meeting his intense hazel stare, and their gazes remained locked for a fleeting moment. Without another word, she shut the door and walked briskly toward the playground, crossing the large grassy field and heading for the swings with laser-like focus. Since the meeting was supposed to be a coincidence, she paused on three different occasions to play nonchalantly with Phoenix, point at the swings, and pretend to notice everything around them, *except* the approaching gray sedan.

Ramsey's muscles twitched as he sat in the cab of the SUV, watching her, even as his heartbeat grew eerily calm and steady. He had wanted Tiffany to be in position before the couple arrived, but *oh well*. Things rarely went off as planned. He bided his time, glancing back and forth between the sedan's tinted windows and his *destiny*, waiting for her to secure Phoenix in one of the park's two allocated baby swings.

It seemed like it took forever.

The sedan finally pulled to a complete stop, and a nervous, skinny woman stepped out of the passenger seat, looking both timid and afraid.

Once again, Ramsey's hackles rose, but he didn't quite know why. This wasn't the same instinct as before. It was something ominously different. He growled deep in his throat as he watched her approach the swings, all the while preparing to dematerialize from the Escalade and insert himself in the boyfriend's car. *Damnit all to hell*, he thought, just as abruptly. The woman had barely gotten out of the car, and the boyfriend was already pulling away from the curb. He didn't have time to watch Tiffany's interaction before he took chase…

He hesitated.

Sons of the original house of Jadon, something was simply wrong.

Amiss.

Unexplainable.

As foreign as it was… *familiar?*

He stayed a moment longer than he should have, watching the female approach the swings, letting the sedan pull away and gain speed. He couldn't help it. There was something inexplicably *off* about this woman. Something he just couldn't put his finger on.

The female made it to the circular enclosure, the gravel pit beneath the swings, and she seemed to sigh with relief—it was as if her entire body relaxed with the awareness that she had finally broken free from her abusive boyfriend, that he had finally, albeit unwittingly, let her go. And then Tiffany whispered something in her ear, and the two of them turned toward Ramsey's Escalade and watched him, together, even as he continued to watch them, right back.

Tiffany glared at him then, growing increasingly impatient.

Apparently, she assumed he could see her expression from a distance, and naturally, he could. She smiled, waved, and cocked her thumb in the direction of the sedan, trying to hide the gesture from the woman, while simultaneously indicating that she wanted him to follow the car and take care of the boyfriend. "We're fine." She mouthed the words, and he sharply inhaled, willing his mind to believe her…

Because his heart was simply *not on board.*

He hesitated a moment longer, growing increasingly uncomfortable, and then he watched as the woman—Tawni, right?—gave Tiffany an awkward hug, glanced in the direction of the disappearing BMW, and shuddered as if she were still terrified by the very thought of her tormentor.

And truly, nothing stood out as amiss.

Her posture was submissive; her countenance was meek; and her expression was appreciative. But her energy was inexplicably dark, almost primitive—*or savage?*—in a way that just didn't fit.

This female was damaged to the core.

Ramsey tilted his head to the side, trying to place the vibration, trying to make sense of what his sixth sense was telling him.

There was no explanation.

He just couldn't pin it down.

For all intents and purposes, she was a five-foot-six, fairly scrawny human female, with ghastly black-and-red dyed hair; and she was clearly terrified of the man who had just driven off in that car. No one could fake that kind of terror.

Maybe the best thing to do was to get the whole business over with, as quickly as possible, so he could retrieve his *destiny*, secure the prince, and send the poor broken woman on her way before anything could go wrong.

The man would be no problem.

Ramsey could catch up to his car, head him off on the roadway, and be in the fool's backseat faster than the bastard could say, *Who the hell are you?* He could erase his memories and implant a suggestion—time to get the hell out of Dodge—just as swiftly.

And the sooner he got that done, the better.

The sooner he could get Tiffany away from the strange, enigmatic woman.

He shut his eyes and tried to concentrate, struggling to dismiss his apprehension, whatever it was, and then he shifted the SUV into gear and pulled out of the lot at breakneck speed, whispering an inaudible prayer to the sacred star of Gemini, his own ruling twin lords:

Sacred Geminorum, watch over my mate and protect my prince while I finish this silly task. Please safeguard their immortal souls.

fourteen

Brooke Mondragon tightened her grip on the steering wheel of her dark sapphire metallic Jaguar XJ and watched the odd scenario unfold through her dim, tinted windows.

Ramsey and Tiffany had arrived at the park and chatted a bit at his truck. Despite herself, she couldn't help but giggle as Tiffany seemed to be giving the fearsome warrior the *what for*, and he seemed to be, amazingly, taking it in stride.

Well, as much as Ramsey Olaru could take anything in stride.

And then the unhappy human couple had pulled up, and Tiffany had rushed to the playground, secured Phoenix in a swing, and given him a gentle push—*aw, it was so sweet to watch*—before placing her body squarely between the baby and the strange woman, who had summarily approached them. Brooke had no doubt, whatsoever, that human or not, Tiffany would tear out the throat of anyone who ever tried to hurt little Phoenix. So that's not what had given her pause…

What had seized her attention was what had happened next.

The boyfriend had immediately driven away, a scenario Ramsey had anticipated—at least it was one of the scenarios Tiff and Ramsey had mentioned earlier—but Ramsey had not immediately followed. Rather, he had sat there in his SUV, watching the *woman* like a hawk, his intense hazel eyes deepening with interest.

And concern.

Brooke had sat up rigidly then, her back arched, her muscles taut. She had leaned over the steering wheel and braced her hands on the dash, focusing one hundred percent of her keen vampiric vision on the slender human female in order to take in every subtle nuance of the lady's behavior. The woman had spoken softly with Tiffany, or vice versa, and then she had given her an awkward hug. And for all intents and purposes, she appeared to be exactly as Tiffany had described: a somewhat distracted person with an unusually anxious demeanor, who was desperate to get away from her boyfriend and probably just a little bit neurotic. She was obviously rattled. She was clearly afraid. And her posture was both appreciative and nonthreatening.

But there was something inexplicable in her eyes.

Something just *not-quite-right* and certainly unusual.

Her pupils were haunted with shadows, but not the kind cast by nightmares, not the reflections of terrible memories or recollections of being battered. They were haunted by unseen demons.

And the demons were *her own.*

Brooke knew that it didn't make sense, that this ad hoc, *psychic tea-leaf* assessment, this sudden rush to judgment, was not in any way supported by the poor woman's actions, but just the same, Brooke felt it in her bones.

And apparently, so did Ramsey Olaru.

It was not until Tiffany finally waved him away, giving him an enthusiastic thumbs-up and a not-so-subtle signal to *get going*, that the seasoned Master Warrior had driven off, but even then, he had seemed hesitant to do so.

Now, as Brooke watched the two women standing beneath the swings, talking in hushed, amiable whispers, she hoped Ramsey would hurry back.

She rolled down her window, just a bit, in order to listen in on their conversation. Although she was several blocks away, she could still see and hear everything as acutely as if she were standing right there. Score one for the Vampyr.

She closed her eyes and tilted her head to the side: Tiffany was telling the woman, *telling Tawni*, that Tiffany's boyfriend, Ramsey, was going to follow *Saul* from a safe distance, make sure he didn't do a U-turn and head back that way, before they whisked Tawni out of there—they didn't want to take a chance that this Saul guy could find her.

Hmm, Brooke thought, *Tiffany's boyfriend, Ramsey.*
Interesting.

Now Tawni was asking Tiffany if Ramsey could protect himself.

Brooke laughed and opened her eyes.

"Don't worry about it," Tiffany said. "I promise you: He can hold his own, and you will never see Saul again."

All of a sudden, the woman drew back in alarm, asking if Ramsey was crazy enough to confront Saul, and Tiffany laughed. "No," she reassured her in that feisty, clipped way that she had. "He's just going to watch him from a distance, follow a little ways, and then he'll be right back."

"But what if Saul sees him?" Tawni asked.

"He won't," Tiffany said.

"But what if he does?"

Tiffany sighed. "Don't worry," she insisted, "one way or the other, it'll all be fine. Trust me, Ramsey can take care of himself, and he can be very persuasive when he has to be."

"Mmm," the woman said. "But then so can my boyfriend. Very, *very* persuasive."

Brooke narrowed her eyes and blinked several times in confusion. *Now that was strange.* Was the nutcase defending him now? And after everything he had done to her?

Tiffany seemed momentarily caught off guard by the odd

reaction as well as the protective statement. She took a deep breath, as if preparing to respond, and then she abruptly stopped short and took a reflexive step backward.

Brooke leaned forward.

What the hay?

Tiffany was staring dazedly at Tawni's eyes, and she looked like she had just seen a ghost.

Brooke shifted her bottom in the seat, absently scooting back and forth, as if she could get a better purchase, and consequently, a better look. Tawni's eyes were noticeably bloodshot and incredibly intense—she probably hadn't slept well in weeks—but they didn't seem all that interesting, unless one considered…

Holy shit!

Her eyes weren't bloodshot.

They were blood red.

As crimson as the petals of a dark velvet rose, and their origin was all too familiar.

Vampyr?

Tiffany backpedaled a few steps further, unconsciously shielding Prince Phoenix with her body, and her gaze dropped lower, dipping from Tawni's eyes to her mouth.

Brooke's gaze instinctively followed, and that was all she wrote. The woman's lips were curled back into a wicked snarl, the reedy flesh twisted into a thin line just above the tops of her teeth, and her gums practically twitched with anticipation as her canines grew sharp, long, and *deadly*… as they extended into fangs.

For a moment, Brooke could only sit there and stare, stunned into inaction, all the while wondering: *What the heck is this?*

After all, it simply wasn't possible.

There were no female vampires in Dark Moon Vale, none but the *destinies* who had been chosen for the males in the house of Jadon, those converted by their mates, and this sure as hell was no female *destiny* she had ever heard of.

It only took a moment for her body to catch up with her

mind, for her concern to override her confusion, for her heart to synthesize the information.

Who the hell cared what, why, or how?

The woman was turning feral right before Brooke's eyes, and she was only moments away from lunging, from sinking her teeth into—

Oh, dear goddess, Andromeda!

The woman had her sights set on Phoenix.

In her haste to get out of the car, Brooke wrenched the handle right off the door. When she could no longer get it to open, she flung her shoulder into the panel, shoved with all her might, and fell from the Jaguar, sending the driver's-side door spiraling into the night.

She sprang to her feet and sprinted toward the playground, willing her muscles to move faster, ordering her body to take flight as it had never done before.

"Tiffany! *Tiffany!* Look out! *Get the baby!*"

*

Ramsey Olaru pulled onto the main county road, about five or six blocks beyond the park, watching for the dark gray sedan. In the absence of a visual cue to lead him, he had his window cracked open, and he was concentrating on the distinctive purr, that deep, rumbling drone made only by a BMW's engine.

Sure enough, the familiar hum was about five hundred yards in front of him.

He stepped on the gas and sent a powerful mind-command to the driver, even as he approached the shiny bumper. *Pull the hell over. Now.*

The dark gray sedan slowed down, and the driver pulled over to the side of the road.

Ramsey brought the Escalade to a complete stop, right

behind the BMW, and then instantly teleported his body from one vehicle to the next.

He was just about to snatch the despicable human by the neck, pull him into the backseat, and get the whole sordid business over with, when the driver instantly vanished before his eyes.

What the hell?

He hadn't even gotten a good look at the guy.

Although what he had seen, if only a momentary profile, was more than a bit unsettling: long dark hair that fell from a widow's peak, masking deep sapphire eyes beneath thin, arched brows, and the hair appeared to be dyed partially red.

The hairs stood up on the back of Ramsey's neck, even as his senses quickened.

The sedan was filled with the faint scent of sulfur, the telltale signature of a sorcerer, and the air practically hummed with preternatural power. Not to mention, the vibrations were way, *way* off.

Errant.

Supernatural.

Evil.

Before his mind could even register the data, he heard a faint, terrified cry from a distance—it was coming from a female, and it had to be close to the park. "Tiffany! *Tiffany!* Look out! *Get the baby!*"

Son of a bitch!

That was Brooke Mondragon's voice, and the *baby* was none other than Phoenix Mondragon, the prince of the house of Jadon!

Ramsey was just about to will his molecules to dissolve, to hurl his body in the direction of the park, when he suddenly thought better of it: He scrambled to the back of the Escalade, punched through the glass, and withdrew three weapons: a sheathed dagger, which he tucked inside his belt; his familiar trident, which he melded to his hand; and his AK47. And then he took to the skies like a vampire of old, his rich, flaxen wings punching through his back as he spiraled toward Tall Pines Village Park, and his mind at last made the final connections.

Sweet goddess of mercy.

He knew that profile intimately, and he also knew that smell.

The miserable *boyfriend* wasn't human at all. He was a Dark One.

And by all that was unholy, the bastard probably had a name.

Salvatore Nistor.

fifteen

Tiffany Matthews heard Brooke scream, but there was nothing she could do. Tawni was transforming before her very eyes, turning into something savage and terrifying, something utterly unthinkable.

Impossible.

And she was just about ready to lunge at Phoenix Mondragon.

Tiffany took several quick steps to the left, placing her body more squarely between Tawni and the child, even as her mind raced frantically, spinning in hysterical circles, searching for a viable solution:

What the hell what she going to do now?

What the hell was happening?

Whatever Tawni had become—whatever she intended to do—Tiffany was only human.

And Ramsey?

Holy Virgin Mary…

What a fool Tiffany had been. The warrior had driven away from the park, following the so-called boyfriend at Tiffany's request.

She sucked in a deep breath of air, focused her attention on the matter at hand, and summoned every last ounce of her courage. "Hey!" she shouted, trying to rattle Tawni's bones with the sheer velocity of her voice. She waved both hands wildly in front of the crazy woman's face, hoping to draw her attention away from the child in the swing. *From Phoenix.* "What the hell are you doing?"

Tawni whipped her head to the side in an eerie serpentine motion and snarled. She hunched her shoulders in an unnatural arc, and her breath came out with a hiss. "I'm simply following my master's orders"—she paused long enough to smile—"now move away from the prince!" She drew her right arm over her left shoulder, preparing to strike, and Tiffany instinctively threw up an elbow to block the blow.

It was an utterly useless maneuver.

The powerful backhand landed halfway between Tiffany's elbow and her shoulder, instantly launching her off her feet and sending her spiraling through the air, soaring across the playground, and heading straight for a huge wooden fort.

Tiffany was just about to slam, spine first, into the main post when Brooke appeared out of nowhere. The queen leapt into the air, caught Tiffany around the waist, and then spun them both around in a nimble display of prowess, setting her evenly back on the ground. "*Run,*" Brooke snarled. She didn't wait for an answer. She released her hold on Tiffany, dropped into a crouch, and then launched herself at Tawni from nearly twenty yards away.

Tawni dove at Phoenix.

Brooke dove at Tawni.

And in a clash of flesh, bone, and willpower, the two enraged women hit the ground with a thud and began to tussle like a pair of wildcats, each vying for supremacy, each seeking the other's throat.

Tiffany gasped as Tawni sank her wicked fangs into Brooke's forearm, yet Brooke ignored the pain. She fisted a handful of Tawni's hair, wrenched the woman's head forward, and then slowly, deliberately, sank her own deadly canines deep into Tawni's throat. Brooke snarled and bit down harder, whipping her head from side to side like a crazed dog worrying a bone, trying to break Tawni's neck.

Tiffany gawked for a few heartbeats longer, unable to tear her gaze from the terrible sight, and then she took her best friend's warning to heart and took off like a bat out of hell.

There was simply no point in sticking around to watch.

She would only get in the way.

And if she became a liability to Brooke, she would further endanger the prince. Besides, Ramsey had told her in no uncertain terms to make her way back to the spot where he had parked the Escalade if anything went down. Surely, the Master Warrior could not be that far away. Surely, he would hear the feral snarls, savage bites, and life-and-death struggle ensuing in the park, and he would come running.

Tiffany glanced over her shoulder, even as she continued to make tracks toward the small, circular parking lot. The battle behind her was as vicious as it was shocking. The women were trading blows, bites, and lunges. Brooke's arm was torn open and bleeding, the flesh hanging loosely from the bone, and Tawni's throat looked like someone had run it through a meat grinder.

In the blink of an eye—if only for *one* opportune moment— Brooke gained an advantage: She kicked Tawni in the chest, knocking the wind out of her sails, and then she sprang to her feet, rushed to the swing-set, and unfastened her son. In a series of movements that could only be described as a transient blur, she lifted Phoenix out of the harness, turned to face Tiffany, and promptly launched the child into the air, tossing him across the park in an effort to get him out of imminent danger.

In her haste, her aim was way off target.

At best, the child would land fifty feet to the right of Tiffany.

Prince Phoenix squealed at the top of his lungs, his little arms and legs flailing wildly in the air, as if he were desperate for someone to catch him, something that was *not* going to happen. His eyes grew wide as saucers, and his little throat convulsed with screams as he flew like a missile toward a hard, barren patch of grass.

Tiffany turned to run in his direction, all the while praying for divine intervention, and then just like that, something primordial must have kicked in, because his thick down jacket exploded into a dozen spiraling pieces of cloth, and the most perfect pair of obsidian wings shot through his back and began to flutter wildly in the air.

Phoenix floated gently to the ground, where he curled into a ball and began to sob.

"Oh, baby," Tiffany whispered, desperate to get to him quickly. "It's okay, sweetie. Auntie Tiff is coming."

"Get behind me, and get down!" A deep, commanding voice brought her up short, and Tiffany whirled around to see Ramsey standing right in front of her. He was clutching that gruesome pitchfork in his left hand and some perilous-looking machine gun in his right, and his eyes were literally ablaze with fury.

"But, Phoenix," she tried to argue. "He's—"

"Get behind me, *now!*"

Tiffany scrambled behind him and dropped to the ground just in time to see a *Dark One* appear before him.

"Greetings, son of Jadon," the wicked vampire snarled. "It did take you quite a while to figure this whole little scenario out." He bowed infinitesimally and gestured toward the swing-set, where Brooke and Tawni were still going at it, both women now balanced on their feet, knees bent and arms locked around each other's wrists, both trying to gain an advantage, waiting for an opportunity to let go of a wrist and strike. "Mmm, I trust you've met my bride?"

The left side of Ramsey's lip twitched rapidly, several times in a row, as if someone were yanking a string attached to his flesh, and then his smooth, ivory canines descended from his gums like two brandished daggers, long, lethal, and menacing.

Tiffany shivered and scooted even further back as a deep, feral purr rumbled in his throat, and then he abruptly angled his body toward the swing-set, leveled the gun in the females' direction, and shouted an implacable command to his queen: "Brooke, let go and drop down!"

The compulsion must have done its job because Brooke didn't hesitate.

She released Tawni's arms, fell to the ground, and covered her head, even as Ramsey began to unload the clip into Tawni's fully exposed torso.

Tiffany screamed.

Salvatore lunged at Ramsey.

And Ramsey dropped his pitchfork, caught the Dark One by the throat, and continued to spray what were obviously diamond-tipped bullets into Tawni's chest and head. His body hit the ground, and he fought to keep the automatic weapon steady.

"*Oh God, oh God, oh God!*" Tiffany panted, scrambling backward to put more space between her and the vampires. "Please don't let him hit Brooke. Please… please… *please.*" She watched in utter horror as Tawni's body jerked this way and that, convulsing in the air like a jackhammer torn free of its handler, and the bullets struck home, again and again… and again.

After several terrifying moments, the park grew silent.

The clip was empty, and Tawni's bloody carcass slumped to the ground.

Brooke stood back up and headed straight for Phoenix, even as Ramsey turned his full attention on Salvatore. The dark vampire was chewing his way through Ramsey's extended arm, frothing at the mouth and spitting like some kind of rabid dog.

Ramsey dropped the machine gun, drew back his good arm, and punched the Dark One, dead between the eyes, sending him spiraling backward from the force of the blow. The incensed sentinel then rolled across the grass, grabbed his pitchfork in mid-turn, and sprang to his feet, his mangled left arm hanging limply at his side.

He tossed the pitchfork with a flick of his wrist, twirled it around like a baton, and rotated it into the center of his hand. And then he stalked toward the Dark One with a murderous rage in his eyes, his body moving more like a machine than a vessel of flesh and blood.

His muscles twitched.

His chest heaved with determination.

And his knuckles turned white from his murderous grasp on the weapon.

And then everything happened at once.

The north end of the park virtually filled with Master Warriors, vampires from the house of Jadon, materializing like Vikings from a prehistoric sea previously masked by fog: Napolean, Santos, and Saxson; Julien, Saber, and the Silivasi brothers; even Kagen and his new mate, Arielle, drove up in their jeep, appearing on the fringes, ready to treat whoever was injured.

Clearly, Ramsey must have called for the Calvary.

Tiffany was just about to get up, head for the safety of the warriors—*check on Brooke and Phoenix*—and leave the Dark One, who was clearly doomed, to Ramsey and his capable band of brothers, when Tawni Duvall stirred.

In fact, she didn't so much stir as *rise*, like a ghostly apparition from a grave.

A brittle leaf, left over from autumn, crunched beneath Tiffany's hand, and then the unthinkable occurred: Tawni ascended to her feet, dropped low into a squat, and vaulted the full distance of the park at Tiffany, her clawed hands extended in front of her, her sharp fangs protruding from her mouth.

Tiffany gasped at the terrifying sight, and she even tried to scream, but the sound got caught in her throat. She thought she saw Ramsey pause to glance over his shoulder, but there wasn't any time.

What seemed like minutes actually happened in a fraction of a second. It simply transpired in the blink of an eye. Tawni landed in front of Tiffany, dropped into a squat, and gently grasped her by both of her trembling cheeks, the pads of her inhuman fingers massaging Tiffany's jaw.

It was almost like a lover's embrace.

Tawni cocked her head to the side and smiled, and then she swiftly flicked her wrists, rotating each to the left in perfect unison.

There was a pregnant pause before the snap, the sharp, crackling *pop*, as Tiffany tried to speak. She wanted to say to someone, *Hey, I think she's about to break my neck*, but the words never came out.

The thought never reached completion.

The pain was horrendous, yet so short-lived, Tiffany never had a chance to register its intensity.

It was simply and indelibly over.

Her pain, and her fear, and her *life*.

The world and everyone in it disappeared.

sixteen

Ramsey Olaru *felt* Tiffany's fear.

He heard the silent scream his *destiny* couldn't cry, and he registered that finite pause in her heartbeat, that sudden hitch of terrified breath.

Although he knew better than to turn his back on Salvatore Nistor, he couldn't help it. It was instinctual. He glanced over his shoulder to see to his mate, to determine the reason for her dread, and his breath caught in his throat.

Dear sacred twins of Gemini, the Vampyr woman was bending over his *destiny*, cupping her face in her hands, and he knew—*oh sweet Andromeda, he knew*—what was coming next.

Ramsey Olaru was an immortal being. He was capable of moving faster than light or sound; gifted with the strength of a mythological god; notorious for besting the most seasoned of enemies, lycan or vampire, yet he was one step too far away; one heartbeat too late to turn around; one neuron firing too slow to comprehend, the *only thing* that had mattered in his entire, eternal lifetime.

Tiffany Matthews was human, and he was helpless to protect her.

He speared his trident into the ground and lunged toward the vicious female, cringing as he heard the *pop*, praying to any god who would listen that it hadn't meant what he thought, hoping against hope that his *destiny* wasn't dead.

He could feel Salvatore sneaking up behind him, but he just didn't give a shit. Whatever the foul, demented monster was planning to do next…

Bring it on.

All he could see was *red*.

That, and the vile soulless witch who had just snapped Tiffany's neck.

He snatched Tawni by the throat, yanked her off the ground, and glared into her eyes, burning the sight out of her retinas with a crimson beam of rage. "What have you done!" he roared, shaking her like a rag doll. He closed his fist around her larynx, crushed it like a walnut, and then continued to squeeze until her sightless eyes popped out of her head and hung along her cheeks by the optical nerves. He ripped her heart from her body, even as it slumped to the ground, and then he spun around and shoved the organ, along with his trembling fist, right into Salvatore's mouth.

Salvatore choked on the unforeseen offering, spitting out the pieces in a rage. He flew backward, out of Ramsey's reach, and channeled a mystical fire. But before he could hurl the black conflagration at his enemy, Ramsey unearthed the trident, dove forward at the Dark One, and plunged all three stakes in the vampire's chest. He twisted the metal to the right, and then to the left, thrusting it deeper and deeper, until the hooked ends grasped at the heart; and then he withdrew it in an instant.

Salvatore was not a fledgling sorcerer, and he must have felt the inevitability of his demise, because he channeled all his magic into dematerializing and scattered his molecules to the wind.

The errant building-blocks of life coalesced around the trident's forks and then settled ominously in the air like a fog, swirling in luminous circles.

Ramsey shouted in outrage.

The bastard could not get away!

He dropped the trident, now a useless piece of steel, and dissolved his own precious molecules, hurling them into the midst of the sorcerer's sphere. He heard Nachari Silivasi's voice in the background, and he instinctively knew that the powerful wizard was weaving a spell of his own—Nachari was keeping Salvatore earthbound, anchoring his molecules to the park, refusing to let him flee to the colony, to live and fight another day.

Ramsey felt like an egg in a blender as his wits were ruthlessly whipped about. Never before had he dissolved without a clear focus, a predetermined point of re-emergence, or a specific locale for rematerializing already fixed in his mind. To simply come apart and spin was more than disorienting. It was chilling.

Ramsey let go of his body and his consciousness, each one in turn, and focused his attention, instead, on the celestial heartbeat all around him. He became one with the elements, merged with his distant celestial ancestors, and *felt* for his orientation: For the purpose of alignment, the gravitational pull beneath him was south, and the expansiveness above him was north. There was a vibration from the west, coming at 426 pulses per second, which had to be sound, and this told him where the other warriors stood. The corresponding *silence* was east—Salvatore had to be there.

Ramsey felt his own *being* like a ray of light, an internal velocity traveling at 186,282 miles per second, and then he felt for the vacuum, the inherent darkness, the slower, inky vibration that would identify Salvatore's soul.

It was all around him, swirling about him, moving in and out of the air like a ghost.

Ramsey exploded outward. He attached his faster molecules to their slower counterparts; he formed numerous chemical bonds with his enemy; and then he fixed his point of transportation to the west and fought to rematerialize amongst the warriors, praying that Salvatore would come with him.

The sentinel and the Dark One appeared as one, both shimmering into view before the house of Jadon's finest. At first, there were gasps and growls and uneasy snarls as the warriors stepped away from the apparition, unsure which being was which, but then Nachari Silivasi laughed out loud, a wicked scoff of triumph, and all the warriors knew…

The wizard reached into the fresh amalgamation, wrenched his arms around Ramsey's waist, and pulled backward. And just like that, the two beings stood in their natural, visible forms.

Salvatore opened his mouth to protest, perhaps to decry his rage at being bested by a brutish warrior in matters of arcane magic, but he never had the chance to make a sound. Santos Olaru ripped out his heart so quickly that it took a moment before he felt it leave his body. His cruel mouth flew open in surprise, even as Saxson beheaded him with a medieval axe and tossed the skull to Julien Lacusta. The savage tracker retrieved Ramsey's trident and skewered both appendages to the ground, the head on top of the heart, and Marquis Silivasi stepped forward and tore what remained of the Dark One limb from limb, tossing the pieces into the macabre pile.

For the space of one or two seconds, the park was deathly silent, and then Ramsey turned around and knelt on the ground.

He crawled several paces toward Tiffany and gently lifted her head.

Her neck was broken; her eyes were vacant; and her beautiful mouth was silent.

He blinked several times, trying to process what was happening, trying to comprehend… "Kagen," he croaked in a raspy drone, "healer? What can be done?"

Kagen and his mate, Arielle, pushed their way through the crowd of stunned vampire observers and dropped to Tiffany's side. Kagen placed his hand over Tiffany's heart, and then two fingers against her throat, and then he sat back and sighed. "Ramsey, is she still… "

He didn't have to say *human*.

Ramsey simply nodded, waiting to hear what he already knew.

The air left Kagen's body as he folded his hands in his lap. "I'm sorry."

Ramsey shook his head. "No," he barked, his voice growing harsh with anger. *"No!"*

Kagen tried to place his hand on the warrior's shoulder in a gesture of solidarity, but Ramsey jerked it away—and Kagen took no offense. How could he? The situation was beyond an epic disaster or a Greek tragedy: It was an utterly heartbreaking catastrophe. Tiffany was gone, and Ramsey was a dead man walking. What in the world could the healer say?

Kagen cleared his throat, three times, staring at Ramsey's hands. "Uh, we… " He shut his eyes, and his voice came out in a hollow rasp. "Let's heal your broken arm"—he gestured toward the shattered limb— "and then, maybe… and then maybe we can sort this out."

Ramsey cocked his head to the side and glared at Kagen with a vacant stare. "Sort this out?" he parroted. *"Sort this out?"* He glanced at the beautiful blonde before him, scooped her up by the waist, and held her tightly against his chest. "My *destiny* is dead. What is there to sort out?"

Just then, Brooke Mondragon shoved her way through the crowd and flung herself at Ramsey's feet. "What are you saying?" Her frantic eyes shot back and forth between Kagen and Ramsey before settling on her lifeless best friend. "Ramsey?" Her voice raised an octave in terror. *"Ramsey?"* She spun around and grabbed Kagen by the shoulders, heedless of her own bleeding arm. "Do something! Why are you just sitting there?"

Kagen Silivasi grasped her by the wrists and tried to command her gaze. "Milady… " He swallowed a lump in his throat and slowly shook his head. "My queen, there is nothing I—"

"No!" Brooke shouted. She bounded to her feet and frantically searched the crowd. "Napolean! *Napolean!*"

The king immediately materialized at Brooke's side, the little prince asleep in his arms by obvious compulsion. The king's face was a barely concealed mask of horror as he surveyed the scene and his mate's battered arm.

"*Do something*," she implored him.

Napolean looked at Kagen, and the healer shook his head.

"Arielle," Napolean whispered, making fleeting eye contact with Kagen's mate.

The beautiful female stood up quietly, removed the sleeping babe from Napolean's arms, and swiftly strolled away.

The king turned to face his mate. "Brooke." He reached down to assess her damaged limb, and she slapped his hand away with a fury.

"No! Don't touch me!" She knelt over Tiffany's body, grasped her by the shoulders, and gently pried her from Ramsey's arms. "Tiff… *Tiffany*… " She lowered Tiffany's head onto Ramsey's lap like a fragile piece of china. "*Hey, you*; wake up. We need to go home now. Phoenix needs someone to give him his bath, and I… and I have *so much* to tell you." She laughed nervously, as if Tiffany had just responded, her voice rising in anguish. "Napolean and I made a major decision." She leaned in closer to whisper in her best friend's ear. "We're going to have two more children. I know it seems fast, but… what can I say? Gotta protect the throne. Phoenix is too much of a target on his own." Her voice trailed off, and she began to tremble uncontrollably. It was almost as if the part of her that was anchored in denial was warring with the part of her that knew. And then, all at once, she became enormously agitated. She rocked back and forth and moaned. "We can do it together. Go through it together." She grasped Tiffany's hand and squeezed. "Did you hear me?"

Napolean visibly cringed. He knelt behind her, placed his hands on her waist, and leaned closer to her ear. "Sweetheart, I need you to let go now. She's gone."

"No-no-no," she argued, speaking in rapid fire. "She's just sleeping. *She's just taking a nap.* She's not gone." He placed his hand on her shoulder, and the cry that escaped her throat was as guttural as it was raw, the piteous echo enveloping the valley. And then, just like that, she quit wailing, glared at Ramsey beneath tear-stained lashes, and groaned: "What have you done?" Her voice grew hoarse with accusation. "We trusted you. We placed her in your care. *What have you done!*"

Ramsey rocked back on his heels.

He laid his *destiny* on the ground and slowly backed away, still lumbering along the grass. The earth was spinning around him, and there were so many people—*vampires*—staring. He gazed up at the sky. The air was growing thick with clouds, enigmatically dense, and the ground was beginning to shake beneath him, as if any moment now, it might just split open.

The rain began to fall, and at first, he thought it might be his own emotion triggering it. He was struggling to make sense of Brooke's question, to compartmentalize the approaching, threatening wave of guilt before it grew too powerful and destroyed them all, but then he realized that, *no*; it was his brothers. They were literally teeming with pain. Santos and Saxson were standing behind him like two crumbling statues, like they didn't know where to go or what to do next. Their mouths were hanging open; their massive shoulders were quaking; and their faces—*great celestial gods, their expressions*—they were horrible masks of grief.

They knew that Ramsey was dead as well.

That in twenty-seven days, when the Curse came calling, there would be no sacrifice of atonement, that the Blood would have its vengeance.

Ramsey closed his eyes.

It was all too much to take in.

He needed to get away, but he didn't want to leave Tiffany behind, just lying on the ground. He had already failed her miserably. In fact, Brooke was right: He had failed at the only task he'd ever been given that truly mattered.

He had failed to keep his *destiny* safe.

And Tiffany, with all her quick, polished wit and her keen, superior mind…

He drew her closer to his heart and held her.

She would never argue with him again. She would never cringe at one of his comments or stare at him with *those eyes*. She would never grow to love him, and he would never have a chance to love her in return. He had let Salvatore Nistor destroy her, however indirectly, and for that, there could be no forgiveness. He thumbed the hilt of his ancient dagger—it was no longer sheathed but, oddly, nestled in his broken left hand—and he groaned. He opened his mouth to respond to his queen, but there was nothing he could say.

And then, in his peripheral vision, he caught a glimpse of Saber Alexiares slowly ambling forward, and something inside of him snapped.

*

"You son of a bitch!" Ramsey Olaru leapt to his feet in one smooth but furious motion and lunged at the unsuspecting vampire, signaling his rage with a roar.

Saber jerked back and snarled. "*What the hell?*"

The clouds opened up. The sky exploded with thunder and lightning, and the relentless rain turned to hail as Ramsey snatched the incredulous vampire by the collar and clipped him across the jaw with a powerful right hook.

The bone in Saber's jaw snapped audibly, and the male stumbled to the side. He caught his balance, drew back his fist, and lunged forward at Ramsey, like he was about to knock his block off; and then, in the midst of the mayhem and anger, he took one good look at the warrior and blanched.

Saber caught his punch in mid-swing and pulled it back, hissing in both revulsion and surprise.

Ramsey went after him again.

This time, he dove for Saber's throat, but Julien Lacusta moved twice as fast. The hard-nosed tracker jumped between the vampires, wrapped both arms around Ramsey's chest, and abruptly pulled him back. "Stop, brother! *Oh gods*; you've gotta stop."

Ignoring the tracker's cryptic words, Ramsey kept trying to charge at Saber, hoping to break the tracker's hold. He was too far gone to let it go. "I was going to call you for backup, you miserable son of a bitch!" He slammed the back of his head into Julien's chin, but the hard-as-nails tracker didn't even budge. "I was going to ask you to tag along, but I didn't." Spittle flew from his mouth as he spat the words again. *"But I didn't!"*

Saber shook his head in disgust and alarm. "Well, why the hell not?"

"Because of this!" Ramsey shouted. He brought his right arm up, shoved it in Saber's face, and splayed his fingers wide to emphasize the intricate ring wrapped around his fourth finger. And then he shook it like a fist.

Saber took an anguished step back, his face growing pale with mounting awareness. "The crest ring," he murmured, referring to the sacred emblem of the house of Jadon.

"Yeah," Ramsey mumbled, *"the crest ring."* Still wielding his dagger in his broken left hand, he somehow managed to slide the ring off his finger and toss it at Saber's chest. The heavy disk bounced off the stiff leather jacket and burrowed into the grass, settling with a plop. "Keep it," Ramsey snarled. "Maybe two will be your lucky number. Besides"—he glanced at Tiffany's body; *oh dear gods, she was getting drenched*—"I don't need it anymore."

Saber gasped and staggered to the side as if Ramsey had physically struck him. He glanced down at the discarded ring and fought to regain his composure.

And that's when Napolean stepped in. "We are not going to do this," the king said, sternly. "Not here. Not now." His own voice was ragged with emotion. He looked up at the skies and assessed the lightning. The storm was growing worse. "Marquis,"—he turned to the Ancient Master Warrior standing off to the side, and nodded—"drive your queen back to the mansion and heal her arm. Her car is parked on the street." He searched for Kagen's mate and softened his tone, albeit only slightly. "Arielle, take Phoenix and go with them. Carlotta is there if you need her." He appraised the healer next. "Kagen, be gentle with Tiffany—bring her to the Ceremonial Hall. We will prepare her body there." He immediately held up a hand to halt any objections or comments. "And tracker, sentinels"—he eyed Julien, Santos, and Saxson as one—"you need to return to my parlor. This is not the time or the place. Where is Nathaniel Silivasi?" The ancient vampire stepped forward, and Napolean gestured toward Salvatore's remains. "Clean up this mess. Get it out of here. I don't care what you do with it." He spun on his booted heels to seek out the Master Wizard next, his eyes beginning to glow. "Nachari, you need to scan the area, make sure there are no human witnesses—take care of anything you find. And Saber?"

The still-stricken vampire folded his arms in front of his chest. "What?" His voice was as distant as it was angry, and by the look on his face, he had half a mind to simply turn and walk away. He was pissed, and he was hurt. But those weren't his dominant emotions. For all intents and purposes, the vampire looked ashamed.

"Son." Napolean spoke in a much gentler tone, clearly aware of the difficult history—Saber Alexiares had only recently been returned to the house of Jadon after living for centuries with the sons of Jaegar. He had been kidnapped as a baby. "You stay here with Nathaniel. Keep an eye out for any Dark Ones who might still show up." He raised his eyebrows, and his pointed expression spoke volumes: *This is your house. You are one of us. And I am trusting you to stand against our* common *enemy.*

Saber inclined his head. He cast a sideways glance at Ramsey, and the warrior's heart constricted.

Damn.

That shit had been wrong.

What he had said to the former Dark One.

But it was too late to fix it now.

Ramsey nodded once. It was the best that he could do. And then he watched like a helpless child, rather than a full-grown male, as Kagen Silivasi gently lifted Tiffany—*Ramsey's destiny*—into his strong, protective arms and headed for his Rubicon.

Ramsey felt like the very air around him might ignite into flames.

"*Ramsey!*" Napolean barked his name as if he had already called it ten times.

Ramsey looked at the king and frowned. "I'm right here," he mumbled. And then for reasons he couldn't explain, he added, "It's all good."

Napolean reached out slowly, gently, with a tentative but steady hand. "Give me the knife, warrior."

Ramsey furrowed his brow and slowly looked down. He was still grasping the hilt of his dagger in his broken left hand, yet all five inches of the blade were imbedded in his thigh. He must have accidentally stuck himself at some point, although he couldn't remember when. He grunted beneath his breath as he took a closer look.

Son of a bitch.

When had that happened?

His entire front torso looked like someone had played a morbid game of tic-tac-toe on his flesh. There were crisscrossed lines through the front of his arms; deep, ugly gashes up and down his thighs; and wicked, circular gouges carved into his chest, all like a series of *x's* and *o's.* Yet, he couldn't feel a thing.

Why hadn't he felt any pain?

He was supposed to feel the pain!

Whatever the Blood was going to do to him in twenty-seven days, it wouldn't be enough, not nearly enough.

It would never, *ever* be enough.

There was no punishment great enough for what Ramsey Olaru had done to his mate, and by all the gods in the celestial heavens, he wanted to feel more pain!

"Ramsey!" Napolean's voice rang out like a clashing symbol, and his otherworldly eyes sparked red. *"Stop."*

Ramsey took an unwitting step back. The knife was now protruding from his gut. *What the hell?* And what was that on the ground? He bent over to take a closer look and started counting fingers, missing from his broken left hand.

Napolean winced and shook his head. "That's not how we're going to play this, warrior. By all the gods, I swear it: I *will* put you to sleep if I have to."

Ramsey cocked his head to the side. He blinked several times and shrugged. "Where's Tiffany?"

Napolean scrubbed his hand over his face. "Come back to the manse, Ramsey." He gestured broadly at all of Ramsey's wounds. "Let me heal this... *mess*... then come back to the manse. Your brothers need you to be strong."

Ramsey bit his lip and scowled, still trying to make sense of what he was hearing... and seeing... and feeling.

The sky was a dark, angry mass of swirling clouds; the valley was one tremor away from splitting open in a half-dozen places; and the king of the Vampyr—*sacred twins of Gemini*—was Napolean Mondragon *crying*?

"I'm sorry, milord," Ramsey said softly, biting down on his lower lip.

"I know," Napolean whispered. He slowly removed the dagger from Ramsey's flesh and tossed it aside on the ground. "I know."

"I didn't mean for this to happen," Ramsey whispered. His right leg began to shake uncontrollably, and he couldn't make it stop. He stared at it blankly and frowned. Nothing around him made sense.

"I know," the king repeated, yet again, placing a steadying hand on Ramsey's shoulder.

For reasons he couldn't explain, Ramsey stared off into the distance and focused his attention on a pine tree. He felt like he had just been run over by a freight train, and his heart constricted in his chest. "This shit is all wrong." His knees buckled out from under him, and he stumbled to the ground, strangely surprised by his sudden weakness. And then he noticed the color of the grass. It was so incredibly green. So silvery and wet. He reached out to touch it, to see how it felt, maybe rake it through his fingers, and then he chuckled morbidly beneath his breath.

Alas, he didn't have any fingers left.

He threw back his head and moaned, no longer recognizing his own voice. It was much too wretched, primal, and *wrong*. His chest began to heave beneath the enormous weight of his… sobs? And this disturbed him most of all. His *destiny* was gone. His body was ruined. His heart was broken, yet he couldn't *feel* a thing. He was locked inside a vault. Lost. Disconnected. Splintered in two. He turned to face his king. "Help me, Napolean. Something's really wrong."

The king sank down onto his knees. "I've got you," he whispered. He wrapped his arms around the warrior's chest and bent to murmur in his ear. "The earth can't sustain this, Ramsey. Neither can you. You're trying to hold back a dam, but it's going to break. Give me your hand."

Ramsey shut his eyes and tried to swallow his confusion. Napolean was right. There was a tsunami of rage, anguish, and guilt just churning beneath the surface, hurtling toward the shoreline of Dark Moon Vale, and ready to wreak havoc on the land. And when it did, there would be no survivors. The gods themselves could not insulate Ramsey from this much pain. There was nothing left to cut; no digits left to chop off; no flesh, yet unmarred, to self-injure; and no way to hold it back. "I can't let this out, milord. I need you to take it away. *Help me*, Napolean."

The king didn't reply.

He simply raised the warrior's arm to his mouth and slowly

inserted his fangs into the brachial artery. As the razor-sharp incisors sank deep into the vein, he whispered in Ramsey's mind: *Be still, warrior. Just let go.*

Like a cool, gentle breeze on a hot summer's day, an undeserved peace began to sweep through Ramsey's bloodstream, lulling the warrior into a false sense of security. As he embraced the welcoming darkness, his heavy lids began to close, and the turmoil began to fade. The pain, the tsunami—*the nightmare*—simply fell away beneath a king's compulsion.

A king's deceptive illusion.

All became silent.

All became still.

And then Ramsey Olaru heard the sweetest word of all: *Sleep.*

And he did.

seventeen

Salvatore Nistor came awake with a shout, his lungs burning as if they were on fire. His entire body felt like it had been pulverized in a food-processor, and something was terribly *wrong*.

He had no sense of his corporeal form in time and space.

He felt lost and disoriented, strangely out of place.

And there was a cavernous emptiness in his chest where his heart had once been.

He blinked several times, trying to open his eyes. The ether around him was inexplicably dark, not like night, but like the total absence of *good*, like there was no longer a war between good and evil. Evil was all there was. The air was as thick as fog, and it contained a strange, skeletal density, like fingernails scraping over an ethereal chalkboard, wraithlike, yet tangible. He shivered, trying to regain his bearings.

Just then, a dark hooded form bent over him, and despite knowing that he was a powerful, immortal being, Salvatore instinctively shrank back, his entire soul trembling. The hooded figure reached out with a clawed hand and traced an odd figure-eight over his brows.

"Welcome, my son."

Salvatore shot up from the ground and sprang into a squat. "Who the hell—"

A deep, rumbling growl brought him up short, and he bit a hole in his lower lip, trying to pull back his words, lest he offend his unidentified host.

"Better," the creature snarled.

And then, all it once, it became crystal clear just who Salvatore was staring at—the dark vampire would know those features anywhere: the oily, tangled hair, matted to the creature's brow; the cloven hooves where his feet should have been; and the viscous, acidic drool, dripping from the corners of his evil mouth. It was the dark lord Ademordna, and his eyes were glowing orange beneath the dark, bulky hood.

Salvatore's teeth began to chatter as he slowly glanced around. He appeared to be outdoors, in a courtyard or a glen, but there were no clear, identifiable markers present, no way to determine his location… or identify his fate. The ground was slate-gray and black, like the remnants of volcanic ash, and there was a tall iron gate behind him, with spiked finials atop, reaching toward the heavens. *But there were no heavens.* There was no sky and no moon. It wasn't night, and it wasn't day. It was an endless expanse of darkness, cloaked in a thick, unholy blanket of fog.

Dear lords of the underworld, he was in the receiving courtyard of the Valley of Death and Shadows.

"Mm, precisely," Ademordna drawled. He removed his hood, revealed his hideous features and his glowing orange eyes, and then he smiled. "Welcome home, my son."

Salvatore bowed his head out of respect—*and fear*—curbing his instinct to run. Although he worshipped the dark lords with all his heart, he certainly had no desire to spend eternity in their midst. "Thank you, master," he whispered. *Oh great prince of darkness, am I dead?*

"You are," Ademordna answered, reading his mind with ease. He wrinkled up his nose and flicked his snake-like tongue, in and out, several times, as if he could taste his fear. "And what a grisly death it was. Ramsey Olaru seems to have bested you at your own wicked game." He wagged his long, bony finger three times in the air. "Tsk. Tsk. Tsk. I must say, I'm disappointed." With that, he lunged at the vampire, made a seal over Salvatore's mouth, and forced thick, burning goo, like acid, down the Dark One's throat.

Salvatore struggled like a helpless baby caught in the demon's arms. He kicked his legs and flailed while choking on the sludge. It burned like volcanic lava, coated his esophagus, and then slowly began to attack his internal organs, one at a time, eating him from the inside out.

He gasped at the pain, or at least he thought he did. His throat no longer worked properly. And all the while, the most hideous visions flashed through his mind: images of vampires from the house of Jaegar being tortured in all manner of cruelty and imagination. One male was chained to a tree in the jungle territory of the Northern Province, and he was consumed day and night by a swarm of demonic beetles and bloodred scorpions. Another was impaled on a rusty spike in the western mountain territory. The stake was erected in the midst of a fire, and the demons roasted and dined on the vampire's flesh, night after night, peeling tasty morsels from his bones. Yet another vampire was thrashing and bucking in a huge cauldron of bubbling magma, unable to escape or die, and the surrounding demons took turns using medieval implements to force his head under "water," watch the skin peel away, and then carefully reconstruct his face. The demon who could recreate his features the fastest, with the most accurate representation, would don his scalp as a crown and dance around the cauldron, victorious in the game.

Salvatore recoiled at the macabre vision, and then the space where his heart should have been constricted. *Oh dark lords, deliver me!* He knew that handsome face, the vampire in the kettle. Salvatore was staring at his beloved little brother, Valentine, trapped forever in a prehistoric vat. And somehow he just knew: Those same demons would soon have Salvatore in their clutches. *No, milord,* he whimpered in his mind, hoping to appeal to Ademordna's blackened conscience.

By all that was unholy, this could not be his fate!

The demon lord withdrew his fetid kiss, threw back his head in triumph, and roared with wicked laughter. He released Salvatore from his grasp and flung him to the ground like so much garbage, spitting out the aftertaste of their mingled saliva. "What did you think would happen when you finally made it home?" he hissed. "Welcome to hell, Mr. Salvatore Nistor." His voice rang out like thunder, reverberating across the barren expanse, and the sheer might of his brogue rattled the vampire's bones.

"My lord?" Salvatore curled into a ball and shivered. "But I have always, *always* served you faithfully. I have worshiped you with fidelity… and love."

Once again, Ademordna thundered with laughter, this time, clutching at his sides to withstand the humor. "Love, dear Salvatore? *Love?* What does one of your ilk know of love?" He pressed his decrepit hands to his lower belly and took three deep breaths to regain his composure.

Salvatore began to retch uncontrollably.

He dropped his face into the dirt, writhed in the vomit, and began to choke on the vile mixture, on his fate, and on his future.

Just then, the ground began to rumble beneath them as a peculiar-looking demon approached from the side. The genetic mutation appeared to be a rodent of some sort, perhaps a weasel or a rat, but he hopped instead of walked, like some barbaric kangaroo, and his mouth was a wide slit, full of dozens and dozens of teeth, each tusk filed to a ghastly, sharp point. "Hehehehehe," he giggled like a fool. "What do we have here?" He rubbed his hands together, and *dark lords,* he sounded like Renfield when he spoke.

Salvatore scooted away. *Ew. Just… ew.*

The rat-thing smiled at the demon lord, flashing at least sixty of his hideous teeth. "This is the sorcerer?" With his curious accent, the word *this* sounded like *thes.*

Ademordna cleared his throat. "What brings you to the Middle Kingdom, Veratchi? Is there no garbage to rummage through elsewhere?"

The rat hunched over and laughed, causing his back to bow and his bones to crack. "Eeeh, yes, yes. Of course there is."

Ademordna rolled his eyes. "Well then?"

The rat stood up straight. He tried to gesture imperiously at the vampire on the ground, but with such short stubs for arms, it looked more like a convulsive tic. *Follow the yellow brick road,* Salvatore thought. *I'm sure you're needed in Oz.*

The little mutant tried to bow next, and the gesture was equally ridiculous, as his overripe belly did not allow for the bend, and he bounced instead. "My great, imperious, all-powerful, maleficent, preeminent, majestic, resplendent—"

"Shut the hell up," Ademordna cut in. "What do you want, Veratchi? As you can see, I am rather busy with a new arrival."

Veratchi licked his hairy lips. "Ah, but of course." Ademordna growled, and the rat suddenly found his voice—and a much quicker pace. "Milord, if you would, I have simply come to point out the obvious: Napolean Mondragon still lives, as does the prince-child, Phoenix. And the house of Jadon still thrives. The celestial gods will celebrate this Dark One's death"—he snickered into his paws, the best he could—"in other words, they'll be laughing their asses off at you, and it will make us all look weak." He glared at Salvatore then, and for the first time, he actually looked formidable. "I mean, with all due respect, your prized sorcerer was dispatched by a caveman with a pitchfork. And I might add: The Neanderthal usurped his skills with black magick." He shook his head as if deeply ashamed. "Oh, it is a dreary day, indeed, for evil everywhere. Might you just… patch him up and send him back?"

Ademordna took a judicious step backward, and his hands

began to shake. He curled his lips in a parody of a smile. "Ah, so you came here to die?" He bent over the rat-thing, removed its left eye with a claw, and transformed into his pure, demonic form, instantly losing his hands. Still ten feet tall, Lord Ademordna hovered over the demon-rat in a rage. "There are rules, you ignorant fool. Free will and all that. We appeal to our subjects, we corrupt willing minds, we lead those who seek our guidance; but we do not interfere with those who inhabit the earth, without first being summoned. We do not alter creation itself!" He gestured wildly with his serpentine head, his voice growing increasingly frenetic. "It would disrupt the eternal balance of good and evil. Nay, the repercussions could ricochet all the way to the gods. Would you risk our own eternal existence by altering the laws of the universe?"

Veratchi hunched his shoulders and softened his voice, trying to speak plainly in spite of his pain. He didn't dare retrieve his eye. "Says who?" His voice quivered slightly.

Ademordna blanched. "Says power. Says wisdom. Says history. Says every existing pantheon of gods from time immemorial."

"Ah," Veratchi sighed, "the gods, of course, not the Dark Lords." He was brave for a one-eyed, about-to-die fool.

Ademordna frowned, and his glowing orange eyes began to leak blood. He transferred back into his typical demon-lord form, snatched the rat by the throat, lifted him off the ground, and bit off his ear. Spitting it aside, he snarled, "Just what are you trying to prove?"

Veratchi squealed in pain and wriggled in the air. "My intelligence is meager compared to yours, my liege. Alas, there is nothing I can prove to you. I would only endeavor to advise and suggest: Are you not a god in your own right? Is your power not equal to those who reside in the celestial realms? Do you honestly fear the earthlings' god or your celestial twins? Isn't it time we asserted our dominion on all the planes of the various worlds—in heaven, hell, and on earth?" His small beady eyes sparkled with delight, and for a moment, Salvatore thought he might actually be... *affected*. Could demons incur brain damage at birth? Did they actually suffer from their own brand of mental illness?

Ademordna dropped the rat.

He glared at Salvatore, who was now cowering on the ground, as if the vampire had given the *touched rodent* the idea. Ademordna paced a slow circle around the two of them and bit his lower lip. "The Dark One could not return as he is. I have not the power to create new life."

Veratchi smiled, a wicked, duplicitous grin, in spite of his missing ear and eye. "No, but he could be patched back together, perhaps like Frankenstein? Imbued with demonic essence, instead."

Ademordna spun on his heels, his cloven hooves sinking deep into the ground from the furious motion. "Send him back to earth as a demon in a vampire's body?" He assessed Salvatore's ethereal form, and it was clear what he was thinking: Dead as Salvatore was, his ghostly body looked whole, but his earthly body had been torn into pieces—just what would that look like?

Veratchi shrugged. "Why not?"

Salvatore remained deathly quiet. This was the most ridiculous conversation he had ever witnessed, the most idiotic idea he had ever heard. Even *he* knew that the laws of the universe could not be altered without severe consequences, that all of existence was constructed in balance: Light was the continuum of shadow; good was a counterpart of evil; and each shared its flux and reflux with the other. In essence, they were halves of the same whole, just a different manifestation, summoned by an opposite vibration, and they could not be separated out any more than day could be separated from night. Balance would *always* be restored. And while the gods may have created the laws, they were also the origin of the laws, bound by their formation as they were one in the same. To destroy their creation would be to destroy themselves.

All of existence would cease to be. In plain speak; Ademordna would never get away with such a thing.

But, then again, who was Salvatore to argue if it would get him out of there, even for a minute?

Maybe he could find a way to exact his own vengeance on the house of Jadon, reclaim his vampirism while back on earth, or at the least, discover a form of suicide that left the soul in limbo, neither dead nor alive, so he never had to return to this valley. At the least, he might take advantage of the rat-thing's stupidity and Lord Ademordna's pride before all hell literally broke loose, and the gods found themselves at war.

Ademordna bent low, over Salvatore's quaking body, and peered into his petulant eyes. "I suppose I could replace your physical ears and your nose, perhaps borrow a limb, here or there, from the suffering vampires, maybe implant a demon-heart, along with your manufactured soul."

Salvatore furrowed his brows. Despite his determination to stay out of it, he couldn't help but speak. "But Dark Ones don't have souls, milord?"

Ademordna harrumphed. "'Tis true, in a sense." He linked his hands in front of him as if he were prepared to give a speech. "All beings, on all planes, have a soul at inception, and these souls are linked to their Source. It simply means that they have the potential to choose good or evil—even the most depraved among them can eventually seek redemption. You, however, are a son of Jaegar." He shook his head and frowned. "And this means that your ancestors traded their souls for power. It is not the same as simply turning away from the light. When the Blood cursed Prince Jaegar's house, it forever severed their souls from their Source. There can be no redemption for your kind."

Salvatore took a moment to process the demon lord's words. He thought he'd heard it all. He thought he understood it all, but this was something new. "And Prince Jadon's house? Were they not equally guilty of spilling so much blood?" His heartless chest seethed with anger... and envy.

Ademordna cocked his head to the side. "Indeed. But salvation is not a question of guilt or innocence. It is a question of *mercy*, and Prince Jadon pleaded for the same. He *wanted* to retain his soul." A wicked smile crossed the dark lord's face. "Who do you think supplied the Blood with the power to wield the curse? The celestial gods?"

Salvatore's mouth fell open as awareness slowly dawned... "No. The dark lords."

"Indeed," Lord Ademordna said. "We became the Source for the house of Jaegar's missing souls—we provided your continued animation in exchange for an eternal claim on your lives."

"And yet, you allowed the house of Jadon to retain their redemption, to remain connected to their Source, the celestial gods, to receive the four mercies... *why?*"

Lord Ademordna shrugged. "We had to barter with something. The depravity of your kind was so extreme, all the remaining souls were so lost, that you would've floundered in darkness for eons, just trying to recognize a hint of light. The road back to redemption would've been long and winding, indeed, and all but a few would have been lost. The celestial gods did not want to lose their offspring or their legacy. They did not want to see all they had created lost to eternal darkness. Vampirism, a firstborn child, and the continuation of the Curse were the lesser of two evils. They bought their precious sons some time."

"And you—"

"We brought our precious sons *home*."

Salvatore shrank back from the dark lord and shuddered. He had never known goodness or light, mercy or regret. He had never had a kind thought in his long, degenerate existence, yet something deep inside of him recoiled. Indeed, they had been doomed from the start. He shrugged it off. It was of no matter. He would rather spend a dozen lifetimes in the darkness than one weak, pathetic day in the light. Such was the reality for one with a *severed* soul.

He turned his attention to Veratchi, who was watching the entire exchange with great interest, and waited to see what would come next.

Veratchi held both paws up in supplication and smiled. "Well, milord? What do you think? Is it time to make a universal statement among *all* the various gods?"

Ademordna licked his lips and bent down to scratch the rat beneath the chin. "Perhaps it is time, my little rat. After all, *what the hell.*" He separated Veratchi's gums with two fingers and peered inside his mouth. "Our Frankenstein will be needing teeth; I believe we will start with these."

The rat jolted in surprise and tried to hop backward in retreat, but the demon lord moved too quickly. In the space of a heartbeat, he snatched the rat by the neck, popped his head off his shoulders, and held it at arm's length as he slowly began retracting the teeth, one at a time, and tossing them on the ground.

Salvatore quivered in fear and anticipation as the demon lord stayed focused on his task.

"I do so deplore insolence and arrogance," Ademordna drawled, in explanation of the murder. He laughed then, a rich, imperious sound. "Unless, of course, it's my own."

Salvatore Nistor wrapped his arms around his waist and tried to quiet his mind. He tried not to think of what was to come next, his reanimation as a demon-rat-vampire…

Frankenstein.

None of that mattered now.

He would remain centered on his temporary reentry to Dark Moon Vale.

After all, his time would be severely limited, whether Ademordna knew it or not.

He needed to make the best of it.

Quickly.

eighteen

Ramsey Olaru sat silently beside his brothers and Julien Lacusta on one of the long wooden pews inside the Ceremonial Hall of Justice, trying not to think about the body, laid so beautifully—so peacefully and respectfully—on the platform in front of them.

The body of his *destiny*.

Over the last twenty-four hours, Tiffany had been bathed, dressed in a beautiful ceremonial robe of lavender and ivory, and laid in repose on a soft, raised pallet at the front of the circular hall, on the formal dais, while Napolean and Brooke attended to the final details of her funeral and tried to devise a plan to notify her loved ones.

As of that day—twenty-four hours beyond her passing—no one had contacted her family, and the procrastination was causing more than just a little bit of angst: On one hand, they wanted to inter Tiffany's body in the house of Jadon's burial grounds, in the traditional manner of the celestial race. They were confident that she would spend her eternal life in the Valley of Spirit and Light; after all, she had been chosen by the gods for Ramsey, and she did contain distinct traces of celestial blood. *The celestial pantheon would claim her immortal soul.* Yet, on the other hand, she had not been converted—she had passed away as a human—and her parents would want to perform their own burial rites in the human, Catholic tradition.

Thus far, Nachari Silivasi's suggestion had been the best: to use a small amount of DNA to create a holographic replica of Tiffany's body, then to ship the counterfeit remains back to the family with a fabricated story about how she had died. Was it duplicitous and beneath them? Did it feel raunchy and unforgivable on every level? Sure it did. Just the same, the Matthews didn't need to know about vampires and Dark Ones. They didn't need to know the truth of Dark Moon Vale or of Tiffany's vampiric affiliations, namely Ramsey Olaru.

They didn't need to know about the warrior's epic failure as her mate.

Ramsey had never had the opportunity to meet Joe and Rita Matthews, and that's the way it would stay. As far as the warrior was concerned, if they followed Nachari's suggestion, the family would at least have closure. They would have a headstone and a regular place to visit.

They would have a chance to say good-bye.

And he wouldn't have to face them with his guilt and shame.

Ramsey shifted anxiously in his seat, staring straight ahead in the dim lantern light. He could no longer meet any of his brothers' eyes, anyway. And Julien? Well, he just looked terminally pissed off and ready to blow, when he wasn't outright morose.

The fearsome tracker leaned back in the pew, stretched out his legs, and crossed his feet at the ankles in front of him, staring up at the high-domed ceiling. "I can score twenty-six days' worth of H if you want it. Got enough 151-proof cocktail to go with it," he bit out, sounding disturbingly indifferent.

Ramsey furrowed his brow and tried to do the math. Just how much heroin and alcohol-cured blood would that be? He shook his head, not knowing what to say.

"We might," Santos chimed in.

"What the hell," Saxson added.

Ramsey was too overwhelmed to speak. If the awkward silence could have grown any more deafening than it already was, it just did. Never before had Julien Lacusta spoken about his unnatural habit out loud. Never before had he offered to share it with his comrades. It was simply understood that the dark, brooding vampire was *different*, that he handled his pain in an unconventional way. No one approved, but no one questioned him either, just so long as it didn't interfere with his job. Gods knew; it couldn't cause any long-term physical damage. And as for psychological? Well, the male was already interminably messed up.

Julien Lacusta had been dealt an ugly, reprehensible hand of cards from birth.

As a firstborn son, he had spent nine months in his mother's womb with a dark twin, and shortly after the two were born, it had become clear that neither parent was capable of making the required sacrifice, of adhering to the Curse.

Things were different back then, in 1044 AD.

Napolean had his laws, but there was no clear reinforcement—it was just expected that each vampire would comply, understood that they had no choice.

Not the case with Julien's parents.

The grief-stricken vampires had fled from the valley, trying to elude the Curse. They had taken both Julien and his dark twin to what was now present-day New Orleans in an effort to outrun the Blood and start a new life. Needless to say, it hadn't gone as planned. Not even a little bit.

On the last day of their father's Blood Moon, the Blood had come calling for Julien's sire. Not only had Micah Lacusta died a brutal death at the hands of the Curse, but his soul was forever barred from the Valley of Spirit and Light for the betrayal, for his failure to heed the Curse. And still believing that she could get away with the unthinkable, his mother, Harietta, had tried to raise the twins on her own.

Ramsey focused on a smooth, oblong stone embedded in the ancient ceremonial wall, and tried to blend his mind with the gray, to keep from feeling the depth of the macabre story. On Julien's tenth birthday, his dark twin had murdered their mother in cold blood. He would have murdered Julien too, but the boy had fought like a banshee to survive. Just the same, Ian, his dark twin, had stolen away into the night, never to be seen again. A few weeks later, Julien had shown up on Napolean Mondragon's doorstop, still disheveled and dressed in bloody, ragged clothes, and according to the king, there had been such a gnawing, empty hunger in his eyes that the child had seemed all but dead. He had asked Napolean to welcome him into the house of Jadon, to let him be raised as a warrior, and to teach him to be the best tracker the vampires had ever seen so that one day he could hunt and kill his brother.

That one day had never come, despite how hard Julien had tried.

There just wasn't enough to go on.

And somehow, over the endless centuries, the pain of it all—the anger, hurt, and wounded pride—had taken a toll on his soul. A part of Julien was missing; another part lived for revenge; and yet another fragment was steeped in self-loathing and guilt. As far as Julien was concerned, his father and mother had been weak and pathetic. They had betrayed the house of Jadon, and they had betrayed what should have been an unconditional love for their firstborn son. Ultimately, they had chosen the dark twin's missing soul over everyone else's lives, and they had been torn to pieces because of it.

Julien was ashamed of his pedigree.

He was incensed at the wretched brother who had somehow escaped him.

And he was haunted by the knowledge that he couldn't save his mother, his father was "burning in hell," and all of it—*all of it*—was due to the fact that his parents hadn't loved him like they should have, and his sire hadn't been *man enough* to step up to the plate when it counted.

The sentinel buried all that emotion in battles.

He tracked like a son of a bitch when it was needed, and he self-medicated with anything he could get his hands on in order to stay fifty paces ahead of the pain. Unfortunately, Julien was a vampire, and his body was lethally efficient in metabolizing drugs and foreign substances. He couldn't stay drunk, and he couldn't stay high. Over the years, he had found a way to mix liquid heroin into a stiff drink of 151-proof alcohol, followed by a fresh drag of blood. Apparently, the buzz lasted about thirty minutes, before the body kicked it off, but Julien was more than willing to do whatever it took in order to grab that half hour of peace whenever he could. Now, he was offering the same to Ramsey and his brothers, to get through the unimaginable period of time leading up to Ramsey's death at the hands of the Curse. At a half hour a pop, that would be about 1,248 ounces of H and 4,992 ounces of cocktail... per male.

Ramsey cleared his throat. "Shit, J. I don't even know how to respond to that."

Julien shrugged, seemingly unfazed. "Don't judge," he said, "just let me know if you need it."

Ramsey nodded slowly. Yeah, *need it*, indeed.

He rose from his seat and made his way toward the ominous dais for the umpteenth time. He didn't know why he bothered— it wouldn't change a thing. Tiffany was gone, and there was no going back. Nevertheless, he felt like he owed his *destiny* at least that much, and he couldn't stand to sit there with his brothers, watching *them* as they watched *him*, waiting for him to die. They had tried to talk. They had tried to reminisce. But *hell's fire*, what was there to say? Each one of them, to a male, was simply surviving, one brutal, intolerable second at a time.

The whole scene was masochistic to say the least.

Ramsey slowed his pace as he approached the platform,

bowing his head out of respect, and then he reached out to take Tiffany's elegant hand in his and simply held it. *I'm sorry, Blondie,* he whispered in his mind. *I'm so, so sorry.* He kissed the back of her fingers, wishing he could hear her laugh. *Soon, I'll be with you in the Valley of Spirit and Light, and I'll spend all of eternity making it up to you.*

The words should have ripped a hole in his heart, but as it stood, he simply felt numb, unable to feel, unable to *be* in this reality a moment longer.

And perhaps that was as it should be.

He was just about to lay her hand back down at her side when the ancient domed ceiling began to shake; the ground rumbled beneath his feet; and the dim lanterns swayed on their mantels.

What the hell?

And then, descending from the ceiling like some sort of low-lying cloud, was a hideous, massive being—a vampire? A demon? A ghost?—with familiar sapphire eyes.

Salvatore Nistor.

Ramsey couldn't say how he knew. Between the rat-like mouth, full of sharply pointed teeth, the elongated snout, with one too many nostrils, and the mismatched arms, one considerably longer than the other, there was still something in those eyes. The widow's peak was familiar, and the pupils were dilated with hate. It was definitely… somehow… Salvatore Nistor, only the vampire had been changed.

"Greetings, my spoiled-rotten cousins!" His voice rang out like thunder as he descended toward the ground and stopped just short of touching the ancient floor. He hovered like some sort of warlock, his entire aura ablaze.

Ramsey reached for his dagger, even as Saxson, Santos, and Julien appeared, in an instant, at his side.

The *aberration* simply held out his hand; flicked his wrist, as if chasing away a fly; and all the sentinels weapons went clambering across the room.

"Oh, it won't be that easy now," Salvatore droned. "You have finally met your match." Floating above the floor, he drifted toward Tiffany's body, and Ramsey thought he might just come unglued.

The vampire was a dead *thing* walking. Ramsey had absolutely nothing left to lose. And if Salvatore thought he was going to defile his *destiny's* body, then he had another think coming: Ramsey would meet him in hell before that happened. He dove at the apparition, hurling all 240 pounds of his rock-hard body through the air, and slammed straight into an impenetrable barrier, stunned at how easily the vampire tossed him aside.

"Oh, do calm down, my little pet. There is little I can do to her now." He cocked his head to the side and shrugged. "Besides, I would say we could call it even. After all, you murdered my bride, and I murdered yours. Tit for tat. Slut for skank. Oh well." He threw back his head and laughed. "Not to mention, I have bigger fish to fry." And then his eyes became like two glowing irons, sizzling in their sockets, and he roared his fury like a lion. "Napolean! *Napolean! Face me if you dare, you cowardly maggot!*"

*

Ramsey watched in morbid fascination as the floor buckled beneath him, the ceiling began to cave in, and the stones began to shake loose from the walls. As irrational as it was, his first and only instinct was to cover Tiffany's body—he just couldn't watch her corpse being desecrated.

And then the ancient king of the house of Jadon appeared in all his power and splendor. Like a warring angel descending from the heavens, he swooped into the room with glorious wings unfurled and his dark onyx eyes ablaze with fury. His voice was a harsh, unyielding command. "What is the meaning of this?" He stopped, took one good look at Salvatore, and took a cautious step back. "Salvatore?"

The wicked reincarnated sorcerer cackled like a fiend. "Milord." He tittered like a joker. "That is such a stupid title."

Napolean's expression turned to stone, and the sentinels all stepped back. They knew that look in his eyes—it was rare, it was menacing, and it was final. He was going to destroy the evil vampire once and for all, and perhaps everyone else within fifty miles.

Salvatore shrank down into a crouch, holding both clawed hands in front of him, and gestured the ancient king forward with his fingers. "Oh, yes… yes… *yes*. Come. This is positively orgasmic. Come to me, my king."

Napolean stopped dead in his tracks and surveyed his enemy a second time. Undoubtedly, the fearsome monarch was taking more than Salvatore's measure—he was trying to discern just what he was now, how he had returned from the dead, and what it would take to destroy him.

Salvatore laughed like a hyena. "Perplexing, isn't it?"

Napolean didn't wait for further banter. The powerful king sprang into motion, moving so fast that even Ramsey couldn't track his movements. His body was like a neon light, swirling in incandescent pulses, spinning around the Dark One in tight, circular passes, as one by one, vicious wounds appeared on Salvatore's body; blood spurted out, as if from a faulty hydrant; and the cocky interloper began to stagger.

Salvatore called on some unholy power—he must have—because he grew several feet taller; a dark, inky halo began to churn around his head; and his voice grew so deep and demonic that it no longer sounded like the familiar sorcerer's. "You dare to attack me now!" he bellowed. "The undefeatable king of the Vampyr, the legendary patriarch of the house of Jadon. Well, welcome to the gates of hell. You fight the entire forces of darkness!" He threw his gnarled hands into the air, and the very ether began to dance a fiery tango at his command.

The air around them began to pop and sizzle like sparks from a macabre fire. The atmosphere grew inexplicably dense, as if ghosts were swaying rapidly in the background, and Salvatore's palms did not just fill with combustion—they became the flames of hell. He hurled a wicked conflagration at the powerful king, forcing him out of his circular pattern of assault, and then he shoved him hard against the chest, with two flaming palms, sending him spiraling back into the stony wall.

Napolean landed on his feet, as graceful as a lion. He growled deep in his throat, measuring the demon-vampire from head to toe, and then he released a wicked-long pair of fangs, his own blackened pupils beginning to glow.

"The sun isn't out," Salvatore snarled, taking several brusque, long strides in the direction of the king. "You will have to find something else in your bag of tricks."

Napolean's hand went to his beltline, and three diamond-tipped daggers flew through the air, each in rapid succession of the last. The first planted itself in Salvatore's forehead, the second lodged between his nose and his mouth, and the third pierced him straight through what looked like a partly exposed, six-chamber heart.

Salvatore groaned, rolled his shoulders as if to stretch, and shook his body in sweet reclamation. "It's hard to kill that which is already dead!" And then he sprang across the room like a rabid animal: crazed, determined, and insane. He caught the king by both shoulders and spewed some sort of acid from his mouth.

Napolean froze the discharge in midair and sent it careening across the room with telekinesis. He threw a lightning-quick, resounding punch, breaking the Dark One's jaw, and then he withdrew the first knife from the vampire's forehead and staunchly carved out his heart.

Salvatore grew a new one. "That felt... *funny*," he mused.

Napolean took a deep, hesitant breath and glanced askance at his warriors. Ramsey shrugged and transported himself to the king's side, even as Santos, Saxson, and Julien surrounded the seemingly invincible sorcerer in a perilous circle.

They took turns inflicting mortal injuries. Julien crushed his skull. Santos ripped out his entrails. Saxson gouged out his eyes, and Ramsey literally tore his limbs from his putrid body.

The bloody heap rose again.

It reformed itself into another vampire, demon… monstrosity: bigger, stronger, and seemingly more powerful.

Napolean reached for Salvatore's neck in order to wrench it from his shoulders, and by the look of the twin, red-hot beams pulsing from the king's eyes, he had every intention of incinerating the skull to ashes, perhaps eating the ash when he was through. The king intended to burn the Dark One, again and again, until he could finally rise no more. Napolean Mondragon was beyond wasting effort. He was ready to get vicious—he was ready to conjure the devil.

And he never saw the unearthly strike coming.

From the tips of Salvatore's claws grew two hideous forms, each slithering into the night like a singular, demonic serpent, each growing the head of a cobra. They were enormous; they were noxious; and they were clearly possessed, each occupying a pair of malignant fangs that contained the kiss of death.

How did Ramsey know this?

He just did.

Like two hellish entities conjured from the grave, they rose up like specters, drew back their heads, and struck the king at once, each sinking their odious fangs deep into the king's beating heart.

Napolean gasped and staggered backward, a piteous grunt of pain and fury escaping his constricting throat. The sound of the serpents feeding was unlike anything Ramsey had ever heard before—the craving, mania, and thirst.

This just wasn't happening.

It couldn't be happening.

Great celestial gods, have mercy!

In the blink of an eye, Ramsey surveyed the chamber and all of the destruction he had unintentionally wrought: Tiffany was dead. His own days were numbered. And now, Salvatore Nistor, their black-hearted enemy, had returned from the grave, as a result of the sentinel's reckless actions, with some ungodly amount of power. And he was about to destroy their king.

"No!" Ramsey heard himself shout, as if from a distance, as he reached for the necks of the snakes. His brothers and the tracker were right there with him, trying to wrench the king free from the otherworldly bites, trying to destroy the bewitched aberrations.

Napolean sank to his knees, and the snakes followed his motion, tightening their feral jaws as he started to convulse and topple to the floor.

And then the room grew deathly quiet.

The chilling air grew still.

And a light so bright that it pierced the eyes streamed into the room in the form of a funnel, striking like lightning behind Salvatore and the ancient king.

"Cease this blasphemy!" a glorious, thunderous voice resounded through the hall. "'Tis not the will of the gods!"

nineteen

The incandescent funnel of light began to take form like a pillar of fire, planting its foundation in the hall, and out of the brilliance rose the most hauntingly beautiful creature Ramsey Olaru had ever seen.

The female's long auburn hair cascaded from her shoulders like living waters flowing through a stream. Her bare back and shoulders glistened in the torchlight like luminous particles of sand, and her silver gown sparkled like it was made of ethereal jewels. As her snow-white wings fluttered down from her sides to drape behind her like a train, she raised her elegant arms, held a graceful hand in the air, and slowly inclined her noble chin. "Rise, my king," she said to Napolean.

The snakes screeched a terrified hiss, withdrew their fangs, and released the dying vampire, even as Napolean Mondragon stumbled to all fours. He was just about to shift his weight onto his calves in order to do as the woman had bid when his eyes met hers. He winced from the brightness and immediately *fell* to one knee. "My goddess, my lady, my queen. Blessings, Andromeda."

The celestial goddess Andromeda nodded her head in reply even as Salvatore Nistor gasped in terror and tried to retreat. She flicked her wrist in his direction, and he flew backward like a rocket, slamming into the wall, where both arms were immediately pinned to his sides. "*You*, be still… until we sort this out."

She gazed in the direction of the three sentinels and the tracker, and they all dropped to their knees as well, bowing their heads in supplication. "Honor and exaltation, my queen," Ramsey bit out, his voice sounding far too raspy. He had no idea, whatsoever, how to address this original being. He shrank down further toward the floor, hoping he would not offend…

"Children… " she whispered softly. And then she drew a deep, tranquil breath. "Alas, my shadowed brother Ademordna has lost his immortal mind. Brother!" she shouted, shocking the vampires into frozen postures as her voice ricocheted like shrapnel across the hall. "Audience, now!"

The room began to rock to and fro as thunderous, pounding footsteps descended the center aisle of the hall. Ramsey gaped, then looked away as the dark lord Ademordna simply strolled into their midst. "Sista, you seem to fare well." His voice was a discordant, abrasive snarl.

"And you seem to fare like a witless parody of a mule." She wasted no time going straight to the point: She drew back her shoulders and raised a graceful hand, commanding the very ether's attention. "What is it you have done, you fool?" He started to reply, and she shushed him with a glance. "Do not speak in this moment—just listen. There is very little time. You have challenged the laws of creation by reanimating this abomination." She gestured toward Salvatore, still hanging limply from the wall, and Ademordna's eyes quickly followed.

He held up both palms in a satirical gesture. "Oh, he's not that bad." He glanced at Salvatore, winced, and then chortled.

"You laugh?" Andromeda said. "'Tis not funny in the least." She lowered her voice, and it was as if the very walls and the furniture strained to hear her words, as if the very molecules, gathered inside their foundations, responded to her voice. "Gods and lords may be creators—'tis certain that we are—but we are also an extension of creation. It is one in the same, and the laws that brought forth light and darkness; sound and substance—nay, life and death itself—cannot be altered. They are the foundation on which all creation stands." Her voice grew ominously serious. "You have created a rift in the cosmos, Ademordna, a tear reaching back as far as time immemorial. Nay, you have begun to unravel the very threads of creation. You may not undo the design of the universe without undoing the laws." Her voice rose in proportion to her angst. "Without undoing yourself. Without undoing the gods. Without undoing *All That Is*. Do you understand what I am saying, brother?"

Lord Ademordna puckered his rancid lips. He cocked his head to the side and thought it over, and then he cleared his gravelly throat. "I thought I had accounted for that." His chin jutted out in hubris.

"You arrogant ass," Andromeda clipped. She began to move about the hall, pacing rapidly up and down the aisles, staring at the crafty dark lord and the impaled vampire on the wall. "We must act quickly, before there is nothing remaining to act upon. We must restore balance in the universe."

Ademordna frowned, and for the first time, it appeared as if the lights had finally turned on. His hideous face displayed the barest hint of contrition. "I'll take him back with me."

"'Tis not that simple," Andromeda said. "What is done lives on. The energy of a thing, of an action, or a thought—*of an intention*—remains in perpetual motion. One can never remove it, only counter it with something else of equal vibration." She rubbed her forehead, thinking, as she kneaded her flawless temples. "Life and death, eternal souls," she mumbled to herself. "Life for death? Death for life? A soul for a soul?" She spun around on her heels and held her hand out to Ramsey. "My son, arise. Quickly."

Ramsey shot to his feet, desperate to comply.

To obey.

He glanced to his left, then his right, certain she was speaking to someone else. When she simply stood there waiting, her kaleidoscope eyes, which changed with her moods, fixed on his basic hazels, he tried very hard not to tremble. "Yes, my god… goddess… Andromeda."

She chuckled softly beneath her breath. "What has been destroyed today is the result of free will, the power of a single soul's intention, of multiple souls' interaction, to create their own prosperity… or demise. You made ill-conceived choices, as is your right, and the consequences drew nigh; however, what was wrought was undone by an idiot"—she glanced sideways at Lord Ademordna and scowled—"and that must be repealed. Lord Ademordna interfered with the death of Salvatore Nistor, a death the vampire brought on himself. It can only be counterbalanced with an equal death… or an equal life."

Ramsey had *no idea* what the goddess had just said, but he watched with faultless attention as she splayed out her fingers and a golden dagger appeared in her palm, glistening in the light of her countenance like a prism in the sun. "The right of Blood Vengeance is yours, and I grant you the authority to restore the imbalance in the heavens, the netherworld, and on earth. Take this golden dagger and carve out the Dark One's heart, and his death will be permanent; he will return to the Valley of Death and Shadows, and his evil will haunt you no more."

She closed her fist, and the dagger vanished. Then she opened it again. This time, there was a small crystal vial lying delicately within her palm, containing a bloodred substance within its borders. "Or, you may pour this substance into your beloved's mouth, and her heart shall beat again." She gestured elegantly toward Tiffany's lifeless body and swiftly inclined her head. "But decide quickly, or we shall all meet a similar fate."

Ramsey's mouth dropped open in surprise as he immediately began to process the alternatives. He had to make an impossible decision—and *quickly*.

He turned to look at Salvatore, and something inside of him festered. He wanted the vampire's death more than life itself, to carve out his blackened heart and spare the house of Jadon his never-ending atrocities: Blood Vengeance was Ramsey's by right, and he was itching to reach out and take it.

At the same time, Tiffany was his *destiny*, his responsibility, and his life. He had promised to keep her safe. He had gone against his intuition by granting her three more days, and her death was *his* unforgiveable failure. With the potion, he could make it right. He could give her back the life she had lost so suddenly, so needlessly.

So violently.

He clenched his hands into fists, bit down hard on his bottom lip, and locked his jaw in concentration. His heart was beating like a bass drum, rumbling in his chest, as he tried to make sense of his options—*oh goddess, forgive him*, but he needed more information: "My lady," he said reverently to Andromeda, "I must ask one question first: If I save Tiffany now, will the abomination live?" He glared at Salvatore's disfigured form, wanting to spit fire across the room and incinerate him where he hung. "Will he still be just as strong?" He closed his eyes because he dreaded the next question. "Will he be capable of destroying our king?"

Andromeda drew a deep breath. "Aye, my son. He will. 'Tis how my brother recreated him. However, to balance such an act, Tiffany will rise with equal power, also indestructible."

Indestructible…

Ramsey had to let that sink in.

Tiffany would be indestructible. There was nothing he wanted more, but—and it was a major *but*—Salvatore Nistor would be indestructible, too. And unless Tiffany took him on, which was all kinds of wrong on all kinds of levels—not to mention, she couldn't actually destroy him—he would surely kill the king, if not every male in the house of Jadon, one by one. Salvatore would be like a god living among men, an evil, imperishable entity that could never be stopped.

Ramsey groaned inwardly, and for the first time in many, many years, bitter tears stung his eyes and began to roll down his cheeks as he stared at the beautiful woman he had failed to save, lying on the dais. "Tiffany," he whispered with a heavy heart, his shoulders beginning to shake. "My angel, I'm sorry." He unclenched his fists, relaxed his jaw, and squared his shoulders to his *destiny*. "I will be with you soon."

Just then, Saxson Olaru jumped to his feet, took two brazen strides, and grabbed his twin by the shoulder, shaking him abruptly. "Ramsey!" he roared. "We've got this. *We've got this!* We may not be able to destroy him, but we can find a way to contain him, cage him, keep him somewhere locked away. Don't even think of relinquishing your life."

Ramsey frowned, meeting his brother's grief-stricken eyes, feeling as if he was staring into his own hazel orbs. "*Saxson—*"

The male shook his head briskly to cut him off. "*No.* You have a chance to live. Take it."

Santos stood up warily and nodded his head. "Take it, Ramsey. Please."

Ramsey turned toward Julien, who crossed his arms over his chest and shrugged his shoulders in an anguished gesture. "Damn, warrior. That's a hell of a choice to make. Either way, we've got your back."

Ramsey nodded, knowingly. "Can you save Napolean, Julien? In the next five minutes—in the first ten seconds—the instant the deed is done? And Santos, can you swear to me that you can overpower Salvatore and keep our king alive?"

Napolean cleared his throat, capturing Ramsey's attention. "I'm not going down without a fight, warrior."

Andromeda smiled graciously, sweetly, a subtle parting of her faultless lips. "Time, my sons. There is little time."

Ramsey glanced back and forth between his two

choices—Salvatore and Tiffany—several times in a row. His heart was breaking. His chest was hurting. And his soul was literally weeping. Napolean Mondragon had lived for 2,820 years. He had brought the house of Jadon together, raising it from the ashes of the Curse, and he had dedicated his entire life to its service, to making sure that the celestial progeny lived on. Not to mention, Prince Phoenix was so very young. He had not been trained to be a king. Not yet. And the Dark Ones, they were living right below the vale, just waiting to usurp and conquer their reviled cousins. It all sounded so easy, the way Saxson and Santos framed it: Just choose to live, and everything will be all right.

But Ramsey knew better.

Salvatore Nistor would never give up.

He would go after the princesses next, Ciopori and Vanya; he would hunt the warriors one by one. If they couldn't contain him—and who could say with absolute certainty that they could?—the male would be like a swarm of locusts, devouring everything in his path.

Ramsey couldn't take that chance.

He just couldn't.

He was a sentinel.

Yes, he was beholden to Tiffany, first, as her protector and her mate, but he had sworn eternal fealty to the house of Jadon, and he would die as he had lived, boldly and with no apologies, putting his people first.

"Forgive me," he said to his brothers, wishing he had something more than words to convey the depth of that sentiment. He turned to the goddess Andromeda and nodded. "I claim my right to Blood Vengeance. On behalf of the house of Jadon, I voluntarily surrender my life, and I recall the life of Salvatore Nistor."

"Very well," Andromeda said in a sober tone. She closed and reopened her fist once more, and the golden dagger reappeared. "Take this, and do what you must. But first… " She held up her hand to keep the hall silent. Turning to face Napolean, she whispered, "My most beloved child has a question he has always wanted to ask. Speak, Napolean."

The king cocked his head to the side, and his eyes were filled with pure, unadulterated longing. "Forgive me for questioning the gods… "

She waved her hand in a dismissive gesture and smiled, and the entire room lit up from her grace. "Ask what you will, Napolean. I will do my best to answer."

Napolean's eyes were two haunted spheres as he forced his seemingly dry tongue to work. "Why did the gods allow the Curse?"

Andromeda sighed, and her heart rose and fell with the weight of the king's fateful question. "*Allow* is not the correct word, my child. Alas, you of all souls know how creation works. Thoughts are deeds. Desires are actions. *All That Is* exists, in and of itself, as a blank canvas of quantum energy, merely awaiting a creator's brush, the attractive energy of a creator's attention, to manifest as a physical thing. As beloved beings, you were created with unassailable free will, to generate both wonders and horrors as you saw fit, and then to live in the wake of those choices. When Prince Jaegar and his men were sacrificing their women, destroying your civilization, where do you think all that pain and anguish and turmoil went? The hatred and vengeance, the inconsolable sorrow, that festered for so many years? The tangible energy of suffering that beset so many souls?

"You and I both know the first law of thermodynamics: Energy can neither be created nor destroyed; it may only change forms and flow from one place to another. The collective energy of the slain—the fear, anger, and despair—flowed from the blood-soaked hands of your ancestors to the living will of the slain. It magnified, took root, and rose in the form of the Curse. And much like I have done today, the cosmic deities could not interfere with free will. They could, however, see to its balance. For every action, there is an equal and opposite reaction. I believe even Sir Isaac Newton, a mere human being, understood this truth. And so it was then, and shall forever be, Prince Jaegar manifested great destruction; Prince Jadon manifested equal mercy; and the celestial gods and the dark lords played our miniscule roles in allowing balance, *only balance*, Napolean, not the Curse or its vengeful destruction. That wasn't ours to touch."

Napolean shut his eyes and hung his head. "So it may never be undone?"

Andromeda smiled once more, though her eyes were brimming with reflection and even a little sorrow. "On this plane, this earth, time is an agreed-upon construct: the past, the present, and the future. You may use the power of your *now* to create great and horrible things tomorrow, but you may not go back in time. For you are but sentient beings, not gods, bound by the laws that govern the planet surrounding you." Her multicolored eyes lit up with a sudden spark of interest, and she immediately furrowed her brow. Without stopping to explain, she spun around in a harsh circle, glared at Salvatore, and regarded Tiffany's resting body. "Forgive me, my son, but our discussion has come to an end." She cast an almost wicked glance at her brother, at Lord Ademordna, and smirked. And then she turned toward Ramsey Olaru and *smiled*.

"Think quickly, my son. *Be* the warrior that you are. There is yet another way to achieve our balance."

And just like that, the room disappeared.

twenty

Without warning or preamble, Ramsey Olaru was back in Tall Pines Village Park.

He had just emptied his clip into Tawni; Tiffany was crouched down behind him, and Salvatore Nistor—*the vampire, not the demon*—was chewing his way through Ramsey's arm, frothing at the mouth.

Great celestial goddess, Andromeda; it was all happening again!

The deity had turned back the hands of time!

And she had left Ramsey's memory intact!

Ramsey dropped the machine gun, drew back his good arm, and punched Salvatore dead between the eyes, sending him spiraling backward from the force of the blow. And then he rolled across the grass, grabbed his trident in mid-turn, and sprang to his feet, his left arm hanging limply at his side.

Only this time, he didn't stalk Salvatore in order to attack.

He called out to Saber Alexiares on a private, telepathic bandwidth and marshaled the soldier with a shout: *Saber! It's Ramsey. I'm on the* southern *end of Tall Pines Park, battling Salvatore Nistor. Come to my aid at once!*

The soldier shimmered into view so quickly, his appearance took Ramsey aback. "Holy shit!" Ramsey swore, and then he waved the trident in Salvatore's direction. "Keep that son of a bitch busy, no matter what else occurs!"

Saber nodded his head and growled a wicked purr. He cast a sidelong glance at Ramsey, taking note of his damaged arm, and then immediately turned his attention to the Dark One and smiled.

Ramsey chose to let it go, if only for the moment.

He had to leave Salvatore in Saber's capable hands.

The north end of the park virtually filled with Master Warriors, vampires from the house of Jadon, and Ramsey knew they were there in reply to his previous call, an earlier moment in time.

It was of no matter.

He knew what was coming next.

He tossed his trident with a flick of his wrist, twirled it around like a baton, and rotated it into the center of his hand, and then he *pretended* to stalk toward Salvatore, along with Saber. His muscles twitched; his chest heaved with determination; and his knuckles turned white from his murderous grasp on the weapon.

And then just like before, everything happened at once.

Tiffany shifted to get up, and Tawni stirred, rising like a ghost from the grave.

A brittle leaf, left over from autumn, crunched beneath Tiffany's hand, and Ramsey made his move. He sprang into the air, meeting Tawni in midstride, just as the wicked female was hurtling through the park at his *destiny*. Her eyes grew wide with horror and disbelief as Ramsey thrust his trident into her heart. *"Surprise, surprise, witch!"* He twisted the crude implement to the right, and then the left, even as he used a searing beam from his retinas to carve a wicked gash in her throat. He didn't stop until her head fell from her shoulders and her heart sat at the end of his spikes.

Tawni's dismembered body fell to the ground; Ramsey landed softly on his feet, and he immediately made his way to Tiffany.

She was cowering in the grass where he'd left her, her face a mask of unconcealed terror, and her mouth was still hanging open, suspended in a scream.

"Sh," he whispered softly, tossing the trident aside and extending his healthy hand to help her up. "It's over, baby. Everything's okay. I've got you." He pulled her to her feet in one swift tug and crushed her to his chest, tightening both arms around her.

Pain be damned.

Tiffany gasped for air. She arched her back in an awkward curve, her arms hanging to her side, and tried to gain some space. "Thank you, Ramsey." She swallowed convulsively as he held her even closer. "But... uh... um... I can't breathe!"

Ramsey released her waist and cupped her by her cheeks, his rough thumbs caressing her jaw. "*Hell's fire*, Blondie." He stared into her glorious eyes like it was the first time he had beheld the sun and fought to contain his emotion. His eyes were moistening with tears. He cleared his throat and smiled. "Oh, baby," he breathed. And then he swept her once more into his arms.

He just didn't care...

Tiffany stiffened and drew back her head, nearly straining her neck. "Uh, Ramsey? Are you all right?"

He shook his head and smiled. "Yeah, angel. I'm better than I've ever been before." And then he placed one hand on the small of her back, anchored the other in her hair, and bent her over to kiss her.

*

Tiffany reeled from the shocking yet powerful sensation of Ramsey's chiseled lips pressed tightly and ardently against hers, sealed in a nearly desperate kiss, and then she tried not to panic.

What the hell was going on?

Why was he acting like this?

Their relationship had not gone *there*, at least not yet.

She blinked several times, glancing furtively about the park, peeking beyond Ramsey's cheeks. The sentinel seemed to be oblivious, and *holy mother of passion,* the male could kiss like a fallen angel! But still, there were warriors everywhere. They might still be in danger. Ramsey had just skewered and beheaded Tawni, and what the hell was that all about anyway? The woman had turned out to be some sort of vampire!

None of it made any sense.

Her head still spinning from the sudden turn of events, Tiffany planted both hands firmly on Ramsey's chest and shoved him sharply back, breaking the fervent kiss.

He didn't seem at all dismayed.

In fact, he just stood there like a prowling lion, staring at her like she was a steak, and he hadn't eaten for a year.

"Ramsey," she tried again. "What are you doing?" Before he could answer, she started to ramble, her nerves finally getting the best of her. "Oh, gods, I'm so, *so* sorry." She shook out her hands like she had something disgusting on them as she, once again, glanced around the park. "I did all this, didn't I?" She blanched and ran a nervous hand through her hair. "Tawni wasn't who she said she was. Oh my gosh; that's like the understatement of the year! She was a freakin' blood-sucker! But how?" She spun around in an anxious circle, taking in more of the chaotic scene. "And Salvatore; I thought he was going to kill you. *To kill me!* Oh God, where's Phoenix?" She pressed the side of her hand against her brow and strained to get a better look. And then she saw Brooke in the distance, holding the child in her arms. "Brooke! Brookie!" She waved her arms frantically through the air, but her voice got lost in the din with so many vampires all around them. "Holy shit, half the house of Jadon is here." She planted her palms on her knees and tried to calm her nerves. "What have I done?"

Ramsey placed a firm but gentle hand on her back and sent a soothing stream of energy into her core, even as Saber Alexiares approached from the south. "Calm down, Blondie," Ramsey said. "Just take a deep breath." He laughed aloud—*actually made a sound that was akin to joy*—and increased the pressure on her back. "Soldier," he said to Saber, as the arrogant vampire approached.

"Salvatore got away," Saber bit out angrily. He sauntered up to Ramsey's side, his eerie black-and-red locks sweeping the tops of his shoulders as he walked, and planted his feet a shoulder's width apart. "That cowardly bastard took one good look at what you did to that—that *female*— and headed for the hills. I got a few good licks in before he vanished, though." He massaged his jaw with his left hand, drawing attention to several nasty cuts along his cheek. He opened his right fist, and several locks of Salvatore's bloody mane fell from his palm to the grass. "Hell, I think I scalped the piece of shit."

Ramsey's eyes grew dark and enigmatic, unlike anything Tiffany had ever seen in his expression before. He was staring at Saber like some long-lost brother, like the male had wandered for forty years in the desert and had just this moment come home. "Thanks for getting my back." His voice was unusually emotive.

Saber furrowed his brow and shrugged with indifference. "Of course. Always." He snarled then. "Just sorry we couldn't kill the bastard this round."

Ramsey tilted his head in an indulgent gesture. "You didn't have much warning."

Saber nodded. "True. *True*."

And then Ramsey did the oddest thing. He placed his right hand on Saber's shoulder and just stared into his eyes. When he finally decided to speak, he asked him the strangest question: "What do you remember?"

Saber cocked his head to the side. "What do you mean?" He sounded more confused than sarcastic. When Ramsey didn't reply, Saber pursed his lips. "I remember getting ready to *feed* my mate when you ramrodded your way into my head and told me to get my ass to the park, *post haste*. What am I supposed to remember?"

Ramsey looked away and frowned. "Nothing. Not a thing. Just... checking."

Saber raised his eyebrows and frowned. "You good?"

Ramsey nodded. "Yeah... *yep*." He pointed his forefinger at a stiff blade of grass and crooked his finger. The blade snapped loose from the root, shot into the air, and landed in his hand. He stuffed it between his lips and worked it into the corner of his mouth. "You do know," Ramsey said, pausing to consider his words, "that I wouldn't have called you if I didn't implicitly trust you, right?" He sighed and flicked the blade of grass with his tongue. "Not with my *destiny's* life on the line. Not when the queen and the prince were in peril. I mean, you get that, right?"

Saber shifted his weight from one foot to the other and grew quiet. After several pregnant moments had passed, he brushed some grass off his pants, perhaps for a lack of anything better to do. "Yeah, I get it. Why?"

Ramsey cleared his throat. "Because it's important—that you know." He curled his fingers into a fist and placed it against his heart in a rare gesture of affection.

Saber literally started. "Ah'ight," he said. When Ramsey continued to stand there, just staring, he added, "So, what now? You wanna kiss me or something?" Saber's mouth turned up in a smile, or a scowl, depending on one's perspective.

Ramsey barked out a deep, masculine laugh. "Hell no, dragon. I'll leave that for Vanya." He drew Tiffany upright, hauled her to his side, and gave her the most ravenous look she had ever seen. "I've got other... interests."

Okay, so this was getting out of hand.

In fact, it was bordering on exploitation.

On a scale from one to ten, the weirdness was reaching a twelve, and Ramsey was acting way *out of character.* Maybe he had bumped his head in the midst of all the turmoil. Tiffany shot him a questioning glance through her peripheral vision, hoping to send him an unspoken message: *Calm down, Conan.* I'm really not feeling the *Me Tarzan—You My Jane* thing.

Saber pretended not to notice. He gave Tiffany a cursory nod and then turned his attention back to Ramsey. "I get it. S' all good." He held out his hand, and the warriors exchanged some primitive, masculine handshake before Saber turned to walk away. Stopping to look back over his shoulder, he gestured toward Ramsey's left arm with his chin and grimaced. "You need to get that fixed." He shuddered. "That's nasty."

Ramsey chuckled. "Yeah, well, you should take a look in the mirror as well." He drew an invisible circle around his face to emphasize his point, and Saber rolled his eyes. "Be well, warrior," the vampire called in a formal register.

Ramsey nodded in kind. "Be well… *dragon.*"

Saber sniggered, and then he simply disappeared.

Tiffany bit her bottom lip and wrapped both arms around her waist before Ramsey could snatch her up again, or worse, plant another one of those hot-as-hell, but unsolicited kisses on her mouth, and she sighed. "So… are you *really* ticked off, or just a little ticked off?"

He leaned in closer. "At you?"

She nodded, feeling like a heel. "I swear to you, I had no idea. About Tawni, I mean." She twiddled her thumbs. "I can't believe I was *that* stupid. I fell right into their trap." She shuddered, involuntarily. "So many people could've been hurt… or worse."

Ramsey grew unnaturally still. Something dark and ominous flashed through his eyes, and then he purposely pushed it way. "Vampires," he corrected.

"What?"

"So many *vampires* could have been hurt." He spit out the blade of grass and turned to grasp her by both shoulders. "But they weren't." He reached down, took her hand in his, and rotated his thumb along the center of her palm, once again, growing distant. "You weren't."

Tiffany didn't know how to answer. This was not at all like Ramsey, this rare, emotional bent. Sure, he was typically serious as a heart attack about hunting, serving the king, and protecting the house of Jadon, but this was something *else*. She stared at him for a moment, taking careful note of his posture. His shoulders were squared directly to hers in an open invitation. His head was tilted at an attentive angle, as if he was afraid he might miss some subtle signal, and his legs were planted just far enough apart to create a cradle for her smaller body. It was like he was protecting her, *but from what*? Finally, she whispered, "Just the same, I am sorry for creating this mess. I truly am."

He smiled. "It's not on you, Blondie. I should've never let it happen. But trust me, things are about to change."

Tiffany drew back, all at once uneasy. "And what is that supposed to mean?"

He tilted his head to the side and stared at her for a moment, and then he stiffened and blinked. "It means I'm going to talk to Napolean, debrief the other warriors—*spend a moment with my brothers*—and then we're gonna get the hell out of here." He held up his hand to silence any protest as he expanded his explanation. "You go give Brooke a hug and spend a little time with Phoenix, and then I'm taking you home."

Tiffany practically shrieked in alarm. "*Okay*… I get that part, but you're still making me a little uneasy. What are you implying, Ramsey? *Things are going to be different*, how?"

His deep hazel eyes darkened with intensity, and his mouth grew taut and pensive. "It's all about time, baby doll."

She frowned. "What? *Time?* How?"

"Time," he repeated. "There's no more time to play around."

Her mouth grew suddenly dry and she gulped. "What's that supposed to mean?" Her heart restricted in her chest.

Ramsey pitched forward until their bodies were nearly touching, and then he slowly lowered his head, the movement as graceful as it was intimidating. His breath was both sweet and warm as his lips hovered just inches away from hers.

She trembled, afraid to even blink.

Something was clearly different about the male, but for the life of her, she couldn't put her finger on what it was. It was as if he had taken command. As if something deep inside of him, both primordial and dominant, was rapidly rising to the surface. As if the predator had marked his prey. She only knew that Ramsey Olaru was no longer playing games, not that he ever had. The warrior inside him—the sentinel—was clearly taking charge, and he would not be deterred by a woman.

By his woman.

He locked his gaze with hers, and she felt an undeniable stream of energy pass between them. "You are my *destiny*, Tiffany Matthews. The gods gave you to me to protect, to value, and to claim. And I've been tiptoeing around this Blood Moon like a fledgling, trying to take it easy, when it's my nature to take it hard. Trying to move things forward at a laid-back pace, when it's my duty to *get things done*. Trying to give *us* plenty of time, when time is never promised, not to anyone." His voice grew thick with emotion. "No more, Blondie." Perhaps without meaning to, he growled like a leopard, purring deep in his throat, and then he flashed the barest hint of fangs. "I *am* going to make you want me." He leaned in closer, if that was even possible, and the subtle shift in posture was an unmistakable play for power—his body all but enveloped hers. "I'm going to make you *need* me." He reached out, as if it were his gods-given right, and traced the outline of her bottom lip with the pad of his thumb. "By this time tomorrow, you're going to beg me to convert you. And I will. *I will.*" He turned his head to the side, bent over, and whispered in her ear, his voice a deep, husky rasp of promise. "But not before I make you scream my name, so I know that you want it."

Tiffany's jaw literally fell open.

Her eyes grew wide as saucers, and her heart began to race in her chest.

What the hell was that?

She tried to utter a protest, but her voice got lost in her throat. She wrung her hands together and stepped deliberately to the side. "Um, Ramsey." She looked down at the ground, causing her bangs to fall into her eyes. "The last time I checked, it takes two to tango." Her voice sounded weak and unsure.

He smiled, a wicked, predatory grin. "Oh, we will both be fully present. You can bet the farm on that."

She shook her head emphatically. "That's not what I meant." She swallowed her trepidation and forced herself to be strong. Surely, he was just reacting to the situation, to the adrenaline and the danger—he *was* a vampire after all. "You said I could have at least three whole days, remember?"

"I lied."

She jolted. "Whaa... *no*... you can't just... " She shut her mouth and cropped her words, not wanting to provoke him, at least not now. She decided to try another approach. "You know, you're kind of scaring me again." She waited with bated breath, and he smiled another wicked grin.

"You'll get over it." He brushed an errant lock of hair out of her eyes, raised her chin with his hand, and then shackled both of her wrists in his fist, albeit very gently. "Tiffany, *you belong to me. You are* mine. And I want you—all of you—*now*." He narrowed his gaze and sighed. "But I have enough class, or at least enough good judgment, not to take you in this park, in front of the entire house of Jadon. So go touch base with Brooke, spend a little time with Phoenix, and then we *are* going home. Together."

Tiffany took a startled step back. There was nothing she could say. Ramsey was pulling the rank-and-file card at his leisure—*as if!*—and she was utterly helpless to challenge him.

In truth, the male was exactly what she had always believed him to be: a beast.

A powerful, beautiful, terrifying beast.

And he had just scared the wits out of her.

"Don't I get a say?" she whispered.

He raised her left wrist to his mouth and held her gaze in a captive stare. The air around them stirred, grew several degrees warmer, and tangible electricity pulsed between them. *Good heavens, was he doing this with his mind,* using his powers to influence her?

"Yes… and yes," he rasped seductively. "I plan to use everything I have."

She almost bolted and ran, but she was far too captivated, ensnared in his trap, caught in his enthrallment. Tiffany Matthews was like a ball to a chain, only she was tethered to Ramsey's soul.

"You do get a *say*," he whispered. And then he sank his fangs into her wrist, drew a minuscule sip of blood, and swirled his tongue around the twin pin-holes, savoring the flavor.

Tiffany nearly swooned. Her heart fluttered wildly, and her stomach clenched into knots: *Oh, heaven help her*—he wasn't playing fair.

As he sealed the wound with his venom, his eyes bored into hers, and he winked like a devilish fiend. "In fact, *say my name*, right now," he commanded softly.

Tiffany inhaled sharply as her chest rose and fell in distress. Her shoulders began to tremble, and her palms grew sweaty, even as her pelvis flooded with warmth.

That bastard. That caveman. That louse!

That gorgeous, disgustingly masculine… god.

She closed her eyes and shivered. *"Ramsey."*

twenty-one

Tiffany rinsed the shampoo out of her hair and just stood beneath the spray, trying to collect her wits.

What the hell had just happened?

All the way home, the entire ride, she had tried to talk Ramsey out of his *plan*, yet he hadn't budged an inch. The male was bound and determined to get this Blood Moon rolling, and he didn't have a single compunction about playing fair.

In fact, what was it he had told her when she had insisted on taking a shower, at least washing the grime from the park off her soiled body? "I wouldn't get dressed when you're done if I were you, not unless you want to make me undress you."

She adjusted the polished-chrome lever to a much hotter setting and reveled in the immediate warmth. *Who the hell did Ramsey think he was?* She groaned. Oh, hell, he knew exactly who—*and what*—he was: a supernatural being with the power to make her quake, quiver, and *say his name* whenever he damn well felt like it.

Had she really done that?

Had she actually batted her sea-green eyes, licked her quivering lips, and whispered *Ramsey* like some lovesick teenage dolt, just because he had commanded it? She eyed the window beyond the sunk-in jetted tub, wondering if she was small enough to shimmy out of it. How long would it take him to notice?

And then she remembered the episode on the horse…

Not a good idea.

Reaching for the conditioner, she coated her hair liberally and tried to make sense of the drastic change in Ramsey's approach: True, the scene in the park had been grisly. She could have been killed. He could have been killed. Hell, Brookie and Phoenix could have been killed, and Tiffany would have never forgiven herself for her stupidity.

But they hadn't been killed, none of them.

Ramsey had done what he did best, protect the house of Jadon.

She sighed as she reached for the soap.

She had half a mind to sneak her cell phone and call the queen for help. But then, what would she say? *Brooke, get Napolean and come here, quick. Ramsey is determined to ravage me!* Yeah, that would definitely marshal the troops.

Not.

If anything, Napolean would give Ramsey a badge—some sort of dark, vampire, Blood-Moon-rising, way-to-go, atta-boy badge!

She grit her teeth in frustration and maybe a little… arousal?

Oh, hell.

This was maddening.

It was way too soon.

"*Time, baby. It's all about time,*" she mumbled, trying to mimic his voice. That deep, raspy, sultry… voice. "Aaaaarghhhh!" she moaned. *Okay, okay, just breathe. Think! Think and breathe. If you can figure out what's really going on, you can probably get him to see reason.*

Why was Ramsey acting like a caveman?

She reached for a loofah and began to work in the soap. Ramsey was clearly rattled by the entire scene in the park. Heck, he had even treated Saber like some long-lost comrade, showing rare and demonstrative emotion. And his brothers? Holy crap! On one hand, he had tried to debrief them; on the other hand, he had looked like he wanted to crawl into their skin, stand in their shoes, and meld their souls as one. He had looked like he never wanted to be apart from them again—even they had found his behavior strange.

And Phoenix?

How many times did he apologize to the prince? How many times did he apologize to Brooke? Just how many times did he genuflect to Napolean?

Ramsey did not do obeisance. He didn't grovel, and he didn't kiss derriere.

Something was definitely off.

She silenced her mind and tried to listen to her intuition—perhaps she should go back to her most recent dreams. What had Dream Weaver been trying to tell her? Was there a clue she was overlooking?

She jolted beneath the warm spray, all at once making sense of the obvious: Duh! A wolf in sheep's clothing. Dream Weaver had tried to warn her all along, and not about Ramsey, but about the woman, about the ferocious wolf playing the role of a timid sheep, pretending to be a victim while waiting to tear out her throat.

And what the hey was that all about, really?

How in the world could Tawni have become a vampire? She sure as heck wasn't anyone's *destiny*, not unless Satan had recently joined the house of Jadon. According to Ramsey, there was only one way it could have happened, only one way that coincided with the Curse. The female had to have been evil from the start. She had to have willingly relinquished her soul, given Salvatore Nistor permission to convert her. She had to have given herself to the sorcerer.

Ew.

Now that was just the nastiest thing Tiffany had ever heard.

Salvatore Nistor?

Really?

She grimaced and shook her head. She was getting distracted, losing her train of thought.

Back to Ramsey and his blind determination to take her like the spoils of war, turn her promptly into a vampire, and then lock her in her room until, oh, maybe the next century.

What was going on with the terrifying sentinel?

Before she could follow the thought any further, there was a light rasp on the bathroom door. "Blondie?" It was Ramsey's gravelly voice. "Are you going to hide in there forever?"

Tiffany held her breath, hoping he would just go away. When the knock came again, she sighed. "Give me a minute," she called in desperation.

"You've already been in there for forty-five," he said. "I think you've drained both water heaters."

She clenched her eyes shut. *You can afford it*, she said to herself. "Fine," she said to him. "I'll be out in a minute."

He chuckled, deep and low beneath his breath.

Honestly, he was such a brute.

She reached for the faucets with an unsteady hand, each one in turn, and slowly turned the levers to *off*. Then she reached for a large, fluffy towel and wrapped herself up like a mummy, almost restricting her ability to move. She tiptoed to the bathroom door and pressed her ear against the panel, listening for… listening for… what? His breathing? His heartbeat? And just who was she? Wonder Woman?

She sighed and tried to get a grip.

Just get out of the bathroom and get dressed, she told herself. She counted to one hundred, giving him plenty of time to retreat, and then she turned the knob, very slowly, peeking around the doorframe to make sure the massive vampire was gone.

He was.

Thank the Lord.

She stepped out into the guest bedroom timidly, immediately shuffling to the bedroom door to flip the lock. He wouldn't saunter back in if she could help it, as if a measly lock could stop Ramsey Olaru. She shook her head to dismiss the thought. She doubted he would break down the door as a precursor to seduction.

Or would he?

She gulped and scanned the top of the bed, staring at the various piles of clothes she had preselected before her shower: What to wear?

What to wear?

She quickly shimmied into a pair of blue jeans, donned a form-fitting, long-sleeve turtleneck, and then covered that with a large, bulky sweater made of loosely knit wool. It was a ridiculous choice, not to mention way too hot. What was she trying to say? *Back off, Buckaroo! You'll never get through all these layers!* She hurriedly stripped them off and tossed them on the floor.

She grabbed a beautiful, floor-length nightgown next. It was made of soft green satin, a perfect complement to her eyes, and the V-neck didn't plunge too low. She stared at herself in the full-length mirror and grimaced. *Yeah, Tiff, that's exactly what you want: Why not just scream, "Come and get me, big boy!"* She ripped it off with a haste that bordered on frenetic and then reached for a pair of too-large gray sweat pants and an oversized sports tee. Yeah, that worked. Didn't it? She eyed herself from several angles in the mirror. Frumpy. Disinterested. It kind of said, *"Wouldn't you rather paint the garage?"*

She sighed, feeling tears well up in her eyes. What in the world was she supposed to do? What in the world was she supposed to wear? She tried on three more outfits, each one more ridiculous than the last—a red dress, *too street-walker*; a pair of jean overalls, *too redneck*; and a thick pair of flannel pajamas covered in little blue bunny rabbits, *too childish*. She ripped off the pj's and tossed them across the room in a fury. Standing there in her soft yet elegant matching panties and bra, she stared into the mirror and frowned. Good grief, she was a hot mess. Her harshly layered hair had dried without the benefit of a blow dryer—or a brush—and it was sticking up in all directions like it wanted to flee her head. She didn't have an ounce of makeup on, and her eyes looked tired, at least to her. Her pale skin was somewhat mottled from dragging so many layers of fabric over it, time and time again, and she hadn't bothered to put on any lotion or perfume. As if that mattered.

Just then, she heard someone stir behind her.

She heard a distinctly male sound, a vampire clearing his throat, and she spun around to face the empty, adjacent corner.

"Ramsey?"

*

Tiffany gasped as Ramsey slowly shimmered into view.

Had he been standing there all along, watching her from the shadows while remaining invisible?

Oh dear celestial gods, please tell me he hasn't been here this entire time. Please tell me he hasn't traded sentinel *for* stalker.

He eyed the unholy mess covering just about every square inch of the carpet, even as he sauntered toward her, crossing the room in three long, predatory strides. "Sorry," he whispered, his eyes distinctly unapologetic, "I couldn't help myself."

She cringed and bit her lower lip, backing up until the bend in her knees hit the edge of an oversized armchair, and her rump fell into the plush, downy cushion. She snatched a convenient afghan off the back of the chair and draped it over her body, tugged it up to her neck, huddling protectively beneath it. "I can't believe you were watching me this entire time."

He knelt before her as she sat on the edge of the chair, his strong, muscular body resting comfortably on one knee, his left elbow propped against his raised thigh. With his free hand, he reached out to thumb a wild lock of her hair. "I can't believe that you tried on all those clothes, that you put yourself through that many paces, or that any woman alive could possibly be this beautiful." His eyes met hers, and the liquid hazel pools practically seeped into her soul. "What were you thinking, Blondie?"

Tiffany swallowed her trepidation and tried to regulate her breathing. "What was *I* thinking? What were *you* thinking, watching me like that?"

He frowned, and his naturally sculpted brows furrowed ever so slightly, enhancing his flawless features like an exquisite frame. "At first," he said, his voice utterly lacking guile, "I thought, *Gods, she's cute.* Then I thought, *She doesn't need to be this afraid.* Then I thought, *Oh yeah, she should wear that*"—he chuckled—"and now, *right now*, I'm thinking, *I came way too close to losing this woman.*" He cupped her face in his hands, more gently than a body had a right to, and whispered, "I'm thinking, *Gods, she really doesn't know... she doesn't understand... and I don't know how to tell her.*" A thick lock of his chin-length hair fell into his eyes as he pressed his forehead to hers.

Tiffany stared at him through lowered lashes. It was hard to hold his gaze. "What don't I know?" she whispered, realizing her mouth was trembling.

He brushed a finger over her quaking bottom lip. "That I would never, ever hurt you." And then he kissed her. Just like that: soft but firm; commanding but subtle; sweet but seductive. And he watched her like a hawk.

She exhaled slowly, still feeling the electric sensation of his gorgeous lips on hers. "What don't I understand?" Her voice was way too throaty.

Oh, hell...

He pulled back, just barely, and ran his rugged hands along the outline of her shoulders, around the curve of her arms, and down to her waist, lowering the blanket ever so slightly to the bend of her elbows, the frayed ends balancing perilously along the swell of her breasts. "That I only want to worship you." He appraised her openly from head to toe, and his piercing gaze grew dark with… reverence?

She gulped, acutely aware that she was shivering. "Uh, um, what do you want to tell me?" She sat there, frozen like a statue, hanging on his every word despite her misgivings.

His eyes bored into hers. "That it's okay." He bent forward and pressed a gentle kiss against the hollow of her throat. "It's okay," he repeated in a harsh whisper, this time kissing his way along her neck to the lobe of her ear, where he did… *something*… sinfully unnatural.

A kiss.

A nibble.

A stroke of his tongue.

Her spine literally tingled.

He buried his face in the curve between her neck and shoulder, using that thick bottom lip like an artist's brush to paint an erotic stroke of contrast across her skin: blazing fire chilled by arctic ice.

Tiffany drew back. "It's just… " She swallowed hard. "The thing is… " Her eyes darted this way and that, fixing on everything but him. "I'm just not ready, Ramsey."

He took her hands in his and smiled, and heaven help her, but in that frozen moment, he was the single most beautiful *anything* she had ever seen.

"That's my job, Blondie," he rasped.

She inhaled sharply, but he didn't stop.

He grasped the lingering hem of the afghan and slowly inched it down from the swell of her breasts to the flat of her stomach, practically groaning at the sight of her lace-covered breasts. He placed both palms along her sides, his fingers finding a natural station in the grooves of her ribs, as he swept his thumbs beneath the base of her bra, removed the front clasp with uncanny ease, and gently began to tantalize her peaks.

She tried not to moan.

Oh, he was definitely using some sort of vampire-magic, some sort of compulsion or supernatural power. The pads of his fingers were like a taut, gentle bow, and she was like a fine violin. He was tuning her strings to his own vibration, playing the nerves on her skin like sweet, legato notes, tweaking her desire with his hands.

She felt the sensation in her toes.

It was beyond sensual or arousing. It was all-consuming, like he was touching her body, her mind, and her soul, all three domains at once.

"What are you doing?" she whispered helplessly.

"You like?" he breathed huskily. And then he swept his hands down the curve of her waist, grasped her narrow midriff in his massive palms, and hauled her forward with one sharp tug. The afghan slid away; her thighs fell open; and her knees instinctively hugged his hips. The only thing keeping their bodies from pressing together *intimately* was the thin layer of silk on her panties and the coarse layer of denim on his jeans. He rotated his hips and growled.

"Ramsey!"

"Mmm?" He clasped her by the small of her back, pressed his arousal against her, and swallowed her protest with his tongue, sweeping her up into the most profoundly erotic kiss she had ever experienced.

She clung to his shoulders for purchase, feeling utterly exposed and provoked.

Once again, he must have used his preternatural power because there was no accounting for the level of arousal that assailed her. Every nerve ending in her body came alive, and she was suddenly filled with a hunger so intense, an ache so extreme, that she almost shuddered at their contact, coming apart at the seams. He deepened the kiss, his lips, tongue, and mouth making child's play out of her desperate responses. He knew exactly when to tease, how to please, and where to nip or bite. He knew precisely when to devour her mouth, torment her throat, and torture the tops of her breasts, careful to stay away from the most personal zones… almost as a tease.

Tiffany slid further into him, cursing herself for her response. Her hips were beginning to rotate in harsh, beckoning circles, pressing back against his groin. Her back arched sharply, as if by its own accord, and she hooked her ankles behind him, wanting to keep him close.

Needing to bring him closer.

"That's it, Blondie," he rasped in her ear, causing her to tremble in response. "Stop thinking," he instructed. "Just start feeling." He reached down and unbuttoned the fly of his jeans, sliding the zipper open.

She tried to pull away…

Or did she?

She should really voice some protest…

Or should she?

She wanted to tell him that it was way too much, way too soon, that she was losing herself in the moment, and he was utterly devastating her—but she couldn't find the words. When she felt him drag his fangs along her collarbone, swirl his tongue over the vein in her neck, and tighten his grip on her waist like a flesh-and-bone vise, she squirmed wildly. "Ramsey!"

He bit her, and she fractured.

What!?

Oh… no… not this soon!

Not like this.

They hadn't even—

He flung his jeans aside, ripping the denim like it was mere, flimsy paper, and then he dropped his head to her breasts and virtually devoured her flesh. He teased her nipples, flicked the taut peaks with his tongue, and drew her areolas deep into his mouth, where he tasted, suckled, and tantalized the flesh until she felt her tension mounting once more.

He grasped her by the back of the neck, turned her gently to face him, and locked his gaze with hers. "*Again*," he commanded softly, and like a marionette on a puppet-master's strings, her body obeyed his directive: She fractured—*once again*—splintering into a second, wild, uncontrollable orgasm.

"Stop!" she gasped, feeling utterly astonished, undone, and overwhelmed. It was like she had been swept up into a swirling vortex of sensation, passion, and pleasure—a tempest of eroticism unlike anything she had ever known—and she couldn't find the eye of the storm. She couldn't identify the ground. She couldn't make sense of the sky. She couldn't stop spinning with pleasure and sensation, and she had never even seen the tornado approach.

Sensing her confusion, if not her impending panic, Ramsey wrapped her in his arms, held her unbearably close to his heart, and whispered softly in her ear. "*It's okay, baby girl*. I've got you."

Tiffany blinked back pressing tears.

She was simply overcome with emotion.

Never before had she opened herself up to a man like this, not even while making love. There was always some carefully masked, inherently protected, hidden piece of her *self* that she held back and kept guarded.

Kept stored away in a microscopic vault.

But Ramsey had unlocked that safe—exposed it, *touched it*—like he had always held the key. Like the map to her hidden treasure was written on his soul.

And they hadn't even made love yet.

He was leaving her no escape.

"What are you so afraid of, my love?" he murmured, as if reading her thoughts. In one graceful movement, he drew back, grasped his form-fitting tee in his fist, and tugged it over his head, tossing it to the floor.

Her mouth dropped open as she gaped at his utterly magnificent masculine form. Yes, she had seen him, briefly, earlier that day, but this was entirely different. This wasn't a man. Hell, this wasn't a vampire. This was a finely honed, flawlessly defined, living work of art. "You're way too… way too… " The words escaped her.

He hooked his thumbs beneath the elastic bands of his cotton boxers and slid them down his hips. "Way too what?"

Her eyes bulged. "Way too… everything. Too big. Too powerful. Too much."

He slid the boxers past his thighs, over his knees, and to his ankles, where he kicked them carelessly behind him, utterly unashamed of his nudity and the straining erection, so boldly exposed. He bent his head and began to kiss his way along the inside of her thigh, slowly approaching her core. "Stop playing games, baby. *What are you afraid of?*"

Her eyes swelled with tears, and he rocked back on his heels to watch her, his own expression growing ripe with concern. "Tell me." He placed his open palm over her heart and watched as her chest heaved up and down in heightened response. "Because your heart is racing, yet your desire is with me. Your body is on fire, even as your eyes are filling with tears."

She nodded and placed her hand over his. "I know."

He ran his hand down the center of her chest, careful to avoid her breasts, and then paused at the round of her belly. "Then tell me what's going on, Blondie." He lowered his arm, ever so slightly, until the heel of hand pressed gently against her hot feminine core. "You want me as badly as I want you, so what's the conflict?"

She sighed, nearly moaning from the pleasure of his touch. There was no denying that she wanted him. He wasn't wrong in his assessment. Her body had utterly betrayed her, and even as he touched her, now… *there*… she felt her stomach tighten and her desire mount, another climax beginning to coil. "I just… I just… " She grasped his thick wrist with her hand, hoping to stop him from using those fingers more intimately, knowing that she would come apart… again. Her body would be his to command.

"You just?" he prompted, waiting.

Oh, what the hell.

Who was she kidding, and what was she hiding from? Why was she acting like this? Her body was inflamed. Her heart was melting beneath the heat of his gaze, and her soul was swimming in the velvety pool of his masculine beauty—her mind was spinning with the possibilities, the promise of his impending possession...

She was virtually yearning for his invasion, yet something inside of her was reeling, and she had to try to express it, even if she sounded like a fool. "I'm afraid I'll lose something," she whispered tentatively, "that I'll somehow get lost."

His expression changed to one of deep empathy as he slowly shook his head. "No, baby, you won't. You're too strong for that."

"But what if I'm not? What if I lose my way?"

"You can hold onto me, follow where I lead."

"What if I lose my power?"

"You can borrow some of mine."

"What if lose my *self*—my identity?"

"You aren't going to lose that, Blondie. In fact, I think for the first time in your life, you're going to finally find it... *with me.*"

She shook her head in exasperation. "I feel like I'm falling, like I'm drowning, like you're about to consume everything I am. I am powerless in your presence, Ramsey, and not just because you have such a strong personality, not just because you're such a dangerous species. I feel like you're bigger than me, more certain than me, and in the end, if I let you have me, I'll be *nothing* by comparison."

There.

She had said it.

She was afraid that Ramsey was bigger than life, more powerful than she could ever hope to be, and if she submitted her *very being* to him, when it was all said and done, she would be *nothing*.

twenty-two

Ramsey Olaru let out a deep, measured breath and stared at the beautiful, sensual woman before him, trying to make sense of her words. Her usually stylish hair was disheveled in the most adorable way; her deep, sea-green eyes were heavily lidded with desire, even as they were lined with confusion; and his body was getting in the way of his brain. In fact, his manhood was so incredibly strained, swollen, and hard that he was having trouble remembering his name, let alone processing the depth and gravity of what Tiffany was trying to say.

But he thought he got it.

He thought he got her.

She would resist him forever if she could because that solid core inside of her was so carefully contained, so fiercely independent, and so neatly controlled that to give herself completely to another being felt almost like a death of sorts. And Ramsey would never settle for just a part of her personality, a piece of her body, or an arm's-length romp in the hay. The celestial gods had chosen the two of them for one another, and he intended to make them one. Maybe, if she hadn't died and come back from the grave, he might have approached things differently. Maybe, if he hadn't failed her so miserably before, he would not feel the need to claim her so completely now. But Ramsey understood, perhaps for the first time in his long, monotonous life, what a *destiny* truly was.

Who Tiffany truly was.

She was his: his heart, his providence, his other half.

She was his reason for *being*, and he was hers.

And they would never come together if he continued to allow *any* sort of distance between them. The fact that he was a vampire—a predatory, dominant male—and she was yet human, his sensual partner, created to yield, was beyond reasoning or debate. It was simply the way of creation. The will of the gods. And she would come to understand, ultimately, that he was as vulnerable as she was, that their pairing was as revealing for him as it was for her. That with all he might take, he would give even more. In asserting his strength, he would also relinquish control—

To her.

But not if he allowed the procrastination to continue.

"Baby," he whispered ardently. "You aren't *nothing*. You're everything. My sky, my moon, my sun, my air, my life as we go forward. I would die for you. I would die *without you*, and if you give me your trust, all of you—your body, your heart, and your mind—I promise, I will never let you fall. I will never let you sink or drown. And I will never take anything from you that I'm not willing to give back in equal measure. Give yourself to me, Tiffany, *willingly*. Let me take you. Claim you. Let me *love* you."

Tiffany sat forward and looked deep into his eyes. She cupped his jaw in her hands and stared at his mouth for what seemed like eternity, and then she brushed her thumb along the scruff on his chin. "You are so incredibly handsome… so harshly, ruggedly… *beautiful*." She nearly groaned the words. "Your eyes. Your mouth. Your features." She ran the pad of her finger along the bridge of his nose, circled the indentation in his cheek, and then traced the contours of his lower lip. "You are utterly terrifying in your perfection, Ramsey." She took a deep breath and sighed. "I swear, sometimes, it actually hurts to look at you."

He inhaled sharply and grasped both of her wrists in his hands. "Right back at you, Blondie."

She chuckled softly, and then playfully shook her head. "Are you kidding? I'm a mess."

There was nothing playful in his eyes as he tried to convey his appreciation with his gaze, the quirk of his lips, and the slant of his head. "You're *my* mess, baby girl, and I'm just… *gone*. Just utterly and completely gone over you. Not the Curse, not the prophecy, not even the urgency of this Blood Moon. *You*, Tiffany."

Her eyes lit with surprise, and then she quickly glanced away. "If you didn't have to choose me, would you? I mean—"

"Oh, yes," he interrupted, "I want you, angel, more than you can imagine. I want to be inside you. I want to touch your heart and your body with my own. I want you to know me… feel me… *get* how much I need you."

She gulped, as if trying to swallow his words. And his request. She leaned forward and kissed him with abandon, and he responded in kind. She linked her fingers in his hair and breathed in his essence as he deepened their kiss and pulled her to the edge of the seat. She extended her shapely legs for his consideration and waited as he gently removed the remaining vestiges of her clothes and positioned his hips between her thighs.

There would be time for extended foreplay in the future.

There would be nights of wild passion—perhaps even broken furniture and screaming each other's names—as their expression became more natural, their bodies became more familiar, but this was not the time… or the place.

This was their joining.

Their first union.

This was Ramsey's claiming.

Sliding his palm beneath her lower back to support her weight, he thrust himself inside of her, waited for her body to adjust to his, and then slowly began to pump his hips. When her graceful neck arched, her head fell back, and a feminine moan of pleasure escaped her lips, Ramsey growled with satisfaction.

His *destiny* was finally his.

And together, they would find their rhythm.

Together, they would find their way.

Regardless of how it happened—or when it all came together—one thing was for certain: Ramsey Olaru would never, *ever* let this beautiful creature slip away from him again.

twenty-three

Tiffany curled up beneath Ramsey's protective arm and snuggled closer to his heart, turning to the side so she could wrap her legs around his—there just wasn't an inch of extra space in the oversized chair and ottoman, and while the afghan covered her nicely, he was hanging out on both ends.

She closed her eyes and sighed.

Wow. Just… wow.

"You good?" he asked in that deep, raspy voice.

She smiled. "I'm very good at the moment, thank you."

He absently brushed her hair out of her eyes and shifted in the chair, trying to get more comfortable.

"So," she said in a lazy voice, "tell me more about you."

He ran his palm down her arm and then gently caressed her back. "What do you want to know?"

"Everything."

He chuckled. "Could you be more specific?"

She burrowed deeper into his arms. *Let's see, what do I really want to know about this mysterious guy?* It was probably better to start simple. "Red or blue?"

"Excuse me?" he said dubiously. She loved the tenor of his voice.

"Red or blue?" she repeated.

"Blue."

"Why?"

He paused. "It's more mellow than red."

She propped herself up on her arm and gazed into his eyes as if looking for the truth. "You consider yourself mellow?"

He shrugged.

"Fine." She settled back into his arms. "Rock-and-roll, jazz-and-blues, or classical?"

"Rock."

She thought some more. "Hot or cold? The beach or the mountains? Racquetball or swimming?"

He laughed out loud, and the sound was both resonant and melodic, almost inviting. "Where do you come up with these questions? Cold. The mountains. And we have an indoor pool."

She sighed. "Oh yeah, that's true."

"Never racquetball," he added to her surprise, "too frilly for my taste."

"Frilly?" she asked. "How is racquetball frilly?"

"Dancing around with a little paddle in your hand, trying to work up a sweat with some basic hand-eye coordination—not very challenging for a vampire."

"Ah," she said, "so you've tried it?"

"Nope," he answered. "Too frilly."

This time she laughed out loud. "Okay, so the questions are going to get harder."

He waited, clearly undaunted. "I think I can handle it."

"Playful or serious? Happy or sad? Saxson or Santos?"

He shook his head in bewilderment. "Seriously? I don't even know what that last question means."

"Just answer," she prompted.

He sighed. "I can be playful… with someone who knows me. I take a lot of things seriously, but not everything. Happy or sad?" He scrunched up his handsome face. "Damn, Blondie. I guess the first thing I'd say is this: These are all black-or-white questions. In most things, I'm some shade of gray. Happy? Do I skip down the lane, marveling at the birds and the bees?"

"No!" she interjected decisively.

"No," he said more softly. "But do I lock myself in my room, listen to sad violin music, and bemoan the fact that the world's a gloomy place? Absolutely never. Not in a million years."

She pondered his answer. "Because you don't think about things like that?"

He tilted his head to the side, thinking. "I don't *take on* things like that. If I see something that bothers me, I handle it. If I see something I want to change, I change it. If I see something that's none of my business, I keep walking."

Tiffany nodded. "I guess that makes sense."

He sniffed. "When you live as long as I have, you learn a few things about staying sane: The mind can be a paradise or a prison. Depending on what you choose to give your attention to, it can be a place to retreat or a place you need to escape—and then you're in a world of hurt. I don't choose to think about things that don't directly affect my experience."

Tiffany grew quiet, contemplating his words. Once again, this enigmatic male seemed to be so much deeper than she initially thought. "And as for your brothers?"

This time he frowned. "Do I have a *favorite*?" There was a slight hint of disapproval in his voice, but she didn't take offense. None seemed intended.

"No," she said. "Are you closer to one than the other, maybe your twin?"

Ramsey grew quiet on a different level, one of careful introspection. He looked off into the distance as if really thinking it over, and then he cleared his throat. "It's different, the way I relate to each one." His top lip twitched, almost imperceptibly. "Saxson is my twin; so yeah, there's definitely a different bond between us. We've always existed together. But Santos, he's the oldest, and after our parents died, he tried to step in and take some sort of quasi-parental role in our lives: provide stability, act as a mentor, take the lead whether it was needed or not." He chuckled softly. "I think he just tried to stand in the gap."

Tiffany drew a light, zigzagging line over his chest, just above his heart, scarcely aware that she was doing it. "And you let him? Both you and Saxson let him? I mean, as strong and independent as you both are?"

Once again, Ramsey paused for a moment before responding. "I'm not much of a follower, never have been. I don't necessarily have to lead, and I don't follow so well, but with Santos, I make an exception. That role—what he tried to do for me and Saxson—it's part of his identity." He shrugged. "I can't really speak for Saxson, why he went along, but I imagine he had similar reasons."

She nodded and decided to change the subject. "I think, for me, I was an only child, so I never really practiced leading or following. I pretty much just carved out a comfortable place in my own skin, if that makes any sense."

He grunted. "And your parents? Did they spoil you?"

She laughed. "A little, yes, but I wasn't a princess, not by a long shot. My parents, Joe and Rita, inherited a generational farm back in North Carolina. It was a good life, but a lot of hard work. I was especially close to my nana before she passed. She might have spoiled me a bit."

Ramsey brushed an errant wisp of hair out of her eyes, then pressed an easy, unexpected kiss against her temple. "So how did you end up in San Francisco with our queen… with Brooke?"

Tiffany felt her expression lighten as her smile broadened. "Ambition. Inspiration. *Determination*. Brooke and I met in college in North Carolina. I fell in love with graphic design, and she fell in love with marketing, with all things PR. I wanted to go where the best opportunity was, and she convinced me that was San Francisco. We both landed jobs with PRIMAR, right after graduation, continued our education over the years, and I guess the rest is history."

Ramsey pulled her closer, his warm breath wafting across her forehead. "So your parents were supportive?"

"Oh yeah," she answered, emphatically. "They always were. They still are."

He nodded. "And what do they think of you living here, in Dark Moon Vale?"

She sighed. "Well, obviously, they don't know *everything*, but since I've always kind of followed Brooke—in work and play—it wasn't a hard sell. It made sense."

He shifted his weight in the armchair and ottoman then. "And what do you think they're going to make of me? Your new mate—husband?"

Tiffany started, still shocked by the sound of those words and their meaning, still shocked at the easy, blunt way Ramsey had of just putting it all out there on the table. "I think… well… most likely… " She grimaced. "Oh, God."

He laughed.

"You're kind of scary," she whispered, hoping it did not offend him.

He shifted forward on his side, in order to see her more clearly, and flashed a devilish grin. "They're going to love me," he teased. And then his eyes grew dark and shadowed with desire. "And so are you."

She looked up at him and gasped, swearing her heart had just skipped a beat.

"I'm not that scary," he whispered, dipping down to plant a convincing, sensual kiss firmly on her lips. True to his nature, Ramsey went straight to the heart of the matter, taking control as if she were simply *his* to command—at will—and by the way her body reacted, flooding with warmth, heating with instant passion, he had every right to assume it was true.

He brushed her top lip with his tongue and then traced her bottom lip with the same in an erotically playful stroke of invitation. "It'll all work out, baby doll." He breathed the words into her mouth, and then he *growled*, deep and low in his throat.

Ramsey Olaru was done talking.

And so was Tiffany Matthews.

twenty-four

One week later

Tiffany sank deep into the luxurious hot tub, letting her head fall back against a form-fitting pillow. It was a hauntingly beautiful night outside, and the invigorating water was just what the doctor ordered. As she gazed up at the blue-black sky, she couldn't help but think everything was just the way it should be: The moon shimmered like a soft, golden halo, crowning a peaceful scattering of stars; the sweet scent of pine mixed with juniper filled the crisp mountain air; and a soft breeze tickled her skin, cooling the bite of the otherwise sweltering heat.

Just then, someone knocked on the patio door, the elegant glass slid open, and Tiffany sat upright, turning down the jets, to see who it was.

Ramsey would never knock like that to alert her.

Hell, Ramsey wouldn't alert her at all.

He would probably just step right through the glass, using his vampiric powers, and leap into the hot tub from twenty feet away, shocking the breath right out of her. She giggled to herself, thinking of all the amazing things Ramsey could actually do.

Making love was at the top of that list.

"Hey there, you," Brooke called, stepping out onto the patio.

She was clutching the collar of a plush terrycloth robe, and Tiffany almost squealed with glee, realizing that her *bestie* had come to spend time with her.

"Brookie!" She waved her hand with excitement.

Brooke's smile lit up her deep blue eyes as she made her way to the hot tub, laid her heavy robe on a nearby patio chair, and slowly climbed the stairs, entering the water gingerly. "Ah," she moaned as the water began to envelop her, steering a path to an adjacent, corner seat.

Tiffany turned the jets back on, swam across the liquid expanse to give her best friend a hug, and then made her way back to the lounge chair. "I didn't know you were coming," she said cheerfully.

"Yep," Brooke answered, leaning her head back and shutting her eyes. "Napolean wanted to talk to Ramsey, so I thought I'd surprise you."

Tiffany smiled broadly, even though Brooke couldn't see it—she just felt happy. Indeed, all was just perfect with the world tonight.

A moment of companionable silence passed, and then Brooke opened her eyes and regarded Tiffany with her peripheral vision. "So?" Her eyebrows shot up in question.

"So?" Tiffany mimicked, knowing she shouldn't tease.

Brooke let out an exasperated sigh. "So… you're obviously alive."

Tiffany laughed. "I am."

Brooke sat up straight and leaned forward to stare at the woman she considered a sister. "And you're… " She waited, letting the words linger.

Tiffany shrugged, feigning ignorance. "I have no idea what you mean." The corner of her mouth turned up in a mischievous hint of a smile.

"Oh c'mon, Tiff; don't do this. You're… still human? Not human? Part Martian?"

Tiffany laughed. She wanted to draw out the suspense, tease

her friend just a little bit longer, but she knew she could never pull it off. Brooke just had a way of wringing information out of her… quickly. She ran her tongue along her front teeth, pausing to emphasize her canines.

Brooke threw up her hands in true frustration this time. "They look the same, Tiffany! Just tell me!"

Tiffany practically bounced in the water as she shot up in the lounge chair, leaned forward, and exclaimed, "Yes! Yes. *Yes*: It's done. I'm just like you now." She frowned. "Well, maybe with a slightly smaller ass."

"Hey!" Brooke objected, "My *assets* are positively perfect. Just ask Napolean." And then she nearly shrieked with delight, turning to the subject at hand. "Are you serious? Oh my god! *Oh-my-god.*" Her expression turned serious. "Was it awful?"

Now this made Tiffany roll her eyes. Was Brooke kidding? "Um, no," she said, "awful is too soft of a term. *Awful* is a word you use to describe a bitter apple or a poorly acted movie, maybe some really unpleasant weather. Being converted, as you well know, is more along the lines of torturous, excruciating, the Spanish Inquisition in the modern age." She glared at her best friend defiantly. "Yes, it was awful! It was the single most painful, unbearable, absolutely horrific experience of my life."

Brooke grimaced and sank deeper into the corner chair of the hot tub, kindly averting her eyes. "How long?"

"Six hours," Tiffany said.

"Ohhhh, gods… "

"Yeah," Tiffany quipped, and then she thought better of making a federal case out of her experience: After all, Brooke's conversion had been far, far worse. Napolean had been possessed by a demon at the time, and the demon had spared Brooke zero suffering when he'd converted her in a meadow, feverish to inflict as much pain through brutality as he could. The entire ordeal had been a nightmare.

"How was Ramsey?" Brooke asked pointedly, interrupting Tiffany's thoughts. "I mean, how was he with you?"

Tiffany shrugged. Despite herself, she couldn't help but share. "I don't know. I don't really remember his demeanor, although I'm sure he tried to be as gentle as he could." She sighed. "To me, he was just one big set of fangs… and venom… and torture. I'm sure he did all he could to comfort me, but from where I stood—" She stopped short, refusing to relive it.

"That bad," Brooke said solemnly.

"Oh yeah, that bad."

"You wanted him dead?"

"Al Capone," Tiffany said.

"Ew." Brooke grimaced, demonstrating her horror.

Whenever one of them said *Al Capone*, they each knew exactly what the other meant: *I want him* dead. *I want his family* dead. *I want his house burned to the* ground!

Brooke cleared her throat. After a prolonged moment of silence, she finally said, "So?"

Tiffany pretended to be ignorant and rolled her eyes. "So."

Brooke bit her bottom lip. "Have you… "

"Have we what?"

Brooke dove across the hot tub, punched her friend in the arm, and pointed right in her face. "You know what!"

Tiffany hunched forward and giggled, and then they both glanced toward the wall of sliding glass, trying to determine exactly where Ramsey and Napolean were in the living room, wanting to be sure their conversation was private.

"Well?" Brooke whispered, leaning close enough to Tiffany to almost touch noses.

Tiffany drew back. "Well, what?"

"Was it good?" Brooke's eyes were as wide as saucers as she waited for Tiffany's answer.

Tiffany's eyes rolled back in their sockets; she slid down the lounge chair like a limp rag doll; and her tongue lolled out the side of her mouth. "Holy… *shit.*"

Brooke clasped both hands over her mouth, and her bulging blue eyes lit up with intrigue. "That good?"

"Better," Tiffany whispered.

Brooke's mouth fell open. "Maxwell House or KFC?"

Tiffany laughed. "Both. Good to the last drop *and* finger-licking good!"

Brooke squealed. "Maxwell House *and* KFC! Holy shit!"

"Sh!" Tiffany hushed her, cringing as the glass door slid open and Ramsey Olaru, the immortal god of all things sex-related, peeked out onto the deck.

"You ladies all right?" he asked, eyeing them both suspiciously.

Brooke giggled. She stuck her finger in her mouth and made a great show of smacking her lips as she popped it out. "Just perfect," she said, laughing conspiratorially. "Just discussing fried chicken."

Tiffany burst out in laughter, and then abruptly cut it off.

Ramsey frowned, but before he could reply, Napolean stepped out onto the deck and placed a fatherly hand on his shoulder. "Don't ask," he said. "You don't want to know."

Ramsey eyed him sideways. "Are they always like this?"

"Pretty much," Napolean replied.

Ramsey smirked, leveling a heated gaze at Tiffany. "And don't they know we can hear them at will… if we choose?"

Napolean shook his head briskly. "*No,*" he said in a deep, dark tenor, "you don't want to go there, either."

"Why not?" Ramsey grumbled.

Napolean shook his head again. "Because if Tiffany is anything like your queen, then you would be better off dining with a Dark One than eavesdropping on your mate, just because you can."

"We can hear you!" Brooke called out from the hot tub, projecting her voice so it would carry above the jets.

Tiffany smiled. It was true. Even with the jets pumping and the blower circulating air, her new vampiric hearing was impeccable.

"Of course you can, sweetheart," Napolean said, flashing a far too gentle smile at his mate, considering who he was to the Vampyr.

Ramsey furrowed his brow. "So let me get this straight: We can't eavesdrop on them, but they can eavesdrop on us?"

Napolean clapped his hand on Ramsey's back and nodded. "You're learning, son."

"What was that?" Brooke asked, eyeing her mate inquisitively.

Napolean's voice turned to pure, unadulterated silk. "You look ravishing in that bathing suit, my love," he said.

Brooke instantly melted at his words. Her expression turned soft and inviting, and her eyes glazed over with love. "Thank you, my king," she flirted.

Tiffany looked away. *Okay.* Well then…

As the males sauntered back into the house, Brooke squeezed in on the lounge chair, lying parallel to Tiffany. She sighed contentedly.

"You give me hope," Tiffany said wistfully.

Brooke smiled. "How so?"

Tiffany patted Brooke's leg. "Well, if you can tame Napolean, then maybe—"

"Oh, he's anything but tame. Don't get it twisted—Napolean still wears the pants in our house."

Tiffany drew back and eyed her sideways. "So then, how does that work?"

Brooke waggled her eyebrows and grinned for all she was worth. "Because *we* wear the skirts!"

Tiffany laughed, and once again, they fell into a peaceful, easy silence.

After a few minutes had passed, Brooke reached out and took Tiffany's hand, giving it a firm, loving squeeze. "So there's something I wanted to talk to you about."

Tiffany's eyebrows shot up. "Go on."

"It's just an idea, but I think it's a good one."

Tiffany angled her head to see Brooke's expression. "Okay. So?"

"So, have you and Ramsey talked about the pregnancy yet?" She glanced down at Tiffany's stomach. "I mean, I imagine it will be soon considering the Curse and all… "

Tiffany nodded. "Very soon." She paused to reach forward, tap a button on the panel, and reset the jets for another cycle. "Why do you ask?"

Brooke took a slow, deep breath before speaking. "Because I think we should do it together."

Tiffany's left eyebrow shot up like a lone, rebel feature, undoubtedly distorting her appearance. "Uh, that just sounds really kinky, Brooke. Is there some vampire pastime that I'm unaware of? Because I don't really swing that way."

Brooke laughed out loud. "No, silly!" She pinched Tiffany on the arm. "I meant, I think we should both get pregnant *by our mates*, together, at the same time."

Now this caught Tiffany's attention. "When did you… have you talked to Napolean? Where is this coming from?"

Brooke squeezed Tiffany's hand, and her voice grew serious. "Over the last several months. Of course we've talked about it, and it's coming from a couple of places. Just hear me out, okay?"

Tiffany nodded.

"It's not the same, being married to the king. Everything is such high stakes. There's just a lot to consider." She shimmied sideways, trying to secure a little more real estate on the lounge chair. "We've always wanted more children, but more than that, we both agree that we've placed little Phoenix in an untenable position." She sighed. "Like it or not, the poor child practically has a target on his back: Anyone who wants to lash out at Napolean—or to hurt the house of Jadon—can simply go after the prince. There's no other successor to the throne, so to speak. So, yeah, we've talked about how important it is to give

Phoenix some siblings, to take some of that weight *and danger* off his tiny shoulders. And ever since that day in the park, when Ramsey killed that awful woman who was with Salvatore—" She stopped abruptly and shook her head, not really wanting to go there right now. "Besides, what if Phoenix doesn't want to rule one day? What if he doesn't want to be first? Shouldn't he have a choice? And Napolean has *so much* to teach him. He'd be better off teaching several successors at once."

Tiffany swallowed hard, ingesting Brooke's words and weighing their meaning. "That makes a lot of sense, Brookie, but what about you? Are you ready for *two more* children?" Now that the initial sacrifice was over and done with, the royal couple could keep *all* their future children.

Brooke laughed. "Yeah, I am. I really am. Napolean and I are in a really good place, and it's not like we don't have lots of help if we want it. I think it's time."

Tiffany sat up and held her best friend's gaze, trying to process all she was hearing. "So, you want to get pregnant *again*, at the same time as me?"

Brooke's smile was radiant. "Our men can and do command the condition at will, you know? They can name the hour and the minute: Why not?"

Tiffany sank back into the steamy water and simply let the idea percolate in her head. "Huh." *Why not, indeed?* "Do you realize that a few weeks ago, I was just your employee, Phoenix's unofficial nanny, and your consummate best friend forever, of course; and now—"

"Oh, hell, Tiffany," Brooke interrupted. "Less than two weeks ago, you were a total flake who took off into the forest on a giant horse, trying to outrun a vampire. I would say progress has been made on all fronts."

Brooke's words elicited more than a little laughter out of Tiffany, and then she grew suddenly quiet, glanced up at the magnificent sky, and stretched her back. "What do you say we just soak for a while and let it all sink in?"

"Sounds perfect," Brooke said.

As the strong scent of pine rose on the breeze, and the crystal-clear water enveloped them in its tranquil, soothing arms, both women fell into a companionable silence as deep and abiding as their friendship.

*

Napolean leaned forward in the overstuffed living room chair and braced his strong forearms on his legs.

Ramsey squirmed just a bit.

It was odd having the king in his living room, like one of his brothers or the tracker, and since Ramsey wasn't accustomed to social calls from the sovereign ruler, he wasn't entirely sure what to say. He cleared his throat for the second or third time and then reached for his trusty, monogramed case to extract a toothpick.

Napolean's dark, penetrating eyes grew even darker with purpose. "I remember." There was no preamble, just those two ominous words: *I remember.*

Ramsey stuffed the toothpick between his teeth and sank back into the sofa, regarding his king with newfound curiosity. "Come again." He immediately remembered his manners. "Milord."

Napolean chuckled. "Awkward, I realize." He swept his hand in a leisurely arc, indicating their current surroundings. "We don't often meet like this."

Ramsey forced a genial smile. *More like never,* he thought. Not that there was anything wrong with the two males sitting down for a heart-to-heart, but Napolean was a notoriously busy male—ruling the house of Jadon kept him ceaselessly occupied. His stature and his position kept him somewhat aloof.

He repeated the phrase. "I remember, Ramsey. That day in the park—I still remember."

Ramsey's mouth grew momentarily slack around the toothpick as he finally registered the king's words. *Holy celestial goddess,* so time had rolled back; the *ramifications* had been undone; yet Napolean remembered everything. Ramsey winced as he realized the full implications of the king's words: Napolean *remembered* how Tiffany had died. He remembered how his son, the prince, had nearly been attacked, how his wife, the queen, had been placed in mortal danger. He remembered how Ramsey had failed to protect them all. Napolean was acutely aware of Ramsey's unforgivable lapse in judgment. He lowered his gaze inadvertently.

Napolean shook his head, seeming to read Ramsey's thoughts. Truth be told, the ancient vampire was more than capable of doing just that, and doing it with such a feather-light touch that Ramsey would never feel it. After all, he *was* the most powerful being on the planet. "I don't have to read your mind to discern your expression, warrior," the king said softly. "And I'm not here to relive the past or to pass judgment. We are not perfect, Ramsey. None of us." He settled deeper into the chair—and the conversation—thoughtfully. "I am more concerned with the ongoing repercussions, the lingering, persistent energy that still reverberates from the original event."

Ramsey frowned. He hated when the king spoke in scientific riddles, and frankly, he was still stuck on the fact that Napolean remembered.

He remembered.

How could that be?

"Andromeda," Napolean said, never missing a beat. "The goddess allowed me to retain the memories for two reasons." He pursed his lips, considering how to proceed. "First, because the question she answered for me was too important to take away. She didn't want me to lose that knowledge, that wisdom. And second, because manipulating time, altering the past and, thus, the future, is a very tricky thing. The memories are my burden to bear, Ramsey, not yours."

Ramsey was having trouble following Napolean's line of reasoning: Why would *his* actions—his incredibly poor choices—be Napolean's burden to bear? "What do you mean?" His tone was blunter than he intended.

Napolean sighed. He rose slowly from the chair and strolled toward the floor-to-ceiling windows, where he glanced out at the alluring night sky. "Ramsey, have you told Tiffany about that day in the park, about what happened? Have you told her that she died?"

Ramsey sat forward, removed the toothpick from his mouth, and twirled it absently between his thumb and first two fingers, debating what to say. "No. Not yet. Maybe not ever."

Napolean nodded, still glancing out the windows. "Indeed, that would be a very heavy burden for her to bear." He folded his arms in front of his chest. "As it stands, it is a fairly heavy weight for you to carry now."

"I'm handling it," Ramsey murmured.

"Are you?" Napolean asked. He turned around to face the sentinel, and his long, regal hair fell forward, framing his ancient features like an ebony crown. "How many times a day do you dream of hunting and killing Salvatore Nistor—how many specific plots have you hatched in your mind?"

Ramsey didn't answer. *Well, hell*, so the king knew him well.

Napolean flicked his wrist in a slow, dismissive gesture. "Beyond that, how many times a day do you find yourself guarding your words, stopping abruptly, or catching yourself just before you say something careless to Tiffany, something that would reveal the secret?" Before Ramsey could answer, Napolean took several steps forward and regarded the sentinel with scrutiny, making him feel a bit like a bug underneath a microscope. "I'm sure I don't have to tell you that it sucks to start a new mating with a secret, to begin a new life by withholding something so important."

Ramsey frowned: Did Napolean just say *sucks*?

"What happened in that park may very well define your future bond with your mate; surely the horror of it all is like cement, adhering to the very foundation of your communication and interactions."

"English," Ramsey prompted, feeling like his head was beginning to spin.

Napolean smiled, and the kindly gesture softened his otherwise serious features. "I would not have it so, son. You do not need to remember something your brothers have forgotten. You do not need to carry something the entire house of Jadon is unaware of, and you don't need to start a new life with Tiffany based on a secret. While we would all like to see Salvatore dead, you do not need to make his demise your own personal mission of vengeance. At some point, it will lead to taking unnecessary risks."

Ramsey's spine stiffened as he sat upright on the sofa. "Milord, if what you're implying, if what you're *saying*, is that I'd be better off without my memories, then with all due respect—"

"I've already made my decision, Ramsey." Napolean waved his hand in polite but firm dismissal. "When the time is right, I *will* take those memories from you. They will be my burden—and my burden, alone—to carry."

Ramsey choked back a sharper retort. "But I haven't asked you to do that. I don't *want* you to do that. And how is that any different, you keeping a secret from Brooke... from the queen?"

Napolean shook his head and shrugged. "I keep centuries' worth of secrets from the entire house of Jadon, Ramsey, some from Brooke, some from my inner circle, *all* by necessity. It is part and parcel of who I am as a Justice, as your Sovereign... as your king. You have to understand: I am privy to every desire, every fear, every sorrow and misgiving of every member in the house of Jadon. I carry each male and female's blood in my veins, and I feel you, all of you, in my soul." He sighed, almost as if he didn't quite have the words to express what he truly wanted to say. "Yet, I am largely at peace, Ramsey. I have never known any other way. You, however, have a choice. You don't want this burden, warrior, even if you think you do. But more importantly, you don't *have* to carry it."

Ramsey studied the tips of his fingernails, trying to form his own appropriate words, trying to restrain his rising ire. "Doesn't sound like I have much of a choice," he mumbled, thinking out loud, and then his anger flared. "Then why tell me, milord? Why not just come over to my house, sit in my living room, and violate my mind at will? Why not just take the damn memories and leave me none the wiser?"

Napolean grew as silent as a monk, and then the entire room lit up with pale gold, electric energy. "Watch your tone, son."

Ramsey ran both hands through his hair and took a deep, measured breath, trying to do just that. "I'm sorry." He shut his eyes and counted backward from ten to one. *"I'm sorry."*

Napolean sighed, his chest rising and falling with the effort. "So incredibly strong-willed, warrior. You always have been." He crossed the room to the sofa and squatted down in front of Ramsey. "I like that about you, son. It's one of the reasons I placed you in my inner circle. I always know where you stand. I always know that *if and when* you disagree with me, you will clearly speak your peace. And since a king is only as wise as his counsel, it's an extremely important trait. However, we both know that my word is final, that all decisions begin and end with me."

It was a gentle but powerful reprimand, and Ramsey had no intention of pushing the envelope any further. He still remembered *vividly* what had happened the last time he had pushed the king too far—and in a public way. Napolean had swiftly and definitively corrected him in front of all the other warriors, and that torturous *correction* still hurt when he thought about it…

No, Ramsey definitely did not want a repeat.

"Nor do I," Napolean said.

Ramsey furrowed his brows. "King or no, you're not supposed to read my mind, *milord*. Not unless it's life or death, absolutely necessary."

Napolean chuckled softly, and then he winked. "You have expressive eyes, warrior." He stood back up and cocked one shoulder in a sharp, *are-you-kidding?* gesture. "Besides, that was pretty obvious." He strolled back to the armchair and took a seat, looking entirely at ease. "Now then, there are two other matters we need to discuss, and each one is equally important."

Ramsey shook his head. The king still surprised him after all this time. Shifting to the subject at hand, he waited *respectfully* for Napolean to continue.

Napolean linked his hands in his lap and stared off into the distance at some point beyond Ramsey's shoulders. He was obviously contemplating his words carefully. Taking a deep breath and then slowly exhaling, he began speaking in a measured but serious tone. "Despite Andromeda's miracle, turning back the hands of time so expertly, there were still some… ripple effects… from that day in the park."

Ramsey raised one eyebrow. "Ripple effects?"

Napolean nodded. "Yes, some energetic repercussions that still linger. And I'm hoping you can do something to correct them *before* I remove those memories."

"Like what?" Ramsey asked.

Napolean met his gaze directly. "Like your brothers, to begin with."

Ramsey sat up straighter, immediately concerned. "What about my brothers?"

Napolean gestured absently with his hands as he spoke. "They're not doing well." He held up his palm to halt any interruption, asking silently for an opportunity to convey his thoughts. "I have felt a powerful sense of loss and apprehension in both of them, something that borders on irrational fear, illogical uncertainty. Perhaps the impending loss of one so close cannot simply be erased, no matter how cleanly time is manipulated. I think they are each still grieving the tragedy in some indelible way, like some marginal part of their consciousness still expects to lose you at the end of your Blood Moon. Yet they have no idea why they feel as they do, why the fear won't go away, or what it even means." He softened his voice. "I don't know how it happened or why it's still present. I only know that they need to be reassured *by you*. They need to see your face, hear your voice, get a gut-level feeling that you're here, that you're solid, real, that you aren't going anywhere—at least until the pattern finally breaks. Perhaps you could involve them in some of your decisions with Tiffany or invite them to stay with you for a while, make their soon-to-be nephew an excuse. I don't know. It's not my place to tell you how to make this happen. I just wanted you to know that it's needed."

Ramsey rubbed the bridge of his nose, feeling like an idiot.

Napolean should not have had to bring this to his attention, not with a matter concerning the two beings closest to him in all the world, his own brothers. Ramsey *had* noticed something strange over the past eight days. He had thought it was odd, the way both of his siblings kept texting him around the clock, disturbing his thoughts almost randomly, whenever they had the urge, and with such unimportant, telepathic interruptions. Santos had offered to come by the house no less than five times, and Saxson had actually invited Ramsey to check out a movie, *a movie*, knowing good and well that Ramsey had a new *destiny* to bond with, to convert—heck, to get pregnant.

He clenched his fists and cracked his knuckles, each one in turn, trying to relieve some tension. It all made sense now. *Perfect sense.* His brothers weren't being obnoxious or clingy. They were being *brothers*. They were trying to hold onto something they feared they were losing. They were trying to deal with emotions they couldn't begin to understand.

He sighed, wishing he could get a *do-over*.

Damn, he wasn't the most observant male in the house of Jadon, was he?

Meeting Napolean's penetrating gaze head-on, he slowly nodded his head. "I can do that. *Thank you.*" He let a moment of silence linger between them before asking about the second subject—did he really want to know? "There was something else?"

"Yes," Napolean said. And this time, the king's expression turned positively sober. "Saber Alexiares."

"What about him?" Ramsey asked.

"Similar situation. Much deeper turmoil."

Ramsey thought about that day in the park and cringed, remembering the way he had gone after the vampire, tossing his crest ring at his chest, blaming him for Tiffany's death. He had been so relieved that the goddess had erased all that madness, but now, it looked as if it still remained. At least some of it. "Sounds as if the goddess left a few celestial traces behind."

Napolean quickly glanced skyward and then narrowed his eyes at Ramsey. "Watch yourself, son. Be careful."

Ramsey held up both hands in supplication, also glancing skyward in reverence. "No disrespect intended. None whatsoever. I owe Andromeda *everything*." He uttered a quick prayer of gratitude to the goddess before returning his attention to the king. "I'm just saying I thought it was completely erased."

Napolean leaned forward. "I think it was, but I also think that some events are so deeply felt; some conflicts are so deeply rooted; some experiences are so life-changing that they have a resonance all their own. In a sense, you plucked a string that day in the park. Andromeda silenced the note, but the vibration continued to chime."

Ramsey nodded. What could he say?

"He came to the mansion the other day to speak to me."

"About what?" Ramsey asked.

"About that crest ring, about his place in the house of Jadon. He's ready to wear it, but there's more: He wants to be a sentinel."

Ramsey's eyebrows shot up in surprise. "Seriously? I thought he was going to travel with Vanya to Romania, six months each year?"

"He is, but he wants his six months here to be purposeful." Napolean scratched the tip of his nose before lounging further back in the chair. "He wants to serve the house of Jadon. He wants to be the soldier that he is. And I think—he wants to make things up to *you*."

Ramsey frowned. *Shit. Just... shit.* "Okay, so... what can I do?"

Napolean sighed, tapping his fingers absently along the arm of the chair. Clearly, the king had already given the matter a great deal of thought. "I already spoke to Saxson and Santos, just before coming over tonight, and they're both on board with the sentinel angle—what say you, warrior? Do you trust him... *implicitly?*"

Ramsey gave the question the serious consideration it deserved, refusing to answer in haste. After several pregnant moments had passed, he nodded. "I wouldn't be here without Saber Alexiares. Tiffany wouldn't be here. Yes, I trust him completely." He linked his fingers together and placed his hands behind his head. "Do you?"

The king smiled unabashedly then. "With the life of my *destiny* and child, as well as my own. Yes, I trust him." He chuckled softly. "Besides, he's a lot like you. He speaks his mind rather clearly."

Ramsey joined in the king's laughter—truer words had never been spoken. "So I gather there's more to this question than a simple yes or no. What role can I play in mending invisible fences, making all this happen?"

The king looked pleased by the question. "Here's the thing: We both know how critical your Blood Moon is, how important it is for you to stay focused and fulfill the demands of the Curse.

I would never ask you to stray from that purpose, not even for a moment. However, I will simply say to you that Saber *needs* this as soon as possible."

Once again, Ramsey mulled over the king's words, weighing all the various implications carefully. The decision seemed so obvious—the right course of action was abundantly clear. Today was Wednesday. The preparations for an induction ceremony could be made in twenty-four hours, by Friday night, and every vampire in Dark Moon Vale could be gathered together by then.

Ramsey didn't just spit words.

He might not be the most sensitive male in the house of Jadon, but he meant what he said and he said what he meant— he owed Saber Alexiares his life. "Tiffany will understand." He spoke without preamble. "The pregnancy can wait until Saturday. My Blood Moon can wait until Saturday. Saber has waited eight hundred years to come home."

The king regarded Ramsey with unconcealed admiration, almost too moved to speak. "Are you sure?"

Ramsey nodded. "Nothing I said in that park was true. So the male has wrestled with his identity? So he needed some time to sort it all out, redefine his place in the world—so what. The sooner we make this happen, the better."

Napolean's determined expression reflected his equal conviction. "Very well, consider it done. I'll get the ball rolling as soon as I return to the manse tonight." He leaned back in his chair and nodded, looking immensely satisfied. And then he began to twiddle his thumbs. His eyes darted this way and that around the room, and he practically squirmed in his chair.

What. The. Hell?

He blew out a long, anxious breath, and the air whistled as it left his mouth. "Ah, hell," he said, sounding suddenly embarrassed. "There is one more thing."

Ramsey wasn't about to chime in on this one. At least not yet. He sat there, silent as a church mouse, waiting…

Napolean rolled his dark, regal eyes and stuck out his lips like a child. "Your queen has a plan."

Ramsey waited with bated breath. *Oh hell, well, no wonder the king had been reduced to adolescence. This was about Brooke, his female, and more than likely, it included Tiffany...* "What kind of plan?" he asked, practically willing the king to just spit it out.

"Babies," he said.

"Come again?" Ramsey said.

"*Babies,*" the king said more firmly. He stared at his hands as he continued. "We are all going to have more babies." He glanced out the tinted glass in the direction of the hot tub, even though the women were securely tucked out of sight. "But the thing is"— he leveled a helpless gaze at Ramsey, his dark onyx eyes almost pleading for sympathy—"we're going to have them together."

Ramsey stroked his jaw and looked askance at a particularly bright tile on the floor. *What the heck kind of plan was this?* He opened his mouth to speak and then shut it. Finally, wrinkling up his nose, he said, "With all due respect, milord, that just sounds kind of kinky."

twenty-five

Friday night

Ramsey knew he was breaking with tradition by approaching the exterior door to the Ceremonial Hall of Justice in order to see his *destiny* one more time before Saber's induction. The ancient rite would take place in an outdoor clearing, about six hundred acres behind Napolean's manse, while the indoor ceremony, which was really more of a reception, would follow immediately after the initiation.

Traditionally, the males took part in the actual sacrament while the females waited in the ceremonial hall to receive the males when the ritual was over. It wasn't a sexist thing. Rather, it was deeply steeped in centuries of lasting tradition: Long ago, when Napolean began to gather the house of Jadon together, to mold it into a formal, organized entity, there were few *destinies* present, and those who did attend the bestial rite of passage didn't have the stomach for the process. True, it was a different time. These days, women were no longer prone to swoon, nor were men obliged to protect their "delicate sensibilities" at every turn. And Ramsey had no doubt whatsoever that every *destiny* in the house of Jadon could stand proudly through the ceremony, today. Just the same, tradition was tradition. The house of Jadon was born from a Curse, and that Curse followed the male line of descendants, unerringly: "From this day forward, you shall be cursed. And your *sons* shall be cursed. And their *sons* after them… unto all eternity." Bottom line: Females didn't die a horrific death in the sacrificial chamber if they failed to offer the required sacrifice.

Males did.

Ramsey shook his head, quickly dismissing the thought. This was a night of celebration, not morbid reflection. He sent a telepathic request to Tiffany, asking her to come to the outer door—they could speak clairvoyantly now, ever since she had been converted—and then he waited rather impatiently for the heavy iron door to swing open.

Tiffany looked like the goddess she was when she finally opened the door open and stood before him. Her sleek, layered hair was perfectly groomed, expertly styled, and the stark, golden-brown highlights accentuated the natural blond in a way that made her sea-green eyes sparkle and her soft, delicate features stand out. She leaned forward and scanned the darkness, turning her head to the left, then the right. "What are you doing here?"

Ramsey braced a heavy, muscular arm against the upper doorframe and leaned in to get closer. "Just one more kiss."

Tiffany blushed—*she actually blushed*—then she shoved him none too gently in the chest, causing his arm to fall to his side. "*Ramsey*! You are not supposed to be here right now." She glanced over her shoulder and promptly lowered her voice. "Besides, if Princess Vanya sees you"—she made an executioner's gesture beneath her throat with her hand—"it won't be pretty."

Ramsey frowned. "Why? What's going on with Vanya?" He leaned forward to peek inside the hall, but Tiffany blocked his line of vision with her body.

"I'm warning you," she whispered coarsely, "she's wound as tight as a drum." She rose up on her toes to speak conspiratorially in his ear. "She just told Brooke that this separation of males and females is both stupid and unnecessary, that traditions were made to be broken, and that if Saber gets injured in this ceremony, she's going to—and I quote—'unleash a magical can of whoop-ass on the king that will rival the Blood's fury.'" She stepped back and punctuated her words with a nod.

Ramsey grimaced. "*Damn*. She said *whoop-ass?*"

Tiffany put her hand over her mouth to keep from laughing. "Yep. Then Kristina told her to *chill the hell out* before she upsets Saber's mother."

Ramsey chuckled. "Now that sounds like Kristina." He paused. "Why don't you just tell Vanya that Saber's going to be fine: In fact, he's going to be better than before. He needs this."

Tiffany shook her head adamantly. "*Just tell Vanya*, hell! I'm not going anywhere near that woman until this induction thing is over." She crossed her arms over her chest and leaned back in the doorway. "She may be beautiful, and she may be sweet, but that woman does not play around when it comes to Saber. No, thank you. Besides, she knows entirely too much magic for my comfort." She gestured emphatically with her hands. "So if it's all the same to you, I'll keep my distance, *mister*."

Ramsey cocked one eyebrow. "*Mister?*"

Tiffany rolled her eyes.

"Say my name," he whispered.

Tiffany looked away, feigning annoyance.

He chuckled. "Oh, okay. So it's like that?"

Tiffany bit her lower lip and stifled a giggle. "Do you ever stop?"

Ramsey gave her a sly, devilish wink in reply. He knew he really shouldn't tease her like this, but he couldn't help it. She was just so cute, so adorable, so *sexy* with her one-step-forward, one-step-back behavior. One moment, she thought Ramsey was the devil. The next, she found him irresistible. Still, a few minutes later, she treated him like some hybrid between *the big bad wolf* and her own personal centerfold. And all the while, she remained an intriguing enigma: impossible to conquer yet willing to please.

His ultimate challenge and his greatest reward.

He absolutely adored her.

She was everything he could have ever asked for in a *destiny*, and the more he got to know her, the more he believed their personalities were simply a perfect match. "Fine," he said, trying to mimic a pout, and then he dipped down to tempt her. "Kiss me, and I'll go."

Tiffany angled her neck to give him a light peck on the cheek, and he snatched her by the waist, pulled her firmly against his chest, and planted a solid, erotic kiss on her mouth, leaving her gasping for air when he finally pulled away.

Smoothing out the front of her skirt, she groaned: "You're going to be the death of me, Mr. Olaru. I swear, one day, you really are."

He flashed a wicked yet appreciative smile. "And you're going to be the *life* of me, *Mrs. Olaru*. I swear; you already are."

Clearly surprised, she averted her eyes. "We're not *married*."

"Wanna be?"

She glared at him, and then she shooed him away with her hand. "Would you go, already? *Geez!*"

Deep, resonant laughter rumbled in his chest as he consented with a nod, and then he swept his gaze over her body, one last time, tracing the obvious contours of her feminine form oh so slowly, from head to toe, with blatantly hungry eyes. "Later," he said in a dark, husky voice, allowing the word—and its connotation—to linger.

"Maybe," she quipped, quick-witted as always. "Maybe not."

He could hardly contain his laughter as she shut the door in his face.

*

Ramsey entered the sacred clearing behind Napolean's manse from the west, his demeanor as solemn as he was silent. The night was absolutely perfect for the upcoming ceremony: The moon was at full zenith; the air was crisp, cool, and clean; and the copious scent of pine, burning in the towering bonfire, permeated the meadow like swirling fog rising off an ancient sea. The densely wooded forest provided an ominous backdrop for the ceremony, setting a stage reminiscent of Ramsey's beloved homeland: *Romania*.

Saber Alexiares was already standing on the raised platform, wearing a thick mahogany robe with the letters *HOJ* embroidered across the breast in brilliant gold thread, and the combination of texture and color looked positively bewitching against his wild, two-toned hair. To the right of the vampire was an elevated bench made of pure ebony, and resting on the bench were four priceless implements: an ornate bronze tray, forged by King Sakarias's blacksmiths in 820 B.C.; a matching bronze goblet, prefilled with Napolean Mondragon's venom; a thin, iron stylus with a razor-fine tip; and a solid gold dagger with precious jewels embedded in the shaft, purported to have belonged to Prince Jadon a decade before the Curse.

Ramsey copped a lean against a nearby pine tree, tucked a sharp, dry reed between his teeth, and began to survey the crowd: The vampires were gathered in loose, informal rows, fashioning multiple semicircles in front of the stage, like the common tiers of an old-fashioned theatre. They were gathered according to rank or family—or a combination of both.

His heart warmed as he eyed Marquis and Keitaro Silivasi standing nonchalantly in the front row like two peas in a pod. Marquis was not only smiling, but *laughing*. The Ancient Master Warrior had never seemed more at ease, and Ramsey knew instinctively that the burly vampire had gained far more than a father when he'd ventured into Mhier. He had returned with his best friend.

Before Ramsey could begin to feel the loss of his own departed father, Nathaniel and Kagen closed in on either side of Marquis and Keitaro, circling the pair like a team of buzzards, vying for the patriarch's attention. Nachari was right behind them.

Ramsey chuckled beneath his breath, his heart growing light with amusement. It was the darndest thing he'd ever seen, the way the Silivasi brothers, a family of bad-ass vampires, vied for their father's affection: just a wink, a nod, or a glance of approval. There was no insecurity in their actions, just blatant respect and overt admiration. It wasn't about competition or even loss, being apart for so long; they just clearly worshipped the ground Keitaro stood on and were overjoyed to have him back in their lives. Ramsey swore, one day, if he watched long enough, he was going to see one of them raise their hand and exclaim, "Hey, Dad! *Look at me!*" And Keitaro would oblige them.

Damn, they were lucky as hell.

Across from the Silivasis, Julien Lacusta slinked back into the shadows, taking an unobtrusive position between two parallel trees, close—yet not too close—to Santos and Saxson. No doubt, the happy reunion was a bit much for Julien to take, and not because he wasn't happy for the family—gods knew, Julien had a heart of gold—but his own tragic history with his father was just so brutal, so catastrophic.

So completely unresolved.

It had to open some very nasty wounds.

Ramsey turned his attention back to the dais. It stood like a towering column of mystery, looming in the firelight. Rising at least *twenty feet high*, it ascended above the bonfire, and Saber looked like an otherworldly ghost, adjusting the ties on his robe with the help of his nervous father. Hell, they both looked pretty edgy.

Finally, Napolean Mondragon shimmered into view, adorning the stage with his regal presence—*leave it to the king to make a dramatic entrance*—and he held up his hands to silence the throng. The vampires quickly settled down, taking their official places, as Napolean cleared his throat.

He was dressed in an exquisite golden robe with crimson ropes sewn around the edges and intricate celestial symbols embroidered into the lapels. His long, black-and-silver hair fell unevenly about his shoulders as he glanced at the four accoutrements, nodded informally at Saber, and then stepped to the edge of the platform and waved his hand over the fire, turning the hot yellow flames to a deep, scarlet red.

Ramsey inhaled sharply, suddenly reminded of the Ancient One's mysterious, mystical powers; and to think, Ramsey had just sat down with the monarch over the weekend, chatting about *destinies*, pregnancies, and the need for this ceremony. He watched the king like a hawk as the sovereign ruler began to speak.

"As all of you know, this ceremony is long overdue." Napolean glanced at Saber and smiled softly, his expression as fatherly as it was regal. "A male's induction usually takes place on his twenty-first birthday, following his graduation from the Dark Moon Vale Academy."

Braden Bratianu stirred in Ramsey's peripheral vision, swaying uneasily on his feet, and Nachari Silivasi steadied him with a reassuring palm on his lower back. No doubt, the youngster was thinking about his own induction ceremony, just five years away.

"So I guess it's safe to say that we're only about 780 years late," Napolean continued, drawing a chorus of chuckles from the crowd, "but we'll make do with the circumstances we have." He turned to Saber and addressed him playfully: "*Graduate*."

Saber laughed, his mouth turning up in that characteristic smirk that was as much a snarl as a smile. He shrugged, and the crowd chuckled again.

At once, Napolean's voice turned profoundly serious as he turned to face Saber directly. "State your given name before this assembly, as it will be recorded in the annals of history for all time."

Saber turned to glance at his father, who was still standing beside him, and Ramsey nearly held his breath. *Holy hell, this was an awkward moment.* Everyone knew that Saber had kept the name Damien Alexiares had given him at the time of his abduction, and everyone understood why—it was his identity, his very *persona* for eight hundred years. Still, Napolean had to keep to the letter of the ceremony: *Graduate, state your given name before this assembly.*

Saber cleared his throat and looked out from the dais, addressing the crowd in a strong and certain voice. "My name is Saber *Dzuna* Alexiares."

Rafael let out a surprised gasp, and then he quickly regained his composure and nodded his head with pride: Dzuna was Rafael's surname, the name *he* had bequeathed the child at birth. His son had just changed his name from Saber Mikhael to Saber Dzuna.

Napolean turned back toward the crowd, and his pupils were glowing with approval. "Once again, I find myself at odds with orthodoxy." He sighed. "Typically, I would announce the field of study this vampire has chosen for his coming years at the Romanian University." He eyed Saber sideways and shrugged, apologetically. "But I think, in this case, we won't be sending Saber back to school." He tilted his head to the left, and then to the right, in a lighthearted gesture. "Well, other than a few remedial courses."

This time, Ramsey snickered. The king was really putting on quite a show, clearly making an effort to mitigate any awkward moments in the ceremony, for Saber's sake. And actually, he was telling the truth: Saber's mate, Princess Vanya, was deeply committed to the Romanian University. She had elected to record the oral history, revive the magical incantations, and share the ancient spiritual practices that were once only known by the original females. Her dedication was extraordinary, and her work was invaluable. She would singlehandedly return a lost legacy back to the Vampyr, and Saber would be present for all of her classes. He could probably get away with skipping Antiquity 101: The History and Foundations of the House of Jadon.

Napolean smiled freely. "All kidding aside, it gives me enormous pleasure to announce to this assembly that Saber Dzuna Alexiares has made a decision to join the house of Jadon's formal Sentinel Guard. From this night forward, he will belong to my inner circle, and he will dedicate his life to the protection of my family... as well as our people."

The crowd responded with a perfectly timed chorus of three thunderous shouts, and Rafael Dzuna, Saber's father, virtually beamed with pride.

"With that said," Napolean continued, "it is time to move forward with this induction."

Rafael made his way to the steep nearby staircase and quietly descended the stage, making his way across the first row to stand before the dais, front and center, just adjacent to the bonfire.

Everyone knew what was about to take place.

As a son of Jadon, Saber would be required to shed his blood in a symbolic act of sacrifice for the people. As a pledged sentinel, a sworn protector of Napolean and the royal family, he would be expected to do much, *much* more.

Ramsey, in particular, understood the power, pain, and significance of the second half of the ceremony; and he waited with bated breath as Napolean ambled to stand directly behind Saber, lowered the mahogany robe from the vampire's shoulders, and gestured toward the bonfire. Without a sound, Rafael Dzuna approached the raging fire, reached into the flames, and removed a red-hot implement, an iron stylus, to be used for Saber's induction. He ascended the dais once more and set the sizzling implement on the edge of the tray, beside the golden dagger.

The king took the dagger in his right hand and rotated the blade until the hilt was facing Saber. "Saber Dzuna Alexiares, as a loyal subject of this house, will you sacrifice your blood for all those who stand before you? Will you live, die, or bleed for each of our beloved *destinies?*"

Saber didn't hesitate. "I will." He reached for the dagger, raised his left arm high above the platform's edge, his wrist hovering above the raging fire, and cleanly sliced his flesh from the heel of his hand to the crook of his elbow. The vertical incision was deep and jagged, and the blood sizzled as it made contact with the fire, christening the flames.

After a sufficient amount of time had passed, Napolean nodded, and Saber healed the wound himself with his venom.

The night seemed to grow darker as Napolean retrieved the dagger, held it loosely in his hand, and then turned to face Saber, who promptly kneeled before him. "As a faithful sentinel, one whose voice is now my voice, whose hand is now my hand, who is now and forevermore conveyed with the authority to enforce my laws, will you pledge your very soul to your duty by inscribing the name of the *house of Jadon* on your heart, before these witnesses?"

Saber briefly closed his eyes, and the crowd collectively inhaled. Finally, he licked his lower lip and nodded. "I will."

With that, Napolean braced his left hand on Saber's right shoulder, crouched down before him, and drew a deep vertical incision down the center of the male's lean but muscular chest with the dagger, and then he set the implement aside on the tray. As Saber bit down hard, gritting his teeth against the pain, the king placed both hands on either side of the open chest cavity, reached in, and pulled the breastbone apart, exposing Saber's heart to the open air. The organ could still be seen beating. Without hesitation, Napolean lifted the searing-hot stylus from the tray and began to carve the letters *HOJ* into the fragile organ.

Saber stiffened and moaned.

His back bowed; his neck arched until his head lolled backward; and he began to tremble uncontrollably, clutching the king's wrist with his right hand in order to buy a moment's reprieve while he caught his breath.

Undaunted, the king continued to carve the insignia into the vampire's heart, even as Saber continued to groan and shudder from the pain. Yet the soldier did not cry out.

Not even once.

Once the monogram was finished, Napolean set the stylus back down, dipped his hand in the goblet full of venom, and slathered the healing substance over Saber's exposed, beating heart. The male turned three shades of sickly green. He swayed a bit to the left, and then to the right, as Napolean closed his chest and, once again, coated the outer incision with venom.

All the while, Ramsey watched in rapt fascination.

He knew exactly what the male was feeling: the pain, the inevitable panic, and the unexpected shock. Both he and his brothers had been through the grisly ordeal, and it had hurt like a *mother*, no two ways about it.

Julien Lacusta, on the other hand, was another matter altogether.

It wasn't that the tough son of a jackal could not have withstood the agony—on the contrary, he would have probably borne it with a smirk—it was more that he didn't want to deal with all the social requirements of the job, interacting with humans and vampires alike on a daily basis. Julien was a loner, plain and simple. And he chose to remain an honorary member of the sentinels, as opposed to a formal inductee, an adopted brother in the Olaru household and the valley's best and only professional tracker, rather than a sentinel, because he preferred to work alone.

Before Saber could lose his nerve, and just in case the vampire passed out, which had been known to happen, Napolean stepped to the side, locked his gaze with Saber's, and amplified his next question: "Saber Dzuna Alexiares: To whom do you pledge your fealty?"

Despite the agonizing pain, Saber struggled to his feet, turned to face the crowd, and spoke loudly and clearly. "Before the celestial gods and my revered ancestor, Prince Jadon Demir; before all who have come to witness my induction"—his eyes met Rafael's, and for a moment, they glazed over with unfettered emotion—"before my *father*, Rafael Dzuna, and before my noble king, I pledge my eternal fealty to the house of Jadon. And I swear henceforth to protect and serve my people, to uphold and obey the laws of my Sovereign. From this day until my last, I shall live for the betterment of this house."

An approving murmur rose from the crowd even as Napolean cleared his throat. "I accept your pledge of fealty." He placed his hand on Saber's shoulder and smiled. "Breathe, son. It'll heal quickly."

Saber cocked his head to the side, shook it briskly a few times, and then drew in a harsh, ragged breath. "*Shit!*" he swore loudly, wholly unashamed of the outburst.

Napolean waited patiently, as did the crowd, as the wound finally knit back together, the color returned to Saber's face, and the vampire, at last, stopped trembling. "You ready?"

Saber nodded, and the king took a graceful step back, gesturing toward the platform floor. "For the last time, kneel as the son of your father."

Saber fell to one knee, placed his right hand over his still tender heart, and bowed his head in supplication. Napolean extended his royal hand before him, and Saber kissed the imperial crest on the king's ring. Then, in a brief moment of levity, Saber reached into his hip pocket, pulled out the now-dilapidated pouch he had been carrying around for over nine months, and shook it out in an exaggerated fashion, retrieving his own HOJ crest ring. The crowd responded with gaiety and cheers as he made a grand show of *slowly* slipping the precious object onto his right, fourth finger.

Napolean's smile was positively radiant as he squared his shoulders to Saber and simultaneously gestured at the waiting assembly. "Acum inalta-te ca fiul lui Jadon." *Now rise as a son of Jadon!*

Saber stood, and the crowd erupted with jubilation. As the

males began to chant *house of Jadon* over and over, some chanting Saber's name, the emotion in their voices swelled to a deafening peak; the sky lit up with multicolored arcs of lightning; and the arcs crisscrossed like supernatural fireworks exploding in the sky. When Saber held up the back of his hand and displayed the ring proudly, several volleys of fire rained down from the sky, and the vampires snuffed them out with matching torrents of manufactured ice.

Ramsey reached up to brush an unbidden tear from the corner of his eye.

Son of a bitch.

And after all this time…

For so long, he had held Saber's decision to wait against him, not truly understanding what the male must have been going through, yet when it had counted—*really counted*—the vampire had stepped up like a trooper, saved Ramsey's life, and ultimately saved the life of his *destiny.* The male was truly a brother and a friend. He owed him enormous respect.

Hell, he owed the male an apology.

Waiting at the end of the line for Saber to make his rounds— the vampire would head down the left side of the dais and make his way across the front row, all the while accepting well-wishes and congratulations from each of the honored vampires—Ramsey sought to gather his words.

Saber greeted his father and Keitaro Silivasi first; then he made his way down the row to Marquis, Nathaniel, and Kagen before spending an extra amount of time with Santos, Saxson, and Julien. After clapping hands with the youngster, Braden, he turned to Nachari Silivasi and stopped dead in his tracks. Their feral eyes locked in a knowing gaze, and Ramsey watched with guilty interest, knowing he was witnessing a rare, intimate moment.

Ever since their unlikely paths had crossed, Nachari and Saber had formed an unusually strong bond, and there was such raw emotion in each of the vampires' eyes. Watching as the two males publicly embraced, without any unnecessary posturing, without the need to keep things *hard*, Ramsey couldn't help but find it fitting: After all, Saber had lost his dark brothers, and Nachari had lost his twin. Despite the fact that they had lived very different lives, both losses were equally real. Both males knew what it was like to live without a critical part of their identity.

Beyond that commonality, the dragon had spent eight hundred years in the Dark Ones' Colony, while Nachari had spent a little over four hellish months in the Valley of Death and Shadows. There was no doubt in Ramsey's mind that *each* vampire had seen, experienced, and survived a level of moral corruption, and personal degradation, beyond anything he or his *house of Jadon* brothers could imagine. And, as if that weren't enough, when Saber had first been captured, before they knew who he truly was, Nachari had gone to see him in the HOJ holding cell to settle what had happened with Deanna. Despite Nachari's hunger for vengeance, the Master Wizard had not struck out with violence, nor had he cursed the *Dark One's* immortal soul. Rather, he had funneled a four-dimensional stream of his own memories, the time he had spent in hell, directly into Saber's mind, transferring all of his experiences *firsthand*. He had wanted Saber to know *exactly* where he was headed and what he had to look forward to, and in the process, he had unwittingly shared the most intimate, brutal, and painful secrets of his own life.

As things turned out, Saber wasn't a Dark One at all, not in the end, but he still retained every last one of Nachari's vulnerable memories. That had to play a factor in their bond. *It just had to.* Those males had seen and shared some serious shit, and on a deeper level than most.

Ramsey shrugged.

Who knew?

He wasn't a shrink.

But for whatever reason, the two had a clear and unmistakable connection. And now, as they drew back from their masculine embrace and held each other's stares, Ramsey couldn't help but think that all was right with the world.

This night had been worth the wait.

He continued to watch as Saber accepted congratulations from several other members of the house of Jadon and then finally headed his way.

The vampire stopped short, about three feet in front of Ramsey, and smirked. "And to think, all those years I was raised with the hyenas, when I was meant to be a lion. *Damn*, that's rough, brother."

Ramsey cringed and shook his head. "*Ah, hell*, I said that? My bad."

Saber snickered. "You were a rare kind of an asshole, *Chief*. I'm not even gonna lie."

Ramsey chuckled and nodded. "Yeah, I was… " His voice trailed off, and he cocked his brows in question. "And what about now?"

"And now? Now you're my brother."

The words were unabashedly raw, laced with true conviction, and Ramsey had a hard time digesting their content: *Shit.*

Just… *shit.*

Saber held up his right hand to break some of the tension. "I'm wearing it, *Chief*."

Ramsey looked away.

It was just too much.

He brushed his hands through his hair, trying fervently to check his emotions: His gut was lodged in his throat, and he wasn't sure he could speak, not even if he wanted to.

Growling to loosen his windpipe, he met Saber's coal-black gaze. "The other day… in the park… you had my back, and I won't ever forget that."

Saber shrugged and flashed his signature snarl… er… *smile*. "Yeah, well, that day in the red canyons, outside of my cave, you and Nachari had mine. So what'd you expect?"

Once again, Ramsey averted his eyes in shame. All kidding aside, this was brutal in its honesty. "Expect? *Everything.* Deserve? *Nothing.* Hope?" He paused briefly. "To be forgiven." And then he literally held his breath.

"Already done," Saber said.

The words struck Ramsey like a fist, and he wanted to walk away. Who the hell was this dragon, raised in darkness, to forgive Ramsey so easily when all along, Ramsey had harbored a grudge, conscious or not? The lines between *light* and *dark* were suddenly very gray.

Ramsey felt something overwhelming swell in his heart, and he struggled to suppress it: This was way too deep—way too vulnerable and real—for his liking. Under normal circumstances, he would flip the male off, laugh away the moment, and take a graceful exit to preserve his pride. Instead, he reached out with a rugged hand, grasped Saber by the back of the neck, and pulled him into a fierce, warrior's embrace. "You are loved, brother," he murmured in his ear.

Saber hissed like the so-called dragon he was. And then he laughed out loud. "As are you, *Chief.*"

There was nothing else to be said.

This dark bastard was learning to love.

And so was Ramsey Olaru.

Indeed, all was right with the world.

twenty-six

Salvatore Nistor sat alone, on the top of a rocky outcropping, on the outer skirts of the Red Canyons. He dropped his face in his hands and groaned. Honestly, he wanted to puke. He felt so incredibly sick to his stomach, which was virtually impossible for a vampire to be, but he felt it just the same.

So Saber Alexiares had *truly* and *completely* gone over to the dark—*light* side. Salvatore felt his stomach churn, and he waited to see a stream of gooey yellow bile spew from his innards.

Nothing happened.

He sighed.

Not only had Saber Alexiares, one of the house of Jaegar's most illustrious and prized Dark Ones for eight hundred years, just formally joined the house of Jadon as a loyal, *happy-happy-rah-rah-rah, I-can't-wait-to-kiss-the-king's-ass* subject, but he'd also joined the sentinels!

The freakin' sentinels!

And to make matters worse, Salvatore's dark-hearted yet once-beautiful bride was dead.

Ramsey Olaru had murdered Tawni Duvall, and now, the love of Salvatore's life was gone! As much as he wanted to drown in his grief, dive deep down into the agony and swim around in it for a couple of centuries, Salvatore could hardly keep up the ruse.

Oh, hell…

The woman had been a skank.

A twisted, good-for-nothing, utter failure of a skank.

But still, she had been *his* skank, and their brilliant plan had fizzled out almost as quickly as it had gotten started.

He stared off into the distance, scowling at the reddish orange glow that still lit up the night sky from the house of Jadon's bonfire. *A bonfire.* How adolescent was that? He knew of a few marshmallows he would like to roast over that infernal fire: Napolean Mondragon, Phoenix Mondragon, Ramsey Olaru, Saber Alexiares, Nachari Silivasi…

Oh hell, he would roast every dog, cat, and fish in the house of Jadon if he could.

But he couldn't, at least not today…

Resigning himself to the inevitable—Tawni was deader than a doornail, and Saber was gone, gone, *gone*—he rose from his perch and flipped off the sky. "Screw you, Lord Ademordna!" *Now, just why had he said that?* "And screw you, too, Sister Andromeda!" He squared his jaw—at nothing, really—drew back his shoulders in mock satisfaction, and then quickly ducked as a dark, dangerous—*pine cone?*—fell from a nearby tree.

"*Shit*," he murmured, feeling like a fool. And then he thought about his self-indulgent rant. "I'm sorry, Lord Ademordna," he whispered, hoping the deity could hear him. "I didn't mean it." No point in getting his own immortal ass kicked into the underworld out of an intemperate moment.

Salvatore would be back.

The house of Jaegar would never be bested by the likes of those *feminine* blood-suckers. *Weak-ass punks.* One way or another, the house of Jaegar would get to their quarry and balance the scales. And when it did happen, Salvatore Nistor would be right in the middle of things. He would find a way to punish his enemies, even if it killed him.

His stomach roiled… again.

Surely, vampires could get sick, because the very thought of dying, of something or someone killing *him*—Salvatore Nistor— an all-powerful sorcerer and generally gorgeous male specimen, was suddenly petrifying…

Utterly distressing.

Absolutely unthinkable.

Besides, his brother Zarek needed him, and so did his nephew Derrian. The child was growing so quickly…

As much as Salvatore had always wanted to descend into the underworld; meet his heroes and his legends in person; sup at the table of the dark lords, so to speak, he could no longer stomach the thought of it.

In fact, he could hardly even imagine it.

The very concept was revolting, nearly paralyzing.

And just why was that?

He shook his head, not wanting to investigate the feelings any further.

He only knew that he belonged here, *on earth*, safely ensconced in the underground colony, securely tucked away in his private, luxurious lair with his fellow brothers of darkness.

Wrapping his long, muscular arms around his midriff, he shivered as he stood. Thumbing his nose at the distant clearing, the sacred ceremonial grounds of the house of Jadon, he dove head-first from the rock, released his glorious wings, and withdrew from the night.

twenty-seven

Tiffany settled into the soft comfortable bed in Kagen and Arielle's clinic and took a deep, cleansing breath. Although it was highly unusual for a pregnancy and birth to take place in the clinic, as opposed to at home, the king having twins and Ramsey having a son, both at the same time, was a very unusual circumstance. As Brooke had so aptly put it, better safe than sorry. Now, as she stared at her huge protruding belly, she could hardly believe it was happening—yet it most definitely was.

The past forty-seven hours had been a whirlwind: Ramsey and Napolean had commanded each of their *destiny's* pregnancies at exactly 4:00 PM on Saturday—of course, the *deeds* had been done earlier, in private, *thank the gods*—and now, at 3:00 PM, Monday afternoon, there was only one hour left to go.

Tiffany squeezed Ramsey's hand, feeling nervous, excited, and exhausted at once. Certainly, the male had been there the entire time, taking part in the process, blocking any potential pain or discomfort with his mind, and trying to keep Tiffany occupied when Napolean wasn't wheeling Brooke in and out of Tiffany's private room at the queen's behest.

Truth be told, both Ramsey and the king seemed utterly perturbed with the entire event, the fact that the two *besties* were having babies at the same time. What had started out as a grand idea had quickly evolved into a royal pain in both of their necks. One moment, the women wanted to play cards; the next, they were irritated and eager to go for an outdoor stroll. An hour later, they had sudden cravings for odd human foods, sending Saxson and Santos on numerous trips to local establishments to pick up pickled pears, movie-theatre popcorn, and chocolate-covered cheesecake. Still, a couple hours later, they demanded to be alone, to talk in private, a request neither vampire-husband would grant, and in the middle of the night—the first night and the second—there was no place comfortable outside of Kagen's personal hot tub. And so, the hospitable couple had obliged them with much more alacrity than their mates.

Now, staring into Ramsey's tired—*and slightly irritated?*—eyes, Tiffany hoped to lighten the mood. After all, they would be parents soon, and despite the fact that they were still getting to know each other as a couple, still feeling their way through each other's moods, inclinations, and idiosyncrasies, there was absolutely no doubt that they were in it together... for the long haul.

"Penny for your thoughts?" Tiffany whispered.

Ramsey sniffed. "Now, what would I want with a penny?"

Tiffany huffed.

How rude.

The male really did require at least eight hours sleep a day—she had so much yet to learn about him. Just the same, she could be the bigger person, both literally and figuratively at the moment. She would simply ignore the less-than-amiable remark and press on. "So, I've been thinking more about names, and I think I've come up with a good one, something catchy and strong, something familiar, but also unique."

Ramsey raised his perfectly arched brows, and despite his obvious fatigue, Tiffany couldn't help but find him gorgeous. He was truly a stunning, albeit intimidating, work of art. She cleared her throat and spoke the word with enthusiasm: "George."

The room fell silent.

Ramsey didn't say a word.

He didn't light up, and he didn't frown.

He just sat there like a stone statue until, at last, his brow creased in thought. "George?" he echoed, as if maybe he hadn't heard her correctly.

She flashed a tentative smile, and then her mood turned on a dime. She couldn't help it. Her hormones were fluctuating wildly, as if all nine months' worth of a typical pregnancy's *fluctuations* were being packed into these last few hours. Whatever the reason, she didn't like that sardonic look on his face. "What's wrong with George?" she asked, in a tone far too loud for his proximity.

Ramsey drew back in surprise, quickly raising a placating hand. "I didn't say anything," he murmured.

She frowned. "You didn't have to. It's written all over your indignant, smug face."

Once again, he twisted his features, but to his credit, he didn't engage with a hormonal woman. Rather, he rotated his neck on his shoulders, popped it a couple of times in the process, and then scooted closer to Tiffany on the bed, still holding her hand in a firm yet gentle grasp. "George?" he repeated.

"Yes, *George*."

He nodded, and then he looked off into the distance.

What was he staring at? The wall, behind her? How interesting was that? "Well?"

He cleared his throat. "I'm just thinking."

"About what?" she insisted. "George is a nice name. It's reflective of American culture, and it has a solid, pleasant ring to it."

Ramsey snaked his tongue from one corner of his mouth to the other, almost as if he were searching for a missing toothpick, and then he pursed his lips. "It's a perfectly good name." His voice was monotone. "I'm just considering… the broader picture…

you know, like when he goes to the Academy or the University, that type of thing."

Tiffany suddenly felt like crying. *And just why was that? It was only a name!* Holy cow, she was truly on edge. "I don't understand." She tried to keep her tone affable. "I mean, why would that be a problem at school? It's not like the teachers couldn't pronounce it."

Ramsey nodded thoughtfully, this time biting his bottom lip. *Would somebody—please—give the male a toothpick? He was clearly having an oral crisis.*

"Well?" she pressed. He smiled that overtly endearing and devilish grin of his, but it wasn't doing a thing for her at the moment. "Explain," she prompted.

Something flashed in his eyes, something that might have been a warning, a vampire's way of saying, *You need to watch your step*, but whatever it was, it was gone as fast as it had appeared. Rather than glower at her, he locked his thoughtful hazel gaze with her suspicious green one and spoke in a clear, rational tone. "So let's say he's taking a class with the other kids his age, say Medieval Weaponry or Mind Control… "

Seriously?

Were those the types of classes Tiffany's young son would be taking?

She wanted to ask, but now was not the time to interrupt. Besides, she was dying to hear what he had to say. *What was wrong with George?*

"And let's say the instructor is calling the boys out, one by one, for some reason," he continued, shrugging in a noncommittal manner. "You've got Keitaro, Nikolai, Phoenix, Sebastian, Lucien, Ryder… and… *George.*" He quickly threw up both hands to allay any friction. "I'm just saying he might feel a bit out of place."

Tiffany could hardly contain her scowl. *Oh, so now he thought she was an idiot?* She yanked her hand free of his grasp, crossed both arms over her enormous belly, and plastered an unforgiving scowl on her face. "Was *all that* really necessary?"

"All what? I was just—"

"*Lucien, Nikolai, Sebastian... and George.* I'm a highly educated woman, Ramsey. I don't really require Name Categories for Dummies."

Ramsey's jaw went slack and his mouth fell open. He leaned toward her and placed a light hand on her thigh to compensate for the hand-holding contact she had just removed—in order to continue blocking her discomfort, some form of touch was absolutely necessary. At least he seemed committed to that aspect of their union. "Baby," he drawled softly, "you know what? I think you just need to rest for a while. This pregnancy is about as advanced as it's gonna get, and—"

"You know what I think?"

He clamped his mouth shut and shook his head.

"I think you would be happier with some aboriginal, feudal name, perhaps something more antiquated, like Kristoff or Munchauser or—I know—we could name him Beelzebub *after his father.*"

Ramsey visibly flinched. "*Damn.*" His brows furrowed in surprise. "That was a bit *harsh*, don't you think?" He shook his head in a forceful, brisk manner, as if he were trying to flush out his hearing.

Tiffany grew very quiet, her eyes suddenly brimming with tears. *Oh gods*, she was an utter failure at this whole vampire-wife, speed-dating-through-the-process-of-pregnancy thing; and now, Ramsey would probably keep the baby and cast her out, deposit her on a hillside somewhere... with a horse.

What—in—the—hell—was—wrong—with—her?

Seeming to sense her sudden, and latest, change of mood, Ramsey reached for her hand once more and cradled it between his palms. "It's okay, angel," he crooned, almost as if she were a child. "It's all good. It's all gonna work out." He brought her hand up to his striking, bad-boy mouth and kissed her knuckles softly.

"Can I just ask one question?" His voice was infinitely patient and kind.

"What?" she whispered, still trying to rein in the lunacy.

"What the hell kind of name is *Munchhauser*?"

Tiffany burst out in laughter, and then she began to cry. "I don't know," she droned between sobs.

Ramsey repositioned himself on the bed, wrapped a strong, reassuring arm around her shoulders, and pulled her against his chest, cradling her in his arms. "Sh… c'mon, now… don't do that. No tears allowed."

She sniffled and wiped her nose on his sleeve, leaving a goopy streak behind. "I think I've gone crazy. Seriously crazy. I'm certifiable, Ramsey; aren't I?"

He cocked his head to the right and grimaced. "Ah… not so much." He tilted it back to the left. "Okay… little bit, but"—he rushed the next words, giving her a playful, supportive squeeze—"it's almost over, and you'll be stable again soon. Very soon. *Thank the gods*." He murmured the last three words beneath his breath, held her for a while longer, and then extended an arm to fluff the pillows behind her head before gently laying her back against them. He tapped her ever-expanding belly, and his vivid hazel eyes brightened. "I tell you what: You liked my father's name, right?"

She swallowed to lubricate her throat. "Santiago?"

"Yeah."

She nodded. "I do, very much."

"We could go with Santiago George."

Tiffany perked up. *Was he serious? He would actually do that, for her?* She shook her head in remorse. "I can't do that to our child."

They both chuckled, and the much-needed release eased the tension.

"Well, what was your second choice, then?" he asked.

She tapped her fingers on the bed. "Roman. I think I like Roman."

"Okay, so Roman Santiago or Santiago Roman? You choose."

Tiffany couldn't help but smile. Good gracious, who was this guy? Beneath that gritty, exterior, pit-bull shell was a genuine vampire with a heart of gold. Could it actually be true? Had her horrible luck with men finally changed? Could Tiffany Matthews actually be *lucky*?

Blessed?

She sighed. "We'll name him Santiago Roman, after your father, but we'll call him Roman, so he has his own identity."

Ramsey demonstrated his consent with a nod, and the male looked utterly content. "Done," he said.

She beamed. And then her attention turned to a more serious matter, something that had been niggling her since the moment of conception, something she could no longer afford to put off or avoid: Despite all the frequent mood swings and bizarre behavior, Tiffany was well aware of the fact that this was Ramsey's Blood Moon, and it had been brought about by both a blessing and a Curse. While the timing of her pregnancy had been a mutual choice, it had also been mandatory. And by the end of the thirty days, there had to be a sacrifice, an exhibition of atonement made by Ramsey—and now her—in restitution for the original sin of his ancestors. The Blood would demand and take the soulless child, the Dark One, born without a conscience or hope of salvation. While he… *it*… might look human, even act and pretend to be a rightful son, it was something altogether different, predestined… malevolent. If nothing else, asking Ramsey about Julien's story the night before, then hearing the morbid tale, had driven that point home. Tiffany had no intentions of watching the Blood come for Ramsey, nor was she stupid enough to get herself murdered by a ten-year-old "child" in the future. She was not about to mistake evil for good. No, Ramsey had to do what he had to do. He had to hand the dark child over to the Blood, but the real question was this: Would she be able to follow through when the moment of truth arrived?

She narrowed her gaze and spoke in a serious tone. "There is one other thing, Ramsey."

He raised his brows with interest, saying nothing.

"I can't… I don't… " She placed both hands on the fullest part of her belly and sighed. "There's just no way—"

"I've got it," he said. "So it can go one of two ways: You tough it out, and I wipe the memory; or the moment the dark twin arrives, you go to sleep. I make that happen."

Tiffany nodded. She was not a wimp, not by anyone's standards, at least not once she got past all of her initial fears and impulsive antics, and she was coming to understand, all too well, that Ramsey Olaru was a *man's* man. He wasn't just tough on the outside. He was as strong as an ox on the inside. He didn't just pretend to bear the weight of the king's safety and the Vampyrs' laws on his powerful shoulders; he virtually carried them everywhere he went. Hell, the male had HOJ, *house of Jadon,* literally inscribed on his heart. He could, and would, do whatever was required of him, and he would do it with an iron spine.

But that was just it.

Ramsey had always stood on his own two feet, no matter how capable they were.

Only now, he had her, and she was beginning to believe—to actually hope—that she had him, too. That they were truly *in this* together.

She stared at him for a moment, admiring the placid strength within his eyes. "If you need me to be there, to experience all of it with you, then"—she paused to make sure every word she spoke was *truth*—"then I can do it. I will do it."

Ramsey's approving smile was positively breathtaking. He nodded and stroked her arm with appreciation. "I know that, Miss Matthews." He leaned forward then, pressing a soft kiss on her belly. "Just as you know, by now, that taking care of you… *protecting you…* standing in the gap isn't just what I do. It's who I am. This might sound a bit messed up, when it really isn't, but all I've ever wanted from a life with a *destiny*, from a life with *you*, is for the gods to give me a woman who's strong enough to submit, to let me be *her* sentinel. Not always. Not in all things. Not blindly or without question, but yeah, I'm cut from a fairly protective cloth. You fighting me or going through unnecessary discomfort in order to hold *me* up? Nah. There may be times when that's needed, but honestly, baby girl, I want you to *want me* to handle it. Does that make a lick of sense?"

Tiffany squeezed the hand that was now holding hers. If she hadn't been so aware of her topsy-turvy emotions, and so determined to control them, she might have started crying again. "I don't want to endure the experience just to lose the memory. I'd rather be put to sleep."

"You don't need to see him?" he whispered. "For closure?"

She shook her head. "No."

He locked his gaze on hers. "Consider it done."

*

As excited as Ramsey was for the birth of his son—*and after all these centuries*—he was equally serious about the Curse: all business, no play. He understood intrinsically that there was a whole lot of future, and past, and obligation riding on these next critical moments, that he had a critical role to fulfill, and Tiffany was counting on him to keep his promise.

As the dimly lit room filled with tiny prisms of light, and miniature, translucent rainbows began to oscillate through the air, glistening directly above Tiffany's protruding belly, he took a deep breath, closed his eyes, and spoke the necessary cryptic prayer in the old language, the invocation that would call his offspring forth from his *destiny's* womb.

He immediately sensed a dark, disharmonious energy, and he knew instinctively that the Unnamed One was coming first. Locking Tiffany's expectant gaze with his own, he nodded slowly, bent forward to brush the backs of his fingers along her anxious jaw, and whispered a silent command: *Sleep*. As her eyes drifted closed, he sent a telepathic call to his brothers: *It's time*. Since they were waiting just outside the door, it only took Saxson and Santos an instant to materialize inside the room, each warrior standing on an opposite side of Tiffany's bed. "The Dark One is coming first," Ramsey said, without preamble.

Saxson inclined his head. "I'll take him to the Chamber of Sacrifice and Atonement and wait for you there." His matching hazel eyes were stark with determination.

Santos held his tongue. Heck, he appeared to be holding his breath. The Olaru brothers had pre-orchestrated the events, at least as best as they could: Saxson would remove the Dark One from the room immediately, and Santos would remain with Tiffany when Ramsey departed to complete the necessary ritual. Both males were clearly focused and on board.

Ramsey pressed closer to Tiffany's abdomen as a powerful, rushing sound, like a train dashing into a station, filled the room with surround-sound acoustics and gravelly undertones. The halo that arced above the crest of Tiffany's belly was muddy and *angry*, for lack of a better word, and the particles that flickered outward were anything but golden. They were an inky yellow-green. Ramsey bit down on his lower lip and held out one hand, and just like that, the child materialized: dark, malevolent, and thoroughly ticked off.

It was almost as if he knew.

It knew.

His novice fangs were fully developed, and he lunged, sinking them deep into the palm of Ramsey's waiting hand, as if the dominant show of aggression would somehow buy him clemency from his father, as if the aberrant act of bonding could somehow change the Curse.

Ramsey whistled low beneath his breath, refusing to meet the dark child's glowing, demonic eyes. "Take him," he said to Saxson, wrenching his hand free from the tiny demon's bite. *The Blood had certainly contrived a cruel and twisted, everlasting torment...*

Saxson didn't hesitate. He reached out with a firm pincer grip and secured the Dark One's neck with one hand, while bracing the child's torso against his chest with the other, making sure that he couldn't break free.

The tiny creature hissed.

He tried to throw back his head, without success, and his red-and-black banded hair began to undulate around his scalp like a twisted ball of serpents. That was the last thing Ramsey saw as Saxson and the infant vanished from the room.

Ramsey cocked his brows and gave Santos a knowing glance. "Glad that's over."

"The first part," Santos reminded him, his solemn eyes brimming with intensity.

"True," Ramsey uttered, and then a wave of relief swept over him as a beautiful, multicolored halo returned over Tiffany's belly in a graceful arc, and the space above her naval filled once more with shimmering particles of dust; only this time, they sparkled a glorious, brilliant gold. "Wake up, baby girl," he said softly.

Tiffany blinked several times before her soft sea-green eyes opened. She tried to sit up, was immediately restricted by the weight and size of her belly, and fell back into the pillows, all the while seeking Ramsey's gaze. "Is it—"

"It's done," he said. "Your son is raring to get out of there." He inclined his head toward her heaving belly and cast his eyes to the side, listening intently, emphasizing the pure, harmonic tones now filling the room.

Tiffany's eyes grew wide with wonder and surprise. "Oh my gosh," she whispered, reverently.

Ramsey smiled. "You ready?"

She nodded, shook out her hands to release some tension, and then stared earnestly at her belly. "Yes." Her hands became jittery once more, and she wrung them together a couple of times before forcing them down, against the bed, and holding onto the sheets for stability. *"Yes."*

The golden particles rose into a peak, just above the apex of her belly, and then gradual waves of light began to pulse, faster and faster, streaming above her, even as the ambient sound grew louder and louder. And just like that, Santiago Roman appeared.

He did not begin as an outline.

He did not slowly shimmer into view.

He did not ease his way into this new dimension with subtlety and grace.

Rather, and in true *Ramsey Olaru* fashion, he simply ramrodded his way into the room as if to say to all involved: "Hello, family. I'm here!"

In a rare, unforgettable moment, so perfectly timed it could have been orchestrated, Ramsey, Santos, and Tiffany all laughed out loud. And then Tiffany leaned forward, clearly amazed as her large, swollen belly began to rapidly deflate, returning to pre-pregnancy form. "Well, hello, little guy," she cooed. "I see you're just like your father, not lacking for confidence."

The baby wriggled restlessly in Ramsey's hold and reached out for Tiffany.

"Ah, and I see you have good taste." She immediately took the babe in her arms and cradled him close to her heart, her expression lit with joy.

At a glance, Ramsey's heart swelled with affection and pride: Tiffany was absolutely radiant, and her eyes shone with a gleam unlike anything he had ever seen before. They were positively brimming with love.

And then the door to the private room swung open.

"Is he here yet?" Julien Lacusta's gruff, baritone voice pierced the inner sanctum, even as Saber Alexiares swaggered in on his heels.

"Well, come on in," Ramsey barked sarcastically. "Make yourselves at home."

"Aw, shut up," Julien snorted. He strolled to the side of the bed, bent over Tiffany, which made the female flinch, and took a real hard gander at the babe. "Well, would you look at that?" he bellowed. "That sucker's got silver-green eyes." He threw back his head and chuckled.

"And some blond-ass hair!" Saber added, gawking at the nearly opal locks adorning the child's scalp.

"Language, warriors," Tiffany said in a no-nonsense tone. "Sheesh, his first word is going to be a swear word."

"Nah," Julien said, reaching down to test the child's grip.

Ramsey rolled his eyes, and then he gave Saber a sidelong, questioning glance. Julien's brusque, somewhat unorthodox entrance he could understand, but Saber strolling into the room? Now *that* was unexpected.

The dragon shrugged one shoulder. "Hey, you said you loved me. I figured you wouldn't make it without me."

Santos and Julien eyed Ramsey suspiciously, and the Master Warrior shook his head. "It wasn't like that," he grumbled.

Santos's crystal-blue eyes lit up with mischief. "Hey, your business, brother. As long as Tiffany's all right with it—"

Before he could rib him any further, and as if the room wasn't crowded enough, the door swung open again. This time, Brooke Adams-Mondragon entered. She was sitting comfortably in a wheelchair, being pushed by her kingly mate, and both of her long, elegant arms were filled with newborn bundles.

Tiffany shot up straight on the bed, careful to support Roman's head. "Oh my gosh!" Her voice rose to a pitch that made all four males wince. "Bring them over here!"

Santos, Julien, and Saber took several broad steps backward, instantly aware of the royal couple, that they were in the presence of their king *and queen.* Eyes were respectfully averted, and heads were gracefully bowed.

Ramsey scowled: *Oh, yeah, the vamps had no problem showing some decorum when it came to Napolean.* He watched as Napolean wheeled Brooke to the side of the bed and thought absently that she must have been in the chair because the babies were a boatload to handle—her healing would have been instant and complete following "delivery."

Brooke leaned as far forward as she could, without shifting her balance in the chair or jeopardizing her offspring's safety, and Tiffany met her halfway, holding Roman out toward her occupied lap.

"Santiago Roman Olaru," Tiffany said proudly, and Ramsey chuckled inwardly, thinking what the moment would have been like had she murmured, "George."

Brooke sighed with appreciation and wriggled her nose at the child, since her arms were obviously full. "Nice to meet you, Santiago."

"Roman," Tiffany corrected.

Brooke exchanged a familiar glance with her best friend and nodded before turning back to the baby. "Nice to meet you, *Roman*." She glanced down at her own precious cargo and turned her attention to the child on the left. "Prince Paris Mondragon, meet Tiffany and Roman." She raised her arm upward to show Tiffany the baby, then turned her head to the right. "Prince Parker, this is your cousin, Roman."

Ramsey furrowed his brow and shot a questioning glance at Napolean. *They're not cousins.* He mouthed the words.

Napolean shrugged.

Before anyone could reply, Kagen and Arielle Silivasi shuffled their way into the doorway and peered into the room, their obvious curiosity getting the best of them. "Everything good?" Kagen asked.

"Oh… my… goodness!" Arielle exclaimed, unable to restrain from plowing into the room and approaching the babies.

As the women repeated introductions and proudly showed off their children, Ramsey sank back into the shadows, taking a less prominent position next to Kagen and the king.

"When's the naming ceremony?" Kagen asked Napolean, his satiny, good-natured voice as soothing as always.

Napolean shook his head. "Not for a couple of weeks." He turned toward Ramsey and raised his eyebrows as if to say, *Is that all right with you?* "I think my hands are going to be very full for a minute, and it's not like they don't already have names."

Ramsey nodded, understanding. "I can wait a couple weeks for the formal naming as long as we work the mating ceremony in as soon as possible." He gestured toward Tiffany. It wasn't as if she wasn't truly and indelibly *his* in every way possible, but still, she had just given him a son. He wanted it to be official.

Napolean smiled, also understanding. "You get your brothers together, and I'll stop by later tonight to take care of it."

Ramsey inclined his head with appreciation. "Works for me." He turned toward the bed and smiled as he heard Tiffany tell Brooke how much she loved the alliteration—Phoenix, Paris, and Parker—wasn't that creative?

As if Ramsey and Roman weren't sort of the same?

He chuckled and waved his hand in a small arc to get her attention. "I still have something to *take care of*," he said, ignoring all the bystanders in the room. He hoped she would understand what he meant, as well as the urgency. Saxson was still waiting, after all.

Napolean placed a supportive hand on his shoulder, almost absently, and Ramsey couldn't help but think that the king was lucky: He could just enjoy the birth of his sons this time around— there was no dark curse or dark twin to concern himself with.

Tiffany nodded, clearly understanding, and then she met his eyes in an intimate stare, smiled like there was no one else in the room, and gestured him over to the bed. "Come here," she added for emphasis.

Ramsey sighed with relief, not realizing until that moment that he had been feeling a bit left out. He made his way to his *destiny* and child, and stopped just short of brushing up against the bed.

"Closer," she whispered, peering at Roman, who was now lying peaceful and still in her arms.

Ramsey bent over and took a long, critical look at his son for the first real time. Indeed, his eyes were a pale, almost silver-green, as if they had merged somewhere between his light hazel and her sea-green hue, picking up a faint sliver tint from Tiffany's hidden blue. If his hair were any more blond, it would nearly be white, and his features… they were already so refined, so polished. Lords, he was a good-looking kid with a serious hint to his demeanor. He bent down and kissed the child lightly on the forehead, and the vampire sighed contentedly, settling deeper into his mother's arms. Tiffany reached out and wrapped her free arm around Ramsey's shoulder, pulling him gently forward into a private embrace, and then she mouthed the words *I love you* and sealed it with a kiss.

Ramsey's breath caught in his throat as she pulled away, and he stammered over his reply. He had hoped for a more romantic moment, but—

"Thank you for this gift," she whispered in his ear. "I have never felt more content than I do right now."

He pressed his forehead to hers and simply drank in the moment.

What could he say?

He was at a loss for words.

Sometimes a moment spoke louder than a phrase, a thought was too expansive to condense into sound, and a feeling was too deep to identify with language.

This was one of those times…

And Ramsey could only hope that Tiffany felt it all, that she felt him all around her, within her, beside her.

That she felt the *forever* of it all.

twenty-eight

One week later

Tiffany could hardly believe that Princess Vanya had offered to take all of the babies for a day—*all five of the babies, including her own*—in order to give Brooke and Tiffany, and their respective mates, a much-needed break. While Brooke had the whole nanny thing locked up, it would still be nice for the queen to have the manse to herself for a day. Tiffany, on the other hand, was quickly discovering that she was very hands-on, incredibly particular about Roman's care, a little too possessive to share him with a nanny… just yet.

Things with Ramsey were coming along.

There were only brief moments of fear now, when she looked at him and saw a pitchfork-wielding predator, fewer and fewer instances of awkward silence or push-and-pull between them. In reality, the male had an incredible sense of humor and a heart that was larger than life, once one looked past the domineering, blunt exterior long enough to see the brother, warrior, and father within. He had agreed to let her take Roman with her to the Prime daycare a couple days a week, *without Ramsey present,* and she had agreed to let him implant a few extra memories in her parents' minds so they didn't freak the heck out when they learned of her "marriage," which Ramsey and Tiffany were going to present as an elopement, and the newborn babe that went along with the blissful package.

There was really no other way around the conundrum.

Now, standing in the spacious, elegant living room, wearing only her stilettos, panties, and a bra, Tiffany sighed. The whole seduction scene was a little nerve-racking, but she was ready to show her vampire that she was truly *all in*.

As the back door opened—Ramsey was returning from dropping Roman off at Saber's—she grasped the handle of his pitchfork in her right hand—it was the most appropriate prop she could think of—copped a sexy lean to the side, with one foot crossed over the opposite ankle, and tried to look inviting.

Ramsey rounded the corner like the crafty sentinel he was, moving in that silent, vulturine stride, and then he came to a sudden halt. His jaw went slack. His mouth fell open, and he literally purred in a deep, gravelly rumble. "What are you doing, *destiny*?"

She smiled, trying to match his wicked grin, decadence for decadence. "Oh, I don't know. I was just thinking"— she placed the tip of her forefinger in her mouth in suggestive contemplation—"someone once promised me some down-and-dirty, soul-searching, hair-pulling, name-calling, ecstasy-*inducing* animal sex." She took her finger out of her mouth and sighed. "But I can't remember who it was."

Ramsey nearly swayed where he stood. *"Oh, gods of Gemini."* His already wicked smile turned into a broad, wolfish grin, even as his fangs slowly descended from his mouth of their own accord. He immediately strode forward.

"Stop." Tiffany held up her hand in playful protest. *"Wait."*

Ramsey froze in mid-step, eyeing her from head to toe lasciviously. He shook his head in a rapid, brisk fashion, as if trying to clear his vision, and then swallowed hard, tightening his jaw. "For what?"

She laughed, playfully flicking her hair out of her eyes, and then she rotated her weight to the balls of her feet, gracefully raised the pitchfork off the floor, and started to twirl it at her side. Praying that her new vampiric dexterity would carry her through the whole twirling-seduction scene, she spun it faster and faster around her wrist. "Did I ever tell you that I used to twirl baton in my high school marching band?"

Ramsey's gorgeous hazel eyes grew five shades darker with lust. "You did not," he drawled.

She picked up the speed with her wrist and raised the pitchfork over her head. "Mmm… well… a pitchfork is hardly a baton, but I think it'll do."

Ramsey sank into a predator's stance and began to stalk forward once more, growling as she started to back up. "It's a trident," he corrected her, his thick, sculpted lips growing feline and taut.

She squealed.

Despite the fact that this was precisely what Tiffany had wanted—she had planned on it, prepared for it, and even tried to incite this primitive reaction—his looming, animal presence was overwhelming… otherworldly.

Unnerving in its power and grace.

His heart was beating deep and steady, like a resounding bass drum, and his gaze had turned positively feral, crimson with hunger and desire.

Oh shit, Tiffany thought, her own heartbeat increasing.

And that's when her palms grew sweaty, the pitchfork began to wobble, and she lost control of the weapon. "Watch out!" she screamed, but her warning was too late. The ancient weapon shot through the air; pierced Ramsey through the palm of his raised right hand; continued to bisect his left bicep; and anchored both appendages to the living room wall, spearing the Master Warrior like a stuck pig to his own domicile.

He grunted in pain, and then he grew instantly still, trying to keep the prongs from vibrating.

Tiffany stared in horrified shock as three rivulets of blood seeped down the vampire's arm, he rolled his head back, and he groaned.

She sprinted across the living room, trying like hell not to break her ankle or slide across the floor in her six-inch heels; she'd already made a colossal ass out of herself as it was. "Oh Ramsey," she breathed in distress, "I'm so sorry. I'm so sorry!"

Gods, he looked angry…

"Get it out," he grunted, remaining perfectly still as she studied the prongs, traced the entrance wounds with her finger, and tried to figure out the best way to extract the implement without causing more pain.

"I didn't mean for this to happen," she murmured, regretfully, "to spear you with a pitchfork." Her voice grew in pitch as her heart grew in angst. "I'm so sorry, *sentinel*." She hoped to appeal to his formal persona and invoke his professional nature. "Gods, you must hate me now."

"Get it out," he growled again, this time narrowing his gaze on her quivering lips.

She swallowed convulsively, grabbed the steel base, just above the prongs, with both hands, and started to tug—

And that's when he jerked his shoulder, wrenched free from the wall, and spun them both around, slamming her back into the plaster. "What kind of weapon do I use?" he snarled.

She gasped. *Holy Mother of Grace, he was going to kill her.* "It's… it's a… *trident*."

"That's right," he purred. He flexed his right arm in a smooth, backward motion, dislodging the *trident* from his bicep, and groaned as if in…

Pleasure?

Tiffany's eyes bulged as she gaped at the center prong—still protruding from his right palm.

He reached around the impalement with his free hand, grabbed the trident by the center tine, and wrenched it free, tossing it across the living room floor with a dismissive flick of his wrist. And then he slammed both palms against the splintered wall, pinning her between his arms, and pressed his hips into hers. "What's my name, baby girl?"

Tiffany drew in a sharp breath and stared at his tensed, angled jaw. His lips were set in a harshly erotic line; his fangs were positively gleaming in the lamplight; and his eyes were glowing with primal need.

The male wasn't ticked off…

He was *turned on.*

"Oh gods," she groaned as he covered her mouth with his, kissed the thoughts right out of her head, and then pulled back to lock his gaze with hers.

"Wrong answer," he murmured. "What's my name?"

Before she could speak… or whimper… or even formulate a coherent thought, he grasped her by the waist, held her stationary against the wall, and tore through the center clasp of her bra with his fangs. And then he drew one breast after the other into his warm, punishing mouth, leaving her spinning and light-headed from the sudden sensation.

His lips were utterly possessed.

His technique was positively masterful.

And his teeth traded places with his tongue as he nipped and swirled and teased her peaks into taut, stringent flesh, and her hips began to buck against his hold. *Oh dear celestial deities;* was he mad, crazed, or divinely inspired?

She was practically mindless with pleasure, and he was doing it on purpose.

He drew away from her breasts long enough to lock their gazes once again, release her hips, and slice through the outer straps of her panties with his claws. As the lacy garment fell to the floor, he ripped open his jeans, tugged them down, shimmied out of his boxers, and kicked all the offending scraps away from his feet. He pressed his hand to her throat and massaged her larynx. "I want you to get something straight," he said as he continued to work her throat, dipped down to kiss her lips, and growled into her mouth. "I don't hate you." He traced the contours of her lips with his tongue. "There is nothing you could ever do to make me hate you." He pricked her bottom lip with his fangs and swirled the droplet of blood around his palate, savoring the flavor. "I love you, Tiffany Matthews *Olaru*. And I always will."

She flung her arms around him, grasped him by the shoulders, and hugged him closer, burying her head in his chest. Despite her stoutest resolve, her eyes filled with tears, and she knew she was going to cry.

She wasn't sad.

She wasn't hurt.

On the contrary, she was completely overwhelmed…

Overwhelmed with love, overwhelmed with lust, overwhelmed with gratitude that this magnificent creature was hers.

All hers.

And he loved her.

She bent her knee, raising her thigh to his hip, and wrapped her leg around his waist as best she could. And then she arched into him in mindless invitation. Her body had never needed anything, or anyone, more desperately than she needed Ramsey Olaru *right now*. "Please," she whispered breathlessly, allowing the tears to fall.

Without hesitation, he thrust into her, lodging every thick, magnificent inch into her core. He rotated his pelvis against her *pleasure* in a maddening series of harsh, erotic circles, and then he pulled back out, leaving her bereft. "What's my name?" His voice was a raw, guttural hiss.

Tiffany groaned. She clawed at his back, pressed her heat against him, and strained, trying to force him back inside. He rocked away, and she actually whimpered.

"What's my name?" he growled.

"Please," she whimpered, "I'm *begging*." And then she released her own fangs and bit him in the neck.

It was more than he could stand.

He shouted in pleasure, shivered, and entered her again, this time remaining exactly where he belonged as he took them higher and higher, faster and harder, until they were both lost in a nirvana so profound only the gods themselves could have created it.

Holding on for dear life, Tiffany reveled in the taste, touch, and feel of her mate. She luxuriated in every scent, every groan, every thrust. This male was utter perfection, power and beauty personified. And to think, she had once run from him like a ninny, trying to flee their Blood Moon… *on a horse.*

And yet, here they were.

Once again.

Hovering on the edge of a cliff.

Only this time, they went over together.

"Ramsey. *Ramsey.* Ramsey!"

Epilogue

One month later

Julien Lacusta sank deep into the distressed-leather chair, letting the surrounding darkness envelop him, take him, soothe him.

Become him.

A soft knock sounded on the front door, and he slumped down further in the chair.

Come in.

He pushed the compulsion into Shelly's mind, knowing the door was unlocked, and then he waited to see her familiar face—would the gentle human servant be happy to see him, grateful to serve him, or scared out of her wits, like she often was these days?

No matter.

He tightened his fist around the crystal decanter, filled with 151-proof alcohol and liquid H, also called Liquid "O," and waited for the untainted, fresh blood that Shelly Winters would provide. The short-lived cocktail would provide a much-needed escape, however temporary; and after all, that's all life really was: one endless series of short or long moments, always mundane, each following the other.

Shelly's footfalls were soft and timid as she crossed through the threshold, left the door cracked open, and padded through the wide entry, putting her hand out in front of her to feel her way through the unlit space. She knew better than to turn on the lights, and she stopped abruptly when she saw Julien, sitting so quietly in the middle of an otherwise empty room. "Where's the rest of your furniture?"

He glanced around the cathedral-sized great room, thought about the huge, exposed wooden beams above him, the towering moss-rock fireplace behind him, and shrugged. "Got rid of it."

She blanched. "Why?"

He slid down further in his chair, getting more comfortable. "Don't need it."

She blinked rapidly, appearing honestly concerned. "Are you okay?"

He didn't reply.

Julien didn't answer to humans.

Hell, Julien didn't answer to anybody, except maybe Napolean, sometimes, when the king asked an occasional question. Otherwise, he just did his job, and he did it so damn well that no one asked any questions. No one ever really noticed his true… absence.

"Do you want me to call Kagen?" Shelly whispered, referring to the house of Jadon's healer.

The corner of Julien's mouth quirked up in a sardonic smile. *That was sweet.* Shelly was sweet. He shook his head slowly and beckoned her forward with his hand. "I'm fine," he rasped. "Come here, baby." He patted his lap.

Shelly's tongue snaked out to lick her bottom lip, she fidgeted with the collar on her blouse, and then she glanced around the room nervously as if searching for an escape route. "Um, maybe I should go. Come back another time when you're feeling better."

For some reason, this made Julien more restless than angry.

Her voice was like a harsh, clanging symbol reverberating across the quiet room, the empty space, disturbing his fragile peace, when all he wanted to do was add some blood to his cocktail so he could zone out for a while. *Hells minions*, the H wouldn't work without fresh human platelets, and it had to be now.

He needed it now.

Just five minutes of peace

Just one half hour with nothing turning inside his head.

"Sh," he coaxed her softly, this time lacing his voice with a powerful compulsion. "Don't speak, Shelly. Just come forward and obey."

Her eyes glazed over, and her nervousness abated as the compulsion took hold. She kicked off her shoes, sauntered across the floor, and lowered her seat into his lap.

Damn. This shit is jacked up, he thought as he massaged the back of her neck.

He hated to treat her like this—see her like this—but once again, oblivion was calling his name, and he was all too eager to answer. Deciding that maybe *oblivion* was the best destination for Shelly, too, he wrapped one arm tightly around her waist, raised his decanter so he could tilt her head toward him, using the side of the glass, and locked his gaze with hers. "Sleep, angel," he whispered, catching her falling torso as she crumpled sideways against his arm.

It was too loud.

The situation.

The intensity of it all pierced the darkness.

He extended his forefinger, lifting it from the glass, and pointed at the stereo, which was nestled snugly atop a high, built-in ledge, turning the surround-sound on with an electric pulse from his fingertip.

Ah.

Yes…

Without preamble, he took a long, drugging pull from the decanter, testing the various properties of the alcohol and the H on his tongue, and then he sank his fangs deep into Shelly's throat, savoring each drop of her life-giving blood. As the cocktail began to course through his veins, rapidly slithering along the intersecting passageways like a gentle, erotic snake, just waiting to strike—precious poison appeasing his heart—his head lolled back on the edge of the chair, and his lids grew heavy and dense.

Shelly slid further down on his lap, drooping in his arms, and he tightened his grip *on the crystal glass*. Dark, sonorous music began to blast through the speakers, saturating the air all around him, and he nearly moaned from the vibrations as his body absorbed the lyrics:

"There is a house in New Orleans, they call the Rising Sun...

And it's been the ruin of many a poor boy, and god I know I'm one.

My mother was a tailor, sewed my new blue jeans.

My father was a gamblin' man, down in New Orleans... "

Damn, the Animals could really sing that folk song—Burdon's voice was all grit, angst, and brutal melody. A sweet jolt of cocktail rocked him at his core, and he started to drift even further away...

"Now the only thing a gambler needs is a suitcase and a trunk,

And the only time he's satisfied is when he's on a drunk."

Something visceral seized Julien's attention, and he pulled himself away from the music, temporarily: *Shelly.*

Where was Shelly?

She was sliding down his lap, falling over his knees, slumping to the floor—*that wasn't right, was it?*

"Oh mother, tell your children, not to do what I have done,

Spend your life in sin and misery in the house of the Rising Sun."

Julien thought he reached for the female, but rather, he tightened his grip on the glass even more, shattering the crystal into a dozen serrated pieces, each one immediately embedding in his flesh.

As crimson rivulets trickled down his wrist, soaked the pads of his fingers, and stained his nails, he fell back into the chair and dropped the remaining glass.

Nothing mattered in this moment.

Not the pain in his hand. Not the woman on the floor. Not the emptiness in his soul.

There was only darkness, ecstasy, and peace.

That, and the hauntingly beautiful melody pulsing through the dark.

*

Rebecca Johnston tucked several golden-brown wisps of hair behind her ear, out of her tired eyes, as she checked her clipboard one more time. She crossed off the previous address, *619 Golden Antelope Way*, scribbling a messy note in the margin: *No one home.*

What kind of a town was this anyway?

Didn't anyone answer their doors?

She sighed, glaring at the paltry numbers in front of her, the pitifully low donations, and then she checked her watch, feeling the weight of the day as well as the chill of the night.

Yes, it was late.

They had been at it since 9 AM, knocking on doors, beating down streets, practically begging residents to donate to VOSU (Victims of Stalkers United), and she should really give it a rest… but she just couldn't go home without a victory.

Just one victory.

VOSU was an extremely worthy cause, and to be honest, Rebecca was hardly objective about the struggling non-profit organization. Not only had she spent the last five years of her life fleeing from one state to another, trying to escape a violent stalker of her own, but she had also taken a counseling position at a local Denver VOSU support group. At least once a week she donated her fund-raising time, as well as her valuable experience, trying to help victims of stalking.

She frowned, wishing desperately that her colleagues were still with her, still prodding her forward and providing encouragement, still knocking on potentially hopeful doors. As it stood, each one of them had bowed out the moment they had approached Dark Moon Vale. They had simply refused to go one step further than the Silverton Creek border.

It had been so, *so* strange…

Almost as if some invisible hand of doom had dipped down out of the sky and forced them back from their objective, as if it had physically stopped their progression. They hadn't been just hesitant to go on; they had been utterly and inexplicably terrified of crossing the municipal line and entering the secluded valley.

It had made no sense at all.

None.

Dark Moon Vale was a booming tourist town. Hordes of people came each winter and summer to enjoy the ski resort or the spa, the hiking, river-rafting, or horseback riding. Heck, the casino was a huge draw all by itself. And the wealth? Oh good heavens, there was more money tucked away in these wooded acres than in Beverly Hills, the Hamptons, and Wall Street combined. For all intents and purposes, Dark Moon Vale had the potential to be a fund-raising haven, a virtual gold mine of limitless potential; yet and still, her colleagues had utterly refused to step one single foot in the valley.

A sudden gust of January wind swirled around her, tossing light crystal snowflakes into her hair and eyes, and Rebecca grasped the collar of her stiff wool coat, drawing it tighter around her slender shoulders. She hunched forward to preserve warmth, tucked her clipboard beneath her arm, and stared at the large rustic house in front of her—at the long, winding driveway that led up to the distant front door.

Oh, hell, can't anybody live right next to someone else in this place?

As she made her way up the steep, snaking slope, the oddest

thing began to happen: The sky grew ten shades darker, almost as if someone had just turned out the galactic lights, and the most brilliant configuration of stars began to twinkle in the deepening sky, like spotlights projecting cosmic beams at the earth.

And the moon…

What in the world?

The moon looked like it was *bleeding.*

It was fading from white to pale yellow; from pale yellow to rose; and finally, from rose to dark crimson-red.

Rebecca froze, suddenly wishing she had taken her coworkers' advice, that she had never stepped foot in Dark Moon Vale. She was about halfway up the driveway, ready to turn around, when the magic in the sky ironically pushed her forward: *Forget raising funds for charity!*

She needed to get inside.

Whatever was happening with the sky—and she had no idea what it was—it certainly wasn't natural, and she was smart enough not to stand around and gawk. If comets were going to plummet from the heavens, leaving craters in the earth, she wasn't going to stand there and wave, completely vulnerable and out in the open, hoping they passed her by. Surely, someone in this town would give her sanctuary, just until she knew what was going on.

She hurried up the remaining segment of the driveway and hopped over a narrow bed of unkempt vegetation, perhaps some sort of xeriscape, landing on the large, wide-planked front porch. She reached for the brass knocker on one of two thick wooden doors, and paused—

What the heck?

The door was partially open.

In fact, the panel was ajar, and there was a dark, brooding melody blasting through a set of crystal-clear speakers—*wasn't that "House of the Rising Sun"?*—yet all the lights in the residence were off. There wasn't a single flicker of illumination, not even the glow from a warm fire or the dim radiance of a pair of candles on a distant table. Yet the glitter from the dazzling stars above was so luminescent that it flashed inside the doorway like a pair of high-beams from an oncoming truck.

Rebecca crept slowly toward the threshold and then tapped the door lightly to force it further open. She leaned forward and peered inside…

Her breath caught in her throat.

Holy Mother of God.

There was a man sitting in the middle of the front room like an ancient slave from the time of the Roman Coliseum: He was built like a gladiator, at least six-foot-two, all hard, unforgiving muscle, with chiseled granite-like features, and his crystalline, moonstone-gray eyes stared absently at the ceiling above him even as his head lolled back on a solitary chair. His right arm was hanging limply at his side, and his hand—*his hand was bleeding!*—dripping steady droplets of dark red blood, like a leaky faucet, onto the coarse, wide-planked floors. There was no other furniture in the room, just the chair, the stereo, and—

Rebecca screamed, her throat instantly burning from the raw, sudden abuse of her windpipes.

She dropped the clipboard, clasped her hands over her mouth, and gagged, frantically trying to back away from the door. There was a beautiful blond woman lying on the floor at the gladiator's feet. She was clearly unconscious, and her neck was stained with dried, crusted blood. *Oh dear Lord, what had he done to her?*

Rebecca had to get help.

She had to call 911.

She had to get away!

Now.

Before she could turn and run, the man's head rocked forward; his smooth, constricted pupils met hers; and his lips turned up in a dark parody of a smile, as sardonic as it was savage. "Where are you going, *Rebecca?*"

About the Author

Tessa Dawn grew up in Colorado where she developed a deep affinity for the Rocky Mountains. After graduating with a degree in psychology, she worked for several years in criminal justice and mental health before returning to get her Master's Degree in Nonprofit Management.

Tessa began writing as a child and composed her first full-length novel at the age of eleven. By the time she graduated high-school, she had a banker's box full of short-stories and books. Since then, she has published works as diverse as poetry, greeting cards, workbooks for kids with autism, and academic curricula. The Blood Curse Series marks her long-desired return to her creative-writing roots and her first foray into the Dark Fantasy world of vampire fiction.

Tessa currently splits her time between the Colorado suburbs and mountains with her husband, two children, and "one very crazy cat." She hopes to one day move to the country where she can own horses and what she considers "the most beautiful creature ever created" — a German Shepherd.

Writing is her bliss.

Books in the
Blood Curse Series

Also by Tessa Dawn

Daywalker ~ the Beginning (A New Adult Short Story)

Join the Mailing List

If you would like to receive an email notifying you of Tessa's future releases, please join the author's mailing list at www.TessaDawn.com